MIDNIGHT BARGAIN

by

SERENITY WOODS

Copyright © 2025 Serenity Woods

All Rights Reserved

This book is a work of fiction. The names, characters, places, and incidents are products of the writer's imagination or have been used fictitiously. Any resemblance to persons, living or dead, actual events, locales or organizations is coincidental.

ISBN: 9798275531312

CONTENTS

Chapter One 1
Chapter Two 11
Chapter Three 21
Chapter Four 32
Chapter Five 43
Chapter Six 53
Chapter Seven 63
Chapter Eight 75
Chapter Nine 87
Chapter Ten 97
Chapter Eleven 109
Chapter Twelve 120
Chapter Thirteen 130
Chapter Fourteen 142
Chapter Fifteen 152
Chapter Sixteen 163
Chapter Seventeen 171
Chapter Eighteen 181
Chapter Nineteen 188
Chapter Twenty 198
Chapter Twenty-One 208
Chapter Twenty-Two 217
Chapter Twenty-Three 228
Chapter Twenty-Four 238
Epilogue 248
Newsletter 257
About the Author 258

Chapter One

Kingi

The three members of the board of the Ngā Whetū Rangatahi Foundation who are sitting on the other side of the boardroom table all glare at me.

I shift in my seat, resenting feeling like a teenager who's been caught smoking behind the bike sheds.

"I'm sure you see our point." Mikaere is fifty-eight, and his once-dark curly hair is now almost entirely gray. He's the principal of the only high school on Waiheke Island and is well respected in the local community.

"The person who takes on the CEO position needs to be seen as respectable and trustworthy." Koa is a GP with a focus on the health and wellbeing of Māori youth on the island.

"We need someone who's going to be a great role model," Moana adds. A mother of five, a grandmother of eleven, and married to the local vicar, she plays a big role in the church community on the island.

Mikaere gestures at the iPad in front of me. "This is the last thing the Foundation needs, Kingi. Frankly, I'm surprised at you."

I glance at the article from the Kōrero news website, feeling a fresh surge of resentment. The headline reads 'Potential CEO Faces Backlash for Reckless Behavior at Cultural Site.' Accompanying it are two photos taken several weeks ago: one of me jumping off the waterfall at the Waiora healing pool, the second of me holding a whisky glass and looking disheveled. The article already has over ten thousand likes and two thousand comments, many of them yelling in capital letters with angry face emojis. It's going viral in the city and will soon be a national story.

I resist the urge to throw the iPad across the room. "This is pure fabrication."

Mikaere frowns. "There's a photo of you, Kingi. Are you saying it's AI? Because if that's the case, you could sue for libel."

"No, the photo is real. Yes, I jumped off the waterfall. It's hardly reckless behavior. We all know how many kids make that jump."

"You're not a kid," Moana points out, giving me a look that makes me feel an inch high. "You're an adult, a company director, and a well-respected member of our community, or so we thought. And the Waiora is a sacred site. This is damaging to us all ways around."

It's natural for young men to develop aggressive feelings as their testosterone spikes, but part of becoming an adult is learning to control that aggression. It's one reason I enjoy mentoring young men and helping them deal with their hostility with physical exercise, as it can feel overwhelming when you're frustrated and resentful at the world. Violence and anger are never the answer; I know that.

Right now, though, I could easily punch the wall to make a Kingi-shaped hole to escape this farce.

"It was a private party at the Midnight Club," I say, careful to keep my voice even. "I arrived late to discover they'd decided to go down to the Waiora for an evening swim. I went down there, and I had every intention of asking them to leave if they were being loud. As it happens, they were relatively quiet and respectful, just a group of friends having a swim, and we returned to the club shortly afterwards. No alcohol was consumed at the pool. I hadn't had a single drink when I did the jump. The other photo was taken at the club a couple of hours later. This is a personal vendetta, nothing more."

Moana looks over her glasses at me. "You're saying that the supermodel in this article..." She looks at her own iPad. "...Sabrina Pearce, is behind this? She made it up?"

"Yes."

Koa frowns. "Why would she do that?"

I run a hand through my hair and wince. The last time I saw my mother, she told me it needed a cut, and she's probably right. Normally I like it long, but I've run my hands through it so many times it's tangled to shit.

"We dated briefly," I reveal. "And I decided not to take it further."

Koa's lips twitch. "Hell hath no fury?"

"Something like that."

It is, of course, just a glimpse of the whole story, and only a taste of my idiocy. When I met Sabrina at the Waiora, I knew immediately who she was—she's splashed across every women's magazine in New Zealand. In my defense, she's five foot ten, with legs up to her armpits, light-brown skin, long brown hair, and big… eyes. Yes, I am that shallow. I hadn't had sex in a few months, and when she stripped off her glittering Givenchy gown to reveal a skimpy bikini, I was lost.

Yes, obviously, I jumped off the waterfall to impress her. And it worked. When we returned to Midnight, she sat next to me in the club, and as the evening progressed, she made it obvious how attractive she found me. At the end of the party, I asked if she'd like to go back to my suite. And she said yes.

The sex was unimpressive, despite my best efforts to make it otherwise. But she's beautiful, wealthy, and well known in the circles I mix in, so it was a short step for me to give her the benefit of the doubt and suggest a second date. If I'm honest, I've been growing tired of the playboy lifestyle, and a little part of me thought that maybe having a gorgeous girl like Sabrina on my arm on a more permanent basis might not be the worst thing in the world.

Unfortunately I didn't realize at the time that she was a viper in a supermodel's clothing.

Over the next couple of weeks, I began to understand what a mistake I'd made. I learned that her cool, composed exterior hid an aggressive brat. She was demanding, rude, and patronizing, and bitchy and dismissive to anyone she thought beneath her, which appeared to be most people.

She also started laying down ground rules for our relationship, which included me giving up any risk-taking endeavors like rock climbing or sky diving because it didn't look good in the tabloids for her to have a boyfriend who enjoyed hazardous hobbies. And that was the nail in the designer coffin, I'm afraid.

She revealed her demands as we were making our way out of the Midnight Club, and when I lost my temper and told her we were over, she literally exploded—well, not literally, but almost—and screamed to my face in front of a lobby full of guests that nobody, but nobody, turned down Sabrina Pearce and lived to tell the tale. She walked away, and I rolled my eyes and promptly forgot about her.

My mistake.

"So she's doing her best to slander you in the press?" Moana's mouth forms an O. "That's… appalling." Honest and whole-hearted, she has no understanding of how a person could ever do anything to hurt someone in such a manner.

"That is unfortunate," Mikaere says, "although maybe there's also a lesson to be learned there about keeping it in your pants, Kingi."

I haven't blushed since I was twelve and vomited on stage during a production of A Midsummer Night's Dream, but my face heats under the principal's steady gaze.

"Give the guy a break," Koa says mildly. "He hasn't done anything wrong. It's not his fault the woman is so vindictive."

"No," Mikaere says. "But he's twenty-eight, not eighteen. You're a man now, Kingi. You're free to live your life however you choose, of course. But we have to think about the Foundation. About the young lives we're hoping to help. We need a respectable figure at the helm. Someone the youngsters can look up to. Not a playboy who's splashed over the tabloids with a different woman every week."

I bristle with resentment. My father is rich and so I haven't had it as tough as some of the youths who'll come to the Foundation, but I've worked hard to get to where I am. I have a First-Class Honors degree and a Master of Business postgrad. I run my own business with my friend Orson, and I've more than quadrupled the money my father gave me when I turned twenty-one. I hold the Duke of Edinburgh Hillary Award at Gold Level, and I'm also now an Award Leader. I've personally broken several national mountaineering records, and I frequently spend weekends volunteering for Land Search and Rescue New Zealand.

But I don't say anything, because even though it stings, I know he's not wrong. I am often photographed with different models and movie stars. I enjoy taking risks, and I am sometimes reckless. I'm torn between believing you only live once, and wanting to be taken seriously.

Mikaere is right. It's my choice. I can continue to live the way I do. But if I want to be CEO of the Ngā Whetū Rangatahi Foundation—the Youth Stars—I'm going to have to make some changes.

I clear my throat. "I'd like to apologize. You're completely right, and I didn't mean to embarrass the Foundation by acting inappropriately."

Moana smiles. "Aw, Kingi, *Kia kaha, kia māia, kia manawanui.*" It's a saying that means 'Be strong, be brave, be steadfast.'

"We'll back you up," Koa says, "of course we will. We wouldn't have offered you the role if we didn't think you were perfect for it. But we just need you to act a little more… respectable."

That word again.

"People respect stability," Mikaere says. "It would help if you looked like a man who values commitment, not just the spotlight."

Moana nods. "Having someone steady by your side, someone who reflects your values, would reassure our donors. Maybe just bear that in mind, going forward."

"I'll give it some serious thought," I promise.

"*Kia ora,*" Mikaere says. It's used as a greeting, but it also means 'be well'. "We appreciate you giving us your time, Kingi."

"Of course."

We all rise, and I walk with them out of the boardroom and through the offices into the lobby.

Midnight is an exclusive business club and resort run by the Midnight Circle—a consortium of wealthy business people headed by Oliver Huxley, who had the idea of using the proceeds of the club to support local charities. We've all worked hard to make the club a success, and to ensure it's seen as honorable and respectable.

I'm going to have that word engraved on my fucking tombstone. Here lies Kingi Davis. Tried to be respectable. Failed spectacularly.

The three of them say their goodbyes and head off to their various cars. I pause on the steps, reluctant to go back to the office. It's been raining the past few days, but today is a beautiful, blustery autumn May day. Even though it's too late for mountaineering, as there are fewer daylight hours and there will be snow at higher elevations, it's my favorite time of year. Up here, north of Auckland, autumn is a bit of a non-event, but in the South Island—in Queenstown and Arrowtown and Dunedin and Invercargill—the trees are decked in glorious colors, and in the mornings the air will be filled with a delicious bite and the promise of winter.

I need to stretch my legs and think, so I set off toward the path that circumnavigates the site and provides a pleasant kilometer walk. I'm wearing my suit jacket but it's too nice for a coat, and I slide my hands into the pockets of my suit trousers and enjoy the feel of the sun on my face.

SERENITY WOODS

The path runs along the front of the site, past the car park, not far from the private beach, then follows the river that eventually leads up to the Waiora healing pool and waterfall. Before it gets there, though, it turns away and curves gracefully around the back of the site.

Here we've had the grounds landscaped to provide a stunning set of Japanese-style gardens, designed to inspire peaceful contemplation. Stepping-stone walkways wind between numerous vignettes that can't be viewed all at once. There are small wooden pavilions, pagoda pillars, a bridge over a small stream, and a pond full of colorful goldfish. Bamboo shoots are interwoven to form latticework that separates each scene. It's beautifully done and has earned the Midnight Club an Earth Star from the New Zealand Gardens Trust for sustainability.

At the back of the site, the ground rises to provide a natural windbreak. At the moment it consists of mown grass, but the landscaping firm we employ is working on converting that to a series of terraces with flower beds to provide a splash of color.

The firm's employees usually work weekdays, so I'm surprised to see someone halfway up one of the slopes, hard at work in khaki trousers and a pair of mud-coated walking boots.

I slow as I approach. The person has their back to me, and is bent over, busy shoveling earth into a wheelbarrow halfway up one of the slopes. Judging by the shapely ass, it's a woman. Even though she's bent over, I can tell she's small and slender, but she has surprisingly big boobs. I wouldn't be a red-blooded man if I missed the bounce of her breasts beneath her light-green sweatshirt as she digs the shovel into the wet earth. Wow.

As she lifts the shovel of earth into the wheelbarrow, she turns to reveal her face in profile, along with her long red ponytail, and I realize who it is.

"Morning," I say.

"Oh!" She spins around in shock… and that turns out to be her undoing. Her boots are sunk deep into the wet earth, and they refuse to move. She loses her balance, and her arms flail as she starts to fall back.

"Shit." I rush forward, grab one of her hands, and yank her forward. The only trouble is that I forget my own strength sometimes, and I pull her so hard she stumbles forward and falls against me. It knocks me off balance, and I step back, knocking into a heavy bucketful of soil. I slip, lose my footing, and fall onto my ass with her half on top of me, right in the middle of a pile of freshly dug wet earth.

She looks down at me, and we stare at each other in astonishment for about six seconds.

Then we both burst out laughing.

"I think our audition for the Clumsiest Human Olympics went well, don't you?" she teases, pushing up onto an elbow.

"It was rather spectacular. I'd say we're up for the silver medal, minimum." I'm lying on my back in the mud. Jesus, my poor suit. I'm absolutely covered.

I look up into her big green eyes. "Hey you."

"Hey." She smiles.

I've known Francesca Ross since I was about eight years old and Chessie, as everyone calls her, was six. Her father is Joe Ross, the owner of Ross Gardens, a company that offers landscaping services as well as general lawn and garden maintenance. He's been my father's gardener for twenty years, and he used to bring Chessie and her brother, Mark, to the house to play with me and my sister Marama while he mowed the lawns and trimmed the hedges. We climbed trees together, went down to our private beach and swam in the sea, played cricket in the sand, and generally had the perfect Kiwi childhood, right up until I went to boarding school at the age of twelve.

As the years went by, we saw less and less of each other. My life became about rugby trials, studying for exams, and working hard to get through the bronze, silver, and gold levels of the Duke of Edinburgh Award, with all that involved, while Chessie went to the local high school and stayed close to home.

We did meet up occasionally during our vacations though. One hot Christmas, we bumped into each other at a summer garden party at my friend Orson's house. The adults drank champagne on the deck while the youngsters went swimming in the pool. I was seventeen, she was fifteen. We'd known each other for a long time, and I'd always thought of her as a kid, my friend's little sis, but that day she was wearing a bikini (clearly I have a weakness for women who wear them), and for the first time I noticed her maturing figure, and just how grown up she'd become. We splashed each other in the pool, flirted, and teased, and then as it was growing dark, ended up finding a quiet spot behind the garage where I finally kissed her.

Unfortunately, my father had gone to his car to retrieve something, and he bumped right into us. He just cracked a joke, and Chessie walked off hurriedly, more than a little embarrassed. But when she'd gone, he gave me a scornful look and said, "Really? You can do better than that, boy." When I got back to the party, I found her and tried to apologize, but she laughed it off and said it was only a bit of fun, and walked away. And that was the end of that.

It wasn't as if I took my dad's advice to heart. We just ended up in different social circles. At eighteen she chose not to go to university and went straight into her father's gardening business, whereas my career skyrocketed, and I've ended up mixing with the rich and famous. Over the past couple of years I've seen her a few times, and we've smiled and exchanged pleasantries, but that has been the extent of our communication.

The last time I spoke to her, she wore braces. Now, when she smiles at me, she reveals a line of attractive, straight white teeth.

The women I'm used to mixing with are, overall, very wealthy. Their hair is professionally highlighted, straightened, and styled, they have long fake fingernails, they tan their skin on a sunbed, they wear heavy foundation, false eyelashes, and outline their lips so they look like Barbie dolls, and their clothing bears designer labels and is always of that season's fashion.

Chessie's green top bears a faded picture of Ridley Scott's *Alien*, her trousers are torn, her nails are short and have dirt beneath them, her long red hair is naturally wavy, and she's clearly not wearing any makeup, because her skin is covered in freckles. She smells of the autumn air rather than expensive, cloying perfume. She's the classic girl-next-door.

We've been staring at each other for a little longer than is necessary, and she finally drops her gaze before saying, "Oh Kingi, your suit, I'm so sorry."

I look down at the mud-soaked shirt and trousers, and shrug. "Eh, the dry cleaners'll sort it out."

She pushes up, then groans as she also discovers she's coated in mud from her ribs all the way down. "Jeez, look at the state of us."

I get to my feet and extend a hand to pull her up, a little more gently this time, so she just bumps against me.

"I've got a change of clothes in the car," she says, "although I think it might be better if I sit on a black bag, drive home, and shower first. This clay is so sticky." She attempts to peel a clod off her elbow.

"Come back to Midnight," I say. "You can change there."

Her eyes widen. "Oh goodness, I couldn't walk through the club looking like this."

"You won't have to. We'll go back to my suite. We can even take the back stairs if you'd rather."

She hesitates, looking down at her mud-covered arm, and her hands that are now stained a rich red-brown. "Ahhh…"

"Come on. Let's put your gear away first."

She doesn't argue as I collect the shovel and bucket. After tipping the earth out of the wheelbarrow, she places smaller tools into it, then wheels it beside me as I head off to the large garden shed.

"What are you doing here, anyway?" I ask. "I didn't think you worked Saturdays."

"I don't, normally." She tucks a stray strand of her hair behind her ear, leaving a long smudge of earth across her cheek.

"So…"

"I'm trying to help Dad out."

It's only then that I remember that Joe Ross suffered a heart attack a few weeks ago, and he's currently in hospital following a quadruple heart bypass operation. "Shit, I'm sorry, I forgot. How is he?"

She steers the wheelbarrow off the main path toward the shed. "He's had a few complications. Something called Post-Pericardiotomy Syndrome. He has a fever and chest pain. They're giving him drugs, but he's developed an infection in the surgical wound, and…"

She stops by the shed, takes the tools over to an outdoor tap, and starts rinsing them off. I join her, cleaning the spade free of mud with my hands. I glance at her, wondering why she hasn't finished her sentence. Her lips are pressed tightly together. I think she's trying not to cry.

I don't say anything, pretending I haven't noticed, but I take the bucket from her and clean it, rinse the tools, wipe down the wheelbarrow, and place all the tools in their right places inside, leaving her to wash her hands and gather herself. When I'm done, I take the key from her and lock up the shed, then hand it back to her.

My jacket and shirt are filthy. I take both off, then run a cleanish part of the shirt sleeve under the tap. Straightening, I turn to her and wipe the cloth across her cheek, removing the streak of mud.

"Kinda pointless," she whispers, her eyes turning glassy. "But thank you."

I smile. "I think a change of clothes, a hot coffee, and one of our special double chocolate muffins is necessary right now."

"Oh, that sounds like heaven."

"Come on. I smell like a farmyard. I really, really need a shower."

Chapter Two

Chessie

We walk around the side of the resort, back to the car park, and I stop and retrieve my bag with a set of clean clothes and sandals from my car.

"Jesus." Kingi looks at my beaten-up old Volkswagen Beetle. "How is that thing still running?"

"It's held together with Sellotape and bits of string."

"You're not kidding. You've had that thing for as long as I can remember."

I close the door and lock it. "Dennis is the love of my life. We'll be together forever."

"Dennis?"

I gesture at the number plate that bears the car's name.

Kingi grins. "I forgot you christened him. Why Dennis? I can't remember."

"It's the name of Cordelia's ghost in *Angel*. Don't tell me you've forgotten."

"Wow, I'd never have remembered that."

My smile fades a little. Most of the time when we were kids, we'd spend our time outdoors, swimming or playing rugby, cricket, or tennis, but of course sometimes the weather was bad and we couldn't go out. Dad still had to work though, so when it rained, Kingi's dad would open up the sleepout next to their house, which they sometimes used for guests who came to visit, and we'd make popcorn and hot chocolate and watch TV together. One particularly bad autumn where it rained non-stop for about three weeks, we watched all the seasons of the paranormal show *Buffy the Vampire Slayer* and its spinoff, *Angel*, with his sister and my brother. I have such fond memories of those times, and the programs and their characters are etched on my soul... but not on Kingi's apparently.

"Poor Dennis," Kingi says as we begin walking toward the resort. "He must get lonely all the way over there." I always park at the edge of the car park—ostensibly so I'm near the shed, but also because I'm too self-conscious to park near the fleet of new cars close to Midnight. Dennis would never forgive me.

"There's a significant amount of money here," I comment, spotting a Bugatti, a Maserati, and an Aston Martin amongst the Range Rovers, Bentleys, and Teslas. "What are you driving at the moment?"

"That's mine." He gestures at a black Porsche Taycan parked in the VIP section.

My eyes nearly fall out of my head. It's plugged into the charging point so it's obviously electric. It's cutting-edge, eco-conscious, and powerful. I'm betting it cost over three hundred thousand dollars.

"Wow." I'm tempted to cover my eyes to stop them from falling out of my head. I'd forgotten how rich he was.

When the two of us fell over and we were covered in mud, it transported me right back to my childhood, to the days when we used to play together. But of course he's grown up into a wealthy, successful businessman. He's around six-three now, I guess, with hair down to his collar and a big black beard, and he's incredibly handsome.

I blink. Where was I?

"Turbo," he says, interrupting my thoughts. "Nought to sixty in two-point-two seconds."

I laugh. It's such a Kingi thing to say. As a boy he was always into extremes—he wanted to be the fastest runner, the best climber, to hit the cricket ball the furthest. Speed and power were his answer to everything, and his favorite saying was 'no risk, no reward.' It doesn't surprise me that he's now one of the most powerful men in the city, if not the country. He was always destined for greatness.

He's come an awfully long way since our childhood, whereas I'm still the same old Chessie—normal, ordinary, and slightly awkward.

Ahead of us, a group of men and women is making their way toward the lobby. They're all wearing suits, and everything about them screams money, from the guys' handmade shoes and sharp haircuts to the women's coiffured hair and designer handbags.

My step falters, and Kingi glances at me and slows. He looks at the group, then down at his bare chest, then at me. "This way," he says, and he turns and leads me along a side path that curves around the complex to a plain door in the side of the hotel building.

He punches in a code, then opens the door and stands back to let me pass. I have to turn to the side to slip by him, and even though he's right—he does smell a bit like a farmyard—as I move close, I get a whiff of his delicious cologne. Mmm. Gone are the days when he'd smell of supermarket-bought deodorant like the rest of the boys his age. Now his scent is something expensive and classy, with cedarwood, that makes the skin on the back of my neck prickle.

Gosh, I'd forgotten how tall he was. I'm only five-four, and I'm wearing flat walking boots, so he towers over me. My eyes are level with the greenstone pendant that rests on his chest, which would normally sit beneath his shirt. He's almost as wide as he is tall, with huge shoulders and a broad chest covered in curly hairs. I don't think both of my hands together could circle his biceps. His left forearm bears a full Māori sleeve tattoo which is immensely attractive. Wow.

I make it past him unscathed into the stairwell, and he closes the door behind him, then gestures for me to go up. I climb the stairs, with him following me.

"Are you looking at my butt?" I tease as we climb.

"What? No, of course not."

"Fair enough. Nowadays a guy can have his eyes put out for something like that. Did you know that on the London Underground there are signs warning against intrusive staring of a sexual nature?"

He snorts. "That's ridiculous."

"I sort of get it," I say thoughtfully. "I mean it's no fun when a stranger stares at your boobs…"

"My point is that signs shouldn't be required. Young guys should be brought up to be respectful and not stare at strangers' tits on the train."

"Good point. We're not strangers, though."

"True. So I can look at your butt?"

"Feast your eyes, my friend."

We both laugh.

"Actually," he says in a mild tone a few steps later, "you have a rather nice ass."

"I… ah… oh." Words fail me as, with that one sentence, our childhood relationship falls away, and suddenly I'm intensely aware that I'm a grown woman and he's a man, and my pulse starts to race.

But that makes me think about the kiss, and I remember what happened after that, and my heartbeat slows once again. The fantasy will always be light years away from the reality.

We reach the door at the top of the steps, and I open it to reveal a long corridor ahead of us. He leads the way and stops at a door marked with the number 104, touches a key card to it, and goes in.

I follow, letting the door close behind me, and stop to take off my filthy boots. We're in a large suite that overlooks the gardens. It's open plan, with a living room, kitchen, and dining room all in one, and a bedroom visible through a doorway. It's like a hotel suite, and I guess most members of the Midnight Circle have one for when they don't want to go home after a late meeting.

"Interesting design." I leave the boots by the door and walk further in. The furniture is all made from natural materials—bamboo, wicker, rattan—and there are lots of plants, making it feel very homely and fresh.

"It's called biophilic design." He tosses his keys and wallet on the kitchen counter. "The whole hotel is like it. We're keen to be environmentally friendly here."

Obviously, I'm aware the gardens have won a sustainability award, so I know the environment is important to the Circle, but I'm impressed that their interest extends to the hotel itself.

"The bathroom is through there." He gestures at the bedroom door. "Have a shower if you want—you can use anything you find in there, and there are plenty of towels. Would you like a coffee and a muffin? I'll place an order while you're in there."

"That would be great."

"Okay." He winks at me, then goes over to the phone on the counter.

I take my change of clothes into the bedroom and close the door behind me. Then I pause a moment.

Oh my God. I'm in Kingi Davis's bedroom.

I stand there for a moment, looking around me. Kingi is wealthy, powerful, and gorgeous, and he's one of the most eligible bachelors in New Zealand. How many women would kill to be in here? How many have already *been in* here?

To be fair, there's no sign of a woman around. Even though it still features a few plants, including a single orchid on the bedside table, the room is decidedly masculine, from the colors of the bedding—navy with burgundy stripes, to the accoutrements—a suit hanging on the front of the wardrobe; a large, expensive Patek Philippe watch on the dressing table; a biography of Edmund Hillary on the bedside table. The smell of his cologne hangs in the air.

I swallow and cross to the ensuite bathroom in the corner and go inside.

It's clean and neat; I'm guessing a member of housekeeping has already been in. The towels are folded on a wooden rack, and the items beside the sink—deodorant, hair product, a couple bottles of cologne, a mug with toothpaste and toothbrush—are all neatly lined up. A beautiful, large *Chlorophytum comosum*—a spider plant—hangs from a holder in the corner, trailing its stripey leaves almost to the floor.

Feeling oddly shy, I go over to the cubicle and turn the water to hot.

I shower quickly, because my arms and legs and even my neck are covered in mud, using the shower gel in the tubes on the wall that smell of orange blossoms. I don't wash my hair, but it's still damp when I come out, so I take it out of its ponytail to dry while I soak up the drips with a towel.

I pick up one of the bottles of cologne, undo the top, and have a sniff. Immediately it takes me back to the moment I slipped past him in the stairwell. That huge chest and those biceps…

I put the bottle down hurriedly. No, no, no. I'm not going to have sexual fantasies about Kingi Davis. That way lies madness. I've always known that.

After dressing in my clean clothes, I turn the dirty ones inside out and put them in my bag, then go out. "That's better," I say, going into the living room. "Thank you so much."

He's standing by the window, checking his phone, and he looks up, then does a comedic double-take as he sees me. His eyebrows shoot up. "Oh," he says.

"What?" Self-consciously, I look down at myself. I'm wearing a short plain green tunic dress, kind of like a long T-shirt, and my legs and feet are bare. Of course I'm not wearing makeup, and my hair is loose. Ohhh… I must look very different from the models he's had walk out of that bathroom, in designer outfits, having spent hours on their hair and makeup.

I wait for him to tease me about looking like a gardener's daughter. Instead, he says, "Your hair's very long."

I pick up one of the strands that falls to my chest and twirl it in a finger. When I was young, I used to wear it in a pixie cut, mainly because I hated the color. The truth is that I haven't been able to afford to go to the hairdresser for ages. But I don't tell him that. "Right back atcha," I say, smirking at his shoulder-length locks. "I bet your dad just loves that look."

He grins again. When we were kids, his father repeatedly nagged him to get a haircut, but Kingi always preferred to wear it long.

"I'd better have a shower," he says. "Can you get the door when room service arrives?"

"Sure."

He nods and heads off to the bedroom.

I wander around the living room, trying not to think about him in the bathroom, stripping off and letting the hot water wash over that expanse of brown skin.

The plants here are well cared for, beautiful and luscious—a *Ficus lyrata* or Fiddle Leaf Fig with its large glossy leaves; a tall *Strelitzia reginae* or Bird of Paradise, its dramatic leaves topped with gorgeous blue and orange flowers; a *Senecio rowleyanus* or String of Pearls with its quirky, cascading green beads; and a *Philodendron Brasil* trailing heart-shaped leaves from a high shelf.

The room would of course have been designed and decorated by a team, not by Kingi himself, but it still features items that suggest he had a hand in the decor. One of his sister's stained-glass artworks hangs in the window, casting jeweled light onto the kauri-wood floorboards. And on the left-hand wall, there's a large photograph which Kingi would definitely have had a hand in choosing, of Aoraki Mount Cook, beautifully colored, to show the green and brown plains below it, the blue and purple of the mountain itself, and a pink and orange sunset in the background. It's the highest mountain in New Zealand, and he climbed it a couple of years ago, after extensive training. I saw the achievement pop up on his Instagram page, and I commented how proud I was of him. He replied with *Thanks, Chess!* It's probably the most words we've exchanged over the past few years.

A knock on the door makes me jump. I run across to open it and smile at the guy in the white shirt and black trousers who's holding a tray.

MIDNIGHT BARGAIN

Surprise flickers in his eyes as he sees me, but he hides it quickly. "Morning, Ma'am," he says, "would you like me to put this on the table for you?"

"Oh, please." I step back to let him in. He walks past me, over to the small, circular dining table, and places the tray there, then says, "Have a great day."

We don't tend to tip in New Zealand, but for a moment I wonder whether the staff is used to foreign guests slipping them a note at times like this. I don't have any cash on me. However, he doesn't wait and heads for the door, goes out and closes it behind him.

I go over to the table, choose one of the coffees, and sip it. Mmm, piping hot latte. The tray also bears a plate with two large chocolate muffins. When I pick one up, I discover it's warm and it smells wonderful... ohhh, lovely.

"Oh good," Kingi says, coming out of the bedroom. "They've arrived." He's wearing jeans and a navy polo shirt. His long hair and beard are damp. He looks gorgeous.

"Come on," he says, picking up the tray, "let's sit outside."

He walks across to the sliding doors, opens them, and places the tray on the round table on the small private balcony. I join him, taking a seat next to him so we're both looking out at the view of the gardens. They're quiet at the moment, although to one side near the bridge over the stream I can just see a group of guests taking part in a Tai Chi class, moving slowly through the careful poses.

We break apart the muffins, releasing a small cloud of steam, and take a bite. "I'm ravenous," I say, sighing as I chew the moist chocolate cake. "Oh, that's so good."

He chuckles. "They make the best muffins here. And have you tried their apple pie?" He rolls his eyes appreciatively.

"No," I admit, "I've never eaten here."

"Oh, you should. Antoine is a Michelin chef. He's amazing."

I smile politely. I've seen the prices of Midnight's degustation menu, and a four-course meal would easily cost me a day's wages. A wine pairing would cost me two days' work. So yeah, not going to be eating here anytime soon.

He has a swig of coffee. "I'm sorry about your dad. That's tough. So you're filling in for him at work?"

"Yeah. Trying to keep up with his schedule and not let things slip."

"That's tough on you. How many staff does he have now?"

"There are eight of us. But he'd been building up his client list over the summer, and now we're suffering a bit trying to make sure we don't fall behind." I break off another piece of muffin. "Four of the guys are working on a big landscaping job on the east side of the island, which only leaves four of us to do all the regular gardening work." I suddenly remember that Midnight is a client. "Of course we'll always make sure we complete all the projects in a timely fashion."

He quirks an eyebrow at me. "Yeah, because I was about to complain. You're such a slacker."

I poke my tongue out at him. "I just don't want anyone to think I can't cope. I'll get it all done, even if I have to work through the night."

"That won't be necessary. The bank terracing can wait if you have other pressing tasks. We won't just hire another firm if you're a few weeks late."

"That won't be necessary."

"You shouldn't be working Saturdays," he scolds. "Everyone needs time off."

"So what are you doing in the office?"

He blows out a breath. "I was meeting with the board of the Ngā Whetū Rangatahi Foundation."

"Oh, I read about that. You're going to be the CEO, aren't you?" It's an impressive role. The Foundation is relatively new, but there's been a lot of publicity in the press about it. It looks as if it's going to make a significant impact on underprivileged Māori youths in the area, giving them access to opportunities they wouldn't normally have. With Kingi's Māori background, his connection to outdoor activities, his youth and success in the business world, and the fact that he's such a nice guy, he's a natural choice for the role.

"Maybe," he says, and he pulls a face.

"Oh? Problems?"

He sighs. "Have you seen the front page of this morning's Kōrero?"

"No."

He takes out his phone, brings up the page, and hands me his phone.

Trying to ignore the fact that it's a huge, brand-new, latest-model iPhone that must have cost him a small fortune, I read the article. Then I look up at him in shock. "Is it true?"

He frowns. "You mean did I jump off the waterfall? Well, yeah. But I hadn't had a drop of alcohol. I wouldn't do that. Give me some credit."

I've insulted him. "I'm sorry. Of course you wouldn't."

He scratches at a mark on his jeans. "I was showing off. But I wasn't drunk."

I look back at the phone. "Oh, was that where you met Sabrina Pearce?" She's a stunning supermodel, famous throughout the country for having advertised a popular perfume and fashion brand, and she's also appeared in a couple of New Zealand movies. I'd seen photos of them together on Insta, but I wasn't sure if they were still dating.

"Yeah. More's the pity."

"Oh dear. Is everything not rosy in the garden of lust?"

"If you're asking if I broke up with her, the answer is yes."

"You dated the most famous supermodel in the country, and then *you* dumped *her*?" I give him a curious look. "Why?"

He rolls his eyes. "Because she had all the personality of a wet lettuce."

"But you still took her to bed?"

"Well I'm not stupid." He purses his lips. "Actually, maybe I am."

I stifle a giggle. I'm not shocked by his admission. He's always had trouble keeping it in his pants. He's a sucker for a pretty face, a big pair of boobs, and a nice ass, and I'm sure it didn't hurt that every fella in the country would give their right arm for a night in bed with her.

Then something clicks. "Wait, are you saying it was Sabrina who said you were drunk, in retaliation for breaking up with her?"

"I think so, yeah."

That shocks me. Someone would really do that? I think about what he said, about meeting the board today. "The board called you in about the article?"

He sighs, leans forward with his elbows on his knees, and runs his hands through his hair. "Yeah. They said it reflects badly on the Foundation. Which it would do, of course. I'm such an idiot."

"Well, you didn't make her run to the press. She sounds like a nasty piece of work if she lied about you being drunk."

"I rejected her. I need to grow up a bit. I know that." He looks at his hands, and suddenly I can see the child in the man.

"Well… yeah, maybe you need to be a bit more careful choosing your bed partners," I say with a smile.

He gives me a wry look.

"Are they saying they won't give you the position?"

"No… but they did make it clear that I need to act more responsibly, and to look respectable." He pulls a face.

That makes me laugh. "Sorry," I say when he throws me another glare, "but that's plain funny. You, respectable?" I subside into peals of laughter.

He stretches out his legs and huffs. "Yeah, amuse yourself at my expense." But his lips curve up as he takes a huge bite out of his muffin. He brushes his beard to remove any crumbs, then flings me a crooked smile.

He's so incredibly handsome. He's always had the power to make my heart skip a beat, and it's clear that nothing has changed.

I've been half in love with this guy for about twenty years, but I've always known it would never be reciprocated. How could it, when he's destined to date women like Sabrina Pearce? He'll end up with a stunning beauty, someone who knows which fork to use at the dinner table, who is the patron for a major children's charity, and who won't look out of place on his arm at social events. The biggest social event I've been to is a hoedown at a local music festival, and there wasn't a sign of a high heel or a designer label anywhere. I'm like Cinderella to his prince, except that there's no fairy godmother to magic me into a princess, and so there will never be a happy ending for the two of us.

More's the pity.

MIDNIGHT BARGAIN

Chapter Three

Kingi

Sabrina sat in the same chair as Chessie just last week, and she also ate a quarter of a muffin by breaking it into tiny parts and feeding them to herself with her well-manicured fingers.

Chessie has a big bite out of hers, and ends up with a blob of soft chocolate on the end of her nose. She laughs and wipes it off with a serviette, then has another bite. It's nice to see a girl eat something properly.

"What's going on in your life at the moment?" I ask. "Are you still dating Tamati?" I saw a photo of her with the fly half from the local rugby team on social media a few months ago.

She shakes her head. "We broke up a week ago."

"Oh? No chance of getting back with him?"

"He wants to," she admits, studying her muffin. "He's being rather a pain about it."

"In what way?"

"Oh, you know… He won't leave me alone. He sits outside my house, revving his car and annoying the neighbors. He texts and calls me all the time." As she says the words, her phone vibrates where she's left it on the table. She picks it up, puts it down, and gives me a look that says, *Speak of the devil…*

"Why don't you block him?" I ask, puzzled by both the guy's behavior and the fact that she's allowing it.

"I will, if he doesn't stop."

"Are you thinking about getting back with him?"

"No."

"Why did you break up? Did he cheat on you?"

"No, nothing like that. He was just so prickly, so intense and argumentative. I was tired of the accusations and arguments. I just want peace and quiet." She smiles and has another bite of muffin.

I study her while she looks out at the gardens, no doubt checking what work needs to be done. She looks like a nymph, like a tree deity dressed in green with her red hair tumbling past her shoulders. She hated the color when she was young, always wearing it cropped short and even dying it occasionally, but now it's gloriously red, a true Titian, glinting with golden highlights in the sun. She was wearing a sweatshirt when she was digging, probably to keep the sun off her pale skin, and she won't be wearing sun lotion after her shower, so I stand and put up the umbrella in the middle of the table, casting a shadow over the two of us so she doesn't catch the glare of the New Zealand sun, which can be harsh even at this time of year.

"Thank you," she says. "God knows I have enough freckles."

"I love your freckles." I sit and have another bite of my muffin. "I've always wondered if they're all over your body."

She coughs into her drink, throws me a look, then wipes her chin with a serviette.

"Sorry," I add, "did I say that out loud?"

That makes her laugh. "You're incorrigible. No wonder you get into such trouble."

"Life's too short to watch what you say." I lean back, holding my cup, and sigh. "I hate polite society. Actually I don't like people much at all. I'm happier when I'm off on my own in the wilderness and I don't have to worry about talking or, you know, washing."

She chuckles. "I wondered whether the current look reflected a recent excursion." She gestures at my hair and beard.

"I cut it all off for a friend's wedding back in February. Nobody recognized me. So I haven't had it cut since." I sip my coffee, feeling mischievous. "So, are they?"

"Are they what?"

"All over your body? Your freckles."

She snorts. "Wouldn't you like to know?"

I tip my head to the side. The skin on her face and arms is pale, so the rest of her body is going to be even paler. I bet she has freckles all over her breasts. Down her tummy. Up her soft thighs. Between her legs, on that sensitive, possibly hairless skin?

I lift my gaze back to hers. She's blushing.

"Stop picturing me naked," she scolds. "It's weird."

"Why is it weird?"

"You're like my brother, for God's sake."

"I can safely say, Chessie Ross, I have never thought of you like a sister."

It's actually a lie. I used to think of her like that... until I kissed her.

She meets my gaze now, her green eyes wide, her expression clearly baffled.

"I'm sorry," I relent, thinking about the Foundation and feeling suddenly guilty at my behavior. "I'm being inappropriate."

Her lips curve up. "I don't mind the teasing. We've known each other long enough that I know you don't mean it." She chuckles and looks away, sipping her coffee. She honestly thinks I'm joking. She obviously has no idea how beautiful she is. Tiny and perfectly proportioned. She's not tall or stick thin like Sabrina; her muscles are toned from her physical job, and she's pleasingly rounded. Definitely a C cup, maybe even a D.

I catch myself thinking about it and tear my gaze away. What the fuck is wrong with me? See, Kingi, this is what Mikaere and Moana meant when they said you need to be more respectable. You're about to head a foundation that teaches young men how to—including other things—be respectful to women. What kind of fucking role model are you going to be?

I clear my throat. "So... how are you enjoying being in charge of the business? Do you like being the boss?"

She pulls a face. "God, no. I'm terrible at it. I struggle with the paperwork. And I'm no good at managing people. Luckily most of them know what they're doing and they organize themselves."

"What about Mark?" I know that her brother also works for their father's business. "What's he up to?"

She lowers her gaze to her coffee cup. "Let's just say he's not management material." Her lips twist, but she doesn't elaborate.

"Can't you hire someone to do it for you?" I ask, puzzled.

She gives me a strange look, and I can see her debating whether to tell me something. She looks away again though, across to the gardens, and doesn't say anything.

"You can talk to me." I'm concerned. I don't like to think of her struggling with the workload, as well as the emotional stress of her father's illness.

She nibbles her bottom lip. Then she gives a little sigh, as if coming to a decision, and she looks back at me.

"There's a financial issue," she says softly.

I lean forward, my elbows on my knees. "With the business?"

She studies her coffee cup. Then she says, "Partly."

So that's why hiring someone to run it is out of the question. "What do you mean by partly?"

She thinks again. I feel that she's choosing her words carefully, as if picking out the best flowers for a vase. "Dad's had trouble meeting the payments on his house. The bank is threatening repossession."

My eyebrows lift. "You mean his income has slipped because he hasn't been working?"

"Partly."

Another partly.

I wait for her to go on.

She looks at me then, a slightly pleading glance. "If I tell you, you must promise not to say anything."

I frown. "Of course."

"Not to anyone, Kingi."

"*E hine*, I wouldn't." It means 'dear girl'.

"Mark has a gambling addiction," she reveals. "It started in his teens, and it got out of hand in his early twenties. Dad bailed him out then, and we got him some therapy, and we thought it was better. But recently Dad discovered he'd gotten back into it. He's in huge debt."

"How huge is huge?" I ask.

"He's maxed out several credit cards and taken out a personal loan. He got hooked on some online betting apps. And… he's borrowed from some disreputable sources."

Loan sharks. It doesn't get much worse than that. "How much?" I ask again.

"Forty-five thousand dollars."

I frown. It's a significant amount. "So Joe bailed him out again?" I ask.

"Yes. He used all his savings."

"And then fell sick?"

She nods.

I frown. "You said he's having trouble meeting his mortgage payments. Won't the bank give him a payment holiday?"

"Yes, they did… on the first mortgage."

MIDNIGHT BARGAIN

"He re-mortgaged the house?" I'm shocked.

"It's the only way he could raise the extra funds, and the payment holiday doesn't apply to that loan. And he still has to pay rates, insurance, utilities, groceries… One of our ride-on mowers blew up, and we don't have the cash for repairs. We're late paying invoices, and a couple of our suppliers are demanding money. I didn't know all this until Dad went into hospital. Mark's useless at the business side of things and has let it all slide." Her voice is bitter—she's torn between loyalty to her brother and absolute fury at him. "It's all such a mess," she confides.

I can already see the problem—no capital buffer, no debt restructuring, no forward forecasting. The bank has happily lent them money with the house as home equity top-up, but all that's done is threaten the family's stability now they can't meet the payments. The compounding interest is only going to add to their problems, especially from the loan sharks. I doubt she's even thought about that.

"I'm so sorry." I lean forward to catch her eye. "You should have come to me sooner."

She attempts a smile. "I appreciate that, but I'm not just going to knock on your door and tell you all my problems."

"Well, I'd hope you would do that, considering our history, but that's not what I meant. I mean in a financial and business sense. Forty-five thousand isn't that much. I'm sure we can work something out."

Her eyes widen. "It isn't that much?" She glares at me. "It's almost what Mark earns in a year."

My mouth opens, but no words come out. Shit. I didn't think. I've probably got forty-five thousand in my pocket.

"It might be a drop in the Pacific for someone like you," she says, "but to most normal people it's a huge amount of money."

I clear my throat. "I apologize. I didn't mean it to come out like that. I just meant that I'll happily bail you all out until Joe's fit to work again."

Her face falls even more, and her spine stiffens. Oh fuck, could I screw this up any more than I already am?

"I don't need you to point out the vast gulf between our financial situations," she snaps. "That is very clear to me."

Fuck. "I didn't mean—"

"And I don't need your pity or charity."

"I know that. That's not what this is."

"Isn't it? Throwing money at me to 'bail me out'? Do you know how patronizing that sounds?"

Irritation flares inside me. "I was trying to help."

"By insulting me?"

"I didn't mean—"

"No, it just happens by accident, doesn't it? You haven't changed, Kingi. You've always gone through life the same way you go through the bush—hacking your way through and expecting everyone else to get out of the way, and if they get caught by your scythe, well, it's their own fault."

That hurts, because it's true. I've been told repeatedly through the years by family and friends that I speak without thinking.

"I know I can put my foot in it," I say as carefully as I can. "But I do mean well. You don't have the financial experience and training that I do, and I can help."

"No," she says, "I'm just stupid old Chessie, who hasn't even been to university."

I bristle. "Don't talk about yourself like that."

"But that's what you're thinking, isn't it? I know what your family thinks of mine."

"What?" I stare at her, startled.

"'Really? You can do better than that, boy…'" She adds air quotes to it and gives me a mocking look. Oh holy shit. The day I kissed her, she must have lingered and overheard what my father said. That's why she's so angry now. She's aware that the gulf between us is social, as well as financial, and that my father considered her family inferior to his own.

Horror fills me at the thought that she's known that all these years. "Fuck. Chessie. I'm so sorry."

She lifts her chin. "You think I'm clueless, and there's no way I could possibly sort this out myself."

That's not what I meant at all, and it makes me bristle. "You said yourself you were in a mess."

"I just meant it's taking time to sort it all out. I don't need your help. And don't think you can go and speak to your friends at the bank or something and magically pay everything off because I'll know it was you. I'll work it out, even if I have to work every minute of every single day for the next year. I was sounding off, letting off steam. I wasn't asking for your help, and I don't need it." Her green eyes blaze. Wow. She's magnificent, and for a moment I'm speechless.

She puts her cup on the table and gets to her feet. "I think it's time I went."

"Chessie..." I rise quickly as she walks away, catch my big feet in the legs of the chair, and trip over. "Wait..."

But she's striding away. She collects her bag as she passes and heads for the door.

"Chessie!" I jog across the room so I can reach her before she leaves.

She yanks the door open, but I put an arm across the doorway, stopping her from going. "Please," I say, "I apologize, I didn't mean to upset you."

She's breathing fast. "I don't need a white knight dashing in on his charger," she says icily. "Before you think about rescuing someone else, I suggest you sort out your own situation, because that looks primed for disaster."

She bends and picks up her boots, ducks under my arm, and runs down the corridor to the stairs.

I watch her go, because I know no words will be able to convince her to stay, and I can't physically restrain her.

I go back into the room and slam the door with as much force as I can muster, but it's fitted with a hydraulic mechanism and closes really slowly, so it provides none of the satisfaction I desire.

Fuck it. Me and my big mouth.

I stand in the middle of the room, hands on my hips. Dammit. I could really do with getting down the gym now and wearing off some of my frustration, but the clock on the wall reveals it's later than I thought. I told Orson I'd meet him at midday to go over some figures, and there's no time for a workout.

Gritting my teeth, I pocket my phone, then head out of the room and take the elevator down. I stride through the lobby and out through the gardens toward the main building, walking fast, telling myself it's because I'm cross with her, but with some surprise I realize it's not anger I'm feeling but guilt and regret. I insulted her, and I feel bad about that. I'm as bad as my father. She's trying hard to get back on her feet, and she thought she was offloading to a friend. She wasn't asking for money, and even though I was trying to be kind, I should have offered in a much subtler way.

"Kingi!"

I glance over and to my frustration see it's my father, making his way from the car park toward the building. I stop and wait for him. He's also walking fast—a family trait—and he's also glowering.

"Kia ora." After Chessie's revelation, I'm not really in the mood to talk to him, and my words come out clipped. "Everything okay?"

He blows out a breath. "Not really."

As we climb the steps, I ask, "Why, what's the matter?" I'm pretty sure I know. It's Saturday morning and so he'll have come straight from home, so it's bound to be something to do with Mum.

Sure enough, as we walk into the building he says, "That woman drives me insane. I had to get out of the house."

It's tough to know what to say during times like this. Publicly, my parents are devoted to one another. They always appear together socially, and there's never been any hint of scandal. Privately, it's a different story, and they have a very volatile relationship. They've always tried to keep their arguments from me and Marama, but of course it's impossible not to notice when plates are being thrown or raised voices can be heard on the other side of the house.

It happened so often when I was young that I thought Dad had become immune to feeling bad about it. So I'm surprised now when he runs his hand through his short graying hair and lets out a heartfelt sigh. His gaze finds mine, and he gives me a long-suffering look. "Never get married, son," he says gruffly. "It's the road to hell, for sure."

"That's encouraging."

"I mean it. Women are all demons sent here to torture us."

"You're not wrong there," I say gloomily, thinking of Sabrina. My lips twist, but he doesn't return the smile. He stops outside his office and looks away, his chest rising and falling fast. Shit, he's genuinely upset.

"You okay?" I ask, concerned. "Was it a bad argument?"

He huffs. Then he says, "Yeah, pretty bad."

"What was it about?"

He shakes his head. Studies his feet for a bit. Then he says, "She wants a divorce." He looks up again and meets my eyes.

My heart skips a beat. "Seriously?"

He nods.

"Why?" I'm absolutely stunned. "Have you… cheated?"

He glares at me. "Of course not. We've just grown apart. We want different things out of life now. And you know what it's like… it's become so hard to be civil in each other's company. We're just incompatible."

"Have you agreed to it?"

"No. I want us to stay together for appearance's sake. She's thinking about it. But today she's moving into one of the spare bedrooms."

I'm so shocked, I can't think what to say. "I'm sorry," I manage eventually.

He shrugs. "*He rā anō ki tua.*" It means 'there is another day beyond.' Or 'don't worry, tomorrow will come. Things will work out.'

Privately, I'm not so sure. When one partner starts thinking about divorce, I would imagine it's impossible to stop that train reaching the station.

My parents are going to get divorced. I'm surprisingly shocked and upset about that. Maybe because, deep down, even though I know they argue, the fact that they've stayed together has given me hope that marriage works if you put effort into it.

Well, shit.

"You seeing Orson?" Dad asks. When I nod, he says, "All right. Catch you later." He goes into his office and closes the door behind him.

I purse my lips, then walk slowly down to Orson's office. His door is open, and when I go in, I find him sitting in one of the soft armchairs in front of the window, looking at some reports as he sips his coffee. His terrier pup, Bearcub, is lying in a shaft of sunlight in the middle of the office, snoring.

"Kia ora," I say, going in.

He looks up. "Kia ora." He gestures at Bearcub. "Mind Foghorn Doghorn over there. Where the hell does all the volume come from?"

I give a wry smile, step over the dog, and flop down onto the sofa.

He watches me, amused. "What's up? Who pissed in your cornflakes?"

I blow out a breath. "I just saw Dad."

"Oh? What's he doing here on a Saturday?"

"Apparently Mum's asked for a divorce."

His eyebrows rise, and he puts down the report. "Oh, fuck."

"Yeah. I'm stunned." I shake my head. "I never thought they'd get this far. I mean, I know they argue a lot, but I just thought that was the way they showed affection."

"I'm so sorry."

I huff a sigh. "I didn't really need that after this morning's meeting."

"Oh, yes, how did it go?"

"I got a dressing down and a lecture about respectability."

He frowns. "I hope you told them you weren't drunk when you jumped off that waterfall, and that Sabrina was being a bitch."

"I did. But the truth doesn't matter, does it? Only what it looks like."

His frown deepens. "I guess."

"Koa told me they need someone the youngsters can look up to, not a playboy who's seen with a different woman every week."

He winces. "Ouch."

"Wouldn't hurt so much if it wasn't true."

"Well…" He gives me a pitying look.

"They said it would be good if I looked like a man who values commitment, and if I had someone steady by my side. After seeing how miserable my father is, I can safely say that's never gonna happen."

"Not all marriages are miserable." He scratches his cheek.

I lift a brow. "Have you proposed yet?"

"No. But I'm going to."

"Look at you, being a model citizen. You'll start wearing cardigans next." The sarcasm in my voice holds a hint of bitterness.

He chuckles. "You're just jealous.

I glower, because he's right. I've never met anyone I've even come close to settling down with.

"Have you ever been in love?" he asks curiously.

I snort. "Love is something invented by Valentine's Day card manufacturers."

"I used to think that, but it's not."

"Look, with all due respect, you two do seem happy, but it's not going to last once the cold, clear air of reality cuts through the fog of lust."

"Wow. That's some cynicism you got there, my friend." His eyes glint—he's only a little amused.

Fuck, how many people can I piss off today?

"Sorry," I say grudgingly. "It's been a tricky morning. I don't know what to do about the Foundation. I'm not going to propose to someone just so I can look respectable."

Orson grins. "Maybe you should get yourself a trophy wife."

I snort.

But he says, "I mean it. A fake fiancée. Someone to act the role and stave off the headlines. I've seen you play Lysander in A Midsummer Night's Dream. You're not a bad actor. I'm sure you can find a girl who's willing to play the role for a few months until the scandal dies down."

"I don't know a single girl I'd be interested in living with for even five minutes."

"Dude, you don't actually have to be a couple. Can't you think of a friend who might want to help you out? Someone you like? Not all girls are evil. Some are actually quite nice." He's teasing me now.

I open my mouth to reply, then close it again as the vision of someone with bright red hair, pale skin, and flashing green eyes appears in my mind.

Oh God, can you imagine it? Asking Chessie Ross to play the role? She'd bite my fucking head off.

Although… if I were to make her an offer she couldn't refuse… Make her see it as a business deal…

Orson's grin widens. "I can see you like that evil plan."

"Mwahaha. It might actually work."

"Want to share who you have in mind?"

"Not yet. I'll need to think about it first."

He laughs. "Okay, let's get these reports done, then. I've got a gorgeous soft woman waiting at home for me, and I'd much rather spend the day with her than with you."

Chapter Four

Chessie

"Can I get you anything, Dad?" I perch on the arm of his chair. When he was young, he used to have red hair, but everything about him is gray now. His hair, his skin, even his clothing. I should make him change his T-shirt to something more colorful, but I don't think he has the energy to move.

It's Sunday morning, and yesterday afternoon Dad was discharged from hospital. I drove there after I left Kingi and brought him and Mum home. The hospital declared he would recover better at home now he's out of danger, but I'm worried about him. He's on lots of medications, and they say his wound has only a minor superficial infection, but I've looked at it, and I'm not sure it's getting any better. Apparently a community nurse is going to come in every day to check it and change his dressing, but I'm concerned he's not showing more improvement. The list of things to expect after a heart bypass is as long as my arm—fatigue, appetite changes, bruising and swelling, anxiety and mood swings, confusion, depression… He's supposed to go for short walks to prevent blood clots, but he's so tired I have to bully him out of his chair.

"I'm fine," he says, but his smile doesn't reach his eyes.

"Stop fussing." My brother is sitting on the sofa with his wife, Nina. He scowls at me. "He's an adult—he'll soon say if he doesn't feel well."

"Leave her alone," Nina snaps. "She's just worried about him. There's nothing wrong with that."

I get up and sit on the floor with my niece, Thea. She's eight, a super-sweet, bright young thing I adore with every ounce of my being. She's coloring in a picture of Ariel from Disney's *The Little Mermaid*, and as I stretch out onto my front beside her, she pushes the box of pencils over to me. I smile, choose a blue one, and start coloring the sea so she can concentrate on the mermaid.

I feel so sorry for her. Her parents argue all the time, and even though they've said she doesn't know anything about their financial situation, she's smarter than they think. She knows something is awry. Now, as they continue arguing, she glances at them, at me, then back at her book, concentrating on making sure she doesn't go outside the lines.

"Tea anyone?" Mum asks cheerfully, cutting into their argument. "How about you, love?" she asks Dad.

"Please," he says, even though I know he'll only have a few sips to please us.

Everyone else also says yes, so Mum goes off to the kitchen to make it. I think she's relieved to leave the room, and I don't blame her. It's tough to watch your partner in pain, and having Mark and Nina picking at each other all the time isn't pleasant either.

"So how many times have you seen *The Little Mermaid* now?" I tease Thea.

"Thirty-seven and a half," she says. "I didn't finish it this morning before we had to go out."

I laugh and switch pencils to yellow so I can start coloring Flounder. "I bet you know it off by heart. Is it your favorite?"

"Yes." She carefully colors the mermaid's shell top in purple. "You need blue for his fins and tail," she points out.

"Of course. So why do you like it so much?"

"Ariel's pretty. She looks like you."

I laugh, flattered. "That's very sweet. I think she's a lot prettier than I am, though!"

"When you haven't waxed your mustache you look more like Yosemite Sam," Mark says.

I check to make sure Thea's looking at her pencils before I give him the finger.

"Don't be mean," my father says to Mark.

I glance up at him. It's unlike him to say something like that. Normally he lets our bickering flow over him.

"I'm only teasing," Mark says, exasperated.

"Well, you need to think more about how your comments might make other people feel. Take some responsibility for your words and actions for once." Dad glares at him.

I return to the box of pencils and rifle through them, looking for a dark purple so I can color Ursula's tail. Our family has been through a lot, and despite everything, as far as I know Dad hasn't once criticized my brother for his actions. He's always accepted the news of Mark's failures with quiet resignation, blaming himself for a lack of guidance, even though I've told him many times it's not his fault. So it's unusual for him to openly reprimand Mark, especially in front of his wife and daughter.

Mark shifts on the sofa. "There's no need to be like that."

Dad brushes a hand over his face. "Sorry."

"No," Nina snaps, "don't apologize. You were right."

I frown at them. "Guys, save this for later, okay?" I glance at Thea, who's still focused on her coloring.

They ignore me, though. "Don't start," Mark says irritably.

Nina stiffens. "Don't tell me what to do."

"I'm tired of you berating me as if I'm five years old."

"When you start acting like an adult, I'll start treating you like one."

I push myself up to a sitting position, frustrated. Last night I was so tired after a busy week's work, as well as going to and from the hospital, that I decided to take Sunday off, but now I wish I hadn't bothered.

"Come on," I say, "it's Dad's first day home, and this is the last thing he needs."

"Well, maybe Mark should have thought of that before he—" Nina stops abruptly as Mark shoots her a glare.

I frown and look at Dad. He's also glaring at Mark stonily. There's an icy undercurrent, as if the door's open and the autumn breeze is blowing through the house, but the sliding doors are closed, and the coolness is coming from the atmosphere, not the weather.

"What's going on?" I ask suspiciously.

"Nothing," Mark says.

My gaze slides from him to her and then to Dad. He looks at Thea.

"Hey," I say to her gently, "how about you go and ask Grandma if she needs some help?"

She puts down her pencil and says, "Okay," then scrambles to her feet and goes out of the room.

"What's going on?" I ask again, my heart starting to race.

"Nothing," Mark repeats, more forcefully this time.

But Nina has clearly had enough. "A man knocked on our door last night," she reveals.

"Oh?"

"Apparently Mark borrowed money off him, and he wanted the first installment."

My jaw drops. Another loan shark? When my brother confessed his debt to us, we pushed him to tell us all of it, all the credit cards, all the loans.

Nina is breathing fast, and her eyes are filled with fury. My eyes widen. "This is a new loan?" I ask, and she nods. Mark drops his gaze to his jeans and scratches at a mark on them. "You're still gambling?" I ask, incredulous.

He doesn't reply.

"How much?" I demand. When he doesn't reply, I direct the question at Nina. "How much?"

"Another five thousand," she says.

"Five thousand…" Horror fills me. "Mark, how could you?"

Slowly, the resistance seeps out of him, and his shoulders slump. "I only borrowed a thousand," he says. "But they charge a hundred percent interest if you don't meet a payment, and late fees…" He sits forward and puts his face in his hands. Oh jeez. So if the loan isn't paid, it's going to balloon into a huge sum.

"He can't stop," Nina says bitterly. "He's so fucking weak."

"There's no need for that," I tell her, even though at that moment I agree with her.

"You're going to ruin us," Dad says bleakly. I can tell by his face that he already knows about the extra debt. That's probably one reason why he seems so beaten today.

"Don't," Mark says, shaking his head, covering his face.

Emotion wells inside me. "I know you're not trying to hurt us on purpose. You have an addiction, and you need help."

"I'm so tired of it," Nina says, and bursts into tears.

"Look," Dad says to him, "look what you've done. You call yourself a man? What kind of man makes his wife cry like that?"

Nausea rises inside me. I can hear Thea in the kitchen with Mum—they're about to come in with the tea. I can't have her witness this. Mark's shoulders are shaking—I think he's crying too, and Dad's eyes are also shining.

Suddenly, it's all too much. I've done everything I can for my family. I've worked my fingers to the bone to try and help them, and where has it gotten us? We were struggling before, and now we have another five thousand to add to the debt. Well, I can forget about getting the ride-on mower mended. I wouldn't take a wage myself, but I have my own rent and bills to pay. I don't know what to do anymore. I have nothing else left to give.

Despair sweeps over me. I love my father, and I don't want to add to his stress when he's so ill. And I love my brother, and I want to help him. But everyone has their limits, and I've finally reached mine.

"You need to get help, Mark," I say. "Clearly, you have a problem. And it's not up to us to solve it for you. You need to want to be better." I get to my feet. "I'm going to take Thea out for a drive. While I'm gone, you have to think seriously about where you go from here. Because I'm done."

I pick up my purse and walk out of the room, meeting Mum and Thea coming down the corridor. "Come on," I say to Thea brightly. "We're going out for a bit."

Her face lights up. "Oh, okay! Let me just pack up my pencils."

"No, you can do that later." I pick up her hand. "We won't be long," I say to Mum. "I'm sorry, but I can't stay." Against my will, my bottom lip trembles.

Her face falls, but she says, "It's okay, love. You two go for a while and enjoy yourselves."

I walk past her, bringing Thea with me. At the front door, we shove our feet in our shoes, and then we go out, crossing the front lawn to my car.

I open the back door, and Thea climbs in and sits on the booster seat I always have in my car for her. I make sure she's buckled in properly, close her door, and get in the front, and soon we're on our way.

"Where are we going?" Thea asks.

I swallow hard, trying to calm my emotions. "I thought we could go to the Waiora." The waterfall and natural pool is open to everyone. Lately they've been doing some work around it, making it safer and creating some new facilities, but as it's Sunday and out of season, it will probably be fairly quiet.

"Can we swim?" she asks. She knows I keep a bag in the car with a swimming costume and a towel for us both.

"Isn't it a bit cold for that?"

"The sun's out," she persists.

"We'll test the temperature when we get there," I promise. The pool is usually on the cool side because it's fed by the waterfall, but kids never care about how cold the water is.

"Why was Mummy shouting?" she asks.

I glance at her in the mirror. "Don't worry about that."

She glares back. "Everyone always says that. I'm not stupid."

"I know…"

"They argue all the time. They're in trouble, aren't they?"

I hesitate. She's not my daughter, and I don't want to cause problems because I've told her things they'd rather she didn't know. Most people believe children should be shielded from problems and worries.

But I can see her frustration, and her fear. All she knows is that something's gone wrong and her parents are arguing and upset. I can only imagine what she thinks might have happened.

Well, I'm not going to lie to her. We're close, and I want her to think she can always come to me if she needs help.

"Wait till we get to the Waiora," I say, "and we'll talk about it."

She sits back, apparently mollified by that, and looks out of the window for the rest of the short journey.

The main road heads through the hills to the Midnight resort, then curves around it, and I pull off into a public car park close to the waterfall. It's empty, so I doubt we'll find it packed with visitors. I turn off the engine, then get out and open the door for Thea. I collect the bag I keep in the boot, lock the car, and take her hand, and we head along the path toward the waterfall.

I haven't been here for a few months, but I'd heard they were doing some work. I can see evidence of it already. This used to be little more than a muddy track, but they've put gravel down so it will be less slippery in the rain. The trees on either side have been trimmed, and at one point where the slope steepens, they've cut a few steps to make it safer and added a handrail.

We can already hear the river and the sound of the water tumbling over the rocks, and then we emerge from the trees to see the waterfall resplendent in the morning sunlight. I've been here when the river is so shallow that the falls are little more than a trickle, but it's been raining, so the flow is relatively heavy now. Upstream, they've erected a bridge across to the side that belongs to Kahukura, the commune now called The Village, which is much safer than the old wobbly stepping stones and also provides a great viewing platform looking downstream over the falls to the sea in the distance. We stay on the public side, though, and make our way down the new steps to the Waiora itself.

Midnight offered us the contract to redesign the area around the Waiora, but we had too much work as it was and had to pass, so they hired another firm. My gardener's eye passes critically over the new landscaping, but I'm relieved to see they've done a good job. They've kept most of the native bush, and the pool is surrounded by palms and ferns, but they've also installed a concrete slope down into the water that makes it much easier to get in. A beautiful pagoda overlooks the pool, as well as several benches amongst the trees. The biggest change, though, is a brand-new set of changing rooms and toilets, set back and well hidden amongst the greenery.

Thea and I sit on one of the benches and look out at the pool. The bush smells damp and earthy, the mineral-rich forest smell after rain, along with the metallic smell of wet rock. The honey-sweetness of the kōwhai mingles with the sharp herbal tang of manuka, as well as the delicate perfume of the pink camellias they've planted to provide some color.

"Is it bad?" Thea asks, reminding me that I promised to tell her about her parents. "Are they sick, like Granddad?"

"No, no, nothing like that." I put my arm around her. "Do you know what the word debt means?"

She frowns. "It's when you don't have enough money to pay the bills."

"That's right, you're so clever. Well, your dad has run up some debt, and we're trying to help him pay it off. We can do it, but it's just going to take some time, and it's important that he doesn't keep making more debt. It's like someone is digging a hole in the ground, and we're trying to put the earth back in. We have to try to fill it quicker than they can dig it, and so it's much better if they stop digging completely—it means we can fill it faster. Does that make sense?"

She nods. "Is he still digging?"

I stroke her hair. "Yes, honey. And he can't seem to stop."

"Why?"

"It's called an addiction."

She thinks about that for a moment. "Like drugs?"

"Yes. With some people, drugs, or alcohol, or tobacco, or a particular behavior, like gambling, create a chemical called dopamine in the brain. It makes you feel good. Like, you know when you're playing a computer game and you level up?"

"Yes."

"You get a little buzz of excitement—that's dopamine, and it feels good. And some people like it so much that they crave that next buzz. They can't stop. It's not their fault. It's called a chronic condition—it's always going to be there, and it can't be cured. Only managed."

"So… he's got into debt because he's gambling?"

I nod, my stomach flipping. I hope I'm not making things worse by telling her.

But she's calm as she says, "I've heard them talking about loans."

Oh shit, so she does know more than she's let on. "Okay."

"A loan is where you borrow money from someone else, isn't it?"

"That's right."

"And you have to pay it back?"

"Yes, over time."

"Why do people do that?"

"Why do they lend money?"

"Yes. Why do they give it away? I don't understand."

"They charge something called interest. So, if you borrow, say, a thousand dollars, you don't just have to pay a thousand back—you have to pay interest, too. A bank doesn't charge much interest, but there are people called loan sharks who charge a huge amount. Each week you'd pay, say, fifty dollars off the loan, but you'd also have to pay something like two hundred dollars interest. So in the end you're actually paying back something like five or six thousand."

Her jaw drops. "That's awful."

"I know. And if you don't pay each week, you can get into trouble."

"Will he go to prison?"

"No, no, honey, nothing like that." I cross my fingers behind my back. I won't describe the true horrors of what might happen if he doesn't meet his repayments: having debt collectors turn up in the middle of the night to collect their TV and other possessions, being thrown out of their home, or maybe even being subjected to violence.

"But he does need help, so he doesn't keep spending more money than he has."

"So he doesn't keep digging."

"Yes."

"Who'll help him to stop?"

"There are groups and therapists he can go to. But it's important that he asks for help. He has to *want* to stop digging, if that makes sense. Nobody else can make him."

She kicks her legs, thinking.

"I hope I did the right thing telling you," I say. "I'm worried that your mum and dad will be angry with me."

"I won't tell them that I know."

I frown. "I don't expect you to keep secrets from them. If they find out, that's okay."

She shakes her head. "I knew there was a hole. I just wanted to know where it was, so I don't fall into it."

My eyes sting with sudden tears. "You're so smart," I whisper. "You're going to grow up into an amazing young woman."

"I want to be a doctor," she says.

My eyebrows rise. "Really?" Mark works for my dad, and Nina is a checkout operator at the local supermarket. Although my father runs his own business, he isn't well educated, and my mother is a dinner lady at the local primary school. They're all nice people, but they're not professionals, so I'm surprised she's aiming so high.

"I want to help people," she continues. "Do you think I could do that?"

"Of course. You'd have to work hard at school, and then go to university."

"Did you go to university?"

"No. When I left school I started working for Granddad."

"Is university expensive?"

She's already thinking about whether her parents will be able to afford to send her. I feel a fresh surge of frustration and fury toward my brother. I know he can't help his addiction, but I also know he didn't think about his wife and daughter—or the fact that our father has remortgaged his house and could well lose it—when he gambled, and I hate him a little for that.

"It does cost money," I say carefully. "But you can have student loans from the government that would help."

"I'm not having a loan," she says fiercely.

"Student loans aren't the same. The repayments are much smaller, and there's hardly any interest."

"I don't care. I'll get a job and work and save up the money until I can afford to pay for myself." She sets her jaw, and her eyes gleam in the sunlight. I'm sure her parents think they've kept their arguments and misery hidden from her, but she's obviously seen more than they've realized.

"I'll help you," I say softly. "If that's what you want, we'll get you there."

"Hello!"

My head snaps around at the sound of a male voice, and my heart races. New Zealand is a safe country, and I've never felt in danger, even if I go for a walk late at night, but we're alone in the middle of nowhere, and my first thought is of Thea.

Relief floods me though at the sight of Kingi Davis, strolling along the path from Midnight behind us, emerging from the trees like some kind of giant Green Man. He's wearing jeans, and his greenstone pendant rests on top of a black tee. Oh my God, the muscles on the man. He looks delicious.

I press a hand over my heart. "You made me jump."

"I'm sorry." He doesn't sound it. He smiles at Thea. "Hello."

"This is Kingi," I tell her. "He's a very old friend of mine. Emphasis on the old." That earns me a wry look. "And this is Thea," I tell him. "My niece."

"Mark's girl?" He holds out his hand. "I used to be good friends with your dad when we were young."

"Hello," she says shyly, and she slides her tiny mitt in his huge paw. He shakes it gently before releasing it.

"Enjoying the peace and quiet?" he asks.

"We were," I say sarcastically.

He just grins.

"How did you know I was here?" I ask.

"I didn't. I often take a walk to the Waiora. It's a peaceful place."

"We're going swimming," Thea says.

His eyebrows rise. "Really?"

"I don't know." I glance doubtfully at the water. "It's going to be freezing."

"Wuss," he scoffs. "You never used to worry." He winks at Thea. "I'll go in with you."

Her face lights up, and she looks at me for permission. "Can I?"

I frown at him. "You're not planning on skinny dipping?"

"When the water's this cold? I wouldn't be very impressive if I did. I'm wearing boxers—they'll do." He starts unbuttoning his shirt. "Come on," he says to Thea.

She jumps off the bench and snatches up the bag. "Please," she begs me. "Come in with us."

I huff a big sigh to cover the fact that the notion of seeing Kingi Davis in his boxers makes my heart race. "Oh, all right. But don't blame me if we all come down with hypothermia."

Chapter Five

Kingi

By the time Chessie and Thea emerge from the changing rooms, I've stripped and already swum across the pool and back.

Waiheke Island isn't huge, and her family home isn't far from Midnight, so it's not a great surprise to meet Chessie here, but even so, I thank whoever's watching over us for my spur-of-the-moment decision to come here.

I observe them walking toward me, glad I'm in the cold water as my gaze falls on Chessie's curves. She's not wearing a bikini today, but the navy costume is cut high at the legs, and the daisy-covered bodice clings to her generous bust. Her arms and legs are covered with freckles.

She stands at the edge of the water and scoops up her hair with both hands before securing it into a bun with an elastic on the top of her head. Wow, that's sexy. I drag my gaze away and smile at Thea as she approaches the edge of the pool, lets the water lap at her toes, then squeals.

"It's always best to get in quickly," I advise. "Can you swim?" It's usually a redundant question—most kids in New Zealand can swim, and many schools have their own pools, especially north of Auckland—but it's always best to check.

"Yes," she says, somewhat indignantly. "But I can't dive yet," she admits.

"Diving's easy. I can show you how, if you like."

"Kingi teaches other boys and girls lots of sports," Chessie says, also shivering as she puts her toes in the water. "Ooh, that's cold."

"Come on, the pair of you. Just jump in." I splash them, and they both squeal.

Eventually, I convince them that the best way is to take the plunge, and within a few minutes they're both in and enjoying themselves. Thea is an okay swimmer—I'm guessing her family doesn't have the money to pay for private lessons, so her technique could do with improvement.

"Your legs have to move like a frog's," I tell her as she attempts the breaststroke. "Like this." I show her. She watches, then pushes off the side, following my lead. "Excellent! You're a natural."

"Can you show me how to dive?"

"Sure, if you want." First, I make sure she knows how to float and tread water. Then we swim over to a collection of large rocks on the bank. These are good for diving from, as there aren't any other rocks beneath the surface. "Start with the lowest one," I tell her, and she clambers out and makes her way carefully to the rock that's just above the water. "Okay, sit on the edge. That's right. Now tuck your chin down and extend your arms. Look, you're just going to tip forward, all right? You don't need to jump. Just tip forward. I'm going to be right here, okay?"

She nods. I glance at Chessie, who's swimming on her back, watching us. Then I look back at Thea. "Go on, then!"

She looks at the water, aims her hands, then tips forward. It's a perfect sitting dive, and I don't have to help as she kicks to the surface, her eyes shining. "I did it!" she declares triumphantly.

"That was terrific!" I cheer, and Chessie joins in.

"Again," Thea says, climbing out. She does it a couple more times, and then I suggest she squats and tips forward, and then finally she does it with straight legs. Once she gets used to the sensation of falling and the shock of hitting the cold water, there's no stopping her.

After that, the three of us have great fun, swimming around and doing tricks in the pool. Thea jumps off my knees, and I bomb them both from the side and make them squeal. Chessie shows her how to do a handstand, and then I do one, and splash Thea when she declares Chessie's was better.

We spend a good hour in the pool. Thea doesn't want to get out, but eventually Chessie declares she's getting cold, and the offer of a snack is enough to prompt Thea to scramble to the side.

"What are you going to do about a towel?" Chessie asks me. Her lips curve up as I blink. "You didn't think about that, did you?"

"Er, no. I'll have to drip dry."

MIDNIGHT BARGAIN

"Are you going to walk back to Midnight in your boxers?"

I scratch my cheek, and she rolls her eyes. "You can borrow my towel when I'm done. Just give me five minutes."

"Okay, thanks."

She helps Thea get out, then hesitates and looks back at me. The last time we spoke, she walked out on me, but I'm relieved to see no resentment in her eyes. "Thank you," she says. "We both needed that today." Without enlarging on that mysterious statement, she gets out, takes Thea's hand, and picks up her bag, and the two of them head over to the changing rooms.

I swim around, pondering what she could have meant, until eventually they emerge, dried and dressed. I get out of the pool and go over to them, and Chessie holds out her slightly damp towel.

"Thanks." I put it around my shoulders and rub my hair as I watch her lift her bag onto the bench and rifle around in it. She brings out a bottle of water and a box of cereal bars, and Thea claps her hands and starts opening the box.

Chessie glances to the right at the ground, sees my feet, and obviously realizes I'm still there. I haven't dried my legs yet, so I imagine she's looking at the water droplets clinging to my hairs as her gaze slowly slides up, gets to my wet boxer-briefs, which are clinging to me, and hitches before her eyes snap up to mine.

Her cheeks stain a light red. "Go and get dressed," she snaps.

My lips twitch. "Yes, Mum."

She rolls her eyes and returns to making sure Thea's feet are dry before she puts on her socks and shoes.

Grinning, I go into the changing rooms, dry myself and put my clothes back on, and do my best to run my fingers through my hair. It's tangled, though, and in the end I give up. I should really get it cut, and my beard too. There's long and then there's *long*.

I go back out and cross the short distance to them, and throw myself on the ground in front of the bench. Chessie holds out a cereal bar, and I take it and demolish it in two bites.

"Wow," she says, as Thea's eyes widen. "Did that even touch the sides?"

"I missed breakfast."

"Some supermodel keeping you up all night?" Chessie asks tartly.

"No... if you must know, I was down the gym this morning."

"At Midnight? Don't you have a house of your own?"

"I do. A very nice one. But I have an early meeting at Midnight tomorrow with some executives staying at the resort, and I was in yesterday, and sometimes I can't be bothered to make the journey home. I need to learn to fly a helicopter, like Orson."

Thea's eyes nearly fall out of her head, and I suddenly remember who I'm talking to. I look at Chessie, wondering if she's angry at me again for reminding her of the difference in our lifestyles, but she's smiling, so I'm guessing not.

"Can I explore?" Thea asks. "I saw a rabbit on the grass."

"Of course. Just don't go too far."

Thea hands her the wrapper from her cereal bar, jumps off the bench, and heads into the trees. Chessie turns so she's astride the bench and can keep an eye on her, then looks down at me and smiles. "You were very good with her," she says. "I can see why they want you at the Foundation."

"Or not," I say, somewhat gloomily. But I don't want to talk about that again. "What did you mean when you said you both needed that today?"

She sighs and stuffs the empty wrappers back into her bag. "We were at my parents' place. Mark and Nina had come to visit because my dad came home yesterday."

"Oh, well that's good, right? They wouldn't have sent him home if they didn't think he was well enough to cope?"

"Yeah... although you always wonder if they need the beds. His wound is still infected. I'm not reassured by them saying it's minor and superficial. It looks horrible."

Of course, I forgot that they wouldn't be paying privately. New Zealand has a free healthcare system, and Joe's heart bypass wouldn't have cost him a single cent, which I'm sure is a huge relief to them. But the staff is overworked, the wait times are horrendous, and the follow-up care isn't as good as it should be, from what I hear. No fault of the doctors and nurses. Just not enough money in the system.

I sense there's something she's not telling me. I glance at Thea to make sure she's not within earshot, but she's sitting on the grass, watching the rabbits playing beneath the trees.

"So... Mark was there... was the atmosphere not good?"

Chessie unscrews the top from a bottle of water, has a few mouthfuls, wipes the top, then offers it to me. I take it and do the same and hand it back to her, and she screws the lid back on. I can see she's thinking about whether to share something with me.

Eventually, she sighs and says, "It turns out he owes another five thousand."

My eyebrows rise. I've been thinking a lot about what she told me, and her statement that it's almost what Mark makes in a year. It's a significant amount of money for the family to find.

"He admitted he only borrowed a thousand," she says softly. "The rest was interest and late payment fees."

Anger flows through me. I can't stand the type of people who make money from others' misery and weakness. "Fuck."

"Yeah." She lifts her hands to her hair, extracts the elastic band, and lets the red locks tumble around her shoulders. "Dad's really angry. I've never heard him criticize Mark, even after everything he's done, but he laid into him this morning. Nina was upset. And I didn't want Thea to see them arguing, so I took her out." She picks up a stone and examines it, then tosses it away with some force so that it bounces off a tree. "It's all so hopeless," she says bitterly.

I don't want to insult her again, but equally I can't let her get upset when it's such an easy problem to fix. "Please," I murmur, "let me help."

She lets out a heartfelt sigh and rests her face in her hands for a long, long time. I wonder whether she's crying, but when she eventually lifts her head, her face is dry. Her eyes are bleak, though. "Thank you," she says, glancing at me, "but I can't."

"Chessie, don't let pride get in the way of a solution."

"Pride is all I have. I'll sort it."

"How? I bet you're already working a seventy-hour week."

"That still leaves a whole day."

"You can't work without a break. That's a sure way to make yourself sick. Believe me, that's one of the first things I learned."

"I can't take your money, Kingi." She speaks slowly, as if she's thought about it and rehearsed what she's going to say. "It's very kind of you, and I was ungracious before, and I want to apologize for that. Yes, you could have phrased it better, but your offer was very sweet. I just can't do it. My father wouldn't want that either."

"Even if it saved his house? And stopped his son getting his legs broken by some nutcase money lender?"

She bites her lip, but doesn't say anything.

I'm lying on my side on the grass, and I prop my head on a hand. I might as well give it a try. What do I have to lose? "What about if we make a bargain?"

She frowns. "What kind of bargain?"

"I give you money. Enough to pay off Mark's debt and all the money lenders, mend your mower, and make sure everyone's flush. Probably a hundred thousand?"

Her jaw drops. "Dollars?"

"Yeah. And in exchange, you give me something else."

She glares at me. "I hope you're not thinking what I think you're thinking."

I stare at her, startled and indignant. "Fucking hell! Give me some credit!"

She returns my gaze for a moment. Her lips twitch. Then she bursts out laughing.

I sulk for a moment, then give a reluctant smile. "That wasn't funny."

"The look on your face…" She giggles for another thirty seconds, wrestling with self-control.

I would never, ever ask for sexual favors in return for money. But there's no doubt that even though she's very different from the women I normally date, there's something about this girl that gives me goosebumps when she looks at me.

"Sorry," she says, sobering finally. "You were saying about a bargain?"

I clear my throat. "I told you about what the Foundation said."

"About you needing to be more respectable?"

"Yeah. They said it would be good if I looked like a man who values commitment, and if I had someone steady by my side."

Her eyebrows rise. "Don't tell me you're going to propose to Sabrina?"

I snort. "Fuck, no."

She gives a short laugh. "Wouldn't that help matters?"

"*E ipo*, I'd murder her within the first forty-eight hours. I don't think that would help my respectability." The Māori endearment means darling. She wrinkles her nose at me.

"I don't want to get married," I state. I look at the ground and pluck out a few blades of grass. "My parents have put me right off that institution."

"Oh?"

"Dad told me yesterday that Mum wants a divorce." I glare at the grass, then lift my gaze to hers. Her expression has softened.

"I'm so sorry," she murmurs. "That's really tough on you."

I shrug. I don't really want to talk about it. "Anyway, I'm not interested in settling down with anyone. Monogamy is definitely overrated. But it occurred to me that I could fake it for a while…" I give her a mischievous smile.

She blinks. "Fake what?"

"Marriage. Or an engagement anyway."

She blinks again. "What?"

I roll my eyes. "I'm saying I need someone to pretend to be my fiancée. Publicly. To come with me on social engagements, parties, that kind of thing. To make me look respectable."

"That's a mammoth task."

"Haha."

"You're saying I could fulfil that role?"

I shrug. "We're friends, aren't we? We've known each other a long time. From the outside, it's not beyond the realms of possibility that we've been dating quietly."

Her brow furrows. "Kingi, nobody would ever believe that we've been dating."

"Why?"

She looks at me as if I'm crazy. "Because I'm me and you're… you."

"I have no idea what that means."

"We're from different worlds," she says softly. "You date models and movie stars—Sabrinas with designer dresses and high heels who are comfortable in your world. I date rugby players who'd have no idea how to put on a tie, let alone do a Windsor knot."

"I know what you're saying, but you're… I dunno… wholesome."

"Wholesome?"

"Yeah."

"Next you'll tell me I'm comely."

"You are comely!"

"It's an insult, Kingi. Like saying I'm a handsome woman."

"No, it's not. It means attractive, and in many ways it makes sense that after all the Sabrina stuff, I'd fall for a girl-next-door type. You're beautiful, and it's a perfect, natural beauty, not the fake kind. Do you really think women like Sabrina look the same without their foundation and hairspray and Instagram filters? They don't, I can assure you."

Her lips part, but no words come out for a moment. She closes her mouth. Then she says, "You think I'm beautiful?"

I smile. "Of course you're beautiful."

"Oh. Thank you."

"I'd do you right now, but I don't want to put Thea in therapy."

That makes her laugh, and we both chuckle. "You're incorrigible," she scolds.

"I know. Look. I could really do with some help. It's a relatively easy fix."

"So you want me to pretend to be your fiancée?"

"Yeah."

"We couldn't just pretend to be dating?"

"I date all the time. The board wants proof of commitment and responsibility."

"You don't find it ironic that you have to pretend to be respectable?"

I frown. "Honestly? I don't see what all the fuss is about. I desperately want this position. I know I can help these kids. Yeah, I'm not perfect, and I know I've not struggled the way some of them have, but I've worked hard to get where I have."

"I know."

"I'd be there to teach them how to swim and climb mountains, and how to work together. To show them what it's possible to achieve with hard work and determination. Not how to have fantastic relationships."

"Yes, but kids see the whole package. They can read headlines." She dips her head to catch my eye as I look down. "I'm not criticizing the way you live, Kingi. You're young and gorgeous; of course you're going to play the field, and I understand why you're anti-commitment, judging by what you've just told me about your parents. And I do think you have a lot to offer young people. It's just… if you're going to do this, you need to think bigger. It's like being prime minister or president—if you're going to set yourself up as any kind of leader, you're going to have a torch shone on every square inch of your life. Every decision you make will impact your image, and people are always ready to tear you down if you don't meet their exceptionally high standards."

"I get it. That's why I'm asking if you'll help."

She meets my gaze for a moment, a frown flickering on her brow.

"A hundred thousand dollars," I tell her. "Don't you think it'd be worth it?"

She straightens. "What would I have to do?"

Ooh, she's thinking about it. I sit up, arms around my knees. "So obviously we'd have to pretend to be dating. Be seen socially a few times—at dinner, a nightclub, the theater... So when we make the announcement, it wouldn't come completely out of the blue. Then we'd probably have an engagement party, maybe at Midnight."

She swallows. "And after that?"

I shrug. "Just be seen together, I guess. I dunno. Never been engaged before."

She thinks about it. "How long would this have to last?"

"We could agree on a timeframe. At least until I get the position, and probably a little while afterward so it didn't look too suspicious. Six months, maybe?"

"So... we'd have to be exclusive, right? No dating anyone else?"

I hadn't thought of that. "Uh... yeah, I suppose."

Her lips curve up a little. "Do you think you can go six months without dating?"

She means without having sex. Six months of celibacy. "Of course. I'll... uh... just have to give my right hand a good workout."

She gives a short laugh. "Yeah, me too."

Of course, I'm asking her to give up dating and sex for a while, too. Now it's impossible not to think about her sliding her hand under the duvet, over her breasts, down her soft pale tummy to between her legs, and pleasuring herself until she comes. Fuck.

Her lips curve up just a little more, as if she's guessed what I'm thinking.

Then she takes a deep breath and lets it out slowly. "I need some time to think about it."

"Of course. Can I ask that you don't take too long, though? It would be cool if we could get started ASAP. It's possible the board is already considering someone else for the role."

"I understand. Just give me tonight to think about it. I'll let you know tomorrow."

"That's more than fair. But just to be clear—I'd still give you the money without you doing this. You know that, right?"

"I know." She looks up as Thea crosses the grass with something in her hand and smiles at her.

"Look," Thea says, holding out a curled-up fern frond. "It had fallen off, and it was on the floor. It's like your necklace." She gestures at me.

I look down at the greenstone necklace in the shape of a spiral that I have around my neck and lift it in my hand. "That's right. It's called a *koru*—it's based on the shape of the fern. My dad gave it to me when I went to university. It's a symbol of new beginnings." I lift my gaze to Chessie. Her eyes are very green, exactly the same shade as the fern frond and the piece of *pounamu* or greenstone in my fingers.

She tears her gaze away. "We'd better get going." She collects her bag, rolls up the towels and clothes, and puts them in.

I get to my feet. "Well, it was nice to meet you," I say to Thea, holding out my hand

She shakes it, beaming. "Thank you for teaching me how to dive."

"You're very welcome. You can be the star of the show now."

"Thanks," Chessie says. "It's been a lovely morning."

"You'll call me?" I ask.

She nods, tucking a strand of her hair behind her ear. "Come on, then," she says to her niece, putting an arm around her shoulders. "Let's go and get some lunch. I'm starving."

They head up the steps toward the car park. I watch them go, enjoying the sway of Chessie's hips and the way the sunlight paints her red hair with gold.

Then I head back to Midnight, hoping that she decides to take me up on my offer. I can think of worse things than being fake-engaged to Francesca Ross.

Chapter Six

Chessie

"He wants you to what?"

I scratch my nose, trying not to laugh at my friends' reactions to my news, even though it's no laughing matter.

I rent a room in a house in Oneroa, the largest suburb on Waiheke Island, along with two other girls. Lisa is twenty-seven, kind and thoughtful, tallish, pretty, and blonde. Ria is twenty-two, Māori, fun and outspoken, with short, somewhat wild, curly brown hair. They both work at the ferry terminal.

"He wants you to be his fiancée," Ria confirms, jaw dropping.

"His *fake* fiancée," I correct. "There's a big difference."

It's Sunday evening, and the three of us are sitting in the living room, sharing a bottle of wine. It's been a tough day, and it's nice to finally sit down and relax.

After leaving Kingi at the Waiora, I took Thea back to my parents' house to discover them all very quiet and sullen. At least they'd stopped arguing, I consoled myself, but to be honest, the miserable, oppressive atmosphere was even worse. Thea and I chattered away about our swim, but we were met with grunts and monosyllabic answers, and in the end I'd had enough. I said I was going home, gave Thea a cuddle, kissed my father's head, and made my way to the door.

Mum met me there, and, uncharacteristically for her, as she's not a hugger, she put her arms around me and held me tightly.

"Hey…" Alarmed, I rubbed her back and gave her a squeeze. "It's okay. Everything's going to be all right."

"I don't know," she whispered. "I'm frightened, Chess."

"There's nothing to be frightened about."

"We could lose the house. Especially now he's added five thousand more dollars to the total. How could he do that when he knew how bad things were?"

"He's not thinking," I said firmly, drawing back and holding her by her upper arms. "I know it hurts, but we don't even enter his head when he's in the middle of it; nor do Nina or Thea. All he can think about is getting the buzz from the next bet. That's why he needs help. We can't keep bailing him out like this. We're just enabling him."

"He's promised he won't run up any more debt."

"He's promised so many times, Mum. It won't work, because he's an addict, and he can't stop."

She pressed her fingers to her mouth as her bottom lip trembled. "I don't know what I did wrong."

She's even shorter than I am, and I had to bend to look into her eyes. "You haven't done anything. It's like having asthma or being short sighted. It's nobody's fault. There's something askew in his brain, and it's nothing to do with you. He needs to get professional help."

There wasn't anything else I could say, and I left then, insisting I'd pop over on Monday to check on Dad and see if she wanted anything.

I cried as I drove home. I felt as if I was giving other people every ounce of my energy, and there was nothing left for me. And the worst thing was that it didn't feel as if it was doing any good. Mark was no better, and there was no sign to the end of his gambling. I believed everything I'd said to my mother, and I knew we were enabling him, but what could I do? I've heard stories of people being dragged to rehab and relapsing as soon as they're released. You've got to want to be better, you've got to want to stop, or what's the point?

When I got in, both Lisa and Ria were home, and they took one look at my tear-stained face, pressed a glass of wine in my hand, ran me a bath, and told me not to come out until I'd finished the wine and was ready to talk.

After half an hour I emerged to discover they'd ordered a pizza, and we sat and ate and drank more wine as I told them what had happened today. I'd already told them about Mark's problem and my father's health, so it didn't take long to update them.

And then I told them about Kingi's offer.

"So let me get this straight," Ria says. "You're talking about Kingi Davis? The dude who's just broken up with Sabrina Pearce?"

"The very same."

"And you knew him when you were kids?"

"Yeah, Dad used to mow his father's lawns."

"But he's, like, mega-rich?"

"Oh yeah," I say with feeling. "Mega, uber, lost track of the number of zeroes in his bank account kind of rich."

"Fuck." Her eyes are like dinner plates. "So… he wants you to pretend to be his fiancée, and in return he'll give you a hundred thousand dollars."

"That's the long and short of it, yes."

She's sitting at the other end of the sofa, and she moves a bit closer to me and rests her hand on my forehead.

"What are you doing?" I ask, puzzled.

"Taking your temperature. I mean, clearly you're coming down with something if you haven't bitten his hand off."

I push her away and give her a wry look. "It's not that easy."

"Why the fuck not?"

"Because she likes him," Lisa says.

I glance at her. I've never talked about Kingi other than to say I knew him as a kid. I've never mentioned having feelings for him. She lifts her eyebrows at me. I poke my tongue out at her.

"Do you?" Ria asks. "Oh…"

"I don't," I protest. "Much…"

"What does he actually want you to do?" Lisa asks.

I shrug. "He was a bit vague. Basically, to be seen together socially. He mentioned dinner, and maybe a nightclub or the theater. And then an engagement party at Midnight."

"How long would this go on for?"

"Again, he was vague. He has to make sure he gets the position first, obviously. And then we'd wait until everything dies down, I guess, then 'separate' quietly. He suggested six months."

They both think about that. "So you'd be exclusive," Ria asks. I nod.

"How do you feel about that?" Lisa queries. "What if you meet someone else?"

I hadn't thought of that. "I don't know."

"He's always in the news," Ria says, "with one model or another. Do you really think he won't date anyone else?"

"I don't know. If he does, he runs the risk of being seen, and losing the position for good. It doesn't sound as if the board is going to be patient with him if there are negative headlines about him again. So it's kinda up to him." A bit like with Mark, I think. Our future is nearly always in our own hands.

"I still don't quite see the problem." Ria looks genuinely baffled. "You get the money, and you get to live the high life for a while. This gorgeous guy will take you to exclusive restaurants and you'll get the best seats at the theater. He'll want you to look good, so he'll probably buy you some great clothes. You'll get an engagement party—he might even let you keep the ring! What's not to like?"

I put my face in my hands. "It's *Pretty Woman* all over again. I've turned into Julia Roberts."

Ria giggles.

"Don't laugh," Lisa scolds her, topping up my glass with the last inch of wine in the bottle.

"Does he want you to… you know… be his partner in every way?" Ria's eyes gleam.

My face flames. "No! Jeez."

"Then how is it the same as *Pretty Woman*? You're hardly selling your body for money."

"Maybe not sexually," Lisa says slowly, "but anything done in exchange for money is a sale, right? And there are always moral implications to that."

Ria blows a raspberry. "You're both reading too much into it. Look, you're his friend, right? He's genuinely asking you to help him out. In return, all your financial problems will be sorted, and you get to test-drive the billionaire life? I don't see the problem."

I bring up my knees and hug them tightly, still holding my wine glass. "I know what you mean, and you're right of course. Forgetting about Kingi for the moment, it doesn't solve Mark's problem. I could pay off all the loans and make sure Mum and Dad are stable and don't lose their house. It's tempting just for that. But what's to stop Mark thinking that if I've done it once, I can do it again?"

"You have to talk to your parents," Lisa says. "I know it's hard, but you'd have to lay down some ground rules. Emphasize that they mustn't bail Mark out again, no matter what happens. If they do, next time they have to sort it out. Make it clear that after this, you're done. There's no more cash, no more help." Her expression softens. "You can't keep doing this to yourself. You're losing weight. You have dark shadows under your eyes. And I know you're not sleeping well. You have your own life to live, Chess."

"With a gorgeous hunk of a human being," Ria adds. "For six months, anyway."

I give a short laugh. "That's kind of the other problem. I don't know anything about his world. I mean, look at me. I'm hardly a socialite. I wouldn't know where to start with talking to his friends and colleagues."

"They're just people," Ria scoffs.

"No, I know what she means," Lisa says. "The highlight of our week is meeting up down the Pioneer for a beer or going for a curry. I don't know about you, but I've never been to a top restaurant or nightclub. And I've never been the subject of a news headline. It sounds like fun on the surface, but if you agree to this, you'll have to live that lifestyle for six months, whether you want to or not. I think you'd have to be very clear about what is and isn't acceptable. I mean, is he expecting you to move in with him?"

"I don't think so."

"This isn't the nineteenth century," Lisa points out. "Most people live together before they get engaged. Don't you think people will think it weird that he proposed before you even lived together?"

"Um…"

"You could say you don't believe in sex before marriage," Ria says.

We all look at each other for a moment. Then we all burst out laughing.

"No, okay." She wipes beneath her eyes. "That won't work."

"You could move in with him," Lisa says, "but stay in one of his spare rooms. I mean I'm betting he owns a huge house, right? He must have more than one bedroom."

"Yeah, he's got a villa overlooking Little Palm Beach." It's a bay on the north side of the island, well known for the fact that it's the only beach on the island where you can swim naked.

"Nudie Bay?" Ria giggles. "Wow. Yeah, that's a great idea. Maybe he's got staff! Imagine what that would be like. Being waited on hand and foot."

"I don't think he spends his days lying on chaise longues eating grapes," I point out. "I doubt he's got staff." As soon as I say that, though, I remember his parents' home. They have a gardener, a housekeeper, a chauffeur, and I believe a chef comes in sometimes to cook for them. Who wouldn't have all that, if they had a choice?

"Communication is key," Lisa says. "If you decide to go ahead with it, you need to sit down with him and hash out the details. Explain how far you're willing to go, and what your limits are."

"Hard and soft," Ria says, waggling her eyebrows.

I blow out a breath.

"It said in one of the articles that he's six-four," she adds. "Is that true?"

I nod. "He's huge." Her eyes widen, and I hastily say, "I mean big. I mean tall!"

They both giggle. "You know what they say," Lisa teases. "Does he have big feet?"

I bite my lip. "Yes, he does, they're enormous."

We all collapse into laughter. Ohhh… it's good to laugh after the day I've had.

"You never know," Ria says mischievously, "maybe he'll fall in love with you, and you'll actually end up together."

I shake my head sadly. "That's definitely not on the cards. He likes models! And movie stars! Not gardeners. Not every Cinderella gets her prince."

"Well," Lisa says, "I don't think—" She stops and cocks her head.

"What?" I ask.

She's the closest to the front window, and she gets up and crosses the room to peer through the curtains. "Fuck," she says, "I don't believe it."

Ria and I exchange a look, and my heart starts hammering. We both get up and run to the window. Sure enough, Tamati's car is parked out the front, and he's revving the engine.

"Shit." Anger flares inside me. We've already had one neighbor complain that he woke up her baby daughter with his revving and yelling.

"I'll deal with him," Ria says, turning to leave.

But she has a tendency to flirt with him, and I don't want him sitting outside thinking he'll get attention every time he does this. "No." I cross to the coffee table and put down my wine glass. "I'll sort it."

"Why don't we just call the police?" Lisa's angry. "This is harassment. He's stalking you, and it's against the law."

"I will if I have to. I'm going to try one more time."

I walk out to the front door, take my jacket off the hook, and put it on, covering my pajama top. I shove my feet in my Wellingtons and pocket my phone. Then I open the door and go out.

It's nearly seven, so the sun has set, and the street lamps are on, casting pools of orange on the dark pavement. I walk down the short path, go out of the gate, and walk up to the car.

Tamati stops revving the engine as I approach him, and he lowers the window. "Hey," he says, and smiles.

I've come out to talk to him several times before. I liked him a lot, and I was keen to part on good terms, but after the day I've had, my patience is paper thin.

"What are you doing?" I snap.

His smile fades. "I just wanted to see you. And I don't seem to be able to get your attention any other way."

"You've got to stop this."

"Come and get in," he says. "We'll go for a drink and have a chat."

"I'm in my pajamas!"

He just laughs. "This is New Zealand—no one cares about that."

"I'm not going to a bar in my PJs. Tam… I'm serious now. We're done. I'm not going out with you again."

"Babe… come on." His lips curve up. He knows his smile undoes me. He's incredibly good looking, and he has an irresistible charm I can't resist. I found it so hard to break up with him, but every time I told myself I could put up with his faults, he'd do something that would leave me exasperated and unhappy. He picked holes in the smallest things, and we were always arguing. He seemed to thrive on that; I think it turned him on sometimes. But I'm not like that. I take everything to heart. And what with everything else that's going on my life, I don't need the stress. I want him to leave me alone.

And suddenly, I know how to stop him.

"I've met someone else," I blurt out.

He stares at me for a moment. Then his expression turns wry. "Aw, come on…"

"It's true," I say calmly, relieved he's forced my hand. "I've been seeing an old friend of mine. We met up for a chat, and he asked me out."

"Who is it?" he demands.

"His name's Kingi."

"Kingi who?"

"Davis."

His eyes widen. "Kingi Davis."

"Yeah."

"You're dating Kingi Davis?"

"Yes."

"The one who's just broken up with Sabrina Pearce?"

"The very same."

He laughs. "What the fuck does he see in you?"

I don't reply, and after a second, he sobers and adds hastily, "I didn't mean that, I mean obviously you're worth ten of someone like her…"

"Yeah," I say sarcastically, "nice attempt to backtrack."

"Shit, Chess…"

"Fuck you," I tell him heatedly. "He really likes me, and he won't take kindly to you harassing his girl. He's fucking huge, and even if he doesn't want to take you out himself, he's rich enough to employ a whole fucking hit team, so stop fucking harassing me, and leave me alone!" I end on a yell, turn on my heel, march back into the house, and slam the front door.

I stand there, trembling, both furious and upset as Lisa and Ria come running out.

"Are you okay?" Lisa's brows draw together.

"I'm fine." I kick off the wellies, take out my phone, then hang up my jacket. "I'll be back in a second." I march off to my bedroom and close the door behind me.

Once inside, I go over to the bed, sit down, and take out my phone. I bring up messages, pull up his name, type a text, and send it. I'm sure he's at Midnight, partying the night away, so I don't expect him to reply, but to my surprise he comes back in thirty seconds.

Me: *The answer is yes.*

Kingi: *Hey! Really?*

Me: *Yeah.*

Kingi: *Shit! What convinced you?*

Me: *It was a variety of things, including Tamati turning up tonight. I told him we were dating to get him off my back. I'm really sorry about that.*

I send it, feeling a tug of guilt. Maybe he's already changed his mind about his offer, and outing him like that might make him cross.

But he comes back with *Taku tau, that's fine, I'm glad I could help*. It means 'my beloved', and it's a very romantic endearment. Kingi is so openhearted. It makes me smile.

Me: *We should probably meet to talk about it, do you think?*

Kingi: *Definitely. I'd like to draw something up legally, actually. I'll make an appointment with my lawyers and let you know the time*

My eyebrows rise.

Me: *Do we need to get lawyers involved?*

Kingi: *It's always best to when money is involved. It's to protect both of us, and we can discuss the finer details while we're there*

My heart races. Suddenly it feels very real. This isn't him giving me fifty bucks to go on a date at a family function to stop his grandmother nagging him about settling down. We're not eighteen anymore. Kingi is a hard-nosed businessman who lives in the limelight, and we're talking a significant amount of money. The full realization of what I'm doing hits me. For a hundred thousand dollars, I'm going to have to pretend to be getting married to him in front of family, friends, and the rest of the country. People are going to want to take my photograph. Maybe even interview me. And the scariest thing of all is that I'm going to have to be close to him… to pretend to be his… Will he want to touch me? Kiss me?

Kingi: *You okay?*

Me: *You know I'm a terrible liar, right?*

Kingi: *LOL. You don't have to lie*

Me: *Sorry, what? We're going to pretend to be dating*

Kingi: *Look, we're old friends. We'll go on a few dates. Yeah, maybe the engagement will be a white lie, but it's not beyond the realms of possibility that something like this could have happened*

Me: *I guess*

Kingi: *It'll be fine, and I really appreciate you doing this for me*

Me: *You're welcome. I appreciate the money*

Kingi: *Are you all right? Did Tamati shake you up?*

Me: *A bit*

Kingi: *Want me to go around and rearrange his teeth?*

That makes me laugh.

Me: *No, I'm hoping that's done the trick. I don't think he'll be back*

Kingi: *He will*

Me: *What do you mean?*

Kingi: *You're a catch, Chess, and he's lost you. He's going to be mad as hell. I'd be very surprised if he gave up now*

I sigh.

Me: *All right. So you'll let me know about the lawyer?*

Kingi: *Yeah, I'll make it late tomorrow*

Most people would have to settle for whatever time the lawyer was free, but I'm guessing that for clients like Kingi, lawyers make time.

Me: *Okay. I'll see you then*

Kingi: *Sleep well, and don't worry. Everything's going to be fine*

Me: *Night*

I turn off my phone with an impending sense of doom. Something tells me Kingi's talking out of his ass, and he has no idea that this has disaster written all over it.

But it's too late now. I've made my decision. And I have to stick to it, no matter what happens. I won't fall for him. I know he has this reputation for being a womanizer, and he comes across as a real Prince Charming, but I know the real Kingi. The untidy, scruffy miscreant who likes to go a week without washing when he's off on one of his adventures. The one who can eat a sandwich in two mouthfuls, and who can burp the National Anthem after drinking a can of Coke. His charisma is all a facade, put on to charm the Sabrinas of the world, and there's no way I'd ever fall for someone like that.

Chapter Seven

Kingi

"Ooh. I didn't know you'd ordered lunch." I go over to the plates of rolls, sushi, tiny savories, and cakes on the table in Orson's office and help myself to a sausage roll.

"Scarlett's coming in," he says, in the middle of typing on his laptop. "So I thought we'd lunch together."

I look at the half-eaten sausage roll in my hand. "Oh. Sorry."

"I ordered enough for you. I knew there was no way you wouldn't demolish half of it before she arrived."

I snort, finish off the sausage roll, and drop into one of the armchairs. Our city office is in Auckland's CBD, high up in one of the new office blocks, overlooking Waitematā Harbour. Auckland Harbour Bridge is just visible to the west, linking the CBD to the North Shore. The harbor is busy this Monday lunchtime, with ferries transporting passengers to and from the city, tourist boats off on sightseeing tours to Rangitoto Island to spot orcas and dolphins, million-dollar yachts carrying the rich and famous, and fishing boats returning with the catch of the day.

"What time's she coming in?" I ask.

He looks up at the door. "Here she is now." He closes his laptop and gets up. "Hey gorgeous."

"He's talking to me," I tell Scarlett as she comes into the office, and she laughs and comes over.

"I know better than to come between a man and his bestie," she says, bending to kiss my cheek.

I grin, then watch as Orson comes over, pulls her into his arms, and kisses her. He's had a few girlfriends over the years, even lived with one for a while, but I've never seen him like this before. He's completely besotted with her. I'm not saying I don't understand why.

She's beautiful—small and shapely with light-brown skin and glossy brown hair, she has a good sense of humor, and although she's the daughter of his family's old enemy, it wasn't enough to keep them apart. But I'm pretty sure he's going to propose to her, and that's shocked me. We used to joke about marriage and monogamy, and why it was pointless to commit to someone long term, because obviously relationships never last forever, and all you're doing is setting yourself up for trouble by making it legal. And now here he is, on the verge of saying 'till death parts us.' I just hope he's got a good prenup sorted, because when it all goes wrong she could easily take him for half of his fortune.

She sits on the sofa in front of the window, and Orson fetches three bottles of water from the fridge in the corner, brings them over to the table, then sits beside her.

"I won't stay," I promise her.

"This isn't a romantic rendezvous," she says wryly.

"It isn't?" Orson fakes disappointment.

"I can always lock the door on my way out." I wink at her, and she laughs.

"We're just going through some figures for the Village," she says, naming the commune her father set up. They've changed the name recently and don't refer to it as a commune anymore because of the negative connotations that it brings, and the problems they had when her father stole money from the shared accounts. It's all been sorted now, and I helped the Elders set up a new, more transparent financial system, but they told us they want auditing regularly, and to have us keep a close eye on their finances.

"Yeah, well, like I said I'll leave you to it… but I just wanted to tell you about something first." I choose a cheese and salad roll and eat half of it in one bite. "I'm getting married," I tell them through a mouthful of roll.

Orson stops with a piece of sushi halfway to his mouth and stares at me, while Scarlett coughs into her water.

"What?" Orson says.

I try not to laugh. "You inspired me with your idea of a fake engagement."

Orson starts laughing. "Oh yeah, a trophy wife."

"This was your idea?" Scarlett says to him.

"He's kidding." Orson eats the sushi. I lift my eyebrows, and his eyes widen. "You're not kidding?"

"Nope." I eat the other half of the roll. "I thought it was a brilliant idea. It's what the board wants—some kind of commitment to show respectability and responsibility."

"Oh, the irony," Scarlett says. "Sweetheart, what they want is for you to understand the benefits of being committed to someone. Not to fake it."

"No," I say impatiently, "it's all about appearances. Nobody cares what I actually think or feel. It's all about what it looks like."

They exchange glances, then look back at me. "I think you've missed the point," Scarlett says.

"I want to be CEO of the Foundation," I point out, "not Director of Feelings and Emotions. I want to help the kids achieve more in their lives, to inspire them to do better. They don't care about my love life. But I understand that it's about presenting a respectable package, so I'm going to do what Orson suggested and fake it."

"With whom?" he asks.

"Chessie Ross." I help myself to another roll.

"Who?" Scarlett asks, puzzled.

"She's an old friend of his." Orson's lips curve up. "She's Joe Ross's daughter."

"Oh… from Ross Gardening?"

"Yeah. She and her brother, Mark used to play with Kingi and Marama when they were kids."

"She's in financial trouble," I tell them. "Mark has run up significant gambling debts, and Joe remortgaged his house to try to pay them off. But now he's recovering from a quadruple bypass so he can't work, and the bank's threatening repossession."

"Oh no." Scarlett presses her hand to her mouth. "That's awful. What a worry for them."

"Yeah, they just don't have the cashflow to solve it."

"Don't tell me," Orson says, "you asked her to pretend to be your fiancée in return for paying off the debt." He glares at me.

I glare back. "What do you take me for? I offered to pay off the debt first, but she refused. The only way she'd accept it is if we made a bargain."

"And she agreed?"

"Yeah, she texted me last night. She's having trouble with an ex who keeps harassing her, and she told him she'd met someone else to get him off her back."

"And then she agreed to marry you?"

"To *fake* marry me. Yes."

Scarlett rolls her eyes. "Oh, this is going to end well."

I huff at them. "I thought you'd both be supportive. She's a good friend. It's a brilliant idea."

"It's a shit idea," Orson says. "You know what they say—having a female as a best friend is like having a chicken as a pet. You'll definitely eat her one day."

I glower while Scarlett subsides into peals of laughter.

"That won't happen," I state firmly. "There will be no eating of any kind. It's a business proposition."

Orson gives me a sarcastic look. "Are you also planning a dowry or herd of cows to sweeten the deal?"

"For fuck's sake…"

"What's she like?" Scarlett asks curiously.

"She's cute," Orson says. "Red hair, big boobs."

Scarlett laughs again and takes a mini quiche. "Yeah, this is going to be real fun."

I lean back and give them the finger. "Mock me all you like. Like I said, it's a business deal. I'm meeting her today at Whenua Law. Tane has drawn up a document making it all legal and above board." I pronounce his name 'tah-neh.'

"Why aren't you using our usual lawyer?" Orson asks.

"I wanted to keep this separate from work stuff."

Scarlett snorts. "Nothing says romance like a binding agreement with penalty provisions."

"Just make sure you add a force majeure for broken hearts," Orson says.

I grit my teeth. "I'm not going to break her heart."

"I didn't mean her."

I just laugh. "The contract will make sure everyone's on the same page, and keep us both safe."

"How long do you plan on this show lasting?"

"Dunno. Six months?"

"And… what will it involve?"

"I honestly haven't thought about it that much."

"I can see that."

I huff another sigh. "I dunno, going on dates, being seen together in public, and then we'll put on an engagement party at Midnight."

He eats another piece of sushi, his eyes dancing. "Is she going to move in with you?"

"What? No!"

"Don't you think it'll look weird if she doesn't?"

I hadn't thought of that. "Well, maybe she can stay over occasionally or something. The house is big enough."

"So she'll sleep in the spare room?"

"Of course."

He just chuckles.

Scarlett frowns. "Seriously, Kingi, this has disaster written all over it. I know what it's like to be an ordinary girl thrown into this world of glitz and glamor. It's scary and overwhelming. And I don't think you realize how attractive you are."

"I'm right here," Orson says.

She gives him an amused glance. "I just mean he's very charismatic. She's going to fall for him, and she's going to get hurt."

"She won't fall for me," I say, baffled. "She's not interested in me in that way. Her ex is a fly half."

It's Scarlett's turn to look confused. "I'm sorry, your point is?"

"She likes small weedy guys."

"So you only like blondes?"

I think about it. "Point taken."

"Just... be careful," Scarlett says.

"No need." Impatiently, I get to my feet. "It's a business arrangement. I half wish I hadn't told you it was fake."

"Like anyone's going to believe it's real," Orson scoffs.

I bend and steal the last cheese roll. "What do you mean?"

"We all know you too well," Orson says. "Nobody's going to believe you've actually proposed to a girl you've only taken on a few dates."

"Oh, I'll make it look believable."

"How?" Scarlett wants to know.

"How do you think? I can fake adoration. Throw around a few kisses here and there for the tabloids."

She giggles. "This is going to be great."

"I've got an idea," Orson says. "Scarlett's right in that it's overwhelming for someone who hasn't been part of our world to suddenly be thrust into it. Why don't we double date? It might make it easier for her."

"You're just hoping I fall flat on my face," I tell him.

"I'll get the popcorn," he replies.

I give up. Everyone's a critic, but I know what I'm doing.

It's not a bad idea, though, and we agree to a date the following day at seven at a restaurant on the waterfront. I promise to book it and leave the room, hearing them laughing as I walk down the corridor.

*

As it gets near to five, I walk the short distance to Whenua Law. The firm is on Victoria Street West, not far from the Sky Tower. It's a fine afternoon, the bright sun bouncing off metal and glass, although there's a coolness in the air that confirms we're well into autumn, which is confirmed by the orange and purple leaves falling from the occasional sweetgum tree. I bet Chessie knows the Latin name for them, I think as I cross the road and go through the double doors into the building.

I'd hoped to get here before her, but as I walk into reception, I see her sitting on the visitor chairs to one side. Nearby, a female lawyer helps herself to some water from the cooler, while another is talking to the receptionist—they're both wearing dark suits with crisp white blouses and high heels. One has a neat bob, the other has long straightened hair, and they're both wearing lots of makeup.

Chessie looks incongruous in black trousers with Converses, and an oversized bright pink shirt that oddly goes well with her red hair, which is in a scruffy bun. She stands as she sees me, and I walk up to her. She still reminds me of some kind of Greek nymph. Man, she's small. Apart from her boobs.

"Hello," I say, and smile.

She scratches her head and looks up at me nervously. "When does it start?"

"The meeting? At five."

"No, the engagement. I mean, I wasn't sure how to greet you." She glances at the receptionist and the lawyers.

My lips curve up. "I'm more than happy to smooch, if that's what you're asking."

She gives me a wry look. "That wasn't what I was asking. I'm just saying, if we were engaged, we wouldn't just say hello."

"What would be an acceptable greeting, do you think?"

"I don't know, I've never been engaged before."

"Neither have I, as it happens. So… a hug?"

"Possibly."

"Come here, then." I bend, slide my arms around her, and lift her up. She squeals and laughs, then wraps her arms around my neck and hugs me.

I bury my nose in her neck and inhale. She smells of the outdoors, of fresh air and flowers and mown grass. Her breasts are soft against my chest. I like how she's so small in my arms.

"Kingi," she says, "you can put me down now."

I lower her so her feet touch the floor, then see she's looking to her left and follow her gaze. The women at reception are smiling at us.

"Sorry," I say to them. "I got carried away."

"Nah," the lawyer says, "it's *sweet as*. Nice to see." She chuckles.

I look at Chessie. She's blushing.

"Kingi!" It's Tane, and he walks toward us with a smile. "*Tēnā koe, e Kingi, kei te pēhea koe?*" It means 'Greetings to you, Kingi, how are you?' We shake hands, and then we lean forward and solemnly press noses and foreheads together in a *hongi* or traditional greeting. "Sorry to keep you waiting," he says. "I was caught on a phone call." He turns to the woman waiting at my side. "You must be Francesca." He holds his hand out to her.

"Everyone calls me Chessie," she says shyly, and shakes it.

"It's very nice to meet you, Chessie. Come down to the meeting room, you two. Would you like a coffee?"

"I'm okay, thanks," Chessie says, "I've just had one."

"I'm fine, too," I tell him, and he nods and leads the way.

We enter the meeting room, which is just a small square room with a circular table surrounded by four chairs. A closed manila folder rests on the table, along with a jug of water and three glasses.

He closes the door, and we all sit. He's in his fifties, with gray curly hair. He's an old friend of my father's, and I've known him since I was a kid, so even though Orson and I use another firm for our company's legal business, I'm more than happy to ask him to help out. He's more like an uncle, and he's often outspoken and doesn't usually hold back from speaking his mind. I half expected him to tell me this was a dumb idea, but so far he's kept his thoughts to himself.

"So," Tane says, "Kingi has informed me of your agreement, and has suggested that it makes sense to draw up a contract to clarify some issues and make sure you're both on the same page."

Chessie nods. "I understand."

"This is our first draft." Tane extracts the document from the manila folder and slides it across to Chessie.

I sit back and wait for her to read it. It's a cross between a prenuptial contract and a services contract. The first half includes a list of clauses: a clear finish line of December 31st; the financial settlement of a hundred thousand dollars, and a stipulation that she has no further claim to my assets, shares, or company holdings after the agreement ends, and I have no claim to hers; a confidentiality clause that neither of us can disclose the true nature of our agreement—if she were to breach it, it might incur repayment of the financial settlement, whereas if I were to breach it, she would be able to keep the money; a conduct clause stating we both agree to behave respectably to support the image of stability—basically making it clear that neither of us can date anyone else; and that she waives any rights a legal spouse/fiancée might have.

"What rights would they be?" she asks, pointing to the clause.

"You would have no claim to alimony, inheritance, or property," Tane says.

"Of course," she says. She glances at me, her expression puzzled. "I'd never do anything like that."

"Kingi asked me to include what I thought was necessary," Tane says smoothly.

He's lying—I asked him to make sure she would have no claim to any of my finances. I don't think she'd ever try to fleece me, but some women would, and I thought it was better to be safe than sorry. He's covering for me. That's nice of him.

"Um… about the confidentiality clause," she says. "I'm so sorry, I've already told the two women I live with. But I won't tell anyone else, I promise."

"It's okay, I've told Orson and Scarlett," I point out.

"I'll add those exceptions to the contract," Tane says, opening his laptop and then typing in. "What about your families? Are you going to tell them?"

"I won't," Chessie says. "I don't want them to know. As far as they're concerned, this is genuine."

"I won't say anything either," I reply. "The less people who know, the better."

"What about your father?" she asks.

"He won't be a problem." I'm not going to give him a chance to argue.

She looks doubtful, but turns her gaze back at the contract. The second half contains some performance guidelines.

"Appearance Quotas," she reads out loud. "Ms. Ross must accompany Mr. Davis to at least twelve public functions." She looks up. "Twelve? Eek!"

"We have to be seen in public, Chess. That's the whole point."

"I guess... but twelve!"

"Over six months? That's only two a month."

She looks pained. "Please don't make me be sociable."

I chuckle. "I'm afraid I can't move on that. It's the whole point of the bargain."

"I suppose." She narrows her eyes. "All right." She looks back at the contract. "An Affection Clause? 'Displays of affection should be natural but appropriate?'" She looks at Tane. "You want me to sign a contract that says I'll kiss him naturally? Who decides whether or not a kiss is natural?"

"I'll take it upon myself to ensure authenticity," I tell her.

"I'm not kissing you," she states.

I frown. "Is the thought so abhorrent?"

She ignores me and glares at Tane. "I'd like that clause taken out."

He concentrates on pouring us a glass of water each.

"No," I say. "Come on, we can't be engaged and not kiss."

"We'll just say I'm shy."

"There will need to be kissing," I say firmly. "We can include a clause that says no tongues if you like."

Tane coughs into his glass, and I chuckle.

Chessie groans. "This is a nightmare." She looks back at the contract. "What's this about expense coverage? What does that mean?"

"For appropriate clothing and accessories," Tane confirms.

"For 'appropriate' clothes? This really is Pretty Woman, isn't it?"

I frown. "You're insulted because I want to give you *more* money?"

"Because you want to tell me what to wear. I have my own wardrobe, thank you very much."

"We'll be going to some upmarket events." My voice holds a touch of sarcasm. She's indignant because I want to give her a clothing budget? Most women would kill for that. "Ten-year-old jeans, Alien T-shirts, and gumboots won't pass muster, I'm afraid."

She glares at me. I glare back.

Tane clears his throat. "Can I be honest with you both?"

She turns her laser gaze on him. "Please do."

"I've known Kingi a long time," he says. "I can honestly say this is the most hare-brained scheme he's ever come up with, and that's saying something. A hundred thousand isn't nearly enough to justify spending six months with this *roro hūrepo*." It literally means 'brains of mud.' He's calling me an idiot. "So I'd recommend taking as much money as he's offering and crossing your fingers that the next six months go extremely fast."

Chessie stares at him, then bursts out laughing.

"Thanks," I say to him.

"Don't mention it." He taps the contract. "What you've agreed to do here, Ms. Ross—helping Kingi to look respectable so he can get the position on the board—is very admirable."

"It's not that admirable," she mumbles. "I'm doing it for the money."

"I appreciate that, but he told me he offered you the money, and you refused unless he received something in response. That's very unusual in this day and age. Not everyone would have been so honorable. So I've made it airtight, to protect you. Kingi has to behave, and if he doesn't, you get to keep the money."

"You remember that you work for me?" I say indignantly.

"You've never been able to keep it in your pants," he says. "But you're a good lad, and I think you'll be a great benefit for the Foundation. So I'm just offering my advice. Also, it's why I've included the last clause."

"I thought that was the last clause," I say. He forwarded me the contract earlier, and I read through it closely.

Chessie reads out the additional few sentences he's added. "The Parties acknowledge that this Agreement is entered into solely for the purpose of maintaining public appearances and enhancing the reputation of Mr. Davis. Accordingly, Mr. Davis shall, for the duration of this Agreement, exercise self-control befitting a gentleman and refrain from engaging in any physical intimacy, romantic advances, or otherwise inappropriate conduct (collectively, "Prohibited Conduct") toward Ms. Ross. Any breach of this clause shall constitute a material breach of contract, entitling Ms. Ross to immediate termination of the Agreement and to seek such remedies as may be available at law or in equity."

"What?" I glare at Tane. "That's harsh. You make it sound like I can't control myself."

"It's for Chessie's benefit," he states. "I know what you're like."

"Does this mean I need a lawyer present every time I look at her?"

He just gives me a sardonic look. I glance at Chessie. She's trying not to laugh.

"I appreciate you looking out for me," she says to Tane. "And I think it's good to be clear where we both stand. Okay, pass me the pen."

"You're going to sign?" I ask her, astonished.

"I'll sign," she says. "God help me. I really need the money."

Tane makes the changes on his laptop, prints it out, and goes to get the new copy.

"You're sure about this?" I ask her once he's left the room.

She nods. "I admit that, at first, I was a bit hurt that you felt the need to make it legal like this. But I can see how it protects us both, and I appreciate that."

I feel a surge of fondness for her. Her big green eyes are wide and clear. There's something innocent and naive about her that I find very appealing, and I don't want her to get hurt. "All joking aside, I am very grateful for this," I tell her gently. "It means a lot to me."

"And to me, Kingi. Playing at being a rich guy's fiancée is a small price to pay for so much money."

"I'm glad I could help. I just hope that Mark appreciates what you're doing for him."

She scratches at a mark on the table. "I know it could be seen as enabling him. But I can't keep doing it. It's destroying me. I've already decided, I'm going to make it clear that it's the last time. After this, he's on his own, and if Dad wants to bail him out and lose his house, that's up to him. I'm not getting involved."

Her eyes glisten. I can see how it's going to kill her to tell them that, but I'm so glad she isn't going to keep throwing herself under the bus.

"It'll be okay," I murmur. "I'm sure Mark will come to his senses when he realizes he's on his own." Privately, I'm not so sure. An addict can't just stop. He needs professional help, and often only reaching the bottom will force them to ask for it. But my main concern is Chessie, and if I can help her right now, that's what's important.

"I hope so. This... what we're doing... A lot of my hesitation was because I don't want it to go wrong. I don't want to lose you as a friend."

Puzzled, I reach out and covered her hand with mine. "Why would you?"

She turns her hand over, and our fingers close around each other.

"Don't break my heart," she says.

Just make sure you add a force majeure for broken hearts.

I'm not going to break her heart.

I didn't mean her.

"It'll be fun," I say firmly. "That's all. It'll be nice to have a companion for a while. The last clause will stop any... prohibited conduct. The main thing is that we communicate well, and everything will be fine."

Her eyes meet mine, and there's something in them that makes the hairs rise on the back of my neck. She opens her mouth to say something... but at that moment, Tane comes back into the room with the new copy of the contract, and the moment passes.

"Here you go," he says cheerfully. "Time to sign away your sanity."

I resist the urge to give him the finger, pick up the pen, and grumble about wishing people would keep their opinions to themselves as I sign at the bottom.

Chapter Eight

Chessie

"Where's he taking you?" Ria wants to know.

It's five p.m. Tuesday, and Kingi has told me he's going to pick me up at six and take me for a meal on the mainland with his friend Orson and his girlfriend, Scarlett. I've been working all day on the landscaping of the back slope at the Midnight Club, and I'm knackered. I just hope I don't fall asleep halfway through the meal.

I stand in front of the mirror in my bedroom, holding a dress in front of me, and survey my reflection with pursed lips. "Some restaurant called Te Moana on the waterfront."

"Te Moana?" Ria's eyes nearly fall out of their sockets. "Oh my God, seriously?"

I meet her gaze in the mirror. "You've heard of it?"

Her lips curve up. "Chessie… honestly. You're hopeless. It's, like, the most expensive restaurant in the city. Everyone who's anyone goes there."

"I don't know why I'm going, then—I'm nobody." I swallow hard. "I don't want to hear it. I'm already nervous enough." I smooth down the black, knee-length dress. "What do you think? Will this do?"

"You look like you're going to a christening."

"That's good, right?"

Lisa giggles. The two of them are sitting on my bed, watching the show. "Not really. You want to wear something that makes everyone sit up and take notice."

"I really don't. I want something that will make me fade into the background."

"Then that dress is perfect," Ria says.

I stick my tongue out at her. She just grins.

"I don't like wearing dresses," I grumble. "I feel like a newsreader. Or a personal assistant. I'm so much more comfortable in trousers."

"Then you should wear trousers," Lisa says. "But not jeans. What about those navy pants you bought at Christmas?"

"These?" I pull them out of the cupboard. They're high-waisted and tailored, and I like them a lot.

"Yeah, they look good on you."

"In that case, you need a flashier top." Ria gets off the bed. "Hold on." She disappears while I pull the trousers on, then reappears with something from her own wardrobe. It's a sleeveless top in a soft pink with small darker pink, red, and navy flowers and petal shapes. It's really pretty.

It also has a plunging neckline.

"That looks great on you," I tell her. "With your B cups. It won't look so great with my pillows."

"Just try it," she urges.

Grumbling, I pull it on. We're a similar size, so it fits nicely, except for the fact that it dips too far south and reveals my generous cleavage.

"Argh." I try to pull the sides together.

"No!" She laughs and bats my hands aside, then turns me to face the mirror. "I'd kill for your boobs. You look amazing."

"This is Kingi we're talking about," I remind her. "He doesn't need encouragement to look at a girl's tits. If anything I should be trying to distract him. I ought to wear a roll-neck sweater."

"No, she's right," Lisa says. "He's a good-looking guy and you're supposed to be his fiancée. You have to try to look the part."

I roll my eyes and turn back to the mirror. "All right, I'll wear it, thank you. But maybe I should put a safety pin in the middle?"

Ria gets off the bed. "Go and get ready, before my brain explodes."

Lisa laughs and gets up too. "Let us know if you need anything else. The bathroom's all yours." The two of them leave the room, closing the door behind them.

I survey my reflection and tug the two sides of the top together. They refuse to meet, though, leaving the Grand Canyon of my cleavage available for anyone to see.

Huffing a sigh, I take off my clothes, put on a robe, and go and have a shower.

By the time Kingi draws up outside the house in his Porsche, I'm ready. The girls do Paper, Scissors, Rock to establish who gets to answer the door, and a triumphant Lisa goes to answer it when he knocks.

"Hello!" she says.

"Kia ora." He smiles at her. He's wearing cream chinos and a maroon shirt that stretches tightly across his impressive biceps. He's rolled up his shirt sleeves, and his Māori sleeve tattoo is clearly visible. The guy fills the doorway physically and metaphorically. Talk about larger than life.

Lisa immediately turns scarlet and loses the ability to speak.

Ria giggles and joins her at the door. "I'm Ria," she tells him, offering her hand, "and this is Lisa."

"Afternoon, ladies. It's great to meet you." His voice is deep and resonant. He's tidied his hair and beard, but they're both still long. Everything else about him screams wealth, from the car sitting like a panther on the roadside to his large expensive watch. It's not the first time I've thought of him as a modern-day Tūmatauenga, the god of war and hunting.

"I… um…" Ria looks up… and up… and up… and blushes.

"Good grief." I usher both of them away from the door. "Stop charming my friends," I scold him, retrieving my purse.

"I'm just standing here."

"It's the way you're standing."

"On my feet?"

I wave goodbye to them, go out, and close the door behind me. "You know perfectly well what you do to women."

"Well it's not intentional, and I never mean to…" His voice trails off. "Er…" He blows out a breath. He's looking straight into my eyes, but his gaze has an odd intensity.

"Are you trying not to eye-dip me?" I ask curiously.

"Summoning every inch of willpower I own," he replies.

I roll my eyes. "You'll dislocate something if you carry on like that. Just look and get it over with."

"I wouldn't dream of it." He takes my hand.

"You're saying you've never looked at my boobs?"

"I always look at your boobs. I just didn't realize they were quite so… full. That's some cleavage you got there, girl."

I look down at it as we walk to the car. "I wanted to wear a roll-neck sweater, but the girls wouldn't let me."

"Please thank them for me."

"I will, when I'm lying on my hospital bed because you couldn't keep your eyes on the road."

He chuckles and opens the passenger door for me. "Give me some credit."

I slide into the seat.

"I'll only look when we stop at traffic lights," he says, and closes the door, cutting off my retort.

As he walks around the car, I huff a sigh and buckle myself in. He gets in the driver's side, closes the door, and does the same.

Then he looks at me, and we both start laughing.

"Kinda nice to be going on a date with a friend," he says as he starts the engine.

"I know what you mean. There's no pressure."

"Yeah, no awkwardness."

"I hate dating," I grumble.

"Me too!" He turns onto the main road and heads for the ferry. "That moment where the conversation is all awkward and you're feeling each other out."

"On a first date? I can see what kind of girls you go out with."

He chuckles. "You know what I mean. You don't know what the other person is into, so you're telling them about yourselves and trying to discover whether they like the same things you do."

"Yeah. And then you find they like motorsport and heavy metal and they don't like curry, and you're, like, oh shit, this isn't going to work."

"I couldn't date a girl who didn't like curry."

"I know! I couldn't date a guy who didn't like music."

"Who the hell doesn't like music?"

"You'd be surprised. Tamati said he was, but after I started dating him I realized he wasn't really into it. He never understood why I always liked to have it on in the house."

He checks his mirror, then glances at me. "You lived with him?"

"Yeah, for about a year."

"I didn't know that."

I look out of the window. "It wasn't the best decision of my life."

"I'm sorry."

I shrug. "It's done now. No point in regrets." I look across at him. He's resting an elbow on the windowsill, with his fingers on his lips, thoughtful. He's incredibly handsome. And he smells amazing. "People are never going to think we're an item," I joke.

He frowns. "Why?"

"Look at you, Kingi. You scream money and power. I'm a gardener for God's sake. You're lucky I'm not wearing wellies."

"Oh yes! About that. High heels! I didn't know you possessed any."

"Not much call for them when you're up to your knees in mud."

"I guess. But it's good you're wearing them. It'll make it easier to kiss you later."

"Oh God, don't start that again. I'm not kissing you."

"You signed the contract."

"Fuck." I slide down in the seat. "I forgot about that."

"Yeah, it's all legal now. Tane sent you a copy of it?"

"Yes."

"So I don't want to hear any 'I'm not going to do that.'"

I poke my tongue out at him. "That's why you paid me the money straight away, isn't it?"

"Totally." He smiles.

"Thank you for that," I say softly. "I didn't expect you to do it right away."

"I didn't want you to worry about it. And sometimes payments take a while to go through."

"No, it came through this morning. I opened my bank app and my balance was $100,027.43. My eyes nearly fell out of my head."

He stares at me. "You had twenty-seven dollars and forty-three cents in your bank account before the payment turned up?"

"Yeah. A whole twenty-seven! It was a good week." My lips curve up at the look on his face. "What?"

He returns his gaze to the road, taking the turning for the ferry, and doesn't say anything.

"Anyway," I continue, "I went to see my parents at lunchtime."

"Oh… how did it go?"

I shift in the seat as I remember the moment I told them. "Mum just sat there with her mouth open. Dad cried."

He sighs. "Babe, I'm so sorry."

"It's okay. I expected it."

"You told them we were engaged?"

"Yeah. They remembered you. I said we'd been dating for a few months and had become really close. They bought it."

"Really?"

"Yes, they bought that I'd agreed to marry the tall, gorgeous billionaire. Shocking, isn't it?"

He laughs. Then he glances at me. "You think I'm gorgeous?"

"Beneath all the hair? Maybe."

He strokes his chin. "It's probably time I trimmed it."

"You think?"

"You don't like it?"

I smile. "It's very you."

"Not quite sure if that's a compliment." He follows the directions of the ferry assistant, parks the Porsche behind the row of cars, and turns off the engine. "Come on. Let's get a coffee or something."

We get out of the car and he locks it. We climb the steps to the deck, and as we walk past the seating that's gradually filling up to the cabin, he holds out his hand.

I stop walking. He stops, too.

I look at his hand. He flicks his fingers up, Matrix style.

My heart races. He wants me to hold it.

"I don't think so," I say.

He just gives me a look that says, *Contract*. I mutter under my breath and slide my hand into his. He closes his fingers around mine, then starts walking again, pulling me with him.

I follow him, my face growing warm. We're just friends. When we were young, we touched a lot, the way kids do: wrestling, pushing one another, and yeah, even holding hands sometimes. But we haven't been kids for a long time. And I don't have any close male friends now, so I'm not used to the kind of relationship I see on TikTok, where a guy and girl declare they're best friends. The feel of Kingi's warm skin, his fingers closed around mine, brings goosebumps out all over me.

It's just platonic, it's just platonic… I repeat the words in my head frantically as we cross to the bar.

Luckily he releases me as we approach it. "What are you in the mood for?" he asks. "Do you want a glass of wine?"

"I'm guessing you won't be drinking as you're driving?"

"No."

"I'm happy with coffee."

"Don't worry about me." He smiles.

"No, coffee's fine," I say hastily. I don't want to drink alcohol if he's not. I'll end up saying something stupid that he'll still be reminding me about in thirty years' time.

So he orders two coffees, and we take them over to a table by the window.

"Anyway, hopefully your dad won't worry so much now." He sips his coffee. "It might help his recovery. It's amazing how much of an effect stress has on healing."

"Oh, definitely." I give him a mischievous look. "He did wonder why you haven't asked his permission to marry me."

"Uh… Because it's not 1842?"

"Even so…"

"You're not a prize heifer. Or a paddock. You're not property. I don't need permission to take what's mine."

My eyebrows slowly rise.

He lifts an eyebrow. "What?"

"What's yours?"

His lips curve up. "I mean if we were really engaged."

"If we were really engaged, you'd think of me as yours?"

"Yeah."

"And yet you just said I'm not property. You can't see the irony in that?"

He tips his head to the side. "If we were engaged, and you were marrying me, you would be mine, one hundred percent. I assume you would realize that."

His eyes hold a delicious possessiveness that totally takes me aback. "That's very caveman of you," I say sassily, to cover how flustered I am.

"Damn straight."

"And if another man showed interest in me while we were engaged? If he approached me, chatted me up?"

He leans back, one arm along the back of the chair, and gives me a direct look. "I'd rip his arms off." My jaw drops. "What?"

"You're not serious."

"I'm totally serious. My ring on your finger also means a big no-entry sign above your head." His eyebrows waggle at the double entendre behind that.

"No wonder you're not married," I tell him sarcastically. Deep down, though, my heart is hammering. I've never seen this side of him—possessive, intense, and passionate. For a moment, I let myself imagine what it would feel like to be truly engaged to this man. To be his, as he says, to belong to him, one hundred percent.

I blink. I can't. I have no idea what it would feel like. I think my head would explode.

"Oh," he says, his face lighting up, "that reminds me. I have something for you." He glances around to make sure nobody is looking, then extracts something from his trouser pocket.

It's a small velvet box.

"It was my *kuia's*," he says. It's Māori for grandmother. "My mum gave it to me when she died. She said to keep it for when I met Mrs. Right."

I frown. "Again, you don't see the irony in that?"

He looks puzzled. "Sorry, I thought you'd prefer this rather than have me spend another hundred thousand on a meaningless rock, but I'll happily buy you one of your own."

"Jesus, Kingi, no, no, no. This is fine. I just meant… never mind." Heart still racing, I watch him crack open the box.

My lips part, but no words come out as he takes the ring from the box and holds it out to me. It's probably white-gold, and the band wraps around a large central diamond in a koru shape similar to the one he wears around his neck. A smaller polished greenstone sits on either side of the diamond.

"It's beautiful," I whisper, automatically holding out my hand and splaying my fingers as he moves the ring toward it.

He slides it onto the fourth finger, saying, "My *kuia* was small, like you, so I'm hoping your hands are a similar size to hers." He pushes it halfway down, then leaves me to wiggle it over the second knuckle.

"It's a snug fit," I murmur.

"At least it won't fall off." He smiles.

I study the ring, trying to get a grip on my emotions. It's not real. He's not proposing. We're not really getting married. So why do I feel almost tearful?

"Are you sure about this?" I turn the ring this way and that, watching the diamond catch the light. "It feels a bit… disrespectful."

He looks baffled. "Why?"

"Because it was your grandmother's. And she would have wanted it, I'm sure, to be used in love."

"I do love you," he says. "As a friend." He's totally sincere. "She liked you," he continues. "You remember meeting her, right?"

I nod. "We were climbing the jacaranda tree in the garden. She was sitting on the deck with your parents. I fell and banged my knee, and you took me over to the house and told them I'd hurt myself. She gave me a hug and said I was an *Urukehu*." It's a term for a fair-skinned and fair- or red-haired Māori person. "She said they're descendants of Patupaiarehe." They're supernatural beings with red or fair hair, a fairy-like people associated with mist and twilight.

He smiles again. "That sounds like her."

"I just… I feel like an imposter."

He shrugs. "Don't think of it as an engagement ring, then. Think of it as a friendship ring." There's warmth in his eyes. I think he really means it.

"I can do that." I like that idea. We are friends, even though we're not as close as we once were. We've drifted apart over the years, and it might be nice to rekindle our friendship.

"Good." He leans back again, satisfied. "I can relax now that's done."

"Relax? What do you mean?"

"I thought you might refuse it."

I look at the beautiful ring. "Why would I possibly refuse it?"

"I dunno. Some girls would insist on being bought a brand-new one."

"You don't have a very good view of women, do you?"

"Just going by experience."

"What kind of girls have you been mixing with?" I think about Sabrina, and go, "Ohhh…"

"Yeah," he says. "I think you see where I'm coming from now."

"You don't think Sabrina would have worn your grandmother's ring?"

He snorts. "God, no, she would have wanted five carats minimum. Size is everything for women like that."

"No wonder she had her eye on you then."

His eyebrows rise. "Have you been watching me in the locker room?"

"I meant your height! Oh my God…"

He grins. "You're blushing."

"It's warm in here."

"It's really not."

I daren't think about Kingi Davis getting undressed in the locker room or I'll really be in trouble.

"I'm surprised you didn't ask Sabrina Pearce to marry you just to get the job," I say tartly to distract him from my hot face. "Surely she would have been a much more believable fiancée, and she'd have killed to play the role."

"I don't even want to think about being engaged to Sabrina Pearce," he says with obvious dislike. "Just the thought brings me out in hives."

"Fake engaged."

"Even fake engaged. Still hives." He gives a theatrical shiver.

"You'd get sex on demand," I tease. "I thought that would have appealed to you."

"That might be one rare occasion when I'd turn it down."

It's my turn to look amused. "Was she really that bad?"

"You have no idea."

I grin. "You're not going to elaborate?"

He tries not to laugh. "It seems ungentlemanly."

I'm intrigued now, though. "Was she a pillow princess?"

"I don't necessarily mind that."

"Oh?"

"I'm happy to pleasure a woman without receiving in return." His eyes meet mine, hot, amused.

Oh my. That backfired on me big time. I clear my throat. "So… what? Didn't she talk dirty?"

His eyes flare—oh, he likes that thought. "She didn't say anything much at all."

"But she must have enjoyed it?"

"She was a starfish," he confesses. "Even when I gave her some of my best moves."

"You have moves?"

"One or two. Clearly I need to up my game, though. I think she even fell asleep at one point."

I giggle, and he grins. Then he smiles. "Thank you for doing this for me."

"Thank you for the money."

"You know I'd have given that to you anyway."

"I know."

He tips his head, studying me, although I can't tell what he's thinking. "Have you told Mark yet?" he asks.

I nod. "I called him from Mum and Dad's while they were listening."

"What did he say?"

"Not much. Nina cried. Mum cried. I cried. It was a very emotional few hours." It occurs to me then that Mark didn't say thank you. But I suppose he was overwhelmed.

Kingi's brow flickers with a frown. "I'm sorry."

"It's a good thing. You've helped a lot of people. All the debt will be paid off. We'll be able to mend the lawnmower, get straight at the firm, maybe even buy some new equipment."

His expression softens. "You're not going to spend any of the money on yourself?"

"I don't need anything."

"You had twenty-seven dollars and forty-three cents in your account," he reminds me.

"How did you remember that?"

"Luck."

Of course, he's a finance wizard. I forgot he has a head for figures. "Well, you mentioned expenses for clothing, remember? They do some great dresses for forty-nine ninety-nine in the Warehouse, and I'll save the rest."

"For fuck's sake. Look, I'll be taking you to a charity ball soon. I want you to treat yourself to a really nice ballgown. Spend at least a thousand."

"It had better be made of solid gold if it's going to cost that sort of money," I joke.

"I'll give you the name of some superior stores in town," he says, "and I expect you to show up there and buy something suitable."

My smile fades. "You're serious about the ball?"

"Look at my face."

Oh shit. I hadn't considered that I might have to accompany him to something as high profile as that. And all joking aside, I can't turn up in a dress from the Warehouse.

"You're determined to make me reenact *Pretty Woman*, aren't you?" I complain.

He looks puzzled. "Most women would be thrilled to be given money for clothing, and to go to an upmarket event like that."

"I'm not most women."

"Clearly not," he says softly. His gaze slides to the windows. "We're close to the city. Come on. Let's head back to the car."

SERENITY WOODS

As we stand, he holds out his right hand, and I slide my left into it. He lifts it and looks at the ring, presses his lips to it, then smiles.

Oh yes. I'm definitely in trouble.

Chapter Nine

Kingi

"Where's your chauffeur today?" Chessie asks as I drive the car off the ferry and head for the city center. "If he'd driven, you could have had a drink."

"I don't usually have a chauffeur," I reply, pulling up at a traffic light. "I like driving."

"Well, we could have taken a taxi."

"Nah, I'm not bothered about alcohol."

"You don't drink?" Her eyes boggle. "I can't imagine life without wine."

"I do, and I enjoy a good wine or whiskey, but I don't have to have one, plus Orson is going to have a field day with you there tonight, and I need to keep my wits about me."

"What do you mean?" She looks alarmed. "Oh, now I'm nervous."

"You don't have anything to worry about. He's on your side, and Scarlett's lovely. They just think this whole arrangement is hysterical and want to make my life a misery."

That makes her giggle. "Should be a fun evening, then."

"You have no idea." I drive along the waterfront slowly. Even though it's a Tuesday, it's busy here at this time of night. I turn into the car park just down from the restaurant, and I'm relieved to find a space not far from the exit.

"Neat bit of parking," she says as I turn off the engine. "I hear we were fortunate to get a table. Ria says it's usually impossible unless you book three months ahead."

"Yeah. Luckily I know the owner."

"Oh." Her eyes widen.

I chuckle and look at a text on my phone. "Come on. Orson's already there."

We get out, and I collect my jacket from the back seat and slip it on, lock the car, and take her hand. It feels tiny in my big paw, with fine bones. My fingers could easily close around her wrist.

That provokes a vision of me pinning them above her head while I thrust into her. Red hair spilled over the pillow. My brown hands against her pale, freckled skin. Once again, I wonder whether she has freckles all over…

I clear my throat and lead the way across the road toward the restaurant. I mustn't think about her that way. Prohibited conduct, Kingi. For the first time, I thank Tane for his wisdom in including that clause.

We approach the restaurant, threading through the busy crowd outside. There's a queue of people out the front, hoping for a last-minute table cancellation, which they won't get. And I can see at least one photographer, lazily snapping the guests as they approach the door, hoping to capture a headline for the next day.

For the first time, Chessie's step falters. "Oh God," she mumbles.

I look down at her. "What?"

She stops walking, then looks down at herself. "I'm going to stand out like a sore thumb."

My gaze skims down her. Her navy slacks are clearly well-worn, and I have a feeling her top might belong to one of her friends, because it's not quite her style, and it's a little tight across her breasts, although I don't see that as a negative thing. She isn't wearing makeup, as far as I can tell, and she's swept her hair up in a simple twist with a plain clip. Her only jewelry is a pair of simple hoops that could pass for white-gold, although I suspect they're silver.

She's right in that the other women here are likely to have streaked hair, perfect makeup, expensive clothing, and diamond earrings. I should have taken her shopping first and bought her a few outfits so she wouldn't feel out of place.

But oddly, there's something about her fresh-faced, natural look that appeals to me. The word pretentious doesn't exist in her vocabulary, and that's refreshing coming from a world where appearances are often everything, and personality is low on the scale of what's important.

"You look beautiful," I tell her sincerely. "I'd rather have you on my arm than any of the women here."

She rolls her eyes and brushes at her pants as if they're dusty, although they're spotless, so I think she liked the compliment.

"Come on," I say softly. "Let's go and find Orson and Scarlett. You'll like her—she was in a similar position to you. She was brought up in the Kahukura commune."

Her eyebrows rise as we cross the courtyard to the restaurant door. "Oh, I didn't realize that."

"Yeah, so she wasn't used to the lifestyle either. She's had to make a lot of adjustments. It's why she suggested the two of them join us tonight. She thought it might make it easier for you."

She doesn't get a chance to reply, because we're approaching the door. I lead her past the waiting queue of people to the guy in a suit standing at the front.

"Mr. Davis," the head waiter says with a smile, "nice to see you again."

"And you, Marc. I think Orson's already here?"

"Yes, follow me please, sir." He leads the way inside.

I glance at the photographer standing under the large oak tree that arches over the center of the courtyard. He's lifted his camera and is watching us through the lens. Chessie hasn't seen him, but I look straight at the lens and give a small smile, knowing he'll have captured me holding her hand.

We enter the restaurant, and the head waiter leads the way through the tables, which are nearly all full. I can already see Orson and Scarlett seated at one of the best tables, situated in the corner of the restaurant so it has views over both the courtyard and the waterfront. It's a little quieter here, too, which I think Chessie will like.

Heads turn as we pass, and I nod at a couple of people I recognize, and stop briefly to greet a friend from a rival property development firm. I continue to hold Chessie's hand while we exchange pleasantries, which I know that nobody at his table misses.

"Aren't you going to introduce your friend?" the woman next to him asks with a smile.

"Oh of course… Chess, this is Ricky Turner, his wife, Emma, Darren Cunningham, and his wife, Fiona. Guys, this is Francesca Ross."

They all say hello. She smiles back, but oh God, she's actually trembling. I hadn't considered how nervous she'd be.

I slide an arm around her waist. This is the first test of how she's going to react in social situations. If she goes to pieces, we might as well call it a day now.

"*E ipo*," I say easily, "you remember me telling you about the Bay of Islands tour I took last year? That was on Ricky and Emma's yacht."

I wait for her to mumble, look embarrassed, or just not be able to think of anything to say at all.

But as my thumb strokes her waist, she turns and rests a hand on my chest in a familiar way and says to them, "Oh of course, I've heard so much about you. It's so nice to finally put faces to the names." She speaks clearly, without a waver in her voice, and the others smile. Good girl, I think.

"How's the food?" I ask.

"Excellent," Emma says. "You absolutely have to try the oysters, Francesca… the mignonette dressing is to die for."

Chessie smiles. "I'll have to trust you on recommendations. I'm more of a fish-and-chips girl myself."

They chuckle, I excuse us, and we continue across the restaurant.

"I'm surprised you said that," I murmur.

She shrugs. "You said it would make sense to others if you fell for a girl-next-door type. What was it you called me? Wholesome?" She gives me a wry look. "I'm happier just being me anyway."

There's no chance to reply because we're approaching the table. Orson glances around, sees us, and stands.

"Hey," he says, smiling. "Chessie! Long time no see." He takes her outstretched hand in his, then moves forward and kisses her cheek before releasing her.

"Nice to see you again," she says, her face flushing a little.

"Likewise. This is Scarlett." He turns to the woman who has also risen to her feet.

"Hello." Scarlett shakes her hand, "it's lovely to meet you at last."

"You too," Chessie replies.

"Come and sit next to me." Scarlett pats the chair beside her. "I remember how overwhelming it was the first time Orson brought me here. We can agonize over the menu together."

Chessie laughs and slides into the chair beside her. "That sounds perfect."

I exchange a smile with Orson and take the seat next to him.

"Would you like still or sparkling water?" the waiter asks.

"Sparkling, please," I say, and the waiter nods and pours me a glass from the bottle on the table that Orson must have asked for. Chessie just nods, and he pours her a glass too. "Would you like to order a drink now?" he asks, gesturing at the wine menu.

"I've ordered a bottle of Sauvignon," Orson says, meeting my eyes. It's a safe option, something most women drink. I'm guessing he's been through this with Scarlett, and he thought it might save a discussion that Chessie might not feel comfortable having.

"Is that okay with you?" I ask Chessie, "or would you prefer something else?"

"That's fine," she says, looking relieved.

He hands us all a menu, then leaves us to consider our choices. Another waiter comes over with a bottle of Cloudy Bay Te Koko Sauvignon Blanc, a classy Marlborough wine, and pours a glass for the three of them, while I cover my glass and say I'll stick with the water.

Chessie has a sip. "Mmm, lovely," she says. I know she'll have no idea that it costs a hundred bucks a bottle.

"Marc recommended the platter to start," Orson says. "Do you like seafood, Chessie?"

"Yes, I don't mind a bit." She opens the menu and stares at it for a moment. Then, although she doesn't move her head, her gaze slowly rises to mine.

"What?" I ask, amused.

"Nothing."

Scarlett glances at her and chuckles. "I have to admit, when Orson first told me they did a seafood platter here, I assumed he meant fish nuggets and scampi or something."

"Yes," Chessie says, relieved, "me too!" Her jaw sags as she looks back at the menu. "Oh my God."

Along with the Kaipara oysters that Emma spoke of, the platter includes Bigeye tuna tataki with sesame, wasabi crème, and pickled daikon, seared scallops on cauliflower purée with pancetta crumble, and venison tartare with quail egg and sourdough crisps.

"If you'd rather have something else, please say," I tell her.

"No, it looks amazing," she assures me.

"What about a main? Anything take your fancy?" Amongst other dishes, there's pan-roasted hapuku fish with pāua and prawn tortellini, beurre blanc, and sea herbs, and a Canterbury lamb rack with roasted garlic mash, harissa glaze, and seasonal greens.

"I'll have the charred eggplant and mushroom risotto," Scarlett says. "At least I know what that is."

That makes Chessie laugh as she reads the options. I meet Scarlett's gaze and her lips curve up. I wink at her, touched that she's trying to put Chessie at ease.

"The lamb sounds fantastic," Chessie says.

"I want to try the truffle fries with parmesan and aioli," Orson says. "We'll get those as a side."

I nod, and when the waiter returns, we all make our choices, Orson going for a venison dish, while I choose the hapuku. The waiter takes the menus and goes off to relay our orders.

"So..." Orson looks at me, then at Chessie, and then all four of us start laughing. "This is a bizarre situation," he states.

"It's just a business deal," I reply. "That's all."

"You're mad," he tells her. "Spending more time in this idiot's company than you have to."

"Orson," Scarlett scolds.

Chessie chuckles. "I wanted to help him. He'll be wonderful at the Foundation. I think it's a bit unfair to say he's not a great role model."

Touched, I say, "Thank you."

"Well, I think it's honorable," Orson says. "You're a very good friend." His eyes meet mine, alight with mischief.

I remember his statement that 'having a female as a best friend is like having a chicken as a pet. You'll definitely eat her one day.' Is he about to mention that? "Don't you dare," I warn him.

He tries not to laugh, and fails.

"Ignore them," Scarlett says to Chessie. "I agree, it's a shame they said Kingi wasn't a good role model. He's going to be great with the kids. So I think what you're doing is really nice."

"At least I got a ring out of it," Chessie jokes, holding out her hand.

Scarlett bends to look at it. "Aw, it's beautiful. It looks antique—is it a family heirloom?"

"My *kuia's*," I say.

"How sweet. Kingi, you old romantic."

"It's obviously the night for rings," Orson says mysteriously, and smiles.

I stare at him, and then my gaze slides to Scarlett's hand. She waggles her fingers, and my jaw drops at the sight of the large diamond sparkling on her fourth finger. I look up at him, overjoyed. "You proposed?"

He grins. "Yeah. And she said yes!" He blows out a relieved breath.

"Dude…" I laugh and throw my arms around him for a bearhug, while opposite us Chessie squeals, and the two girls also hug.

When I finally release him, I get up and go around the table to hug Scarlett. "Congratulations," I murmur, giving her a squeeze.

She gasps. "Are you able to hug and not break someone's spine at the same time?"

"Sorry." I let her go with a laugh. "Congratulations, though." I return to my seat, saying to Orson, "How did you do it in the end?" He'd told me he was going to ask her to marry him, and we'd talked about the fact that on Instagram it's common to see extravagant proposals. He was considering taking her somewhere special to do it.

"We were watching a program on TV last night," he says, "and this guy proposed to his girlfriend by the Eiffel Tower in front of a crowd. And Scarlett said, 'Eek, how awful, I'd hate that.' So I got the ring and just did it there and then."

"I'd have died in front of all those people," she says.

"Plus I was worried she'd turn me down," he adds. She just laughs and holds out her hand, and he takes it and kisses her fingers.

"I think you were very wise," I say. "I don't get all the pomp and ceremony surrounding the proposal, anyway. And as for the huge weddings, why not just say your vows in a civic ceremony in your jeans and have done with it?"

"That's very cynical," Scarlett chides. "They're important rites of passage that should be marked. What do you think?" She directs the question at Chessie.

"Hmm." Chessie thinks about it. "People place such emphasis on the big day that it's no surprise it often fails to live up to expectations. But it's important to see through all that. It's about promising to love someone for the rest of your life in front of your family and friends, and God, if you're religious."

"I understand why other people are interested in the concept of marriage," I reply. "I'm not knocking it, even though I don't think it's for me. I'm more talking about the over-commercialization of these events. The wedding, Valentine's Day. And some of the proposals you see on social media are incredibly extravagant."

"That's true," Scarlett says. "And personally it's not for me. What is important is the sentiment behind it."

"Otherwise you just end with this," Orson says, gesturing at Chessie's hand.

"Orson," Scarlett admonishes him, glancing at Chessie. "Don't be rude."

I glance at Chessie and see her studying the ring. There's a strange expression on her face, but she smothers it before I can work out what it is.

Orson looks startled. "What? Sorry. I just meant a fake marriage."

Chessie smiles. "You're absolutely right." She gives me a mischievous look. "We should come up with a proposal story though, don't you think? People are going to ask."

"Yeah," Orson adds, "you should work out your timings, too, so you don't contradict each other."

"Fuck," I say. "I hadn't thought about all that. Okay… ah… so how long do you think it makes sense for us to have been dating before you get engaged?"

"My dad proposed to my mum on their third date," Chessie says, and smiles.

I stare at her, startled. "That's keen."

"He's always said he knew he wanted to marry her on the first date, but he didn't want to appear over-eager."

"Aw." Scarlett presses her hand over her heart, "that's so romantic."

"It's nuts!" I laugh. "They probably hadn't even slept together. Why on earth would you propose when you have no idea whether you're compatible in or out of bed?"

"Good Lord." Scarlett rolls her eyes. "The word romantic really isn't in your vocabulary, is it?"

"Nope."

"I'm so glad you're not really marrying this oaf," she says to Chessie, who giggles.

"Look," I say, "back to the question, how long have we been dating?"

"It's only been a couple of months for us," Orson says. "So I think you can keep it shortish and have it believable. Why not make it six weeks? That'll take you back to the beginning of April. That's about when you started the landscape work at Midnight, right?" Chessie nods. "You can say you saw her working there," he continues to me, "and you went for a walk while you caught up. You felt a connection, and decided to see her again. Obviously, this is your first public date, so you'll have to say your previous ones have all been informal—picnics and whatnot, because Chessie isn't used to the lifestyle. I'd play on that. I think the board and the press will find that cute and adorable."

"Yeah," Scarlett says, "the 'wealthy, arrogant tycoon brought to his knees by a normal down-to-earth girl' angle works well."

"Steady on," I say indignantly.

"She's talking about me," Orson replies, and Chessie giggles again.

I grin. "You're right, I think the board would like that."

Chessie frowns. "Wait a minute—they called you in last Saturday, right? If we've been dating for six weeks, wouldn't you have mentioned it at the meeting?"

Orson taps on the table. "Oh that's right… And when did you break up with Sabrina? You have to have started dating Chessie after that."

"Shit." I purse my lips. "I didn't think about that. It was… Saturday the third of May."

"That's only two weeks ago," Scarlett points out.

We all ponder that.

I frown. "I didn't think this through."

"It's all right," Orson says, "in a way it plays right into your hands. So what happened is that after that night with Sabrina, you felt disillusioned with your life, with all the beautiful models and meaningless sex."

"Doesn't sound like me."

"This is fiction, obviously. So you went out for a walk around the grounds, and you met your old friend, someone you connected with years ago. The two of you hung out for a while, and she reminded you of your roots, and you found it refreshing to be with someone who doesn't have any airs and graces, and who cares about the things that really matter in life. So you asked to see her again, and you'd been on, say, three or four dates when the board called you in. You were on the back foot, thrown by their accusations of not being respectable."

"Which is the truth," I add.

"It felt too soon to tell them about Chessie because you weren't even sure how you felt about her yet. But the meeting reinforced those feelings of having lost something, and finding them again with her. Maybe it forced you to examine your life and realize that you do need to grow up and be more of a role model for these kids you want to help."

I give him a wry look. He lifts his eyebrows. I shrug.

"You've spent this week seeing each other," he continues, "and what the board said has played on your mind, and then last night you went for a late-night walk somewhere…"

"To the Waiora," Scarlett says.

"Yes," Orson continues, "perfect, and while you were there you realized you were so in love that you proposed."

I give them a doubtful look. "That doesn't sound believable."

"Well, thanks," Chessie says.

"I mean because it doesn't sound like something I'd do."

"But that's the beauty of it," Orson says. "That's what will capture everyone's imagination. That's how love happens, right? Little Cupid with his bow? He turns up out of the blue, when you least expect him, and fires off his arrows and gets you, right in the heart, and there's absolutely nothing you can do about it." He smiles at his fiancée.

"Aw," Chessie says, as Scarlett blushes.

But I feel an impending sense of doom. My friends and family and work colleagues will never believe that I fell in love and proposed in the space of two weeks. I'm far too cynical and vocal with my views on marriage and monogamy. The board members are going to see right through me, and it's only going to make me look even more conniving and insincere.

"Kingi?"

I turn to look for the source of the female voice calling my name… and see Sabrina Pearce approaching the table. Fuck me. Could this evening get any worse?

Chapter Ten

Chessie

The beautiful woman approaching the table looks vaguely familiar. She's tall, almost six foot in her three-inch heels, slender, and stunning, with long shiny brown hair, immaculate makeup, and a dress that even my untrained eye recognizes as designer. I can't place her, though...

Then I hear Orson mutter, "Fuck," and see Kingi stiffen, and it comes to me in a flash. Oh... This is Sabrina Pearce, the supermodel. Her face is everywhere—on billboards, in magazines, and on TV. She's also the woman he was dating.

He really broke up with her? She must have been terrible in bed. I'm straight, and I'd have trouble walking away from her.

"Sabrina," he says flatly.

"I thought I spotted you coming in." She's talking to him, but she's looking at me. Her gaze slips down me, taking in my lack of makeup, my hair, and clothes with obvious disdain, then returns to my face with puzzled amusement. "Well, aren't you going to introduce us?"

What's he going to say? Will he call me his fiancée?

"This is Francesca," he says. "Francesca, Sabrina Pearce."

She waits for a more detailed description, then when it's obvious one isn't coming, flicks me a smile and says, "Charmed, I'm sure." Despite her smile, her expression is hostile, and I feel a stab of dislike. This woman went to bed with Kingi. He kissed her, touched her, slid inside her, and probably made her come. I feel a little nauseous.

"Hello," I say. He hasn't introduced me as his fiancée. I slide my left hand under the table. I don't want her to see the ring and realize we're engaged in public. She's the sort of person who'd make a scene.

"You've met Orson, I think," Kingi says, "and this is his fiancée, Scarlett."

She tears her gaze away from me and gives them a brief smile, then looks back at me. "I haven't seen you before," she says, clearly confused that she hasn't met me in polite society. "Are you from around here?"

Kingi opens his mouth, but before he can reply I interject with, "I live on Waiheke Island. I'm Kingi's gardener."

The others laugh. Sabrina looks startled, then says, somewhat icily, "A private joke, I'm guessing."

"No," I say, "I'm really his gardener."

"It's nice to treat the staff to a night out occasionally," Kingi says, and I giggle.

"Well, I hope you all have a lovely evening," she states, clearly not amused at being made fun of. "I'm here with John Anderson, you know, the movie director?" She gestures over at her table.

"You up for a part?" Orson asks.

"Lead role in Ocean's Eleven Inches?" Kingi suggests, and then I remember another recent headline that revealed she'd starred in a porn movie when she was younger.

Her smile disappears completely. "That was spiteful," she says bitterly.

"It's called karma," Kingi snaps back. "Remember that next time you feed Kōrero a slanderous headline about me."

"Well," she says icily, "I wouldn't get too comfortable. You never know what's around the corner."

She glares at him, then at the rest of us, before turning her back and returning to her table.

"What did she mean by that?" Orson asks.

"No idea." Kingi's glowering.

Orson clears his throat and asks Scarlett something about her opinion of the restaurant. While she answers, Kingi's gaze drifts out of the window. He looks serious, thoughtful, a slight frown on his brow, and I remember that he didn't introduce me as his fiancée.

I lean on the table and tip my head to catch his eye. "Are you having second thoughts about our bargain?"

His gaze comes back to me, and he turns his glass in his fingers. "Maybe. If it backfires, it'll only make things worse."

My brows draw together. Neither of us has really thought this through. If he isn't able to convince the board members, they're going to be shocked and insulted by what I'm sure they'll see as an immature prank, and he'll definitely lose the CEO role. And if they tell everyone what he's done, if the press finds out… his reputation will be completely ruined. Nobody will trust him or take him seriously in the future.

"I suppose we need to decide whether we can really convince everyone," I say softly. "Or whether we've bitten off more than we can chew."

His lips twist. "It was a fun idea." He heaves a sigh.

I smile. "You give up easily."

He studies me, puzzled. "You thought it was a crazy idea to begin with."

"I did. But I know how much you want this job. And I really think you'll do some good in the role. Plus I want to say thank you for the money." I'm conscious that Orson and Scarlett have stopped talking and are listening, but I feel it's important to clear this up now.

I'm nervous about spending so much time with him, about being a part of his world, being in the limelight, which doesn't come naturally to me at all. I know my own heart, and I'll have to be careful not to believe this picture we're painting for the world.

But I do want to help him. He's my friend, and he's saved my family, and that's no small thing in my eyes. He's genuinely a kind, honest guy. He's just young and oversexed and a little thoughtless because of it, but I can't imagine there are many men in his position—thrust into a world of wealth and beauty—who wouldn't be the same.

And now I really want to do it to spite Sabrina. The way she sneered at me annoyed me. She's a nasty piece of work, and posting that headline about Kingi was uncalled for, even if he was clumsy about how he handled their fling.

"I think we should do it," I announce.

His eyebrows lift. "Seriously?"

I shrug. "Yeah. I wasn't convinced… but now I've met Sabrina, I really want to do it. What she did was cruel, and you didn't deserve it. The kids at the Foundation will benefit hugely from you being around. And besides, I don't have anything better to do over the next six months, so…" I shrug again and grin.

Orson and Scarlett have stopped talking and are waiting for Kingi's reaction. He glances at them, and his lips slowly curve before he looks back at me.

"You're sure?" he asks softly.

I nod.

"Okay." He takes my hand, lifts it to his mouth, and kisses my fingers, just above where the ring sits.

To my confusion, Orson makes a sound like a chicken, "Bwah... bwa, bwa, bwa..."

Kingi gives a short laugh, lowers my hand, and says, "Fuck off," to him.

"Why are you calling him a coward?" I ask Orson, puzzled.

He just chuckles, and then I'm distracted as the waiter arrives with our platter.

Oh my... Scarlett was right; even though I saw the menu, I was totally expecting a pile of deep-fried prawns and fish pieces, and the only tuna I've eaten came in a tin. Here, though, it's cut into thin slices, and when I dip it in the wasabi crème, it tastes amazing. I've never eaten a quail egg either, so that's a novelty, and although I've had oysters, these are served with a gorgeous dressing that floods my mouth as I tip the oyster in. Everything is beautifully presented, and it all tastes fantastic.

"That's the best food I've ever eaten," I declare as I eat the last seared scallop.

Kingi watches me, smiling. "It's nice to see a girl enjoying her food."

My eyes widen, and I pull an *eek* face. "Oh crap, I suppose I should be nibbling politely at everything."

"Rubbish," Scarlett says. She's been eating as enthusiastically as I have. "What's the point in coming to a restaurant like this and having a bowl of steam?"

I giggle. I like her. The fact that she's not as used to this lifestyle makes me feel better, because it obviously doesn't bother Orson.

The waiter comes and takes our plates away, then tops up our glasses with wine. I need to be careful not to drink too much, but I can usually handle a couple of glasses without making a fool of myself.

We chat for a bit, and then the waiter brings over our mains. The Canterbury lamb rack comes with roasted garlic mash, harissa glaze, and seasonal greens, and it smells amazing. Do women like Sabrina nibble at their dinners and only eat half of it before declaring they've had enough? Well, I don't care if it does mean I have extra curves, I'm not going to let a piece of this go to waste. I tuck in, enjoying every

MIDNIGHT BARGAIN

mouthful of the tender lamb and vegetables, and dipping into the extra truffle fries with parmesan and aioli that Orson ordered.

Outside, the moon is rising, shining her light down on the people still queuing for a table and the people walking by who linger to catch a glimpse of any famous faces. Usually I'm the one outside looking in, not just physically but metaphorically, and it feels strange today to be sitting at the table with two rich guys, drinking what I've discovered is the most expensive Sauvignon on the wine list, and eating exquisite food.

And not only that, but I'm going to be doing it for the next six months! I can't believe my luck. Ria was right—why shouldn't I grab this opportunity with both hands and run with it? I'm helping Kingi out by pretending to be his fiancée, so it's not like it's charity. It's hardly going to be a chore to act like I'm in love with this guy. It's easy to look as if I'm hanging on his every word, because I kind of am. He's warm, funny, friendly, and gorgeous, and he makes me feel as if I'm the most important person in the room when he looks at me.

Of course it's all for show; I have to remember that. But it's fun to pretend it's real.

After our mains, Kingi asks what I'd like for dessert. I declare that I'm full, so he suggests the four of us share a plate of desserts, and I can have as little or as much as I'd like. I insist I couldn't eat another bite, but when it arrives, it's impossible not to nibble on the hokey pokey crème brûlée with almond biscotti, the manuka honey panna cotta with poached tamarillo., and the Valrhona chocolate fondant with salted caramel ice cream.

Afterward, Kingi talks me and Scarlett into having an Irish coffee, and we sip from our glasses and give ourselves cream mustaches while the guys entertain us with stories about their schooldays together. The ambience, the food, and the company are all delightful. I thought I'd be far too nervous to have a good time, but I'm surprised to discover I'm really enjoying myself. The two of them have known one another a long time now, and of course they work together too, so it's no surprise they're at ease in each other's company, like a double act, bouncing off each other and easily able to make Scarlett and me laugh.

We're close to finish off our coffee when Scarlett says, "Oh, I've had a brainwave! We should have a double engagement announcement!"

Orson grins. "That's a great idea." He smiles at me. "It would take some of the focus off both of you that way."

"I'd love that," I say with relief. "I admit the thought of being the center of attention terrifies me." I look at Kingi. "What do you think?"

"Sounds fun," he says. Then he says to Orson and Scarlett, "Are you sure it's not…" He hesitates.

"What?" Orson asks.

"I dunno," Kingi says softly. "Your engagement is real. I wouldn't want you to feel that we're making a mockery of your commitment."

Orson looks amused. "Are you getting soft in your old age?"

"No… well, maybe." Kingi shrugs. "Obviously I didn't know you were going to propose yesterday, and I guess your sincerity shines a light on our…" He looks at me, pained.

"Deception?" I reply. "Hoax? Scam? Wicked and fraudulent fake?"

His lips curve up. "Yeah, I guess that sums it up."

"Well, I don't care," Orson states. "Scarlett?"

"I wouldn't have suggested it if I did," she replies. "Guys, it's not like you're doing it to con someone out of money or something, and it's not going to hurt anyone else."

"I don't think faking a relationship is what the board had in mind," Kingi mumbles.

She frowns. "Maybe not, but you know you'll do a great job, right? If it's all about appearance for the press, surely it doesn't matter whether it's real or fake? What does matter is that the kids have the right person at the helm, someone who's going to show them what they can achieve if they're determined and work hard."

"I agree," I say.

"All right." Kingi gives a wry smile. "I give in."

"Actually," Scarlett says, "I've had another genius idea. Why don't we announce our engagements at the ball next weekend?"

"Ball?" my eyes bulge. Kingi had mentioned it, but I hadn't realized it was so soon.

"Yeah," Scarlett says, "there's going to be a charity ball at Midnight."

"It does make sense to announce then, while everyone's there," Orson adds.

"Ball?" I say again, my heart hammering. "At Midnight? Oh my God."

MIDNIGHT BARGAIN

Scarlett giggles. "Don't worry, I'd be there with you. And it would save you having to go to two events."

"That is a very good point." I look at Kingi.

He shrugs. "Sounds like a good idea." He pushes his chair back. "Well, today's my treat as you two are also celebrating an engagement."

He rises and goes over to the till. I watch him walk away, not surprised to see that he draws the eyes of most of the women in the room as he passes them. He's so tall and he has such broad shoulders, and there's just something about the way he holds himself that screams wealth and power and confidence.

I give a little sigh, then look back at Orson and Scarlett to discover them both watching me with mischievous smiles.

"What?"

"Nothing," Scarlett says, but her eyes twinkle.

"I was just... um..."

"Admiring the view?" she asks.

Heat rushes into my face, and I know I've turned the color of a tomato.

Kingi comes back to the table, looks at me, and his eyebrows rise. "Everything okay?" he asks.

"Yes of course." I clear my throat and get to my feet as the other two rise. "Thank you for the meal. It was amazing."

"You're very welcome."

As we head toward the door, someone opens it to come in, and a blast of cool evening air wafts over us. "Ooh," I say, shivering, "I knew I should have brought a coat."

"Here." Kingi slips his jacket off.

"Oh you don't have to do that..."

He places it around my shoulders and turns the collar up. "Not a problem at all."

I glance at Scarlett, who catches my eye, and I have to fight not to blush again. "Thank you," I mumble, pulling the two sides close around me. Mmm, it smells of his cologne. It's almost like having his arms around me.

We go out of the restaurant into the cool evening and walk past the queue, then stop in the middle of the paved courtyard. "I've called an Uber," Orson says. "He's coming that way." He points the opposite direction to where Kingi parked.

"Okay, well thanks for a great evening," Kingi says, and the two of them exchange a bearhug.

Scarlett and I also hug, and then Orson kisses my cheek. "It was a great evening," he says, and the two of them smile and head off to their Uber.

I go to walk off, but Kingi doesn't move, so I turn to face him. "Everything okay?" I ask, wondering whether he's left something in the restaurant.

"Yeah." He has a mischievous look on his face. "Don't look over, but the guy under the oak tree? He's a photographer for Kōrero."

My jaw drops. "Seriously?"

"Yeah. He caught us going in. I thought it best not to mention it at the time."

"Yeah, I'm glad you didn't."

"I was thinking…" He's trying not to laugh. "I wonder whether we should put on a show for him."

I blink. "A show?"

"Yeah."

"You want me to sing and dance?"

"Not quite." He takes my hands in his and moves a few inches closer. "You remember that clause in the contract?"

"The one… um… about property?"

"Nope."

"The one about confidentiality?"

"No…"

I swallow hard. "Oh…"

"Yes, Francesca, my darling fiancée. I think it's about time we had our first kiss. Only it mustn't seem like our first kiss, of course."

"I… oh… um…"

"Displays of affection should be natural but appropriate, remember? You signed the contract."

"Did Tane put in a clause about no tongues?"

He chuckles. "He didn't get around to it."

"Oh my God."

He tries not to laugh. "Are you ready?"

"I need to prepare myself."

"In what way? Are you worried about the angles or something? You need a protractor?"

"I mean mentally," I say, exasperated. I'm trembling a little. "Are you sure we should do this? I thought people didn't like public displays of affection."

"They do if you're famous. They lap it up. And they enjoy seeing people in love. It makes them feel good. So the more besotted you look, the better." He grins.

"You're enjoying this far too much."

He chuckles. "Just pretend I'm Tamati."

"You don't want that."

"Why not?"

"You want me to slap you?"

He laughs. "Pretend I'm Tamati before you broke up, is what I meant."

I frown. "In what way?"

He cocks his head at me. "You were in love with him, weren't you?"

"Um..." I think about it. "It's hard to remember what I felt like when we first met. I found him attractive. But by the end all I felt was irritation."

"How romantic."

I just shrug. Then I say, "Have you ever been in love?"

He snorts. "No."

"Then how do you know how to act?"

"I've seen plenty of rom-coms. You know, looking into her eyes, all that shit."

That makes us both laugh.

He moves a little closer to me, and my pulse immediately starts to pound at the thought of him pressing his lips to mine.

"Chess," he murmurs, "you're the most beautiful woman in the world, and I'm the luckiest man on earth to be marrying you."

"Nobody's listening," I berate, my cheeks flaming. "You can just get on with it."

"I'm warming up."

"My face is warm enough for the two of us."

He observes my flushed face with interest. "Why are you blushing?"

"Because you're going to kiss me!"

"It's just me," he points out.

I don't know what to say to that. He thinks of me as a friend. We're just two friends, having a bit of fun. There's nothing romantic in this for him. Nothing sexual. He's not turned on by it. He's not attracted to me.

It's as if he's thrown a bucket of cold water over me, and I stiffen. It's a game. He said that we should put on a show for the photographer. All the world's a stage, and all the men and women merely players, right, Shakespeare? This is all about getting him the CEO job at the Foundation, nothing more.

I force a smile onto my face. This is for the benefit of the photographer, and also for anyone else who might be watching; in fact, I think Sabrina is still at her table. It'll be fun to put on a performance for her.

"Let's do it," I say, feeling a surge of rebelliousness as I remember how she sneered at me. I move closer to him and rest my hands on his chest. It's not just about us pressing our lips together. It's about convincing the crowd that we're in love. "Hello, gorgeous," I say, lifting my face.

He chuckles. "Hello, beautiful."

"You have amazing eyes," I say sincerely. They're the color of amber, with dark brown flecks. I wonder what treasures they hold captive within them?

"So do you." He studies them with interest. "They're a really bright green. You're not wearing lenses?"

"No."

"They're stunning."

"Thank you."

He slides his arms around me. "You're so tiny."

"I'm five four."

"That's a foot shorter than me!"

"Do you want me to get a box?"

He laughs. "That won't be necessary." He bends, and before I can react, he picks me up as if I weigh little more than a cushion and wraps my legs around his waist the way Ryan Gosling did with Rachel McAdams at the MTV Movie Awards. A cheer rises around us, and everyone turns to look.

I squeal, then laugh, despite the fact that my face is now burning. "Kingi!"

"That's better," he murmurs. Our faces are now level, and his lips are only an inch from mine.

I go to turn my head to see who's watching, but he says, "Don't look at them. Look at me."

I focus on his face, my lips curving up. "Well, someone's feeling bossy."

"That's my bedroom voice."

"You have a bedroom voice?"

"I do." He speaks firmly and lifts an eyebrow.

"Ooh," I say with genuine interest.

His gaze slides to my lips. "You like that idea?"

"I do. It's very sexy." I moisten my lips with the tip of my tongue.

He studies them for a moment, and then his gaze comes back to mine. This time, there's a touch of heat in it. "Do you like your men dominant in bed?" he murmurs.

"Depends. Do you like your women submissive? Because I'm not submissive."

"No?"

I give a little shake of my head. "I won't come quietly."

He exhales, his breath whispering across my lips. "But you will come." It's a statement, not a question.

My breath hitches at his double meaning. At the thought of letting this man pleasure me. Of having him give me an orgasm with his fingers, with his tongue.

Someone whistles, and all of a sudden I'm conscious of the crowd and the photographer. "Are we still acting?" I ask, my heart racing.

He blinks. "Of course."

"Good." I need to get this over with so I can escape with my marbles intact.

Most of my marbles, anyway.

I take his face in my hands and touch my nose to his gently in a hongi. Our breaths mingle, exchanging the *hā*, or breath of life. He shivers, which surprises me. Maybe he's not as unaffected as I thought. It warms me through, and I tilt my head a little to the side and lower my mouth to his.

His lips are warm and firm, and a tingle goes through me from the nape of my neck all the way down my spine. I slide my hands into his long, thick hair, and he murmurs something, I'm not sure what, but we exchange a long, luscious embrace that most definitely does not require any acting on my part. I enjoy every second of it—of the electric sensation of his lips touching mine, the smell of his cologne, and the feel of his arms tight around me, easily holding me against his chest.

He doesn't use his tongue, though. And by the end, I'm very disappointed with that.

When I finally lift my head, the crowd cheers again, and we both laugh as we look over. He'd turned a little, I realize, so we're side on to the photographer; no doubt he got an excellent shot.

Kingi lowers my legs until my feet touch the floor. I glance at the window of the restaurant and catch a brief glance of Sabrina's pale face, her mouth open as she watches us. And then Kingi takes my hand and leads me away.

"Do you think that worked?" I ask. My voice comes out as a squeak.

He clears his throat. "I think it did the job."

"That's great. Do you think it will be in Kōrero tomorrow?"

"Almost certainly. I need to call the board and tell them about our arrangement. They might want to meet you. Would you be up for that?"

"Of course," I say sincerely. "That's the whole point, isn't it?"

"Yeah." He glances at me, and there's something strange in his eyes, but he looks away before I can fathom it out.

We don't speak again on the way back to the car. My heart is still racing though.

I have six months of this. Of being by his side. Of pretending to belong to him. Of kissing him.

But only in public, of course.

It's only for show.

Chapter Eleven

Kingi

"Well, I have to say, this is a surprise." Moana studies us with more than a little suspicion.

Chessie and I are sitting before the board of the Ngā Whetū Rangatahi Foundation —Mikaere, Moana, and Koa. They called me in after the article appeared in Kōrero speculating about our relationship—along with a photo of Chessie and me kissing outside the restaurant, and a zoomed-in view of her hand, which clearly showed the ring.

"I know it must seem that way," Chessie says. She's sitting beside me, and she holds out a hand to me and smiles as I slide my hand into it. "And it's true that it has been a whirlwind romance. But we're both very happy."

The three of them continue to look unimpressed. "Kingi," Mikaere says impatiently, "it's impossible not to think that our previous conversation has something to do with this engagement. And you know how that looks, don't you?"

I release Chessie's hand and lean forward, my elbows on my knees. We knew this was going to be difficult. I'm surprised how nervous I am, though. I respect these three elders, and I feel ashamed to think I'm pulling the wool over their eyes. But I'm doing it for the good of the kids.

"Honestly," I say, "it *is* connected with our conversation. After our last talk, I went away and had a good think about what you said. I felt ashamed of my behavior." I shift on the chair. It makes me uncomfortable to say that, but it was Chessie's idea to throw myself on my sword and tell them I was sorry, and I know she's right. "I'm twenty-eight, and you were right—it's time I grew up and acknowledged my responsibilities. I do want this position because I feel I have a lot to offer the kids, and I want to be a good role model in every way."

"So you went home, called an old friend, and proposed?" Koa asks, amused.

I find myself tongue-tied. I can close million-dollar deals without breaking a sweat, but suddenly I feel awful for lying to them.

Maybe I should admit I made it all up. Perhaps they'll see it as cute and adorable and a sign of how much I want it.

Or maybe they'll throw me out the door in disgust and called Kōrero and tell the whole world what an idiot I am.

"If I may," Chessie says to me softly. I can't think what to say, so I nod. "We know how it looks," she says to them. "But it really wasn't like that. We've known each other a long time, and we've always had feelings for each other. Kingi has actually asked me out many times, but I've always said no, because… well… his world is very different from mine, as you can imagine. I'm a gardener! And he's high profile, and I'm not really comfortable in the limelight. I knew the kind of women he dated, and of course I'm nothing like them. I mean, look at me." She gestures at herself. She's wearing cut-down jeans and a plain white tee. Her long hair is drawn back in a ponytail, and the only makeup she's wearing is a touch of lip balm, because her lips look glossy.

"But a couple of weeks ago," she continues, "I was working on landscaping the bank behind Midnight, and he was out walking, and we bumped into one another. We got talking and decided to go for a coffee to catch up. I was a bit emotional, you see… My father had a quadruple heart bypass recently."

"Oh no…" Moana murmurs, and the two men frown.

"His wound was infected," Chessie continues, "but the hospital was sending him home anyway, and I was worried about how my mum was going to cope, and whether the infection would get worse. And Kingi was really nice and said it was going to be okay and made me feel better, and it reminded me how much I liked him. So when he asked me out afterward, I said yes."

"How is your dad now?" Koa asks.

"A little better, thank you," she says. "Kingi helped there too—my dad was worried about his business because he's been unable to work, and there were a few outstanding bills, and Kingi settled those for us, which made Dad feel so much better."

"That was kind of you," Moana says quietly.

It's amazing how Chessie is managing to hide the lie amongst the truth. I look at her with renewed admiration. Nobody would ever think she was lying. She's so genuine and warm.

"Yes, and so we saw each other every day for the week after that," she continues. "I wasn't comfortable being seen in public, so we just went for a few picnics and walks, but we talked for hours, didn't we?" She throws me a smile.

I nod, determined to play along and not let her effort go to waste. "It's hard to explain how different it felt to talk to Chess. She jokes about not being like the other women I've dated, and it's true, but not in the way she thinks. She's so unaffected and natural." I realize as I say it how true it is. "Then the article came out about me jumping off the waterfall. I was worried about it because it mentioned Sabrina, but Chessie was so supportive, and she said that of course I wouldn't have done it under the influence of alcohol, and there was no doubt in her voice at all."

"He'd never do that," she says. "We jumped off the waterfall a lot when we were young, didn't we? And we were always very respectful of the power of nature."

"You've jumped off?" Moana asks her, surprised. "I could never do that!"

"She's done it many times," I tell them. "She's completely fearless. That's one thing I love about her, that and her openness, the fact that she never pretends to be anyone else. Being with her felt so natural."

"What I don't understand is why you didn't mention that you were dating when we called you in last week," Mikaere says.

"We'd only been dating a week," I reply. "I didn't feel it was appropriate to talk about a new girlfriend. But after I left you, I talked to Chessie about it because I felt terrible."

"We talked for ages that night," she says, "didn't we? Well into the early hours. He really opened up," she tells them. "He talked a lot about missing me when he went away to boarding school, and how he hated that we'd grown apart as he got more caught up in his new world. I realized how unhappy he was deep down. He told me how bad he felt after your meeting, and that he was ashamed of what had happened with Sabrina. He was very sweet about it and said he was worried about hurting me, and… I don't know… we just sort of connected, didn't we?" She looks back at me, and her face flushes. She's implying we slept together that night for the first time.

I reach out and tuck a strand of hair behind her ear, and just smile.

"After that," she says, "it's been such a lovely week. We've spent so much time together, and we've talked a lot about the Foundation, and the work he wants to do with the kids there."

"I'll be honest with you," I say to them, "we discussed your comment about me making some commitment to show respectability and responsibility. And Chessie laughed and said maybe we should get married then, and it was like a lightbulb came on. I've never thought about it before. I couldn't imagine settling down with anyone. But the thought of being with her for the rest of my life just filled me with joy. And so I proposed there and then."

"I was stunned," Chessie says. "Of course I said it was ridiculous—we'd only been dating a fortnight. But it's been such a magical couple of weeks, and I'm so head over heels for him that I just had to say yes. I made it clear, though, that we should wait a while before we get married, so we're both absolutely sure that it's not a flash-in-the-pan thing, and he was happy with that, but he wanted me to wear the ring straight away."

"I told Orson," I say, "and he revealed that he'd asked Scarlett to marry him, too! We both thought it was hilarious that we'd done it within a day of each other, and we decided to go out to dinner to celebrate, and so the girls could meet each other. And that's when the photographer saw us."

"You weren't exactly hiding it," Koa says, smiling.

"No." I pick up Chessie's hand again. "I admit I wanted to show her off."

"Aw," Moana says.

Mikaere gives a short laugh. "Well, it's a very romantic story. And at least you were honest in admitting you took on board what we said, and that it might have influenced your decision."

"Oh, it definitely did," I say, "but only in a positive way."

The three of them exchange glances. Koa and Moana both nod and smile. Then Mikaere says, "Okay, so we had a talk beforehand, and we'd like to offer you the CEO role."

I inhale with surprise, and joy fills me. "Really?"

"Oh my God!" Chessie turns to me and throws her arms around my neck, and I laugh and hug her back.

"Thank you," I say over her shoulder. "I'm so pleased."

"You're one of the good guys," Koa says. "It wasn't a hard decision. I hope we can all work together to improve the lives of these kids, and it's good to have you at the helm to steer the ship."

Chessie moves back, and I stand and lean across the table to shake their hands.

"We'll set up a meeting in a week or so to start thinking about what direction we're going to take this in," Mikaere says. "I'm guessing you'll officially announce the engagement soon?"

"At the Midnight Ball," I confirm.

"Then we'll put out a press release on the following Monday."

"Okay. Thank you. You won't regret it."

"I hope not," Mikaere says, meeting my eyes. My stomach flips. He still doesn't believe me a hundred percent. But the other two are smiling, and I guess he thinks it's worth the risk.

Chessie slips her hand into mine, and we lead the way out of Midnight's boardroom. In the lobby, we say goodbye to them, and they head out of the front doors.

We wait for a moment, then turn to each other and blow out a long breath.

"You want a celebratory coffee?" I ask her.

"God, yes."

I ask the barista to make us a couple of lattes, then take her back along the corridor to my office. Once we're inside, I pull her into my arms for a big hug.

"Thank you so much," I tell her with feeling. "I don't know how you did that, but you were spectacular."

"It was ninety percent the truth," she says. "Don't worry."

I move back and look down at her, amused. "Why do you say that?"

"I know you well enough," she scoffs. "I could tell you were about to spill everything. Guilt got you, didn't it?"

I nod. "I felt bad lying to them. They're good people."

"So are you, Kingi. You have to remember that." She looks up at me, and for a moment I'm lost in her big green eyes. It reminds me of when I picked her up outside the restaurant. Our brief conversation about my bedroom voice, where she admitted she's not submissive in bed. The thought made my heart leap, because I have no interest in women like Sabrina who are sexually passive. I like women who enjoy challenging me, and the thought that Chessie is like that makes my heart leap. Our kiss was electrifying, and it took incredible willpower to end the kiss and lower her to the floor.

I want to kiss her again.

I can't, though. Scarlett warned me that I had to be careful not to hurt Chessie. I know girls like sex as much as guys do, and it's possible that she might be interested in a short fling, but we're friends, and if she ends up developing feelings for me, I could lose her, and I don't want that. I value her friendship, and I need to be mature about this and remember it's all an act. I can't use her and move on the way I normally do.

The thought makes me uncomfortable, and I lower my arms and move back. She waits for a moment, a frown flickering on her forehead, then goes over and sits on the sofa by the window.

"So have you had anyone else mention the engagement?" I ask, taking one of the armchairs.

"Yeah. Practically everyone I know." She studies her nails.

"Something bothering you?" I ask.

She shrugs. "They're all incredibly shocked. 'Oh my God, Chessie, I don't believe it, how on earth did you manage to hook someone like that…'" Her lips twist.

I frown, baffled. "You're kidding me?"

"It surprises you?"

"Well, yeah. You're gorgeous. You could have any man you laid eyes on."

She gives a short laugh. "I really couldn't." Her expression softens. "But that's very sweet. It just makes it clear to me how different our backgrounds are, though."

"I'm not sure what you mean. You're talking as if I'm some kind of lord and you're a serving wench. There's no class system here."

"Isn't there? We might not have lords and serving wenches—nice description of me, by the way—but your family is exceptionally wealthy. Mine is very poor. How much money we have bleeds into every part of our lives. It shapes who we are."

"You're saying we have a socioeconomic class system," I say.

"Am I? I guess."

"Where social standing is based on wealth, income, education, and power. Yes, you're probably right, we do have that here."

"There's no probably about it. We're not the same, Kingi. I mean, I knew that, especially as your father mentioned it, but I didn't realize the difference was so marked."

I look over as there's a knock at the door, and nod as the barista comes in with our coffees. "Thanks, Nate," I say, and he leaves them on the coffee table. "Can you close the door behind you?"

"Sure." He glances at Chessie, smiles, then goes out and closes the door.

She shifts on the sofa. "I should get back to work."

"Not yet," I say softly, picking up my coffee and gesturing for her to do the same. "Come on, talk to me."

She picks up the cardboard takeaway cup and studies the Midnight Club logo on the front.

"I don't like you saying we're not the same," I tell her. "Money is nothing. It's ephemeral, and it can be lost as easily as it's gained." As I say the words, I remember that her brother is a gambler, and wince. "Sorry, I know you're more than aware of that. But my point is that it's not important in the big scheme of things."

"That's so easy to say when you have it! Of course it's important, Kingi. I don't blame you for not understanding; you've always had it, and it's impossible to understand what it's like to not have something. But when you don't have money, it's all you think about. Your whole world revolves around it. Do you have enough to pay the rent? Are you going to wake up tomorrow to a new bill, or will something break down that you have to fix—the car, the washing machine? You've never known what it's like to have to choose whether to eat or pay the electricity bill."

"Jesus, Chess..." The thought that she's had to do that horrifies me.

"That's the kind of decision people like me have to make every day. My decisions aren't where I'm going on holiday this year, or which car should I buy, or how many dresses do I need? My choices involve how much money I can afford to give my parents and still have enough to pay for my room. Saving up the coins in my purse for Christmas presents at the end of the year. Fighting the urge to put it all on my credit card, because it's so easy to do that..." She's becoming tearful.

"Do you have a lot of debt?" I ask gently.

She rubs her nose. "I'm not too bad. Not as much as some of my friends. I don't have a student loan, which makes it easier. I do okay, and the money you gave me will help me pay off what little debt I do have. I'm very grateful for that, thank you."

"You don't have to keep thanking me."

She sips her coffee. "I suppose I'm just surprised that our worlds are so different now. When you're a kid, you don't think about money. You're all equal. And of course I've watched you grow up, and seen the Midnight Club being built, and read the headlines. I knew you were on a different path... I just didn't realize *how* different. And talking to the board, I suppose it sank in how vast that gulf is between us. I could see that Mikaere didn't believe us."

"That had nothing to do with our financial situations. Mik knows I've had a lot of girlfriends, that's all. He knows how much I want the role, and that I have a reputation for getting what I want by whatever means. It's nothing to do with you."

She fiddles with the lid of the cup.

"I understand what you're saying," I tell her carefully. "But it's all so superficial. What really matters in life are the relationships we make, and how we treat our friends and family. You can be the richest person in the world and not have any love in your life."

She lifts her gaze to mine. "You did not just say that."

"What?"

"Did you get that from the back of a cereal box?"

I glare at her. "I'm trying to say that money can't buy everything."

"Only a person who has money would say that."

We glower at each other across the coffee table.

"I don't know what you want from me," I say carefully. "It's not my fault I have money. I was born into it. I'm sure you're right that it's impossible for me to understand what it's like not to have it. But I do my best to help others less fortunate than myself."

She blows out a long breath. "I'm sorry, you've been very generous, and it's not fair of me to criticize you."

"I don't mean with you, Chess. You know that the Club is run by the Midnight Circle? A group of wealthy business people in the city?"

"Yeah."

"It's not just a resort for rich people. Once all the bills are paid, the majority of the proceeds go to charity."

She stares at me. "What?"

"That's why we built it. Oliver Huxley runs a club in the city, and he had this idea of bringing in a group of investors to create an exclusive resort that would attract the wealthiest sort of people in the country, and we'd use the profits to help local charities."

"I didn't know."

"We don't make it public because we'd be overrun with requests. We pick the charities carefully. One of them is Kāinga Kore. It attempts to help the homeless have access to laundry, showers, and find a place to stay. Another is Aotearoa Life, which aims to help people living in hardship have better opportunities and futures. I personally deal with the boards of those charities, and I visit them frequently and talk to the people who need help. It's why we're having the charity ball next weekend. I'm not oblivious to the problems of having no money, Chessie. And I try to help where I can."

Her eyes brim with tears, and she presses her fingers to her mouth. "I'm sorry."

"Hey, it's okay." I didn't mean to make her cry. I get up and go and sit next to her on the sofa. "I just don't want you to think I'm some kind of playboy who only thinks about having a good time, that's all." Something strikes me then. "Do you think badly of me for pulling the wool over the board's eyes just to get the role?"

"I get why you're doing it," she whispers. It's not answering the question, though.

I put my arm along the back of the sofa, not around her, but trying to give her comfort. "I understand. I'll be honest with you. I was pissed off with the board because I felt they were judging my behavior, and I didn't feel that any of them was in a position to throw the first stone. Mikaere had an affair about ten years ago."

"Oh shit, really?"

"Yeah, nobody's supposed to know, but Dad told me. It was with Mik's sister-in-law, and it caused a real rumpus in the family. He and his brother had a huge fight over it, and it was so bad that the police had to be called. His brother eventually moved to the South Island."

"My God."

"Koa has six kids by three different women, so yeah, it felt a bit harsh for him to be judging my way of life."

"Really?"

"Yeah. Moana, at least, practices what she preaches in terms of fidelity, but one of her sons just got done for drunk driving. She doesn't exactly have the perfect home life either. And she spends half her time preaching about cultural integrity, but she drives a bloody

Range Rover. Tell me that's not selling out. I mean, that's life. None of us is perfect. I understand that better than anyone. But it's just hard to be lectured by people who are supposed to be pillars of the community, but are also flawed, you know?"

"Yeah," she says. She lifts her gaze to mine. Her eyes are glassy, full of emotion. "I'm sorry. I'm too quick to judge, and it's not fair."

"It's okay, I'm far from angelic."

Her lips curve up. "No, angelic is one word I don't associate with you."

We study each other, smiling.

"Don't take any notice of anyone else," I say softly. "Our story is perfectly plausible."

"I guess."

"You don't think so?" My gaze slides to her mouth. She's so eminently kissable.

"I think you're very sweet, but you don't have any idea of how you appear to others. You're such a big personality, Kingi, larger than life in every way possible. You're like the sun—when you come into a room, you outshine everyone else. I'm just a comet shooting through your system. I'll be gone in the blink of an eye, but you'll still be there, blazing your way through the universe." She tears her gaze away. "I should get going."

"Not yet. I wanted to ask you about your ballgown."

"Don't worry," she says. "Scarlett, Lisa, and Ria are taking me shopping on Monday. I rang the shop you suggested and booked an appointment for four p.m."

"Good." I nod with satisfaction. "Well, I hope you enjoy it, and have some fun."

She swallows hard. "We'll see."

"One more thing—the guest list. The announcement of an engagement is a joint affair. I'd like you to invite your friends and family. It's going to be a huge affair anyway, so a few more won't make any difference to the numbers."

She blinks. "I'll think about it."

"No, Chess, I want you to do it."

"Yes, sir."

"Don't be cheeky."

"Then don't order me about. I told you I'd think about it, and I will."

"Okay, well, when you've thought about it, give our Events Organizer a list of names and numbers and she'll contact them with an invite."

"No, it's okay, I'll do it myself."

"Chess…"

"Stop bossing me about. I'll speak to you later." She softens her words by blowing me a kiss, then gets up and leaves the office.

Huffing a sigh, I finish off my coffee, then go back to my desk. I've got work to do, and this is all becoming too much of a distraction. Time to put it out of my mind and get stuck into the financial report that's been sitting on the desk for several days.

Then I think of Chessie's glassy green eyes and her light-pink, soft mouth, and groan as I sink into my chair. It's like trying not to think of the number seven—an impossible task.

Chapter Twelve

Chessie

"Wow." Ria's eyes are nearly falling out of her head. "This one is five thousand dollars!"

"I don't need any help feeling nervous." My heart bangs on my ribs. None of the dresses hanging on racks in this shop are less than a thousand dollars. Most are over three thousand. And some of the more heavily beaded ones displayed on mannequins are close to ten.

The shop is in a mall, with a hair stylists on one side and a beauty spa on the other, and all three work together to produce a finished package for women who are going to posh events.

I'm here with Ria, Lisa, and Scarlett. When we first came into the shop, we were shown past the glittering gowns to a private nook with a squishy cream leather suite, where a bottle of champagne was waiting on ice for us. Scarlett is a little more used to this way of life now, and she spoke to Clara, the assistant, about what we were looking for, while the three of us nervously sipped our champagne and tried not to giggle.

Clara informed me that Kingi has instructed them to put my purchases on an account. He's apparently told them to supply me with everything I need for the ball, including shoes and handbag, and I'm also to come here on Saturday, when they'll do my hair and makeup for me. And there's no limit to price. Eek!

She suggested we start by having a look through the gowns to see if anything appeals to me, and once she knows what kind of gown I'm interested in, she can suggest others I might like.

"What about this?" Scarlett says, lifting one off the hook and turning with it against her. "It would look good with your red hair." It's emerald green, with a big skirt. It looks like a grass-flavored meringue.

"Oh my God." I feel a wave of panic. "I could never wear something like that." I blow out a shaky breath.

"Do you need to put your head between your knees?" Lisa asks.

I'm actually close to hyperventilating, and I glance at Clara, wondering if she's going to be smirking behind her head with the other assistant in the shop. But the other assistant is busy with some paperwork, and Clara's expression is kind rather than being like the haughty assistants in *Pretty Woman* I'd dreaded so much. She's in her forties, tall and elegant, and she comes up now with a gentle smile and says, "That's okay, it's good that you're clear about what you'd like. So you don't want a traditional ballgown skirt. And you'd prefer a less vivid color?"

I nod. "I don't want people looking at me."

Her lips quirk up. "With that hair, my dear, you will always have people looking at you."

I touch my ponytail self-consciously. "You mean the color?"

"Yes, and it looks beautifully soft. I think you should wear it down for the ball."

"I never wear my hair down."

She looks astonished. "Why not?"

"It draws too much attention. I used to dye it."

Her jaw drops. "My dear, women would kill to have hair that color." Then her expression turns kind. "But I understand you're uncomfortable being in the limelight. We need to find you a gown you feel comfortable in. Something that makes you want to show yourself off rather than hide away."

Privately, I can't imagine a dress exists that would make me want to show myself off, but I don't say so.

"We'll try a variety of styles," she says, "until you find one you like."

Leaving the other three to sit and chat with the champagne and a plate of chocolate-covered biscuits, Clara and the other assistant collect a dozen gowns from around the shop and take me into a huge dressing room.

I know precisely zero about fashion, and I hadn't realized there were so many silhouettes, as she calls them. A-Line, Mermaid, Trumpet, Fit-and-Flare, Slip, Sheath, Column, Empire, High-Low, Drop Waist. She goes through them all, taking her time. God knows how much Kingi has paid her for our appointment.

SERENITY WOODS

I try on all the different styles, parading the results in front of my friends, who are having the time of their lives. Gradually, I begin to whittle the style down. I don't like anything with a flowing skirt, and surprise myself by preferring the close-fitting styles. I feel they suit the fact that I'm on the shorter side, and even though I don't have a small bust, and I don't normally like drawing attention to my figure, I much prefer the simple Mermaid, Column, and Slip-style dresses.

The color is more difficult. Everyone wants me to wear bold tones like bright red, emerald, and sapphire, but I'm not comfortable in those. They're too gaudy, in my eyes. They scream that I want to be looked at, and I really don't.

"Can't I wear black?" I ask.

"Nooooo," they all say together, and laugh.

"I need something more subtle," I beg the two assistants. "Please."

"Oh," the other assistant says suddenly. "I have an idea." She whispers to Clara, who nods and smiles, then walks over to a rack and brings out a dress.

"Ooooh," the girls all say.

My jaw drops. "I can't wear that," I whisper. But even I can hear the longing in my voice.

"Why don't you just try it on," Clara suggests with a smile.

So I do.

And it's perfect.

*

Thirty minutes later, we're done. I have the gown, and I've been talked into buying new underwear, pretty sandals, a clutch bag, and jewelry. I have everything in several bags which are almost as beautiful as the items inside, except for the dress, which remains in the shop. Clara has booked me into the hairdresser's next door on Saturday afternoon, and then I'll be going to the spa to meet a beautician who'll do my makeup for me before I finally put on the dress.

I thank Clara and the other assistant, and then we leave the shop and stand in the mall. I feel a little dizzy after all that.

"You'll have to take a video of Kingi so we can see his face when he first sees you," Ria says with a grin.

"I wish you'd both come with me," I say wistfully. We've had this discussion already. Neither Ria nor Lisa can afford a ballgown. I

MIDNIGHT BARGAIN

offered to buy them one from the money Kingi gave me, as I know he wouldn't mind if I treated my friends, especially as he's asked me to invite people I know to the ball. But despite being tempted, they both declined, and I haven't pushed them. I wouldn't have accepted a handout either if I was in their position, plus I know they're both intimidated by the thought of going to such a high-profile event at the Midnight Club.

"At least you'll have Scarlett," Lisa says.

"Yes," I reply, "and—"

"Whoa." The male voice from behind me stops me in my tracks. "What the fuck?"

I spin around, alarmed to see Tamati and a couple of his friends.

He looks with amusement at the bags in my hands. "Have you been in there?" He stares at the shop in amazement and then starts laughing. "Dressing up for Kingi Davis? I hope he realizes there's no point in putting lipstick on a pig." He glances at his friends, who all snigger.

My face flushes. Scarlett slides her arm through mine. "Let's go and get a coffee in Espresso." She turns her back on him. "I fancy a piece of chocolate cake."

"Yeah, coz she needs a few extra pounds on her hips," Tamati states.

I'm hardly obese, but who doesn't carry a few extra pounds? He's aware that I'm sensitive about my curves. He knows exactly where to slide the blade between my ribs to get at my heart.

I want to slap him, or even punch him—Kingi taught me some boxing moves when we were young for self-defense purposes, and I'm pretty sure I could do some damage with a good right hook.

But with some surprise, I realize I'm done with him. I'm not going to lower myself to his level. I'm better than that. Nothing I can say or do will hurt him the way he's hurt me. So I'm not going to even try. He's beneath me. He doesn't even exist for me anymore.

I look at Scarlett and smile. "Yeah, come on. Let's get a coffee."

As if he's invisible, and we haven't heard a thing he's said, we turn and walk off down the mall toward the Espresso coffee shop.

Behind us, Tamati calls out something, but I ignore him, concentrating on the feel of the bags in my hand. A handsome man has just bought me a gorgeous ball gown. And when I asked him, *You think I'm beautiful?* He replied, *Of course you're beautiful.* Kingi thinks I'm beautiful. Nothing else matters.

The other two girls catch up with us, and together we walk into the cafe.

"I have to say," Lisa says as we approach the cake cabinet, "that was the most elegant put-down I think I've ever seen."

"Very nicely done," Scarlett says. "He didn't deserve a retort."

"That's what I thought." To my surprise, though, I'm trembling. It's the shock of seeing him, and his comments stung. We were close once, and the knowledge that he wants to hurt me makes tears prick my eyes.

She notices and rubs my arm. "Come on. A cup of coffee and something sweet to eat, and you'll be right as rain."

She's right. I drink my coffee and polish off a chocolate muffin, and the girls talk about all the ball gowns and the other things I've bought, and soon I feel a lot better.

Tamati and I are done. He will gradually lose his power to hurt me, especially once I meet someone else.

I think about Kingi, and the way he kissed me outside the restaurant.

It was just for show, Chessie. Just for show.

*

The week passes quickly, mainly because I'm super busy at work. It's odd, but when I first took over from Dad I felt as if I was floundering all the time; now, though, I'm starting to find my feet. Kingi has given me a few tips to sort out our finances, and the books are in order for the first time in years. I've paid all the outstanding bills, and the ride-on mower is up and working again. I've talked to each member of our staff, and everyone seems happy with their work and the way I'm running things. Although I'm scared of jinxing it, it's going well.

I see Kingi a couple of times, but there are always other people around—we meet once at Midnight, for a drink with Orson and Scarlett and a few others, and go for dinner again later in the week to a local vineyard.

Most of the time, we talk about the Foundation. He's in the process of putting together a document to present to the board, laying out the organization's strategy and vision, talking about ideas for fundraising, and ways he can foster the internal culture to ensure the Foundation's success. I knew he was smart, but his knowledge, drive, and authority impress me. I suppose before this I thought his appointment was as a figurehead—he's a young, handsome, successful, and wealthy Māori guy, a perfect role model for the troubled youths, especially now he's 'engaged'. But I can see I've been unfair. He's a sharp businessman, and he's bringing more than good looks and a heap of charisma to the table.

He obviously wants to talk about it, and so I let him bounce ideas off me. In return, he listens when I talk about my father's gardening business and gives me some pointers for things I can do to help make it more stable, which are really useful.

Afterward, though, when I've gone home and I'm lying there thinking about the evening, I realize how the two of us have used our work as a shield to deflect the chance of our conversation turning personal. It's also served to remind me how we exist in such different worlds. We're friends because of a past connection—it's history that holds us together, and, forgetting about sexual attraction, I know he likes me, too, the way I like him as a person. But yet again it reminds me we're not compatible partners.

It's for the best, I tell myself. But it makes me feel sad.

On Saturday, I wake feeling as if a thunderstorm is looming, then remember it's the day of the ball. Oh God.

Lisa and Ria think I'm crazy. They don't understand why I'm not embracing the billionaire lifestyle, and making the most of Kingi's world, and his money.

It's hard to describe why I feel so reticent. Part of it is terror at being found out, and as a result of that, fear at the thought of having to make it convincing, whatever that involves. The rest of it is just being so uncomfortable around all that money. Each time I've called in at Midnight to see Kingi, I'm consistently shocked at the wealth on display. The brand-new, flash cars; the clothing and jewelry the customers are wearing; even the food they consume on a daily basis. Have these guys ever eaten a burger and fries, or do they have caviar for breakfast?

I'm also repeatedly surprised by the attitude of these people. Their sense of entitlement is shocking. They make demands of the staff without a second thought and rarely say please or thank you. Even Kingi and Orson have a degree of expectation, although I suppose it's slightly different for them because they own the club, so they anticipate that their staff will do as they ask. But it's just such a different world for me.

I feel as if all these people live on a stage, in the glitter of the spotlights, heavy with theatrical makeup and costumes. And I live in the wings, aware of the pulleys and trapdoors, and the people waiting to give prompts, conscious of how fake everyone looks when they're not in the limelight.

Unbeknown to Kingi, I haven't invited anyone to the ball. Nobody I know could afford it, and even if they could, I don't think they'd want to come. My father isn't well enough, and my mother wouldn't go without him. I know Kingi would like to meet Mark again, but I feel uncomfortable about him coming. He's behaved oddly since I told him about my engagement to Kingi. I thought he'd be relieved to know Dad isn't going to lose his house, and thrilled that all his debt could be paid off. But he's been distant and quiet. I'm hoping beyond all hope that he's not gambling again. Nina and I talked to him about seeing an addiction counselor, and he agreed it was necessary. I've made it very clear there will be no more money, and that he has to think about the mental health of his family. But did it sink in? I'm not an addict myself, so I don't understand how the need to gamble can take over even the wellbeing of his wife, daughter, and close family.

But I don't want to think about it today. I have other things on my mind.

I work in the morning, but at one p.m. I head home, have a light lunch, and take a shower. At 2:15 p.m., Ria and Lisa give me a hug and make me promise to tell them all about it later, and then they squeal as they look out of the window and see a black Mercedes-Benz S-Class pull up outside the house.

"Fuck," Ria says, "who's that driving? Does he have a chauffeur?"

"Um, yes, it's his assistant." I blush as they both squeal again. "Kingi insisted."

"You're really like Cinderella," Lisa says, eyes wide.

"That makes us the ugly sisters," Ria points out, and we all giggle.

I give them a final hug, then head out to the car. I've met Rob, his assistant, before, at Midnight, and when he gets out and opens the door for me, I give him a wry smile. "You don't have to do that."

"Part of the job, ma'am."

"Oh God, call me Chessie, please."

"Yes, ma'am."

I roll my eyes as he grins, get in the car, and he closes the door.

It's beautiful, sleek and quiet, and the journey to the ferry is smooth and uneventful. On the ferry, I have a coffee in the cafe and try to read, but I'm too nervous. My stomach is bubbling with nerves about the event and my outfit. What if I've picked the wrong sort of gown? Clara insisted it was perfect for the ball, but maybe everyone there will be in big meringue ballgowns, and mine is a much sleeker style. Oh well, it's too late now.

I'm glad when the ferry pulls in, and that the shop is only a short drive. Rob drops me off outside and promises to pick me up at six, and heads off into the city.

First, I'm having my hair done, so I go into the hairdressers. She gives me a trim and blow dry, then spends the time curling my long tresses so they hang past my shoulders in waves.

Afterward, I go into the beauty spa and meet the beautician. She gives me a manicure and a pedicure, painting my toe and fingernails a shade that will match my dress, and then sets to work on my face.

I've never worn much makeup. I can't afford it, and it seems pointless to worry about it when most of the time I'm on my own and up to my armpits in mud. "I don't want anything too heavy," I tell her. "But…" I hesitate and study my fresh face in the mirror, thinking about Kingi.

"But you want to knock his socks off?" she asks brightly. Clara has obviously told her that I'm getting engaged.

I give a short laugh, meeting her eyes. "Kinda."

She grins. "We'll stay mainly with earthy tones, but add a few extras because it's a ball. How about that?"

"It sounds great." Oh. My. God. What on earth have I got myself into?

*

I arrive at the Midnight Club a few minutes before seven.

Rob pulls up in front of the steps, behind the cars also dropping off their passengers.

I've done a lot of gardening work here, so I know the place well, but it looks entirely different at night. The solar lamps that line the drive and steps are all alight, along with hundreds of strings of fairy lights that have turned the place into a stunning blaze of light.

The staff is dressed in black trousers, white shirts, and silver waistcoats to distinguish them from the guests.

And the guests… oh wow. The men all look handsome and wealthy in black tie. And the women… well, one good thing is that my dress doesn't look out of place. A few are wearing dresses in the flouncy ball gown style, but most are a variation on A-Line or sheath, so at least I'm not going to look out of place.

"If you would like to wait a moment," Rob says, "Mr. Davis asked me to call when we arrived so he can come out and meet you."

"Oh goodness, no, that's okay. I don't need an escort." I fumble at the door catch.

Rob leaps out to open it for me and watches as I get out. "He won't like that I haven't rung him," he says nervously.

I give him a wry look. "I'm sure you'll survive. Where am I likely to find him, do you think?"

"He and Mr. Cavendish will be in the lobby, greeting everyone."

"Thank you, Rob. Have a great evening."

"And you, ma'am."

Stuffing the clutch under my arm, I lift the front of my dress a little so I don't trip over it and climb the short flight of steps to the open front doors of the lobby.

My mouth has gone dry. I'm not cut out for this. Not the performance, not the setting, and certainly not the people. I'm a gardener, for God's sake. Most of the time I work on my own, with my earbuds in, listening to music or audio books, and sometimes I hardly speak to another person all day. What the hell am I doing here, at a high society event, announcing that I'm engaged to a fucking billionaire?

I take a deep, shaky breath and let it out slowly. I'm here for Kingi. He gave me a hundred thousand dollars in return for making him look respectable, and that's what I'm going to do. He purposefully picked me because I'm not from the same background as him. And although I don't think he realizes that's a little insulting, I understand why he did it. I can't back away now.

Lifting my chin, hoping I don't pass out because my heart is racing so much, I approach the lobby. There's a queue of people out the front, and I join them, holding the clutch with both hands and fighting the desire to turn and run back down the steps. Gradually the queue moves forward into the lobby, and then I see Kingi and Orson standing there with the other members of the Midnight Circle, shaking hands with everyone as they arrive.

They're both wearing black suits with crisp white dress shirts, black bow ties, and polished dress shoes. Orson looks as handsome as ever. But it's Kingi who immediately draws my eye.

Oh holy shit. He's had a haircut, and he's clean shaven. I honestly can't remember the last time I saw him look like this. It was probably when he was about thirteen.

I wait in the queue to approach them, and I'm only a few people away when Orson glances over and sees me. His eyebrows shoot up, and he nudges Kingi and gestures at me.

Kingi looks over, and his gaze falls on me.

He stares.

And then his expression lights up with the most beautiful smile I've ever seen.

Oh... My heart leaps. That was worth every minute of the effort I've put into my appearance.

Chapter Thirteen

Kingi

When Orson first nudges me and gestures across the lobby, I look down the line of guests waiting in the queue, wondering who he's seen. And then my gaze screeches to a halt at the sight of a woman waiting on her own, not talking to anyone as she studies the rest of the guests.

She's average height, although as I watch, she lifts the skirt of her gown a little, revealing that she's wearing high-heeled sandals. It looks as if her ankle strap has come undone, and she drops the skirt and frowns as if she's trying to think how she's going to do it up.

The gown is Mermaid-style, so it cinches right in at the waist, clings to the hips and thighs, and flares out at the bottom. It's also off the shoulder, its tiny sleeves just about covering her upper arms, but the bodice is low across her generous breasts, exposing a large amount of the pale, creamy skin of her neck and shoulders. But it's the color and fabric of the gown that really stand out. It's velvet, and it looks almost black until it catches the light, and then it shines a deep ruby-red.

Her hair is down, hanging in curls all the way past her shoulders, the beautiful Titian color accentuated by the ruby gown. Her lipstick matches her dress and fingernails, and I can see she's wearing long fake eyelashes.

She's absolutely stunning.

I leave the line of Midnight members who are greeting the guests and cross the lobby, only half-conscious of the photographers on my left, taking shots of the clientele, and the other guests who are watching me pass.

I stop in front of Chessie, and she looks up at me with her breathtaking green eyes. The emerald green shadow along the top of her lids sparkles in the lights.

"What are you doing?" I find myself saying.

She blinks, those long dark lashes lowering gracefully before rising again. "Nothing. Just standing here."

"You've been standing in the queue?"

"Um, yes."

My lips curve up. "You're such a crazy girl."

Her eyebrows rise. "I didn't want to jump in front of everyone else when they've been waiting…"

I chuckle, move closer to her, and cup her face with my hands, looking into her eyes. "Look at you," I murmur. "You take my breath away."

"I brush up okay, don't you think?"

My smile fades a little. She believes she looks good tonight. But she thinks it's the costume that makes her look beautiful. She doesn't realize all it's done is bring her natural assets to life.

Her gaze slides away, then comes back, and color appears in her cheeks. "Everyone's looking at us," she whispers.

"They're looking at you."

"And you. You're pretty good looking without all the hair." She looks aside again. "There are photographers here."

"I know—I organized them."

"Oh."

"They're here to promote the charities, and also because we're going to announce the engagements."

"Of course."

"Everyone's keen to see which stunning woman has landed the mighty Kingi."

"Like a fish."

"Kinda."

"Hooked in the lip and dragged to shore."

"Have you been drinking?"

"Carla gave me a glass of champagne at the shop because I was shaking so much."

"On an empty stomach?"

"I'm not drunk, if that's what you're asking."

I stifle a laugh at her indignation, and stroke her cheeks. "So… photographers… you know what this means?"

Her eyes widen. "Oh!"

"Are you ready?"

"No."

"Too bad." I lower my lips to hers.

She stands there stiffly as I kiss her, obviously too self-conscious to relax. A cheer goes up around us, and I hear Orson laugh… I can almost hear her panicking at the thought that she needs to act 'natural' and return the kiss and convince everyone we're madly in love, and I'm sure her head is whirling with a thousand thoughts, worrying that everyone watching is thinking I must be mad to be getting married to a girl like her…

I lift my head, look into her eyes, and say, "Just breathe."

She exhales in a whoosh, and my lips curve up. "You're so fucking beautiful," I murmur.

She blinks. "Oh."

I lower my lips again, and this time, she closes her eyes and relaxes a little. I only kiss her lightly, not wanting to wipe off her carefully applied lipstick. She smells gorgeous, of a sensual scent, no doubt recommended by Carla. Her lips are super soft.

When I finally move back again, I blink a few times. That backfired on me. I can't go getting hard in front of everyone—there will always be one sneaky photographer who'll capture it.

It occurs to me then that she's alone. Where are her friends and family? I look around and say, "Where is everyone?"

"What do you mean?"

"You didn't come alone, surely?"

"Um, yeah."

My eyebrows fly up. "What? Why?"

"The people I know wouldn't feel comfortable here, Kingi." She lifts the front of her skirt and examines her left sandal. "My strap has come undone. I need to fix it."

Frowning, I take her hand and walk her a few feet away to a row of chairs. She lowers into one, and I drop to my haunches in front of her. I lift the hem of her skirt to expose the sandal and raise her foot to rest on my thigh while I do up the strap.

"I can do it," she protests.

I ignore her as I fasten the buckle. The symbolism of this doesn't escape me. Cinderella's glass slipper was more than an item of clothing. Obviously, it illustrated her journey from rags to riches. However, it also revealed the connection between her and the prince, showing him that she was his one true love.

I shake off the thought. "What do you mean, they wouldn't feel comfortable?"

"Kingi, they would never be able to afford clothing like this." She gestures at us, then at the rest of the people in the lobby.

I look around. That hadn't occurred to me. "You should have said something. I would have been more than happy to cover the cost."

She gives me a strange look. "You can't clothe all my friends and family, honey. They would never accept that. And they wouldn't be comfortable here, don't you understand?"

We've had this conversation before about our class differences. It irritated me then, and it irritates me now. "I didn't realize you were such an inverted snob. Nobody here cares about your social standing except you."

"Sorry, but I don't agree with you."

I grit my teeth as I lower her foot to the floor. "We can't announce our engagement without any of your friends and family here. That makes no sense at all."

"Nobody's going to be interested in my friends and family," she scoffs.

"Chessie, I was looking forward to seeing them again. It's been years since I saw Mark and I haven't seen your parents for ages. And if we were really getting engaged, don't you think it would be odd that you've come here alone?"

"I'm not bringing my family here to have these snobs point their fingers at them. I don't want to read the headlines tomorrow about which high street store they bought their clothing. It's bad enough that I have to go through it; I'm not going to make them suffer as well."

We glare at each other.

"Don't you think you'll hurt their feelings when they find out we've announced the engagement, and they realize they weren't invited to the ball?"

She gives a grumpy shrug. "I'll just say it was for club members only or something."

"I'm going to have to meet them at some stage, honey. It's only polite. What's your father going to think about the fact that I've asked you to marry me when I haven't talked to him about it? You did say he wondered why I hadn't asked his permission."

"I was kidding."

"Even so. I'm very disappointed, Chess."

She lifts her chin. "We'll both have to live with your disappointment, won't we?"

I hold her gaze, breathing hard. Her eyes flash in the light from the fairy lights. She's so stunning she takes my breath away. I swallow hard and force my irritation down. "Let's forget about it for now. We'll just have to say this is an official party and we're having a separate informal get-together that includes your family."

"That makes sense."

"It doesn't," I say, pushing up to my feet. I hold out a hand and pull her up, then keep a hold of it as we start walking back to Orson, "but it'll have to do. Come on… unless you don't think you need to be here either? Do you want to skedaddle now?"

"Don't tempt me."

We both force a smile on our faces as we approach the other members of the Midnight Circle.

"Everything okay?" Orson asks, his gaze sliding from me to Chessie. "Maybe I should ask the staff to turn the heaters on. The temperature's turned a tad chilly."

"It's all good." I smile at a couple who are waiting patiently to say hello. "Ruth, Jan, great to see you again. This is Chessie. Chess, Ruth is the CEO of Underwood Enterprises, and this is her wife."

"Oh, hello." She shakes hands with both the women and gives them a smile. She's trying. As they chat about the weather, I think about what she said, that her friends and family would feel uncomfortable here. I look at the two women before me, noting for the first time the diamonds in their ears, their coiffed hair, their designer dresses. Chessie wears jeans and T-shirts on a daily basis, as do all the people around her. It's no wonder she feels intimidated. And it's not just what they're wearing. Chessie stands out because she's not supercilious— she never looks down on others. She's not spiteful or cruel. The celebrity world must feel very different for her, where everyone is highly critical of every segment of your life.

Even so, I'm still cross that she didn't bring anyone.

"Congratulations on your engagement," Ruth says. "We were so surprised to hear that someone had finally lassoed the indomitable Mr. Davis. How on earth did you manage that?"

Her words imply a girl like Chessie isn't enough to tempt someone like me. I bristle, and I'm about to say something when her hand tightens on mine.

"I have no idea," she says with a delightful blush that looks genuine. "I'm just me."

"And that says it all," I tell them, forcing a smile. "How's Lennon?"

"He's just started at the grammar school," she states. "Thoroughly miserable, but he'll get over it. Good luck this evening, I hope the ball goes well and brings in some significant funds."

"Thank you, have a great evening."

The two women move on.

Chessie lifts an eyebrow at me. "Her son's name is Lennon?"

"She's a big Beatles fan."

"At least she didn't call him Ringo."

"Don't make me laugh," I say, "I'm still mad at you."

Orson glances at me, then smiles at Chessie. "Why don't I take you to Scarlett? She can introduce you to a few people she knows. She picks out all the nice ones."

"I'd like that, thank you." She lets Orson lead her away and doesn't look at me as they walk across the lobby to the doors of the nightclub. A sign states there's a private party at the club tonight, and a bouncer stands on the door, ready to deter anyone who doesn't have an invitation.

I remain where I am, greeting guests, Orson rejoining me after a few minutes, and it's only as the flow dies down that we decide it's time to join the party.

We've worked hard to turn the Midnight Club into a suitable venue for the ball. Gone are the flashing laser lights and the dance music we play most nights. Later, there will be some dance music, but right now a four-piece band is up on the stage playing tasteful jazz, and it's not loud enough to drown out the conversation. The navy and silver decor is classy and elegant, and we've emphasized it with the same color balloons and streamers everywhere.

On the back wall behind the band, above the huge clock, is a banner that declares this is a charity gala. Mostly, we keep it quiet that we funnel the majority of the profits from Midnight into charities, but word gets out, and tonight we're quite open about our wish to help others less fortunate than ourselves.

There is a dance floor, and a few people are attempting to swing dance, but mostly everyone is sipping from champagne flutes and nibbling at appetizers from plates carried by smartly dressed waiters, who slip carefully between the guests. There are lots of nooks where groups of friends are meeting up to chat. There'll be entertainment and dancing later, but at the moment, mostly people are mingling and exchanging pleasantries. Midnight is a place to make connections, to meet other people in business, and that is no different tonight.

"There she is." Orson leads me across the room to where I can see Chessie talking to Scarlett and my sister, Marama, as well as a few others. All the women here are wearing ball gowns, and Scarlett and Marama both look stunning too, but Chessie still stands out in her ruby-red velvet gown, with that gorgeous copper-colored hair.

I don't want to remain mad at her for the rest of the evening, and so I slide my arm around her waist and kiss her cheek. "How are you doing?"

She blushes. "I'm good, thank you."

"Have you had something to eat?"

"Yes, Dad."

I give her a wry look, and Scarlett and Marama both giggle.

"We need to circulate," Orson says, holding out his hand to Scarlett.

"Yes, us too," I tell Chessie. "Are you up for it?"

To my surprise, she says, "Let's go for it," and takes my hand. She's holding a glass of champagne, so I'm guessing a little Dutch courage is involved.

I half expect her to stand quietly at my side as I introduce her to my business associates, but to my surprise she throws herself into the role with gusto. Holding her hand, I take her around the room, introducing her, and she shakes hands and kisses cheeks like a pro, telling little jokes about our relationship and leaning against me as if we've been dating for months.

I thought it might be annoying to have someone acting as if they own me, but it doesn't feel like that. Weirdly, it's comforting to have her at my side. It's as if she's got my back, and that's an unusual feeling for me with women. With men... yeah, I have my father and Orson and other friends and business associates to back me up, but my relationship with women has always been... difficult. I've always felt as if they wanted something from me, whether that was my attention, my connections, or, most likely, my money.

I don't get that feeling with Chessie though. I suppose because she's an old friend, I just feel comfortable with her. I know she was overwhelmed by the amount of money I gave her, and she obviously has no intention of trying to milk me for any more. All she wants to do is help me, and I'm genuinely touched by that selfless act.

She's a little nervous when it comes to meeting my parents. I understand why, as she overheard my father's put-down all those years ago, but I've told her that, to my surprise, when I told them we were getting engaged, although they were both surprised, neither of them said anything detrimental. Now, they both give her a big hug and tell her they're sorry to hear about Joe but are glad he's on the mend. My mother then leads Chessie away with Scarlett and Marama, saying she wants to talk weddings, which, "isn't a conversation for men's ears."

"Like I wouldn't be the one getting married too," I grumble to Orson.

"Oh, leave them to it," he says good naturedly. We've both had a few whiskies, and he's pleasantly mellow. "Girls like weddings. They'll have fun planning ours. Maybe we should have a joint wedding, too." He looks genuinely pleased at the thought.

"Dude." I frown. "I'm not actually getting married, remember?"

He blinks. "Oh. Yeah. You two look so good together. I forgot."

I give him a wry look, convinced he's taking the piss, but he just grabs a crab puff from a passing waiter and eats it, looking out over the crowd.

My gaze slides back to Chessie, who's sipping her champagne as she listens to my mother waxing lyrical about invitations or dresses or something similar. Her face is a little flushed, maybe from the alcohol or the fact that it's warm in here. Even though she's convinced she's not a patch on the other women here, she doesn't understand how she stands out with her natural beauty, both in body and spirit. She has a positive outlook and a gentle nature, and it shines from her like a beacon. She might be a gardener who's more at home in shorts and boots with her hands in the earth, but tonight she's like a lighthouse in the center of the room, radiating grace. I can't take my eyes off her.

"We should do the engagement announcement soon," Orson advises. "Before we get stuck into the entertainment."

"Yeah, probably not a bad idea."

"Ellen's got us a cake," he says, naming our Event Organizer.

"Do you think we're going to have to cut it with a sword or something?"

"Dude, we're not in the SAS."

"And our country can breathe easier because of that."

He opens his mouth to reply, then stops as someone says, "Good evening."

I turn at the sound of the woman's voice from behind us, and my heart skips a beat. It's Sabrina Pearce.

Her blonde hair is swept up in an elegant chignon. She's wearing a skin-tight gown made of a shiny material that looks like liquid silver, and it's clear that she's not wearing any underwear beneath it. Her foundation is so pale, and her makeup so carefully painted, that she looks like a doll. She's beautiful, but in a way that now leaves me cold.

"What are you doing here?" I snap.

"Charming." She looks amused. "I had an invitation."

"Wasn't me," Orson says when I glare at him.

It must have been one of the other Midnight Circle members who invited her. She is on the board of some charities, and she holds a highish position in a fashion business, so I guess someone thought she should be invited.

"I've heard an interesting rumor," she says. "Someone told me there's going to be an engagement announcement tonight."

I don't say anything. Orson glances at me, then says, "Yeah. I proposed to Scarlett. I'm thinking of a Christmas wedding."

She ignores him and keeps her gaze fixed on me. "I also heard it's a dual announcement." The smile she normally keeps pinned on her face fades. "You fucked me less than a month ago," she says bitterly. "And now you're announcing you're getting married? To your gardener?"

"I need some landscaping done," I tell her. "I thought I'd get better service this way."

Her eyes narrow. "You think you're so smart," she whispers. "But you're not. You think you can take whatever you want, then discard it when you tire of it."

"Kingi," Orson warns, but I ignore him.

"I got tired of you even before I took you to bed," I snap.

Her eyes blaze into mine. "Well, I have something to tell you that might make you want to put the brakes on." Her gaze slides briefly behind me before returning to mine. Then she lifts her chin and says, with a horrible smile, "I'm pregnant."

I stare at her, my heart banging. Orson's jaw drops.

There's a long silence, during which Sabrina raises an eyebrow, her smile turning smug.

And then I feel a presence at my side. I glance across and see Chessie, and it's immediately clear she heard every word.

Icy fury creeps through me, and I glare at Sabrina. "That's bullshit."

She gives a small shrug. "You can say what you like. It doesn't change the truth."

I feel a complicated whirlwind of emotions—anger, frustration, dislike, and hurt. "Why are you doing this?" I demand. "Why are you so determined to ruin my life?"

"You're so fucking selfish." Her bitterness is back. "You treat me like shit and then wonder why I react badly?"

Her words imply that I'm right—she's doing this on purpose to hurt me. So is she telling the truth? Or is she making it up?

"I'm going to tell the press first thing tomorrow," she says. "It'll be interesting to see whether my news or yours is the top headline."

I clench my hands into fists by my side. "I bet a pregnancy didn't even cross your mind until you found out about the engagement. Nobody's going to believe you. And anyway, even if you are pregnant, and I know you're not, I bet there are ten other men who could claim to be the father."

She flushes. "Are you slut shaming me now?"

"Just stating a fact. You were hardly saving yourself for me, Sabrina."

"Our relationship was very public. Who do you think the press is going to assume is the Pāpā?"

Fury billows through me. I open my mouth with no idea what I'm going to say, but I know it's going to be cruel and unpleasant.

Orson obviously sees the look on my face, though. "Whoa… okay." He moves between us, takes Sabrina's arm, and physically turns her away. "Let's take a walk over here, shall we, before we all say or do something we regret."

He manhandles her away, just as people are starting to notice the altercation and look around.

I watch her go, silently fuming. Around us, people are leaning together and murmuring behind their hands. No doubt they overheard at least some of that conversation. Did anyone hear her say she was pregnant?

I feel nauseous, and I'm physically trembling both at what she said and her level of bitterness. But it's not just that. I'm furious that she's hurt Chessie. What I have with Chessie isn't real. I'm not getting engaged, or married, to her. But for some reason I feel gutted that she's been humiliated like this.

Chessie meets my gaze for a moment. Then she turns and walks away, heading for the exit.

I stride after her, and we walk silently out into the lobby. She doesn't stop, continuing to the front door, and although someone calls out a hello to me as we pass, I ignore them, catching up with her just before she goes to run down the steps.

"Wait," I say. "Chessie, please."

She wrenches her arm out of my hand. "Why? We can't go back in there. We can hardly announce our engagement now!"

"That's what she was planning on," I tell her with determination. "She wants to ruin me. That's why she invented the pregnancy."

"You don't know that, Kingi." Her eyes shine. "She could be telling the truth."

"She's not. She heard about the engagement, and she decided on the spot to make something up to stop it."

"You can't be sure."

"I can. I used a condom every time."

She blinks. "Condoms break."

I glare at her. I know she's right, and it can happen. "I am not going to let that woman bring me down." I jab a finger at the club. "And I am not going to let her spoil what we have."

"We don't have anything," she says tiredly. "This is all fake, remember? Pulling it off was always going to be a long shot. I think it's time we admitted it hasn't worked."

She turns to walk away, but I grab her arm again, panic rising inside me. "I'm not giving up that easily."

She pulls her arm away again. "It's not up to you." She starts walking down the steps as she takes her phone out of her clutch. "I want to go home. I'm going to call for an Uber."

"Chessie, please stay."

"I don't want to. I'll talk to you tomorrow."

"Don't go. I'll just come after you." I'm determined not to let her leave.

"Stop." She's close to tears now. "I don't want to talk to you. I'm upset, and I need to go. Please, just let me. And don't follow me. I've had enough of that from Tamati. I don't want it from you."

She turns and runs down the steps, heading down the drive for the main road.

I watch her go, and this time, I don't stop her.

After blowing out a long breath, I turn and walk slowly back up the steps. I can't force her to stay. And I mustn't go after her and try to force her to talk to me—I don't want to be like her ex.

She's genuinely upset about this. I don't know why. Is it that she's conscious of the story coming out tomorrow, and how embarrassing it will be for her?

Immediately, I know that's not the reason. She doesn't care about what other people think of her. The news hurt her personally. She has feelings for me. I suspected that was the case, but this just confirms it.

I need to talk to her. I might be able to sneak off early, but I have to stay here for a little while at least and make sure the ball is going well. Then I'll call her, and hopefully I'll be able to sort out some of this mess.

Chapter Fourteen

Chessie

Lisa and Ria were both going to the local bar tonight to meet some friends, so when the uber pulls up and I go inside, I'm surprised to see Lisa sitting on the sofa, watching TV, a glass of wine in her hand.

She puts it down when she sees me and gets to her feet. "Chessie! What are you doing here?" She takes one look at my face and says, "Oh no, what happened?"

"Nothing." Then I burst into tears.

"Babe…" She comes over and gives me a hug. "Aw, come on, it's okay…"

"I'm not upset," I sob. "I'm furious."

"Oh God. What happened?"

I move back and rub my nose. "I'll tell you in a minute. I want to get this fucking dress off."

I go into my room, take the dress off, and throw it into a corner. I scoop my hair up into an untidy bun and pull on my PJs, go into the bathroom and remove my makeup with some wipes, then scrub my face hard with soap until my skin is red.

When I'm done, I go out to the kitchen. I retrieve a wine glass from the cupboard, take it into the living room, and sit beside Lisa on the sofa. She pours me a hefty glass from the open bottle of Sauvignon. The wine is the cheapest brand we can buy at the supermarket and doesn't even come close to the champagne I was drinking earlier, but I don't care and knock back a few mouthfuls. "Where's Ria?"

She studies her glass. "Still out."

That's unusual; normally we stick together when we go out. Then my eyebrows shoot up. "Did she meet someone in the bar?"

"Yeah. Kinda."

"Kinda?" I frown at her. "What's going on? Is she okay?"

"Maybe we should talk about this after you tell me what happened tonight."

"No, come on! I want to know."

She purses her lips. "She went home with someone."

I give a short laugh. "She's so bad. Who was it? Anyone I know?"

Lisa doesn't reply. And then, finally, she lifts her gaze to mine and says, "It was Tamati."

I stare at her. For the second time that evening, I feel as if I've been punched in the stomach. "She went home with him?"

"Yeah. He was in the bar with his mates, and he came over and asked where you were. We said you were with Kingi. He looked sort of upset for a bit, and Ria told him it was time he moved on. And he pulled up a stool and said 'Oh, do you have anyone in mind?' He started flirting with her. And she flirted back. And..." She shrugs.

I look at my wine, feeling a whirlwind of emotions. On the surface of it, there's nothing wrong with what they did. Tamati and I are over. Ria knew that, and I told Tamati the other day, when he sat outside in the car. Our relationship was done, and I think they both knew I had no intention of going back with him.

So why does it sting so much? I can't figure out my feelings. It feels as if they've both betrayed me, and that's silly when they've done nothing wrong.

"I'm sorry," Lisa says miserably. "I told her she shouldn't do it, but she said you didn't want him so why shouldn't she have him?"

I have a big mouthful of wine. "She's right. There's absolutely no reason they shouldn't see each other. Apart from the fact that he's a bastard. She's seen what he's like. Why would she want him?!"

"I know! But that's not the only issue. It's not the done thing to go with a friend's ex. We all know that. She didn't know a hundred percent that you'd never get back with him—how could she when you don't even know yourself?"

I suppose that's it. Even though I've convinced myself it's all over, even after what he said outside the dress shop, he's my ex. We were in a relationship, and we had feelings for each other. It takes a while to sever those ties.

But I have no intention of getting back with him. "I'm glad," I say fiercely. "She's done me a favor. I can move on properly now."

"Are you sure?" She gives me a doubtful look.

I nod. "Tamati and I were done, but it's like pulling a fly off a spider's web—all these sticky threads stretch for a minute until finally it comes free. I'm free now, though. It stings a bit, but I'm glad."

She rubs her nose. "I was so upset when I got in."

"Oh honey, it's all right, it's not your fault."

"I know, but the three of us get on so well, and I didn't know what would happen when you found out."

Good places to rent are hard to come by, and the three of us were relieved when we found each other. Lisa will be worried that we've upset the applecart, and that's not fair on her. I have to be the adult here.

"I know what Ria's like," I say firmly. "She's impulsive and she doesn't always think things through. But she's loyal. She didn't do it to hurt me. It's not as if she slept with my boyfriend. She would have told herself that Tamati and I were over and put me out of her mind. It's okay. Everything's going to be fine."

Lisa looks relieved. "Okay, I'm glad you feel that way. So, come on then. What happened at the ball?"

I tell her everything. By the time I finish, her brows have drawn together, and she looks almost as upset as I feel.

"How awful," she says. "What a bitch."

"Yeah," I reply with feeling.

"Do you think she really is pregnant?"

I hesitate. "He said she's just trying to ruin him, and that she came up with it after she heard about the engagement. But, I mean, he would say that, wouldn't he?"

"I suppose. But think about how she spread the story that he'd jumped off the waterfall drunk. You believed him then?"

"Yes, but I knew he wouldn't have done that. It's not about whether he's trustworthy. It's whether she is."

"I wouldn't trust her as far as I could spit," Lisa says, and I have to agree.

She tops up both our glasses, finishing off the bottle. I haven't eaten much, but I welcome the fuzzy feeling of inebriation. It eases the pain a little.

"Sabrina, Kingi, Tamati, Ria…" I give a heavy sigh. "All these relationships are so complicated."

"So stressful," Lisa agrees.

"I don't want the stress," I say fiercely. "I didn't want all this tonight. Even though I was nervous about going, I thought I'd be like Cinderella, and everything would be magical when I got to dance with the prince. I didn't even make it till midnight!"

"I know."

"I'd like to have seen the clock strike twelve—apparently they release balloons and streamers from nets in the ceiling, and everyone cheers and celebrates."

"And now you've turned back into a pumpkin."

"It wasn't Cinderella who turned into a pumpkin. It was the stagecoach."

"Oh yeah. Well, your dress and shoes have disappeared, anyway."

"My fairy godmother has fucked off," I say gloomily. "For a little while I got to play at being a rich guy's fiancée. And now I'm just plain old Chessie."

"You still have the ring," she reminds me.

I hold it up and look at it. "Yeah." Slowly, I slide it off and put it on the table.

"Aw," she says. "Are you sure it's all over?"

"We were supposed to announce the engagement tonight, but obviously we couldn't after Sabrina's revelation. I don't see how we can do it now, if she's going to insist he got her pregnant. He's probably lost the job at the Foundation, too. They're not going to take him on if he's engaged to one girl while he's knocked another up. That's hardly promoting family values." I have a big mouthful of wine. "Maybe he'll propose to Sabrina. Make an honest woman out of her."

"God help him."

The thought depresses me. If she is pregnant with his baby, it would make perfect sense to marry her. Even if it was all for show, the baby would be legal and have his name. It would all be above board, and look great for the Foundation. They could act happy, even if they were spitting feathers behind the scenes. He doesn't need me anymore.

It crosses my mind that neither I nor Lisa have mentioned the fact that it's supposed to be a fake engagement. When did it stop feeling fake?

Beside me, on the sofa, my phone buzzes, announcing a call.

I lift it and look at the screen. "It's him," I say.

We both look at the phone.

"Are you going to answer it?" she asks.

"Nope." I end the call and put it down.

Thirty seconds later, it rings again. I stab the red button.

The next buzz announces a voice message. "I'm not listening to it," I snap as if he can hear me.

"Maybe we should open another bottle of wine," Lisa suggests. "But I can't get up."

"I don't think I should have anymore." The room isn't quite spinning, but I'm not far off being drunk.

My phone buzzes again. This time he's sent a text.

Him: *Please talk to me*

I pick it up and text back.

Me: *No. Go away*

Him: *Chessie please let's just talk*

Me: *Go back to the ball with the mother of your child*

Him: *Jesus*

Me: *Don't bring him into it*

Him: *She's gone I swear, Orson asked her to leave. I had to stay and make sure everything was going okay, but I'm in my suite now*

Me: *Alone?*

Him: *OMG*

Me: *Is that a yes?*

Him: *OF COURSE IT'S A YES*

Me: *Don't yell at me*

Him: *I'm not yelling, I'm being assertive. I swear I'm alone. I just want to talk*

I sit there for a moment, looking at my wine glass.

"Talk to him," Lisa says softly. "You owe him that."

"I don't owe him anything."

"He's your friend. He hasn't done anything wrong, has he?"

It's true; it's not his fault that his ex was unpleasant tonight, any more than it's my fault that Ria has gone home with Tamati.

"All right," I say. "I'm going to bed."

"Goodnight." She hugs me, and I get up. "Good luck," she says.

"Thanks. For everything." I blow her a kiss, grab a bottle of water from the fridge, go down the hall into my bedroom, and close the door.

As I get into bed, sitting up against the pillows, another text comes through.

Him: *You still there?*

Me: *Yeah just got into bed*

Him: *I'm glad, I thought you'd gone*

Me: *No I'm here. What do you want to say?*

Him: *I want to apologize. I'm so sorry for what happened at the ball*

I let out a long sigh.

Me: *It wasn't your fault*

Him: *I know, but I'm still sorry. It was embarrassing for you and humiliating*

For some reason, it makes me feel better that he realizes that. He could have said this was all fake, and so it shouldn't have had an impact like that on me. But he understands that even though it's not real, I still have feelings for him. I'm human, and because we've kissed and we're in this strange No Man's Land between having a relationship and not having a relationship, Sabrina's actions have affected me.

Me: *Thank you*

Him: *You know I'd never knowingly hurt you*

Me: *I know*

Him: *Good I'm glad you realize that*

Me: *What are you going to do? About Sabrina, I mean?*

Him: *There's nothing I can do except ignore her and deny any accusations she makes*

Me: *It'll be a scandal, though*

Him: *Yeah*

Me: *Do you think she'll still tell the press even though we didn't announce the engagement tonight?*

Him: *I don't know. I suspect not. I think she only did it to stop us announcing, and it had the desired effect, so…*

I unscrew the lid from my bottle of water, have a few mouthfuls, and replace the lid. I sit there for a moment in the semi-darkness, thinking about what he said.

Thirty seconds later, the phone buzzes again.

Him: *You okay?*

Me: *Yeah, just thinking*

Him: *She's not pregnant. And if she is, it's not mine*

Me: *You can't be sure of that*

Him: *I am sure. The condoms were mine, and new. I never used an oil-based lubricant. And the sex wasn't energetic enough to break any of them*

I bite my lip to stop myself smiling. It's not a smiling matter.

Him: *The breakage rate is 1-3%*

Me: *1-3% means it happens to someone*

Him: *I get that. But I suspect it covers those people who don't use it properly and don't admit it. I know how to use a condom*

I glare at my phone.

Me: *I'm sure you do*

Him: *Ouch*

I blow out a breath.

He's quiet for a while, and then a long message comes through.

Him: *I'm just saying, I know it didn't break. Look, I have several colleagues who are trying to get pregnant, and it's not as easy as it seems. Technically yeah, of course it could happen anytime you have sex, and it can happen the first time. But it's extremely unlikely while wearing a condom and using it right, with no breaks, no slippage etc. If there was any obvious issue we'd have discussed using the morning after pill. I'm convinced I couldn't have made her pregnant. I was very, very careful about it.*

The message is carefully typed and punctuated. He's trying hard.

Tears prick my eyes. I want to believe him. But am I just being naïve? He's trying to convince me, and himself probably, that he couldn't possibly have done it, but when you have sex, whether or not you use a condom or any other form of protection, if a man comes inside you, there is a risk of pregnancy.

Him: *I don't want to lose you over this*

I frown at the phone.

Me: *You mean lose the job at the Foundation?*

Him: *No. I mean lose you*

Me: *You mean lose my friendship?*

There's a pause, and I imagine him looking out of the window, thinking.

Him: *That as well*

Me: *I don't know what that means*

Him: *Me neither*

Jesus, this is painful. Why can't men just say what's in their hearts?

Him: *All I know is that I've really enjoyed seeing you over the past couple of weeks. And I'm gutted about what happened tonight.*

I think he has feelings for me. But he has no idea what to do with them. If that's the case, I'm sure he's genuinely really upset and frustrated about what Sabrina's done. No guy wants an unplanned pregnancy forced on them at the best of times, and certainly not accompanied by the intent to blackmail.

It's pointless to go into it now. I've had too much to drink, and I'm sure he has too, as he and Orson were drinking whisky all the time I was there.

That makes me wonder what happened at the club tonight.

Me: *Did Orson and Scarlett announce their engagement?*

Him: *No. Scarlett said to postpone and Orson agreed. She didn't want to do it without you*

Me: *Oh no I feel bad about that*

Him: *It wasn't your fault at all*

I run a hand over my face.

Me: *All right, don't worry about it. We'll talk about it tomorrow, maybe*

Him: *Are you okay?*

Me: *Yeah, just tired and a bit tipsy*

Him: *Me too. You looked so good in that dress tonight*

My lips curve up.

Me: *Well thank you*

Him: *I mean it. You were the most beautiful woman there. The bell of the ball*

Me: *I think it's belle*

Him: *I dunno, you looked very a-peal-ing*

That makes me laugh.

Me: *That's very sweet*

Him: *Oh, I'm not thinking sweet thoughts, believe me*

My heart skips a beat.

Me: *What do you mean?*

Him: *Aaaaah, I probably shouldn't have said that. Blame the alcohol*

Me: *No, come on, what did you mean?*

Him: *You know what I mean. You looked super hot*

My face flushes, and I slide down the pillows a little, pulling my PJ top up to my nose. I feel a tad pathetic at being thrilled, but I can't help it. He's a gorgeous, young, wealthy guy. It's Kingi Davis. I've been in love with him since I was six. And he's saying he finds me attractive.

Me: *You really think so?*

Him: *I do. You have amazing boobs*

I giggle.

Me: *I'm not sending you a pic of them, if that's what you're asking. That's not in the contract*

Him: *I should have put a clause in*

Me: *Compulsory boob shots*

Him: *I would have if I thought you'd have signed it*

Me: *Hehe*

Him: *I'd offer to respond but I'm guessing the last thing you want is an unsolicited dick pic*

My heart skips a beat at the thought of seeing Kingi in all his glory.
Me: *OMG!*
Him: *You only have to ask*
Me: *OMG!!*
Him: *LOL*
Me: *I feel a bit faint*
Him: *Want some mouth to mouth?*
Me: *OMG!!!*
Him: *Hehe*
Me: *You're such a terrible flirt*
Him: *You started it*
Me: *Are you sure about that?*
Him: *Hmm, no, LOL*

I chuckle. I like him flirting. Tucked here in bed, under the duvet, nice and warm, I feel safe and secure and… loved? Is that too strong a term? Maybe not. He does make me feel loved, as a friend.

Him: *Can I ask you a question?*
Me: *Of course*

I wait for him to ask something about our next public engagement together.

Him: *What color are your nipples?*

Shocked, I give a short laugh.

Me: *Kingi!*
Him: *What?*
Me: *Jeez*
Him: *I'm curious*
Me: *I'm sure you are*
Him: *So? What's the answer?*

I feel a surge of naughtiness, born no doubt out of the champagne and wine.

Me: *They're very, very light pink*
Him: *Fuuuuuck*
Me: *Does that meet with your approval?*
Him: *Now I have a hard on*

I inhale, my heart banging. Kingi Davis with an erection… over me… oh my God. This conversation has taken a distinct turn. I should bring it to an end right now, before it degenerates into something I regret in the morning. I'm not blind drunk, but I know I'm tipsy enough to erase some of the concerns that I'd otherwise be having right now.

Oh, fuck it. Tamati wasn't a great texter, and it's nice to message someone who has good spelling and grammar, and is sexy and has a sense of humor. What a great combination.

Chapter Fifteen

Chessie

Me: *Pics or it didn't happen*
Him: *Don't tempt me*
Me: *Then I don't believe you*
Him: *Girl, you shouldn't tease me*
Me: *Or what?*
Him: *Or I'll shock you*
Me: *I think you're all talk*
Him: *I'm really not but I know you're tipsy and I don't want you to regret this conversation tomorrow*

I snort.

Me: *I'm not drunk*
Him: *You sure about that?*
Me: *Do you want me to text in a straight line to prove it?*
Him: *Haha very funny*
Me: *Please send me a pic*
Him: *All right you asked for it hold on*

I wait, heart hammering, then cover my mouth as I see he's uploading a photo. With a squeal I put the phone face down. I can't look. Oh God.

I fight with myself, half laughing, half panicking.

Then, curiosity gets the better of me and I turn the phone back over.

It's a photo of him holding a cucumber in his crotch.

I burst out laughing.

Me: *For a moment I thought that was real*
Him: *Honestly this cucumber's huge, if you used this, you'd know about it in the morning*
Me: *Don't give me ideas, my vibrator's run out of charge*

Him: *Fuuuuuuuuuck*
Me: *LOL what?*
Him: *The thought of you using a vibrator*
Me: *That turn you on?*
Him: *Of course it turns me on I'm a guy and I'm straight*
Me: *I'll have to see if I can find something else I can use*
Him: *Go and take a photo of something you think is the same size as my cock*
I laugh.
Him: *I'm expecting a pic of a thimble or something*
I giggle.
Me: *Challenge accepted*

I get up and look around my room but can't see anything appropriate. I poke my head out of the door. The main lights are out; Lisa's gone to bed. She's left the small lamp on for Ria, although I'm not sure she'll be home tonight.

Refusing to think about that, I look around the kitchen and finally see something that makes me laugh. I take a photo of it and send it to him, then make my way back to bed as I wait for him to come back.

Him: *LMAO*

The pic I sent was of Lisa's Nutri Bullet blender with the large cup attached.

Me: *Not big enough?*
Him: *That's very flattering*
Me: *I can't imagine you're a small man*
Him: *You imagine me a lot do you?*
Me: *Honestly?*

There's a slight pause. Then he comes back.

Him: *Really? Or are you teasing me?*
Me: *Are you asking if I've fantasized about you while I touch myself?*
Him: *Maybe I am*
Me: *The answer to that is yes*
Him: *Fuck*
Me: *Yes Kingi that was part of the fantasy*
Him: *OMG*
Me: *Hold on, I'll send you a photo of my pussy*

Giggling, I text him a picture of a cat.

Him: *Jesus, you nearly gave me a heart attack*
Me: *Hehe*
Him: *Okay now I have to ask, does the carpet match the drapes?*

Me: *Kingi!*
Him: *I'm curious*
Me: *It does <wink emoji>*
Him: *Fuuuuuuck*
Me: *LOL*
Him: *I am so horny right now*
Me: *Me too*
Him: *If I send Rob back to get you will you come over?*
I chuckle.
Me: *Now I know you're teasing*
Him: *Only partly*
Me: *Our sexual relationship will have to remain long distance for now*
Him: *For now?*
Me: *It was a figure of speech*
Him: *Damn*
I smile and wriggle down the pillows a bit. I'm thoroughly enjoying myself, and I suspect he is too.
Me: *Sorry I've got you hot and bothered*
Him: *It's a permanent condition when you're around*
Me: *That's a sweet thing to say*
Him: *I'm serious. You're hot*
My face warms.
Me: *Well thank you*
Him: *You want to know the truth? I fantasize about you too*
I feel a thrill at the thought of him picturing me while he touches himself.
Me: *Really?*
Him: *Yeah frequently*
Me: *How often do you DIY?*
Him: *Most days. You?*
Me: *Same*
Him: *Wow*
Me: *I have to admit it's very hot to think about you doing it*
Him: *Likewise*
Me: *You wanna know a secret?*
Him: *Sure*
Me: *I used to think about you when I did it as a teenager*
Him: *Really? I thought about you too*
Me: *LOL and neither of us realized*

MIDNIGHT BARGAIN

Him: *You sure you don't want to come over?*
Me: *Haha I don't think that's a good idea*
Him: *I think it's a great idea imagine the fun we'd have*
Me: *Sigh*
Him: *Aw why the sigh?*
Me: *It's been a while that's all*
Him: *You only broke up with T a month ago right?*
Me: *Yeah but we hadn't had sex for a while before that*
Him: *Jesus why not? I'd fuck you three times a day if you were mine, I wouldn't be able to help myself*

I inhale, and for a moment I don't think I'm going to be able to stop breathing in. What a thing to say! I should accuse him of being unromantic, but the raw, honest declaration makes my heart race.

Him: *Sorry too much?*
Me: *No you took my breath away that's all*
Him: *It's the truth. I wouldn't be able to keep my hands off you*
Me: *Ohhhh*
Him: *I've been imagining you here sitting opposite me in your PJs and thinking about what I'd do to you*

My heart bangs against my ribs. I'm having trouble getting my head around this. But of course we've had a few drinks; it doesn't mean anything. He's just having some fun.

Me: *Does it involve the PJs being removed?*
Him: *Eventually but first I'd like you to come over to the sofa and sit astride me*
Me: *I think that could be arranged*
Him: *Ahhh now I'm imagining you sitting on my thighs and leaning down to kiss me*
Me: *Slowly at first, just pressing my lips against yours*
Him: *Yes please*
Me: *My soft lips teasing yours, light butterfly kisses*
Him: *Fuck yes take your time*
Me: *Kissing from one corner of your mouth to the other before I touch the tip of my tongue to your lips*
Him: *Jesus that got me hard in seconds*
Me: *Oh Kingi that was so easy, wait till we get to the good stuff*

I send it before I think about it, then blink and re-read my words with a racing heart. Am I really sexting with Kingi Davis? How far am

I going to take this? I've never done this before, not like this, not explicitly explaining what I'd do to a guy.

Him: *While you kiss me I'll slip my hands beneath your top and rest them on your back*

Naughtiness flairs inside me. Fuck it. I want to see how far I can push him.

Me: *Mmm please, while I ease my tongue into your mouth and give you a really slow, dirty, filthy kiss*

Him: *Oh yes*

Me: *I cup your face then slide my hands into your hair while I do it, scrape my nails lightly over your scalp*

Him: *God yes that would be amazing, while I stroke up your back and feel your warm skin*

I tingle at the thought of him doing that, his fingers brushing up my spine.

Me: *I'd love that*
Him: *And around your ribs*
Me: *Mmm*
Him: *To your breasts*
Me: *Fuck*
Him: *Yeah baby I want to feel them in my palms*

I close my eyes for a moment, imagining him touching me like that.
Me: *Oh please yes*
Him: *Your nipples would be soft until I tease them with my fingers and thumbs*

I suck my bottom lip. I'm getting turned on, and I don't want it all to be one way.

Me: *Oh yeah, I move up your thighs so I'm pressed against you*
Him: *I'm already hard for you, baby*
Me: *I rock my hips so I can feel you against me, arousing me*
Him: *Yeah I position myself so I'm rubbing right on your clit*

I cover my mouth with a hand. Holy shit, am I really doing this?
Me: *Mmm I continue to kiss you while you do that, nice deep wet kisses*
Him: *Fuck yes and I tease your nipples with my fingers*
Me: *I arch my back and push my breasts into your hands and moan*
Him: *Yeah baby tell me what you like I want you to be noisy*
Me: *No problems there I'm very vocal in bed*
Him: *Fuuuuuck*
Me: *I want you to unbutton my PJ top*
Him: *Very happy to do that, slowly undoing the buttons from top to bottom*

Me: *I take it off and let it drop to the floor*

Him: *Oh yeah, I drink in the sight of you topless, your beautiful breasts just begging to be kissed*

Me: *Mmm kiss them, Kingi, kiss my nipples*

Him: *I cover each of them with my mouth in turn and suck until they tighten*

Me: *Fuck, LOL*

Him: *Am I turning you on, Chess?*

Me: *Just a bit*

Him: *Are you wet?*

I blink and inhale again. Wow this escalated fast. Biting my bottom lip, I slide my hand beneath the elastic of my PJs and slip it over my stomach and down into my folds.

Me: *Yes*

Him: *Are you touching yourself now?*

Me: *Yes*

Him: *Good girl*

Me: *Fuuuuuck don't say that*

Him: *You want to know what I'm doing now?*

Me: *What?*

Him: *I'm stroking myself*

Oh God…

Me: *That's so hot*

Him: *Not as hot as the thought of you doing it*

Me: *Mmm I'm imagining what we'd do next*

Him: *I want you to take off your PJ bottoms*

Me: *In the fantasy? Or in real life?*

Him: *Both*

I pull my PJ top off over my head, then slide the bottoms off. I suppose we could just call each other, but there's something sexy about reading what he'd do to me in his own words.

Me: *Okay I'm naked now you do it*

Him: *Okay give me a sec*

I wait for a moment and then he comes back.

Him: *Okay sitting here on my sofa naked lol hope nobody out at sea has a telescope trained on my suite*

Me: *Haha so imagine me sitting astride you now with both of us naked*

Him: *Fuck yes that would be amazing*

Me: *Me kissing you while your hands slide over my skin*

Him: *Feeling how soft your breasts are*

I switch to speech-to-text, balance my phone in my left hand, and slide my right down under the covers. Mmm, I'm swollen and slippery, and when I swirl my middle finger over my clit I moan out loud.

Me: *Are you touching yourself?*
Him: *Yeah, I'm so hard right now*
Me: *That's such a turn on*
Him: *I'm leaking precum*
Me: *Fuuuuck I wish I was there*
Him: *I want to be inside you*

I inhale again—when he says things like that it makes me need to suck air into my lungs.

Me: *I'm going to lift up and let you guide yourself into me*
Him: *Oh yeah, I slide the head into you and feel you close around me*
Me: *That feels amazing*
Him: *So warm and wet*
Me: *I move my hips, just a little, to tease you while I keep kissing you*
Him: *Oh I'll let you torture me for a while but not for long be warned*
Me: *Not much you can do about it, boy*
Him: *You sure about that?*
Me: *I do it for as long as I can bear it and then slowly sink down onto you*
Him: *Argh fuck*
Me: *Impale myself on you*
Him: *You're driving me crazy here*
Me: *That's the plan, Kingi, I want to make you come*
Him: *Oh that's a definite*

A thrill runs through me.

Me: *Really?*
Him: *Oh yeah but get ready because I'm going to give you an amazing orgasm*
Me: *Is that so?*
Him: *Yeah I think you've done enough teasing*
Me: *Watcha gonna do about it?*
Him: *I'm going to lift up and move onto my knees and then lower you onto your back on the carpet*
Me: *Ohhhh*
Him: *Yeah you thought you were in charge but you're not*

My fingers move faster at the thought of him taking control like that.

Me: *What would you do then?*
Him: *I'd lift your legs around my waist and start thrusting inside you*

Me: *Ohhh*
Him: *You want me to fuck you, Chessie?*
My face grows hot.
Me: *Yes*
Him: *You want to feel me inside you?*
Me: *God yes*
Him: *You want me to fuck you hard?*
Me: *A million times yes*
Him: *I'm going to take your hands and pin them above your head*
Me: *Oh*
Him: *And hold you there while I fuck you*

Holy shit, this is backfiring on me big time. I can feel my orgasm waiting to take me over, like an actor impatient in the wings.

Me: *Do it*
Him: *I'll hold you down and fuck you and there's nothing you can do about it*
Me: *Oh God yes*
Him: *Plunging down into your beautiful soft body while you look up at me with those stunning green eyes*

I'm having trouble forming words.

Me: *Yes*
Him: *Sucking those amazing light-pink nipples*
Me: *Ohhh*
Him: *Grinding on your clit so I'm arousing you with every thrust*
Me: *Ohhhhh*
Him: *Are you wet for me, honey?*
Me: *Yes*
Him: *Are you going to come for me?*
Me: *Yes*
Him: *Coz I'm so close*
Me: *Me too*
Him: *I'm fuckng close*
Me: *Yes*
Him: *Jesus*

The thought of him pumping himself, about to come, tips me over the edge. Everything starts tightening inside, and I can barely even see the phone, let alone text.

Me: *I'm going to*
Him: *Yes baby grl*
Me: *I*

Him: *Fuckjh*
Me: *Fuck*

I come hard, pressing my thighs together and stifling a squeal, and groaning at the wonderful pulses that feel so blissful, so amazing, especially because I'm sharing the pleasure with him, knowing he's feeling the same. I wish I could be there and watch him come, see the fierce frown on his face, feel his cock twitch inside me. Ahhhh…

It's a few minutes before I finally feel my phone buzz beside me. I pick it up and read the message with a smile.

Him: *Jesus*
Me: *Wow*
Him: *Did you come?*
Me: *Yeah. God.*
Him: *Fuck that's hot*
Me: *Now I need a cigarette and a pizza*
Him: *LOL I need a tissue hold on brb*

I flush at the thought of him having to clean himself up and wait for him to come back. I stretch and yawn, then turn onto my side, snuggling down into the duvet. Did that really just happen? I pull the duvet up to my nose, tempted to pull it over my head so I can hide. Shit, I'm going to have to see him tomorrow after doing all this. How will I face him?

Him: *Sorry about that I had to clean up the carpet*
I giggle. *You came on the carpet?*
Him: *I overshot*
Me: *Hahahahaha*
Him: *:)*
Me: *Wow that was so nice*
Him: *It was amazing*
Me: *Thank you*
Him: *You are so welcome*
Me: *Do you think we'll regret this tomorrow?*
Him: *Ah you shouldn't it's all harmless fun*
Me: *You think so?*
Him: *Well it's not like we really slept together*
Me: *I guess although it is intimate*
Him: *And I have seen your pussy*
I laugh. *And I got to see your cucumber*
Him: *I'd send you a real pic but it's not as impressive as it was*

Me: *LOL*
Him: *You'll have to wait till next time*
My heart bumps. *Next time?*
Him: *Yeah*
He doesn't elaborate.

I stare at the screen for a moment, then lie back and look up at the ceiling. We can't make this a regular occurrence, because… well. I don't know why, but somehow it doesn't feel as innocent as he's making out. Arousing each other, even if only by words, is still…

Still what, Chessie? I mock myself. Still making love?

No, okay, not making love, but it is still having sex, of a kind, right? But maybe he doesn't see it like that. I bet he's sexted lots of girls in his life. And he won't realize that this is the first time I've done it.

My phone buzzes and I lift it up.

Him: *You okay?*
Me: *Yeah just ruminating*
Him: *Don't start doing that. It'll be okay*
Me: *Yeah*
Him: *You're a beautiful girl Chess and I'd love to take you to bed in real life, but I know it would only complicate things*
Me: *It would*
Him: *I know I need to be more responsible*
Me: *Respectable?*
Him: *Exactly and I'm being serious now*
Me: *Ooh*
Him: *Don't mock me, I mean it. I know I need to grow up and the last thing I want is to lose your friendship*
Me: *That will never happen*
Him: *I'll make sure it doesn't even if it means my carpet has to suffer*
That makes me laugh. *I'd like to have seen that*
Him: *Next time I'll film it*
Me: *Oh God stop it I'm going to sleep*
Him: *Hehe okay*
I smile. *Thank you again*
Him: *See you tomorrow?*
Me: *Yeah night*
Him: *Night honey sleep tight*

I turn off my phone and slide it under my pillow.
I think for a bit.

Then I go over to the door, open it, and peer through. The coast is clear.

Creeping out, I go over to the coffee table. The engagement ring sits there, glittering.

I pick it up and put it back on. Then I return to bed and slide under the covers.

I fall asleep with a smile on my face, warmed through at the thought of him saying *You're a beautiful girl Chess*.

Chapter Sixteen

Chessie

The next morning, the first thing I think when I open my eyes is Oh My God. I didn't really sext with Kingi last night. Did I? I snatch up my phone and open it hurriedly, and it goes straight to the messages page. I scroll up in disbelief, my face growing hot as I re-read some of the things he said the night before.

I'll hold you down and fuck you and there's nothing you can do about it.
Are you wet for me, honey? Are you going to come for me?

Oh God oh God oh God. What have I done?

I roll onto my back and stare up at the ceiling. Deep breaths, Chessie. It's okay. It's not the end of the world. It's not as if you really had sex with him.

But I vaguely remember thinking last night that it *was* like having sex with him. It was so intimate, just the two of us in our own private virtual world, voicing our fantasies about each other, exchanging the most personal details. I think about him coming on the carpet and press my lips together to stop the giggle that threatens to leak out. It's not funny.

But it is funny, just a bit. Maybe I'm being too strait-laced about this. I let out a long breath. Jesus, Chessie, lighten up a bit. Ultimately what harm has been done? I feel as if I'm wearing a black bra beneath a white top—my inexperience and naivety is showing through. People do this all the time. But you can't catch a disease from it. You can't get pregnant. It's cheeky and naughty, but in the end it's harmless. The worst that can happen is that one of you takes more meaning from it emotionally, and obviously that's going to be me. I just have to open my eyes and accept the reality. We'd both had too much to drink, we're two young healthy people who are currently without partners, and we got carried away. He's not madly attracted to me. This isn't the romance of the century. It was a one-off bit of fun that doesn't mean a thing.

Content that I've partitioned it off into a box from which it can't escape, I decide it's time to get on with my day and slide out of bed.

I shower and dress, pulling on a tee and a pair of cargo pants. It's Sunday, and I don't normally work on Sundays, but I took a few hours off yesterday, and I want to make up for it this morning.

Lisa is in the kitchen, buttering some toast. "Morning," she says as I come out.

"Morning." I go over to the coffee machine and turning it on.

"How did it go with Kingi last night?" she asks. "Was it a good conversation?"

Suddenly, I don't want to tell her the details. In the past, with Ria, we've sometimes discussed our sex lives, maybe laughed over a silly incident or talked over something we're concerned about. But what happened last night feels like a very sweet, private moment. It's not something I want to share.

So I say, "Yeah, we had a good chat. I said we'd catch up maybe later today and talk a bit more about it."

"Oh, that's good. I checked Kōrero by the way, and there's no sign yet of anything about Sabrina."

I feel a surge of relief. Of course it's still early, but she did say she was going to tell them first thing. Has she changed her mind? Was it really just a threat to throw Kingi off guard?

After tipping the espresso into my takeaway cup, I steam some milk, pour it over the hot coffee, and give it a stir. "Oh, I forgot to ask, did Ria come home?"

She studies her toast for a moment. Then she lifts her gaze to mine and gives a small shake of her head. "I'm sorry," she murmurs.

I shrug. "Makes no difference to me." I give her a smile. "I'll see you later."

"Yeah okay, have a good day."

I go out, get in Dennis, and head over to Midnight. I'm going to do a final bit of landscaping on the back terrace; I've had some hebe 'wiri mist' delivered to put between the lavender and flax, and it's a nice May day, perfect for planting.

While I drive, I let my thoughts linger on the fact that Ria didn't come home. The sad thing is that Tamati hasn't surprised me at all. To be honest, neither has Ria—I know what she's like. I suppose it's more that I'm sad about the harsh finality of it all. I didn't want to get back with him. He was very cruel to me outside the shop, and he killed any remaining feelings I had for him. I don't know why it was such a shock to hear about the two of them. I suppose there's no understanding the human heart. It feels what it feels. We can't always analyze our emotions. They just are.

It doesn't take me long to get to Midnight, and I park Dennis in his usual spot at the end of the car park. I get out and lock him, then head to the shed. Sure enough, the hebe plants are waiting outside on a trailer, delivered by another member of Dad's team yesterday. They're native to New Zealand, hardy, low maintenance, and beautiful all year round, producing white or lilac flowers like a froth of lace that attract bees and butterflies.

At least plants don't let you down. The thought comes to me with a wave of emotion that rises inside me. It's so stupid! Why am I upset? I'm so mixed up right now. It must be hormones or something.

But I know what it is; I can't deal with the complexities of other people and their actions and emotions. This is why I prefer my own company. It's just too hard to fathom people out.

I drop to my haunches to test the moisture in the pots with my fingers, examine the plants, and inhale the delicate scent. Then I push up and turn to fetch my spade…

…and bump straight into someone I hadn't realized was standing behind me.

"Oh!" I hadn't heard anyone approach and my heart hammers.

And then I realize who it is, and I slide my arms around his waist and bury my face in his neck.

*

Kingi

"Oh!" Surprised at her reaction, I close my arms around her. I'd half expected her to slap me around the face. "Good morning."

"Morning." She's buried her face in my shoulder, and the word is muffled by my tee.

"Hey." I rub her back. "Everything okay?"

She nods. Then she looks up at me. Her eyes shine as she shakes her head.

"What's up?" I lower my arms, but she refuses to let go, and in the end I hug her again. "Sweetheart, what's going on? Is it your father?"

"No, he's fine, as far as I know." She clears her throat and moves back a little. "I'm okay."

"Tell me," I say firmly. "Is it about last night? Sabrina, and… what we did?"

"No, not really." She takes a deep breath and lets it out slowly, a little shakily. "Ria and Tamati hooked up last night."

"Ouch." Did I say that because I can imagine how it's hurt her? Or because it feels as if her reaction stabs me in the heart? "I'm sorry to hear that." I lower my arms, and we separate.

She rubs her nose. "It's okay, it's stupid really, I mean it's not like we were just on a break; it was definitely over."

I tip my head to the side to look at her face as she studies her shoes. "Are you sure?"

"Oh yes. I had no intention of getting back with him. But it's just so… final. It was a shock. I don't know why."

"Sometimes what we tell ourselves and what we feel aren't the same thing." I choose my words carefully. She still likes Tamati, and I think she was hoping they'd get back together.

But she insists, "That's not it. I didn't tell you, but I saw him outside the dress shop, and he was quite cruel to me. I didn't want anything more to do with him. It's more that it felt like the closing of a door, you know? The final page in a chapter. And I want to be a tough, confident, independent woman, and be made of rubber and bounce back without a second thought, but I'm not. I feel as if I'm made of porcelain or glass. I'm so weak, and I hate it."

"Weak?" I stare at her. "You're not weak. You're the strongest woman I know. It's been an incredibly tough few months for you, with your breakup, your dad being so ill, having to cope with Mark's addiction, and all the financial issues that came with it. You've been under huge pressure, Chess. It's no surprise you feel vulnerable and fragile. But that doesn't mean you're weak. It just means you need to give yourself time to heal and recover. You're going to be fine. What's that Japanese art of repairing broken pottery with gold? Kintsugi? It highlights the cracks rather than hiding them, right? It symbolizes that your scars are part of you, and they give you beauty and resilience."

Tears well in her eyes, and she presses her fingers to her lips as she fights not to let them fall.

"You're going to be fine," I say softly, reaching out to tuck a strand of hair behind her ear. "My beautiful wood nymph."

"Tamati never called me beautiful." Her voice is little more than a squeak. A tear spills over her lashes.

"Then he's a fucking idiot. Come here." I pull her into my arms, and she buries her face into my neck again. "Silly girl," I murmur.

She turns her head and rests her cheek on my shoulder, letting her emotions settle like leaves coming to rest after being swept up in a breeze. I think maybe she's just exhausted from everything that's happened. She's asking too much of herself. She really has been through it, and what's happening between us is pushing her over the line.

I kiss her hair. "I'm sorry if this whole fake engagement thing was a step too far for you. I didn't think about that. I always assume everyone's like me, and I forgot that you might not enjoy social engagements."

"Nobody's like you, Kingi," she says wryly.

I chuckle. Her hair is in a ponytail, and I run it through my fingers. It's like red silk.

"And I'm sorry about Sabrina," I add. "Sorrier than you'll ever know."

"It's not your fault."

"It kind of is. I'm not excusing what she did or how she did it. But I hurt her, and she wanted to hurt me in return. I can understand that."

"Lisa said there's no sign of anything on Kōrero."

"No. I'm hoping that means she's changed her mind."

"Because we didn't announce the engagement. So if we do, she'll then retaliate?"

"I don't know."

She moves back a little and looks up at me. Her eyes are like green pools, shining in the sunlight. "Maybe you should go and see her."

My eyebrows rise. "You think that's a good idea?" My voice is full of doubt.

"I don't know her the way you do. But I'm sure she's not all bad. You must have seen something nice in her apart from her boobs."

I think about it. "Not sure about that."

"You hurt her feelings when you dumped her," she says softly, "and maybe if you apologize, it'll make her feel better. If after that, she still decides to go through with it, at least you won't feel so bad about it."

I don't like the idea of seeing Sabrina again, but I trust Chessie. Her instincts about things like this seem to be spot on. So I hug her again, and we stand there like that quietly for thirty seconds, while she gathers herself.

"Are you okay about last night?" I ask eventually.

She clears her throat. "Yeah. It was just a bit of fun, right?"

"Oh yeah. It's just… I thought you might feel odd about it."

"Nah, I'm okay. I feel sorry for your carpet though."

I laugh, and she smiles, puts her hands on my chest to push back a little again, and looks up at me. Last night was a lot of fun. I've sent naughty messages before, but I've never had a sexting session like that, leading to both of us coming. It was hot and erotic, and a shock that the shy little Chessie I used to know is a firecracker in bed.

I can't help but wonder what she's like in the flesh, so to speak. I guess it's relatively easy to make up a story, but would she be as passionate face to face? I kinda think she would, and now I'm desperate to find out.

I remember the clause in the contract that stated I have to exercise self-control befitting a gentleman. Well, I blew that one last night. So in for a penny, in for a pound, right?

I lift my hands to cup her face and brush my thumbs across her cheeks to dry them. "Don't cry."

She swallows and nods.

I scan her face, and my gaze eventually comes to rest on her mouth. "Can I kiss you?"

Her lips part in surprise. "Why?"

"Why what?"

"There's no one around. Why do you want to kiss me when it's not for show?" She looks genuinely puzzled.

I run my tongue over my top teeth. "You really have to ask me that?"

"Uh…"

"You can't think of a single reason I might want to kiss you?"

She stares at me blankly. She genuinely doesn't realize how gorgeous she is.

"Crazy girl," I say. And then I lower my lips to hers.

She inhales sharply, but she doesn't pull away.

The sun is bright and unseasonably hot, and I can smell her new plants and the lavender she put in the ground just days ago. A tui bird is chirping from one of the Pohutukawa trees.

Slowly, she closes her eyes, and I do the same.

I tip my head to the side, changing the angle of the kiss, and brush my tongue across her lips. Outwardly, I appear calm, but inside my heart hammers and my blood races around my body. I don't move, though, and I don't breathe, afraid of breaking the spell.

She parts her lips, and I slide my tongue inside her mouth, against her tongue. In answer, she gives a little involuntary moan, and that's enough to fire me up. I move one hand to hold the back of her head and wrap the other arm around her, pulling her closer, tight against my body.

The heat between us rises by several degrees. She's already resting her hands on my chest, and they tighten on my tee, her fingers scrunching the material. She lifts up a little so she's on tiptoes, leaning into the kiss, and I murmur my approval, thrilled that she hasn't pulled away. That she wants to kiss me.

Oh fuck, this is getting out of control. I can't help but think about our conversation last night… The things she said… Is she thinking the same?

She slides her hands up to my face and then further up, into my short hair, curling her fingers in it as she kisses me. It's the sweetest, sexiest kiss I think I've ever had, the two of us warmed by the sun, and I want it to go on forever.

Eventually, though, I tear my lips away before I'm tempted to throw her onto the soft earth and kiss her all over.

She looks up at me with huge eyes. "I don't understand."

"I know." I give a short laugh. "That's what makes you *You*."

My phone has already buzzed in my pocket once, and now it does it again. I step back, pull it out, and check the screen. "Ah, I have to go, I have an appointment."

"Okay."

I smile at her. "Are you going to be all right?"

"Fine." Her voice is a squeak, and I try not to laugh.

"We'll talk later." I bend and give her a final kiss. "How about we go out for dinner tonight?"

She flushes. "Okay."

"All right. I'll pick you up at seven."

"Okay. Are you going to see Sabrina?"

"I suppose."

"Well, good luck."

I roll my eyes. "I'm not particularly looking forward to it."

"Just remember the fable about the North Wind and the Sun—persuasion is always better than force. She had you, and she lost you. I can only imagine how that feels."

My lips curve up. "Yeah, okay. Bye."

I walk away, heading for the club. Already, doubt is setting in. I shouldn't have kissed her. I can comfort myself that the contract stated that kissing would be necessary at times, but Chessie's not as good at lying to herself. Is she already worrying about what it means?

Glancing over my shoulder at her, I see her bending to look at her new plants, and I can just hear her voice joining in with the sound of the tuis and fantails—she's singing.

I turn the corner and head off to the lobby, smiling.

Chapter Seventeen

Kingi

On the way back to my office, I send Sabrina a text and ask whether she's in this afternoon, and if she'd be willing to meet up for a coffee and a chat. I expect to either hear nothing or to get a rude text back, but to my surprise, less than five minutes later she replies to say yes, she'll meet me, and suggesting the coffee shop in her apartment block at 3 p.m.

I put it to the back of my mind while I meet with a couple of city execs who want to talk about the development of a new office block in the CBD, then catch up on some work while I have lunch at my desk—a perfect Caesar salad made by our French chef.

While I eat, I realize how little I know about Sabrina. We only dated for a few weeks, and in that time, we didn't have any heart to hearts. We mostly met at parties and restaurants, or when other people were present, and even when she did come back to my place, after we had sex we still didn't talk much. I feel a bit ashamed of that now.

Wanting to be prepared, I do a Google search and click on a few links, and what I find totally shocks me. I sit in stunned silence for a while, Chessie's words playing over in my mind: *Remember the fable about the North Wind and the Sun? Persuasion is always better than force.*

Hmm. Maybe she's right.

Eventually, I pick up my phone and call Mikaere from the Foundation to run an idea past him.

After that, I go out to my car and head for the ferry. It's a gorgeous May Day, and I park the car, make my way up to the deck, then get a coffee from the shop. It's not long before we get going, and I lean on the railing and sip my latte, looking down at the dolphins swimming alongside the boat and thinking about Chessie.

I'm sure it was difficult for her to mention going to see Sabrina, but I think she understands that I need to put this ghost to rest. I behaved badly with Sabrina, and for some reason, Tane's clause about acting like a gentleman stung. He might well have had Sabrina in mind when he wrote it, and I understand that. She was right at the ball—I treated her like shit and then wondered why she reacted badly. She's a person with feelings, and she obviously liked me and wanted our relationship to develop, and I discarded her like an old sock without a second thought.

I'm ashamed, and I need to try and put it right. Will Sabrina be amenable to a truce? Or will she continue to be spiteful after she realizes I'm not going over to try and win her back?

I ponder on that as the ferry draws into the terminal, and I make my way back to the Porsche and head the car out.

The lower half of her apartment block is a hotel, with the upper half containing very upmarket apartments going for a couple of million and more. I park the car just down from the block, walk to the building, and find my way to the coffee shop. I've just ordered myself another latte when I glance over at the door and see her come in.

I don't know what I expected; she's always been dressed to the nines every time I've seen her, usually with perfect hair, nails, and makeup. Today, though, she's wearing a light-gray tracksuit, albeit a designer one. Her hair is in a ponytail, and instead of high heels she's wearing trainers. Her makeup is still immaculate, but done with neutral shades rather than bright colors.

"Hey," I say as she approaches. "Thank you for agreeing to meet me."

She slides her hands into the pockets of her tracksuit top. "What do you want?"

"Can I buy you a coffee?"

She looks past me at the assistant behind the counter and says, "Trim cappuccino please."

He nods and starts making it.

"How are you?" I ask her politely.

"Fine."

I wonder whether I should point out that if she's pregnant, she shouldn't really be drinking coffee. I decide that's probably not a good way to start the conversation.

MIDNIGHT BARGAIN

We wait in silence until our drinks are ready, then take them over to a table by a window overlooking a side garden. We sit and sip our coffees. I'd run through several conversation starters in my head, but now she's sitting here before me none of them seem to work.

"You look nice today," I say, meaning it.

She looks down at herself. Then her lips twist. "I thought you'd like the outfit."

Oh… Realization sinks in. She's dressed this way because she wants to look like Chessie. She thinks this is what I want.

"Sabrina," I say gently, "I'm not here to try to win you back."

She has cool gray eyes, quite beautiful, and they scan my face now as if trying to see whether I'm telling the truth. She blinks, then looks down at her coffee cup. "I know." She picks it up, has a sip, and flicks me a brief smile. "It was worth trying, though."

It's flattering to think she still wants me back, and kinda crazy too considering what happened at the ball. I can't work out if she's vulnerable and hurt or just a psycho.

I decide to give her the benefit of the doubt and go with vulnerable and hurt. I lean my forearms on the table and look her in the eyes. "I wanted to see you to apologize."

She surveys me cautiously. "For what? For sleeping with me?" Her brow furrows.

"No. I don't regret it." It's a lie, but I make sure to hold her gaze. "We had fun, didn't we?" She gives a small nod. She might not have been enthusiastic in bed, but I made sure she enjoyed it, and I'm pretty sure she didn't fake it.

"I thought you liked me," she says in a small voice.

"I did. I wouldn't have taken you to bed if I hadn't. You're beautiful and spirited, and you deserve much better than me."

She blinks, and her eyes turn a little glassy. Then she lifts her chin and says, "Yes, I do."

"You absolutely do."

I read the headlines, too. She lives her life in the spotlight, and I have no doubt she's been used by many men. I remind myself of what I discovered online this morning. I'm convinced she is just vulnerable and hurting.

I decide to opt for honesty, as far as I can without admitting everything about Chessie.

"There are many times in my life where I haven't behaved well," I begin. "Money does that to you. It makes you think you're above other people, and that you have the power to take what you want, and then cast it away when you're done. After the headline about me jumping off the waterfall drunk, Mikaere at the Ngā Whetū Rangatahi Foundation gave me a dressing down about my behavior and said I need to step up my game if I'm going to be a role model for the young people in the community, and he's right. He said I need to act respectably, and to be someone who values commitment, not just the spotlight. And he suggested that having someone by my side who reflects my values would reassure our donors."

Her eyebrows lift. "That's why you proposed to Francesca?"

"Obviously, it's not the only reason. But it was a factor. It was an odd coincidence; I left the meeting with the board and went for a walk, and literally bumped into Chessie. We went for a coffee and got talking, and we got on really well. I know she's not part of our world, but that's kind of the point—does that make sense? She's down to earth and practical, and she grounds me." With some surprise, I realize it's true.

Sabrina nods slowly. "I can see that."

"We dated for a few weeks, and I just fell for her, and it was like everything slotted into place. I didn't set out to hurt you, although I know I did."

She looks down at her coffee cup and scratches at a mark on the lid.

"I really want to help these kids," I say softly. "There are so many young people out there who are struggling, and who don't have the opportunities I was born with. I think you know all about that."

Her gaze snaps up to me, and she stares at me for a moment. Then she shrugs. "I guess it's not difficult to track me down on the internet."

I'd assumed she was born into money, but after researching this morning, I discovered she was born in one of the poorer suburbs of Auckland and is the daughter of a single mom. Her Māori father has never been in the picture, and her mother raised her single-handed. After she left school she became a dancer in a nightclub, made a few risqué movies, then met a rich older guy, and married him at eighteen. He paid for her to go to university to study fashion because it was her dream, and she stayed with him for four years before he died out of the blue of a heart attack. So she's known her share of tragedy and grief.

"I'm so sorry to hear about your husband," I say. She was eighteen and he was forty-one, so I suspect he was also a father figure for her.

"He was a good man," she replies simply. "Everyone thinks I married him for his money, but I didn't. I loved him."

"I'm sure you did."

"I got where I am because I've worked fucking hard."

"I know."

"I know what everyone thinks of me," she says fiercely. "That I don't have a heart. But I didn't date anyone for two years after he died. I loved him terribly, and I still miss him every day. But I'm not going to spend the rest of my life alone."

"You don't have to explain yourself to me. I'm the last person to pass judgement on someone else's life. My point is that you weren't born into money and opportunity. And you know how much difference it makes when someone gives you a helping hand. I want to do that for others. And that's why I'm here. To ask for your help."

I drop my head to catch her eye. "I know you're on the board of Te Rangi Ataahua Foundation." It means The Beautiful Sky, and it provides opportunities for young Māori women to learn about traditional weaving, and from there gives them an entrance to the fashion industry. I've read what she's done for the group, and how hard she works to help young women.

"Rather than sabotage what I'm trying to do, I want to bring you on board the Youth Stars," I say. "We want to offer you the role of Director of Outreach and Youth Mentor. We want you to use your story to inspire Māori youths—girls especially. Who better to teach them about resilience than someone who's climbed their way out of poverty and worked super hard to get where you are?"

Her cool gray eyes survey me, slightly puzzled. "You want to do that, even after what I've done?"

"I don't want us to be enemies. You're smart and resourceful, and you work damned hard. That's the kind of energy we need at the Foundation."

"And in return... you want me to retract what I said about you being drunk? And not announce I'm pregnant?"

We study each other for a moment.

"I'm not asking anything of you," I say carefully. "I want us to be friends, that's all."

She's still for a while. And then she leans back, a small smile on her face. "You really love her, don't you?"

"I do." And it's true. I do love Chessie as a friend.

She sips her coffee. Then she says, "I'm not pregnant."

I feel a huge sweep of relief. Holy shit. Thank God.

"Okay," I say as calmly as I can. Sun, not North Wind. "Thank you for telling me."

She bites her lip. "I know I shouldn't have said that. It just really stung when I saw you there with her, and someone said you were planning to announce your engagement."

"I understand. I'm sorry I hurt you. So… will you think about it?"

She sips her coffee, watching me. "Whose idea was it to bring me on board?"

"Honestly? It was Chessie who gave me the inspiration. She said to be kind, and it started me thinking about what we could achieve if we were friends rather than enemies."

Sabrina looks away, across the coffee shop and out at the view of the street. I wonder whether that's taken her by surprise. In our world, it's common for people to be focused on themselves and not to care about others' feelings.

Her gaze comes back to me. "All right," she says softly. "I'll do it."

I hide my shock with a big smile. "I'm so glad."

"And I'll retract the statement about you being drunk."

"That would be very nice of you," I say carefully. "And we'll make sure we have a photo taken of us shaking hands when you officially come on board."

She meets my gaze. "It must have taken a lot of courage for you to say that today."

"Chessie has inspired me to be a better person," I say honestly. I wonder if she's done the same to Sabrina?

"So what are your plans for the Foundation?" she asks.

I talk for a while about my long-term vision for it. She listens and offers a few suggestions, which, with her insight into public relations, prove to be useful suggestions. She explains how she does a lot of fundraising for Te Rangi Ataahua, and we talk about some ideas for projects we could work on together.

When I eventually check the time, it's with some surprise I realize that an hour has passed. She's smart and knowledgeable, and maybe because of her upbringing, she has a savvy side to her that I'm sure will prove useful in business.

"I'd better get going," I say eventually. "I've got a few jobs to do, and then I'm meeting Chessie for dinner."

"Okay."

"Thank you for agreeing to meet me today, and for listening, and being gracious."

"I don't know if that word is in my vocabulary," she says with amusement. "But you're welcome. And I do appreciate the apology."

"Friends?" I say, holding out my hand.

She slides hers into it. "Friends." She hesitates. "I'm glad you're not angry with me."

"Of course not." Not anymore, anyway.

She releases my hand. "I'll wait to hear from you."

"I'll be in touch soon." I give her a smile and leave the cafe.

As I go out into the bright May sunshine, a wave of relief washes over me. I feel as if I've avoided a landmine.

Chessie was right. I'm sure some men might have gone in guns blazing, tried to force her to withdraw her announcement of being pregnant, accused her of being spiteful, maybe even threatened her. I'm not like that, but it would have been easy to let anger win.

Instead, we seem to have an uneasy peace, and I think that's a very good start, and a lot more than I expected coming here today.

I get in the car and take the ferry back to Waiheke, then on impulse drive over to my parents' house. I still have a few hours before I have to pick Chessie up, and I haven't seen my folks for a while. They normally go to church on Sunday morning, then return home for Sunday lunch and a quiet afternoon, so I'm sure they'll be at home.

Dad told me they've talked about divorce, but I haven't had a chance to talk to them about it yet, so I don't know how the discussion has developed.

When I arrive at their house, I park out the front, get out, and make my way around the side of the house to the back deck. I find Mum sitting there, looking out at the magnificent view of the Pacific, lost in thought.

It's extremely unusual to find her doing nothing. She's one of those people who's always on the move. She's a member of numerous institutes and groups, and she's always working on her laptop or making phone calls to one of her many friends. So it's with some consternation that I approach her and say, "*Kia ora, e te whaea.*" It means 'Hello, my mother.'

She turns and sees me. "Kingi…" She wipes her face. Oh fuck, she was crying.

"Hey…" I go up and give her a hug. "What's up? What's the matter?"

"I'm okay. Just a bit emotional." She looks tired, which again is unlike her, as she normally has boundless energy.

I take the seat next to her. "Where's Dad?" I'm guessing her current emotional state has something to do with him.

She drops her gaze. "He's gone out."

"Have you argued?"

She doesn't reply, so I know I guessed right.

"Mama…" I frown. "What did you argue about?"

"He wants to stay together for appearance's sake. He's concerned about his public image." There's a touch of bitterness to her voice.

I understand Dad's concern. When you run your own company, and your success relies on appearing in control, things like this can affect how people see you. It's why Mikaere keeps on about being respectable. Image is everything. But she's hurting, and I'm not going to say that to her.

"And you don't want to stay together?"

"What's the point?" She looks out to the ocean again. "The relationship is dead. And I don't want to live the rest of my life like this. I'm only fifty-three. I want to be happy."

"I understand." My throat tightens. "You deserve that."

"I do, and I deserve to be loved. He hasn't loved me for a long time."

I shift in my seat. It's not easy to hear that about my father. I respect him and I look up to him. I don't like hearing that he hasn't been good to my mother.

"He must still love you if he wants to stay here," I say.

But she shakes her head. "It's all about appearances. Did you know that it's been two years since he even kissed me?"

That shocks me. "Seriously?"

She meets my eyes then. "He's having an affair."

I stare at her. "I asked him if he was, and he said no."

"He's lying. He's been seeing her for over a year."

My jaw drops. "How do you know?"

"Kingi, a woman always knows. The secret calls, the texts, the sneaking around, her perfume on his clothes, receipts in his pockets... He's not as careful as he thinks he is."

I'm genuinely shocked. Fuck, I'm naïve. I completely trusted him when he said he wasn't cheating.

I sit back, not sure what to make of that information. I feel hurt and betrayed too, which is ridiculous when I'm not the one he's cheating on, but I can't help it. To deny it to my face... and to cheat on my mother... Anger rises inside me.

She notices, and her expression flickers with guilt. "I shouldn't have said that."

"Of course you should."

"No, he's your father, and you're only getting one side of the story. Don't do anything silly."

She knows what I'm like. I take a deep breath and blow it out again. "What do you want?" I ask, leaning forward, my elbows on my knees.

She looks around. "I don't know. I love this house. I'm comfortable here. And he's the one who's cheated. I think he should leave. But he refused. He said if I want a divorce, I need to be the one to leave."

What a fucking mess.

"I'll talk to him," I tell her.

"No, Kingi..."

"I'll talk to him," I repeat firmly. "You're right—he should be the one to leave. He's worried about the business, but this is the twenty-first century, and it's not going to crumble just because he gets a divorce. You deserve the chance to find happiness again." A tear runs down her cheek. "Ah, Mama, don't cry, that kills me."

"I'm sorry," she says, but she can't help it, and she starts crying for real.

I pull her into my arms, feeling as if someone's slid a knife into my ribs. There's nothing worse than seeing your mother cry, especially when it's your father who's made her do it.

I will talk to him, and I'll make him be the man and sort this out.

Fuck. Relationships are so complicated. While my mother sobs in my arms, I think about how relieved I am that I seem to have come to some agreement with Sabrina.

And then finally I think about Chessie, and how easy it is to be with her. She's so calm. So kind. So down-to-earth.

SERENITY WOODS

When Dad first told me about the possibility of them getting a divorce, it felt like a symbol of my own determination not to settle down with one person. But oddly, right now, I wish Chessie was at my side. I feel that if she was here, we'd feel like a team. We'd support each other. And it's a nice feeling.

I lift my face to the breeze from the Pacific, and close my eyes.

Chapter Eighteen

Chessie

It's nearly one-thirty, and I decide I've done enough work for the day. I lock everything in the shed and head back to Dennis, then drive home. Lisa is out, and Ria's bedroom is still empty, so I have the house to myself. I should have some lunch… but I'm not that hungry, so I spend a couple of hours doing some chores, including my laundry and some general cleaning and tidying.

As I move some books from the living room back to my bedroom, I spot a bag by the side of my armchair and remember that I bought some new coloring books for Thea a few days ago. I was saving them for when I next see her again. On impulse I decide to call in at Mark and Nina's place. I have time before Kingi picks me up at seven. That way I can give Thea the books and also check up on them all and make sure they're doing okay.

When I paid off Mark's debt, I made it very clear to him that this was going to be the last time I would do it. I told him I wasn't trying to be cruel, but I'd been under a lot of pressure lately, and if I carried on I was going to make myself ill over it. Deep down, however, I'm nervous that it made no difference, and at some point I'm going to discover that he's been gambling again. I talked to both him and Nina about him getting therapy for his addiction, but when it comes down to it, he has to be the driving force behind his recovery, and although he's close, I don't know whether he's hit rock bottom yet.

So my heart is already racing a little when I turn onto his road… and it doesn't improve when I see an ambulance in front of his house.

Heart hammering, I park Dennis, cursing as I hit the curb, turn off the engine, and get out. Please don't let it be Thea… oh God…

I cross the road, only then realizing that my parents' car is parked just down from mine, and run up the garden path to the front door.

It's open, and as I go into the hall I can hear voices to the left, in the master bedroom.

"Chessie?"

I look to the voice, which came from the living room to my right, and I walk a few steps forward. My mother is sitting on the sofa with Thea, who's crying. When she looks up and sees me, Thea gets up, runs up to me, and throws her arms around my waist. She's obviously not the one who's hurt.

"What's happened?" I ask Mum, trembling.

"It's Mark," Mum says. "He took an overdose."

My jaw drops. "On purpose?"

"I don't know."

"Is he…" I swallow hard.

"He's alive," Mum says, "but unconscious." She meets my eyes, and then she bursts into tears, covering her face with her hands.

"Oh, Mum…" I bite my lip hard so I don't start crying as well. That's not what she and Thea need right now. "Where's Dad?"

"In with the paramedics," she says in between sobs. "They're putting Mark on a stretcher."

"Okay." I rub Thea's back. "All right, sweetie, everything's going to be okay."

I look over as I see movement in the bedroom doorway and see a paramedic backing out, guiding one end of a stretcher. Mark is strapped to it, and he has a drip in his arm. They get him through the doorway, then stop in the hall. My father comes out, his arm around Nina, whose face is white as a sheet.

I go to move Thea to my mother, but she won't release her tight hold around me, so in the end I take a few steps toward the paramedics with her still attached. "How is he?" I ask. "I'm his sister."

"Hello," the first paramedic says with a warm smile as he sees Thea looking, "he's okay, we're going to take him to hospital and try to make him better."

My mother stands. "Did he do it? Did he take the overdose on purpose?"

The second paramedic, a woman, also looks at Thea and says brightly, "Let's get him to hospital, and then we can work out what happened, okay?"

I look at my father, though, and he meets my eyes and gives a faint nod. Mark tried to kill himself. Oh God.

The first paramedic says, "We've also taken a look at your father's surgical wound, and we're a bit concerned about the fact that the infection isn't better, so we're going to take him in as well to get him checked out."

I'm not surprised; my father looks gray again, although that's probably as much from the shock as from the infection. But I'm glad they're taking it seriously.

"What should we do?" I ask. "Should we come too? What about Thea?"

Nina comes over and gives her daughter a hug. "It's all right," she says, "he's going to be okay. But I need to go to the hospital with him, and I don't want you to come." She looks up at us pleadingly.

"Why don't I drive you there," Mum says immediately. "And Chessie, you can look after Thea."

I open my mouth to object, feeling as if I should be the one doing the driving, because they're both going to be out of their minds with worry. For the past few months I've been the one organizing everyone, and it feels natural for me to take charge now.

But to my surprise Mum says firmly, "It's okay, love, I've got this. You've done enough. Nina needs to concentrate on Mark, and Thea loves being with you." She strokes Thea's hair. "Is that okay, sweetheart? You go and stay with Chessie for a bit?"

Thea looks up at me. "Can I?"

"Of course. Don't worry about her," I say to Nina. "You can call me if you want to talk to her at all. I'll make sure she's all right."

"Thank you." Nina hugs me. Then she says to her daughter, "Come on, let's quickly pack you a bag." The two of them go off to Thea's room, while the paramedics continue taking Mark out on the stretcher to the ambulance.

"Are you going to be all right?" I say to Mum as she gathers her things.

"I'll be fine." There's a flinty hardness to her gaze. "I can't believe he tried to take his own life," she says quietly. "With a young daughter. What was he thinking?" She's not just upset. She's furious. "I've had enough of this," she snaps. "We're going to get this sorted once and for all."

Dad comes up, and I give him a hug too. "Are you okay?" I ask, concerned about his color. "You don't look well."

"It doesn't seem right to complain when there's all this happening," he says, "but I feel a bit rough, I have to admit."

"That's the infection. I'm glad they're taking you in, Dad." I put my arms around him, fighting against the overwhelming urge to cry. When you're young, you feel as if your parents can do anything, and as if they're going to be around forever. I miss the innocence of being a child. Adulting sucks.

Nina comes out with Thea, both of them having packed bags, and there's a flurry of activity as one of the paramedics comes back to get Dad, and Mum and Nina promise they'll follow in the car. Nina gives me a spare key to their house. Then they all head off, leaving me and Thea standing there, watching them go.

I turn to Thea and give her a hug. "It's all right," I whisper. "Everything's going to be okay."

"Will we go back to your house?" she asks.

Lisa and Ria won't mind her staying with me, although we don't have a spare bed as such, so I guess she could have mine and I'll sleep on the sofa. I go to say yes, then remember that I'm supposed to be seeing Kingi this evening. "Let's get in the car," I tell her, "and then I need to make a quick phone call."

Once she's buckled into her booster seat in the back, I call Kingi.

"Hey gorgeous," he says.

"It's me," I reply, not thinking straight.

"I gathered. I don't reply to every caller like that."

I'm too upset to smile. "I'm not going to be able to see you tonight." My voice has a slight waver, and I stop talking and bite my lip.

Immediately his tone turns serious. "What's up?"

"It's… it's Mark. The… the ambulance has taken him to hospital, and my dad too because he's not well, and Mum and Nina have gone in the car, but they asked me to look after Thea…"

"What happened to Mark? Was he in an accident?"

"No. He…" I'm suddenly conscious of Thea sitting in the back. Oh God. She's only eight.

"Where are you?" Kingi asks.

"At their place."

"Mark's?"

"Yeah."

"Are you okay to drive?"

"Yes, yes, I'm fine."

"Okay. I'm heading out of Midnight now." I hear his footsteps, and him calling out to his PA that he's leaving for the day. "You know where I live, right?"

"Um…"

"Matapana Road near Palm Beach. The house is called Kārearea." It's a New Zealand falcon, sleek, fast, and rare. It doesn't surprise me he picked that. "You can stay the night," he says. "I have several spare rooms."

My eyes sting. "You don't have to do that…"

"I want to. You sound like you need a hug."

"I do." I sniff.

"Good." He's smiling. "I'll meet you there in about fifteen minutes, okay?"

"Okay."

"Drive carefully." He ends the call.

I program the location into Google Maps, then look over my shoulder at Thea. "You remember Kingi?" She nods. "We're going to go and stay with him for the night. Is that okay? He lives in a big house overlooking the beach."

"Okay."

I start the car and head off into the traffic.

"Mum said you and Kingi were engaged," Thea says. "Are you going to marry him?"

Suddenly, I can't bring myself to lie to her. I know there was a clause in the contract that said I mustn't tell anyone, and if I tell her, she'll probably tell her mum, but right now I don't care about that. I know with certainty that Kingi won't mind.

"I'm going to tell you a secret, okay? I'm not going to ask you not to tell your mum and dad because that wouldn't be fair, but not many know this. Kingi and I are pretending to be engaged."

"Why?"

As I drive, I explain about the Foundation, and that the board told him it would be best if he was in a committed relationship. And I tell her that he asked me to be his fake fiancée in return for money.

"I wanted to help him," I say, "and I also wanted to help your parents, and Grandma and Grandpa, and the business. So I said yes."

"Couldn't he have just loaned you the money?" she asks sagely. "If he's really rich?"

"He would have given me the money," I say softly. "But I didn't feel comfortable taking it from him without giving something in return."

"Why?"

I consider her question, looking at the trees to the left of Pacific Parade as I drive. "Money is an odd thing," I say slowly. "Everyone says it doesn't buy happiness. But the truth is that it does. Or at least, it buys comfort and contentment and peace of mind. Those who do have it will never understand what it's like to struggle without it. There's this assumption that you're poor because you're not working as hard as they do. Or you're not as dedicated as they are. Do you know what it means when you say someone is superior?"

"They think they're better than you?"

"Yes, that's right."

"Is that what Kingi's like?"

I open my mouth to reply. Then I close it again. To say yes would be unfair, because he's not like that at all. "No," I say eventually. "He's not. I… I think the fault's mine, actually. He called me an inverted snob, and I think he's right."

"What does that mean?"

"It's a person who criticizes things liked by people who they see as richer or cleverer than them. I was self-conscious going to the Midnight Club. I thought I stood out because I'm not wealthy or university educated. He said I'm the only one who was bothered by that."

"Was he right?"

"No… Everyone is very conscious of where they are in the social ladder. We all know when other people are richer than we are, or better educated. It's impossible to hide the fact that we don't have money or education, so we say we're proud of being where we are, and claim we're content to stay there."

"Everyone wants to be rich," she says.

I smile at her in the mirror. "Yes, you're right."

"I don't understand something."

"What's that, sweetheart?"

"You gave Dad money didn't you? To give to the men to pay off the loans?"

"Yes."

"Then why wasn't he happy? Why did he take those pills?"

My throat tightens. "I don't know. But it's important that you know it's nothing you've done."

"I know. Mum said he's mentally ill."

"Yes. It sounds horrible, I know. It just means something isn't working right in his brain, that's all. It's nobody's fault."

According to Google Maps, we're close to Kingi's house, so I slow Dennis, then indicate to turn onto Kingi's drive. It snakes behind some trees, then turns back on itself, and the house opens up before us.

Fuck me.

It's enormous. As I park and get out, I can see it's on the top of a slope. The back of the house, where we are, is on one level, and the front that overlooks the ocean is on two. The view is going to be magnificent.

I get Thea's bag out of the back, only then realizing that I should have gone home first and collected some of my own clothes. Oh well. It's only for one night. Hopefully he'll have a spare toothbrush I can borrow.

Thea gets out, and I lock the door and take her hand. Together we walk along the path that curves around the side and descends to what appears to be the front door.

"He's like a king," she says, wide-eyed, as we ring the doorbell.

"Don't tell him that to his face," I advise. "He won't be able to get his head out of the door."

She giggles, and then we hear footsteps, and the door opens.

My brain's been busy with other things today, so I haven't thought much about our kiss this morning. But as I see him standing there, dressed in a white tee and navy shorts, brown-skinned and dark-haired and gorgeous, I feel a wave of longing so fierce it takes my breath away.

"Hey," I say, my voice a squeak.

He meets my eyes, then looks at Thea and smiles. "Hey, honey. It's great to see you. Come in."

To my surprise, she goes up to him and slides her arms around him, burying her face in his chest.

"Aw..." He meets my eyes, his brows drawing together. There's obviously something about him that makes her feel safe and comfortable. He puts his arms around her and hugs her back, then he holds an arm out to me. I join them in the hug, letting him engulf us both.

Chapter Nineteen

Kingi

I don't know what's happened with Mark, but it's clear that both the girls are upset, and at the moment it's probably not a good idea to talk about it.

"I've got a surprise for you," I say to Thea. "Come on." Releasing them, I gesture with my head to the stairs that lead down toward the living room on the floor below, and Thea starts descending.

"This is a beautiful house," Chessie says as we follow Thea down.

"I bought it a couple of years ago. I looked around hundreds of houses, and nothing felt quite right. Then I walked into this one and I knew immediately I wanted it." The stairs curve to the right, entering the back of the living room, and when Chessie gasps I know she's having the same reaction that I did when I first came here.

The whole front of the house is glass, overlooking the Pacific Ocean. There's a generous lawn circled by a small fence, and on the other side, steps cut into the hillside lead down to the beach.

The living room is large, bright, and full of sunshine today. The walls are painted a pale lemon yellow, the floorboards are kauri wood with lots of rugs, and the furniture is comfortable—a big soft sofa and chairs, and a wooden dining set at the other end, although I don't use that much because I don't entertain here. The kitchen is pine, big and practical, with a square pine table and chairs in the middle. I either eat there, or out on the deck.

By the window, in a crate, is a Parson Russell Terrier puppy, approximately five months old.

Thea squeals, runs over to the crate, and drops to her knees beside it. "Oh, he's gorgeous!"

"Kingi!" Chessie goes over to and bends to look at the pup, who's wiggling his tail frantically. "I didn't know you were getting a dog."

"He's not mine. He's Orson's—my friend's," I explain to Thea, joining them at the crate. "I dogsit sometimes if he's going away." I smile. "I'm guessing you're okay with dogs?"

"I love them," she says with enthusiasm.

"His name's Bearcub." I wink at Chessie, undo the sliding catches holding the crate door closed, and the puppy pushes it open and dashes out. He jumps straight onto Thea's lap, and she falls backward with him, laughing.

"Aw…" Chessie holds her hands out for the puppy to sniff, then strokes his soft ears as he goes back to play with Thea. The little girl retrieves a rope toy from the crate and starts playing tug with him.

"He's just had his final vaccinations," I advise Thea, "so he's not supposed to go to public places for another couple of weeks, but you can take him out into the garden if you like." I unlock the sliding doors and open them, and she and Bearcub go onto the deck, then negotiate the couple of steps onto the lawn. "Here," I call, and toss her a ball, and soon she's throwing it for Bearcub, who trots around looking up at her as if she's a princess.

"Is Orson really away?" Chessie says as I lead her across to the kitchen.

I give her a wry smile. "Busted. No. But I do dogsit for him, so Bearcub knows the house. I asked to borrow him for the night."

"That's very sweet of you." She climbs onto a barstool at the breakfast bar.

I gesture at the coffee machine, and she nods, so I start making us both a cup. "I'm glad you came over." I set the espresso pouring and retrieve some milk from the fridge. As I pour it into the jug, I glance at her. "You sounded as if you'd had quite a shock."

"Yeah." Her smile fades and she scratches at a mark on the countertop.

"You don't have to talk about it if you don't want to."

She glances over her shoulder, makes sure that Thea is still in the garden, then looks back at me. "Mark took an overdose."

I nod slowly and swap the cups. "I thought that might be the case."

Her eyebrows rise. "Really? I was so shocked. Why did you think that might have been it, and not an accident or something?"

"Because of what's been happening, with the money and everything." Once the second espresso has poured, I set the milk steaming, and turn and face her, folding my arms.

"I don't get it," she says, clearly confused. "I paid off the debt. He had no more worries. All he had to do was concentrate on getting better. It was a new start for him. He has everything—a job, a wife, a daughter, a roof over his head. Why would he try to kill himself?" She's close to tears.

"I don't know," I say carefully, "but I imagine he was ashamed."

She blinks. "Ashamed?"

"He enjoys gambling. He likes the buzz it gives him. But he knows it's wrong. The fact that he likes it, and that he can't fight it, will probably make him feel weak, and maybe worthless or stupid."

"But it's not," she says, her brow furrowed, "addiction isn't a character flaw."

"Well, you and I know that. But being ashamed of an addiction is very common. People will try and hide it, deny it, rationalize it, do anything rather than face it and address it."

I pour the steamed milk over the espresso, stir it, and slide hers across to her. "He's a guy, Chess. You can tell us we're equals until you're blue in the face, but we all feel it's our responsibility to be the man, to look after our families, and to provide for them. He let his family down. He risked his parents' home. He caused his wife stress and anxiety and probably lied to her, too. He was a bad role model for his daughter. And he forced his sister to go against her better judgement for money because she wanted to help."

"He doesn't know it's a fake engagement," she whispers.

"Most people won't guess, but he's a smart guy. He knows we haven't seen each other for a while. And then, out of the blue, at a time he needs you most, we bump into each other, get engaged in a fortnight, and then you miraculously produce enough money to pay off his debt? Believe me, he knows." She should probably have told her family the truth from the beginning, but the stupid contract took away that option, and now we're caught up in this web of lies.

I can see understanding sinking in slowly like a stone tossed into the ocean. And I know immediately what she's thinking.

"No," I say firmly, pointing at her, "don't go down that road."

"But… if I hadn't tried to help…"

"You can't blame yourself, Chess. He's an addict. He's fucked up. It's nobody's fault, not even his, and certainly not yours."

It's too late, though. Her face crumples, and then she covers it with her hands and starts crying.

"Ah... fuck..." I walk around the breakfast bar, go up to her, and wrap my arms around her. She's still sitting down, and she buries her face in my chest and sobs.

"It's okay..." I rub her back and kiss the top of her head. It must have been a huge shock to her.

I'm surprised she didn't go to the hospital considering her dad has gone too. But someone has to look after Thea, and it wouldn't surprise me if her mother suggested it. I know Chessie has been working super hard to try to keep the family on its feet, and I'm sure her mother knows the impact it's having on her mental and physical health, and is trying to give her a break.

A skittering noise on the floorboards causes me to look over, and I watch Thea come in with Bearcub, whose nails clack on the wood as he trots in to have a drink from his water bowl.

"Chessie?" Thea asks, approaching us. "Are you okay?"

Chessie nods but doesn't look around.

"She'll be all right in a minute," I say to Thea. "Do you want to give Bearcub a treat? They're in that box over there. He can't have too many or he'll get fat, but you can give him one if you like."

She looks at Chessie, obviously decides from my casual manner that it's nothing to worry about, and goes over to get a treat.

"Tell him to sit," I advise as the puppy approaches her.

"Sit," she says firmly, and the puppy obediently drops his bottom to the floor. "Good boy!" She bends and gives him the treat, and he chews it, then gives a delightful burp that makes her giggle.

Chessie rests her forehead on my chest, then pushes back a little and wipes her face. "I'm okay," she says as Thea looks up at her. "Sorry."

"Nothing to apologize for," I say cheerfully. It's important in Māori culture to show emotion. "*E kore te pāraire e hoki mai i te tangi.*"

She lets me stroke her hair. "What does that mean?"

"The bellbird will not return from its cry. It means once emotion is released, it cannot be undone. It's natural and necessary to let it out. That's how you heal."

She nods and gives Thea a shaky smile.

"Drink your coffee," I tell her. "Now, Thea, what about you? Would you like a drink? I've got juice, milk, or bottled water."

"Juice, please."

Bearcub has flaked out on one of the rugs, so I leave him there rather than put him in his crate. I pour her some orange juice from the carton into a glass, add some cold water from the fridge to water it down, drop in some ice cubes, and slide in a straw, then pass it to her. "Now, what about dinner tonight? I can send out for something if you like, or I don't mind cooking, if you're brave enough to try it." I pull a face at her, and she giggles. "What do you like? I do a mean spaghetti Bolognese."

"That's my favorite."

"Then that's what we'll have." I check my watch; it's four thirty. "I'll start soon. But there's time yet. You want a snack?" I open the fridge, and we both study the contents. "A chicken sandwich?" I suggest. She agrees, so I get out the bread, cold chicken, and Lurpak, and proceed to make her a sandwich. "Do you want one?" I ask Chessie. She shakes her head, although I suspect she hasn't had lunch today. I make an extra one anyway, and when Thea climbs up onto the stool next to her to eat hers, I have a bite out of the other sandwich, then push it toward Chessie. She looks at it, then picks it up and starts eating. I wink at Thea, and she winks back.

"Chessie told me you're pretending to be engaged," she states.

I lift my eyebrows at Chessie, who pulls an *eek* face and says, "Sorry."

I chuckle. "Yeah. But you mustn't tell anyone, okay?"

"Yes, I know it's a secret." Thea has a bite of her sandwich. "Did you get the job?"

"At the Foundation? Yes, I did, because of Chess."

"What job is it?"

I tell her a bit about it while we eat the sandwiches and drink our coffee and juice. I explain that I'll be helping young people, providing opportunities for them to improve their health, wellbeing, and futures.

"Kingi likes mountaineering," Chessie tells her. "He's climbed Aoraki Mount Cook."

Thea's jaw drops. "Really?"

I nod. "A few years ago."

"Wow."

I smile. "It was quite an experience."

Chessie goes to say something, but then she says, "Oh," and pulls out her phone. "It's Grandma," she says to Thea. Putting the phone to her ear, she gets up from the table and wanders over to the window as she talks quietly.

Thea watches her go, then looks up at me. "My dad's in hospital."

I lean on the breakfast bar. She obviously wants to talk about it. I'm sure that some people would try to change the subject, but I've never shied away from difficult conversations. It's one reason why I want to work for the Foundation—because kids need to know it's okay to have feelings, and it's okay to want to talk about them.

"Did an ambulance come to pick him up?" I ask.

She nods. "He'd taken too many pills."

"Yes, Chessie told me."

"I found him," she says.

Oh… fuck. "Thea, I'm so sorry."

She sits with a stiff spine, tearing little bits off her sandwich. "We'd been shopping, and when we got back I went to see him. He was in the bedroom, on the bed. He'd been sick." She swallows hard, but lifts her chin as she looks up at me. Her expression is defiant, and her eyes blaze. "I hate him," she says. "For doing it."

I feel a wave of pity for this poor girl. There's no point in saying it's not his fault. She's angry that he did this to her.

I make sure not to react or look shocked. "I understand why you feel like that."

She blinks, and her bottom lip trembles. She looks at the remainder of her sandwich. "I thought you were going to tell me off."

"You're entitled to your feelings, whatever they are. Don't ever let anybody tell you otherwise. And you can always talk to me. I won't judge you. The only thing I will say is that hate is a negative emotion. It's like a huge wall towering over you and leaving you in shadow. Always focus on trying to find the light, if you can."

She moves the pieces of her sandwich around the plate, thinking about that. "Chessie said something isn't working right in his brain."

"That's right. The important thing to remember is that he doesn't want to be an addict. And he would never want to hurt you. When people attempt suicide, it's because they're in so much pain that they can't think about anything else except stopping that pain. It's as if he's in a box and his emotions are like hedgehogs that are being stuffed in with him, and there are so many hedgehogs in there that there's no room for your mum, or you, or anything else, and all their prickles are really hurting him. Does that make sense?"

She nods, her eyes wide.

"When that happens," I continue, wondering where that analogy came from, "your body goes into what's called fight or flight—you literally can't think about anything else except either fighting or escaping the pain. He's trying to climb out of the box, that's all. He loves you and your mum very, very much, and he would never knowingly hurt you. But when it comes to it, we're just animals, and our bodies are like machines, like cars. Sometimes bits don't work properly."

"Like, I've got asthma," she says. "My lungs don't work properly."

"Yeah, that's right. I'm short sighted—I have to wear contact lenses. Chessie is claustrophobic—she doesn't like enclosed spaces."

"I didn't know that!"

"Yeah. And with your dad, there's something in his brain that isn't quite right."

"Chessie said addiction is something to do with dopa… dopaline?"

"Dopamine, yes, she's right. Gambling makes the body give a high surge of dopamine quickly, which makes you feel good. But we don't quite understand why some people are able to walk away from things like gambling or drugs after trying them a few times, whereas others feel the need to keep going back."

She eats a piece of sandwich, thinking about what I've said. I glance over at Chessie. She's still on the phone, but her gaze is on me. I think she's half-listening to what I've been saying. Her demeanor is calm, so I'm guessing the news isn't terrible. I hope her father is okay, too.

I look back at Thea. I don't think she wants any more of her sandwich. "Would you like to see the room you're going to sleep in tonight?"

"Yes, please."

"Come on, then." I lead her to the hallway, Bearcub trotting at our heels. "That's my study," I say, pausing in the doorway.

"You have lots of books!"

"I do. Do you like reading?"

"Oh yes. I'm reading one called *Wolf Girl*, about a girl called Gwen who gets lost, and she's looked after by four dogs."

"Wow, that sounds amazing! Maybe I should read that one."

She giggles. "What are you reading?"

I lead the way past the small gym room to the end where the bedrooms are. "A biography of Edmund Hillary. Do you know who he was?"

"He climbed Mount Everest."

"You're so smart! That's right. He was a Kiwi, did you know that?"

"No!"

"He also climbed Aoraki Mount Cook, and he went to both the North and South Pole. And he kept bees." I gesture to my left. "That's my room there. Chessie can have this room, so if you need her in the night you know where to find her. And I thought you could have this room." It's next to the one Chessie will sleep in. It's decorated in a pretty light-green and lavender color combination. On the way home, I called in at a furnishings store and bought a couple of plush pillows—one a unicorn, one a purple owl—and also a bedside lamp she can keep on all night that's like a willow tree with small, colorful LED lights.

I show her how she can switch it on just by tapping the base, and she plays with it a few times, then jumps onto the bed and hugs one of the pillows. "Can Bearcub sleep on my bed?"

I hesitate. He usually sleeps in his crate. He can go about five or six hours without needing to go out, but I normally take him out once in the night.

But her eyes are full of hope, and I don't have the heart to say no. "Sure. I'll have to come in and take him out before I go to bed, but I can bring him back afterward."

"Yay!" She bends and lifts him onto the bed, then giggles as he tries to tug the owl out of her arms.

"What's going on here?"

I turn to see Chessie leaning against the door jamb.

"Tug of war," I say. "How are you doing?"

She sighs, then gives Thea a small smile. "Your dad's doing okay. They're going to keep him in hospital overnight and make sure he feels well enough to go home tomorrow. And he's also going to see a counselor."

"Will that make him better?"

She glances at me, then back at her niece. "He'll be okay physically. Mentally it might take a little longer. But at least he's getting help now."

"How's your dad?" I ask.

"Back on IV antibiotics. He'll be in overnight, too." She looks at the plush pillows and the nightlight. "Are these yours?"

I grin. "No, I picked them up on the way home."

"Aw, that was sweet."

"I am occasionally thoughtful."

"Kingi said Bearcub can sleep with me," Thea announces.

"Well, that was kind of him. Are you sure?"

"I can take him out before I go to bed," I say, "and he should be all right until we get up. Okay so I'm going to start the Bolognese so it can cook for a bit. What would you two like to do? I've got Disney+ if you want to watch a movie. Bearcub's fond of *Monsters Inc* and *Toy Story*."

They both laugh as we go out into the living room. "I'm not going to ask how you know that," Chessie says.

"Hey, I love Disney. Actually, *The Little Mermaid* is my favorite, but I don't usually tell other people that."

"I love *The Little Mermaid*!" Thea looks delighted. "I've seen it thirty-seven-and-a-half times."

"Wow."

"Ariel looks like Chessie," she states as we go into the kitchen.

"That's why it's my favorite." I wink at Chessie, who blushes.

I find the movie and put it on, and Thea takes a coloring book and some pencils out of a bag that Chessie gives her, and sits on the floor by the coffee table to color, with Bearcub curled up by her side.

I go into the kitchen and start getting the ingredients ready for the Bolognese: beef mince, a tin of tomatoes, tomato paste, onions, garlic, carrots, celery, olive oil… I turn to put them on the counter, expecting to see Chessie sitting with Thea, and discover her sitting instead at the breakfast bar, leaning her chin on a hand, watching me.

"You all right?" I ask.

She nods. I can't tell what she's thinking, but there's a small smile on her lips. "You're a good man," she says.

I put down the ingredients, then rest my forearms on the bar. I lean toward her… and press my lips to her forehead.

I move back a few inches, and she lifts her face to look at me. I pause, waiting to see if she'll sit back, but she doesn't move. Slowly, giving her time to react if she wants to, I lean forward again, and this time I touch my lips to hers.

She sighs, her breath a whisper across my lips, and tilts her head a little to the right. So I kiss her again, no tongues, just pressing my lips to hers, once, twice, and a longer third time before I finally move back.

She meets my eyes, and we study each other for a long moment.

"Fake engagement," Thea says from where she's sitting at the coffee table. "Yeah, right."

Chapter Twenty

Chessie

Kingi just laughs and finishes off Thea's sandwich, but I bite my bottom lip and study my coffee cup. What am I doing letting him kiss me? Haven't I got enough to worry about, without falling for this gorgeous guy? Kingi has great potential to break my fragile heart. I still believe that this Cinderella will never get her prince, and she'd be foolish to even contemplate it.

I watch Kingi as he starts preparing the vegetables. He does it like a guy—making a mess, slicing unevenly, and then chopping as if he's got a personal vendetta against the onion and carrots, but I'm impressed that he even cooks. Tamati's skills extended to opening a can of beans and putting bread in the toaster.

While I was on the phone to Mum, I half-listened to him talking to Thea. He's so good with children and young adults. He manages to be both approachable and kind of fatherly. He's going to be fantastic at the Foundation.

"Do you want kids?" I ask.

He doesn't look up, busy chopping the celery. "Gotta find a wife first." He gives me a brief smile, then carries on.

"When we were at dinner with Orson and Scarlett, you said you don't think marriage is for you. Is that because your parents are getting divorced?"

He shrugs. "I think it's a lot to ask of people to stay with someone for the rest of their life. The fact that so many marriages end in divorce supports that. And lots of people have affairs. Breakups are hard. Why put yourself through that?"

"I do get that." I lean my head on a hand, watching as he heats up some olive oil in a pan. "But you'd make such a great dad."

"I'm terrible with babies."

"Everyone is at the beginning. Don't you think it would be nice, though, to make a baby with someone? A little piece of you and them to cherish?" I feel a pang inside as I say it, a tug deep inside me I haven't felt before.

He studies the pan for a moment, then tips up the chopping board and scrapes the vegetables into the hot oil. Some of them go onto the hob, and he spends a moment picking them up and popping them in the pan before he starts tossing them in the hot oil.

Is he going to answer me? It doesn't look like it. Is that because he's considering it for the first time? Or because he definitely doesn't want children, and he just doesn't want to say?

I think about that weird tug I felt deep inside. I haven't given a lot of thought to having my own kids, but I've always known I want them eventually. It's the first time I've felt broody, though. Maybe it's just being near such a perfect example of masculinity. He makes my ovaries ache.

"You want kids?" he asks.

"Eventually."

He looks over at me and meets my eyes, and it makes me catch my breath. He holds my gaze for about ten seconds, then looks back at the pan and continues frying the vegetables. He doesn't say anything more, but my heart continues to race for a bit.

"Can you open the tin?" he asks.

I get up and go around the breakfast bar, find the tin opener in the drawer, and open the tomatoes while he starts frying the mince. Once it's done, I take it over to him and lean a hip against the worktop next to the hob and watch him.

"How did the meeting with Sabrina go?" I ask.

"Ah, it went very well, thanks to you."

"Me?"

"Your advice about the North Wind and the Sun proved very useful. She admitted she's not pregnant."

I inhale, and I know my face has lit up, because he smiles. "Oh." Heat rushes through me, along with another wave of emotion. I bite my lip, waiting for it to die down.

"We actually had quite a nice chat," Kingi says, adding the tomatoes to the mince. "And I've offered her a position on the Foundation as Director of Outreach and Youth Mentor, to inspire Māori girls."

"Ohhh... That was a very smart move." He hasn't gotten where he is in business without learning how to make clever decisions.

"She's on several other boards, and she's apparently done very well with them, so I think she'll be able to do a good job with us. But I won't be seeing much of her. I'll let Moana deal with her mainly." He glances at me, his brows drawing together.

I study him, puzzled, as he takes some spaghetti out of the cupboard, measures out a few handfuls, and puts the kettle on to boil. He assumed I wouldn't like him seeing her. He thought I'd be jealous.

"It makes perfect sense to offer her something," I say softly. "To make her feel valued. I think it's a great idea."

"Oh, I'm glad. I didn't want you to think I did it because I wanted to see more of her." He glances at me, meets my eyes for a moment, then looks back at the hob.

This is only a fake engagement. But it's impossible not to wonder what it would feel like if it was real. To have a guy like this at your side, protecting you, supporting you. Loving you. The thought takes my breath away.

I really mustn't think about things like that. But it's impossible to stop my brain once it starts. Imagine being able to hug him whenever I want, to kiss him whenever the mood strikes me.

To make love to him whenever I feel like it...

And now I'm thinking about our sexting, and the way he said he'd tip me onto the carpet, pin my hands above my head, and fuck me hard.

Oh God.

He glances at me then, his amber eyes bright. "Don't look at me like that," he says.

"Like what?"

His lips curve up. "You know like what."

"I was just thinking about our message conversation."

He looks across at Thea, then back at me as he murmurs, "Don't start talking about that, unless you want me to kiss you senseless."

We study each other for a moment, remembering what we said to one another. Is he feeling as breathless as I am?

To my surprise, he reaches out and cups my cheek. "You should go and sit with Thea. I don't want to take advantage of you."

My eyebrows rise. "What do you mean?"

He strokes my cheek with his thumb. "You've had a big shock today. It's natural to look for comfort when you're feeling vulnerable."

I swallow hard. It's true that my emotions are floating near the surface, refusing to be pushed down like a piece of polystyrene in water. That's not why I'm feeling such attraction to him though. Is it? For a moment I feel confused. Maybe it is, partly. The thought of being distracted and spirited away from reality is extremely appealing at the moment. It would be amazing to lose myself in him, and let all my cares float away.

But that's unrealistic, and stupid, because I'd only have to deal with the fallout the next day, as he found out with Sabrina. We try to shove our emotions and actions into boxes, but they're like ferrets; as soon as you lift the lid, they'll sneak a paw through the crack and be running around causing havoc before you can count to three.

So I join Thea in the living room, and I sit beside her and help her color in her picture as we watch *The Little Mermaid*. While he stirs the dinner and sets the table, Kingi sings along to the songs, and we giggle as he gets the words wrong, but it doesn't seem to stop him.

Not long after that, he announces that dinner is ready, so we turn off the TV and join him at the square table in the kitchen. He's prepared Bearcub's dinner and puts it to one side of the kitchen for the puppy to eat, then joins us at the table. He and I sit opposite each other, with Thea on one side between us. He tucks a tea towel into his T-shirt, then offers Thea one to cover her clothing, and she copies him, tucking it into her top to protect it from the sauce that will inevitably stain. I hide a smile as he winks at me.

He dishes us both up a big plate of spaghetti and heaps several spoonfuls of the Bolognese on, then offers us a dish of grated cheese to sprinkle on top. He's also sliced an uncut crusty loaf into thick slices and buttered them.

We dig in, twirling our forks in the spaghetti. I hadn't realized how hungry I was, and I devour the meal with gusto, using the bread to mop up the delicious sauce. Even though the kitchen is a mess, filled with numerous pans and food scattered across the surfaces, I can forgive him because it's so delicious.

Thea takes longer to finish, but we sit and chat while she eats, her mouth stained with sauce. I'm glad she's coping okay. I can't imagine how she must be feeling, but she's a smart girl, wise beyond her years, and she seems determined to try and understand and cope with what's happening.

After she finishes her dinner, Kingi asks if she'd take Bearcub out to the garden. It's dark now, but he has big security lights that come on as she opens the door and goes onto the deck. She takes Bearcub onto the grass while Kingi and I rinse the dishes and stack the dishwasher. Then we make a coffee and take it into the living room. Thea comes back in with the puppy, and we close the doors and settle down to watch another movie.

Thea sits on the floor and colors next to Bearcub. At first, Kingi and I sit at each end of the sofa. I curl up, my gaze drifting out of the window as I think about Mark and my father and wonder how they're doing. Mum has promised to contact me if there's any change in their conditions, but she said it's probably going to be a quiet evening, with both of them getting some rest and recovering overnight.

It's impossible to stop my thoughts sliding into darker places, though. I think about my father, and wonder whether he has the strength to keep fighting, especially after the devastating news about his son. And I think about Mark, and what he tried to do, and what might have happened if he'd succeeded. Will he try again? All of us will worry about that now. Every time I walk away from him, I'm going to fear it'll be the last time I see him. What would we do if he attempted it again, and was successful next time? What would Nina do? And what about Thea?

A movement next to me causes me to glance across at Kingi. He's rested his hand on the sofa cushion between us, and as I look, he turns his palm up and beckons his fingers, requesting I move toward him. Then he lifts his arm up, indicating he wants me to move next to him. His expression is kind. He's seen my emotion, and he wants to comfort me.

I shouldn't... I mustn't...

But I have no willpower left to say no. I want the comfort, and I want to be close to him. So I shift along the sofa, curl up next to him, and slide my arm around his waist as he lowers his around me.

Thea looks up, sees us, smiles, and goes back to coloring.

I stay there like that for the rest of the movie. There's something about Kingi that grounds me and brings me out of my head and back down to earth. His body is heavy and solid. I sneak my fingers beneath the hem of his tee onto his skin, enjoying the warmth, and the way he stirs and murmurs his approval. He smells amazing. Yesterday he was clean shaven, but today he has a little stubble; he's probably going to grow his beard back again. The stubble darkens his cheek and provides a delicious masculine touch. I want to run my fingers along his jaw and feel my nails scrape on the bristles.

I could have lain there like that all night, but eventually the movie ends. "Is it okay if I give Thea a bath?" I ask Kingi.

He nods. "Use the main bathroom—there's a big bath in there. I'll run it for you."

Sure enough, there's a large sunken bath, and Thea squeals with delight when she goes in and discovers it full of bubbles. I help her get in to make sure she doesn't slip, and I wash her hair for her, while Bearcub comes up and tries to eat the bubbles. Thea blows them onto him and then laughs as he races around with them in a big pile on his head.

Kingi sits on the carpet outside the bathroom and talks to us, and when Thea starts singing the songs from *The Little Mermaid* while she plays with the bubbles, he joins in, getting all the words wrong, of course. I smile, listening to them and imagining that one day my life could be something similar to this, with my own husband and child. Is that in the stars for me? And who would play the role of adoring husband?

I can't help but continue my fantasy, and wonder what it would be like to be married to Kingi. He originally admitted he couldn't see himself settling down, especially because of what's happened to his parents, but since then he's made a few comments that have suggested he's beginning to change his mind. Maybe before that, he envisaged being married to someone like Sabrina—a high-maintenance girlfriend who would almost certainly make his life a misery. But perhaps now he can see the benefits of a long-term relationship with someone he truly loves. A partnership where you work together against the trials and tribulations that life throws at you. The thought of having someone at your side to love and protect you in that battle is hugely appealing.

As is the regular sex, of course.

Trying not to think about that, I hold the towel up for Thea as she gets out, find her pajamas while she dries herself, and plug in the hairdryer. I brush and dry her hair for her and braid it while Kingi asks her what she wants for a bedtime snack and gives her a few options.

We go back out into the kitchen, and Kingi prepares her choice: a slice of toast with peanut butter and a glass of milk.

While she's eating that, Nina calls me on my phone. After a brief chat, I pass the phone to Thea, and she talks to her mum while Kingi and I go into the kitchen and unpack the clean dishes from the dishwasher.

"How is everyone?" he asks.

"Dad is doing well and apparently has a bit more color. Nina said Mark has been quiet. He's asleep now."

Kingi nods toward Thea. "You know that she was the one who found him?" He passes me a couple of plates.

I stare at him, my jaw dropping. "Seriously?"

"Yeah, she told me."

I'm stunned. None of them mentioned it when I turned up at the house. Ohhh… the poor girl.

I'm also surprised that she confessed to him. "You say you can't picture yourself as a father," I tell him, "but you obviously have a way about you with kids that makes them open up to you." It's clearly one reason why they want him at the Foundation.

"It's because I'm still one myself," he says with a grin.

I smile, because I'm meant to, but it's a self-deprecating comment, because that's not the reason. It sounds as if he makes them feel that their thoughts and feelings are valid. He makes them feel seen.

I glance over at Thea. She's sitting on the sofa, listening to her mum talk. I don't want her to feel as if I'm eavesdropping, so I turn back to Kingi.

"How are your parents doing?" I ask as I remove the glasses and put them in the cupboard.

"I saw Mum today, actually."

"Oh? How's she doing?"

He hesitates, staring at the dish in his hands. Then he turns to place it in the cupboard. "Not good."

"Oh no, why?"

"It turns out my dad is having an affair."

I stare at him in shock. "Oh no."

"I asked him if he was cheating and he said, 'of course not.' But it was a lie. She said he's been seeing this woman in the city for over a year."

"I'm so sorry."

He sighs and leans back against the kitchen counter. "Mum wants a divorce. She wants him to move out, but he's refusing. I think I'm going to have to talk to him to convince him to go."

"Oh, that's awful."

"Yeah. He's going to be angry about that. He's said that if she wants a divorce, she has to leave. But that's not fair on her. I think he should move into the city and get an apartment. It's not as if he can't afford it. And he's the man. He needs to be the one to take responsibility, admit the marriage is over, and do something about it." His face is hard. He's disappointed and upset with his father, and understandably so. Despite his carefree attitude and his string of girlfriends, I very much doubt he's cheated on any of them. He's not that kind of guy.

He looks past me and says, "She's finished the call."

I turn to see Thea coming into the kitchen, holding out the phone. "Thank you," she says. She's pale, but composed.

"Everything okay?" I take the phone and leaving it on the counter.

She nods. "They've given Daddy something to help him sleep. Mummy said he should feel better in the morning."

"Oh, that's good."

"Someone is going to talk to him in the morning," she says. "About what he did."

"A therapist?"

"Um… she said it was a psy… psych…"

"Psychologist?"

"Yes, I think so. What's the difference?"

I glance at Kingi.

"They're pretty much the same," he says. "Both of them help you to understand why you make certain choices, and to come to terms with trauma. A psychologist has a doctorate—a special degree. They're more highly trained, that's all. It's good. It means your dad will get to talk to someone with a good understanding of mental health issues."

I like the way he isn't afraid to tackle difficult topics head on. He doesn't shy away from problems or emotions.

"Will they make him better?" Thea asks.

"I hope so," I say.

"They'll help him understand why he did what he did," Kingi says. "They'll talk about his feelings, and whether he's depressed. They might give him some pills to help him feel more level and able to cope. And they'll probably find him a therapist for ongoing counselling. It won't be a quick fix. He's not going to get better overnight. But he's obviously been feeling very bad. And now everyone knows, they can start helping him get better. Does that make sense?"

She nods.

"All right," I say softly. "Time for bed, I think. Have you finished your toast?"

She brings the empty plate and glass out while Kingi takes Bearcub outside for a final garden visit. Then we walk them down to the spare bedroom. Kingi lifts Bearcub onto the bed, and once Thea is settled, the puppy turns around a couple of times, then curls up in the crook of her legs.

"I'll come in before we go to bed and take him out for another pee," Kingi tells her. "But I'll bring him back afterward, so don't worry if you don't wake up."

He goes out, and I sit on the bed beside her. "Are you okay?" I ask her. "Anything you want to talk about?"

She shakes her head. "I'm okay."

"Kingi told me that you were the one who found your dad after he took the overdose."

She nods.

"That must have been very hard for you," I say softly. I wonder whether she'll have nightmares about it. "Are you worried about him?"

She thinks about it, then shrugs. "Yes... but Kingi said that now everyone knows how Daddy feels, they can help him get better."

"That's right."

"I love him," she says in a small voice.

"Of course you do."

"I want him to be better."

I stroke her hair. "He will be, sweetie. Try not to worry too much."

She cuddles the owl plushie to her, reaches over and pats Bearcub, then looks at the lamp that's glowing in the semi darkness.

"I'll just be in the living room," I tell her. "And I'm sleeping next door. If you want me at all, just call out and I'll come running, okay?"

"Okay."

"Goodnight darling." I bend and kiss her forehead. "See you in the morning."

She looks so young and small lying there. My eyes sting as I go out of the room, leaving the door open a crack.

I walk down the corridor into the living room, pushing the door partway closed so I can hear her, but we don't disturb her if we have the TV on, and then stand by the sofa, feeling a sudden sweep of emotion.

"Babe…" Kingi was flicking through Netflix, but he gets up now, comes over, and wraps his arms around me. "Aw…"

"So much in our lives is out of our control," I whisper.

"I know." He rubs my back, and I bury my nose in his tee.

"It's horrible feeling so helpless."

"Yeah." He kisses the top of my head.

I rest my cheek on his chest and look out the front window. It's completely dark out, and there's no moon, so the Pacific is just a sea of blackness. As I watch, it begins to rain lightly, pattering against the windows.

"It's going to be all right," Kingi says. "I promise."

My throat tightens, and I move back a little.

He cups my face and looks down at me. I think he's going to kiss me, but he pauses, and I know what's going through his mind. I'm emotional and vulnerable, and he doesn't want to take advantage of me. And that's fair enough.

But what about if I want to be taken advantage of?

I need comfort. I want to be touched. I need someone to show me they have feelings for me. And I want to kiss, and be kissed in return.

Lifting up onto my tiptoes, I press my lips against his. I don't know what tomorrow is going to bring, or whether there's any future for the two of us. All I know is that, right now, I want him, and he's here, and I'm not going to let the opportunity pass.

Chapter Twenty-One

Kingi

I'm twenty-eight, I've had my fair share of partners, and I like to think I'm experienced with the opposite sex. But when Chessie kisses me, I'm so stunned that I stand still for a moment, frozen in place.

I know the news that Thea was the one who found her dad after he took his overdose shocked Chessie, and I could see that when she came out of Thea's room she looked emotional, which didn't surprise me, because when I took Bearcub in there, she seemed so tiny and fragile in the big bed.

So I hugged her as a friend. I wanted to comfort her. But I didn't expect her to kiss me.

Alarm bells ring in my head. I can't take advantage of the fact that she needs comfort right now. I'd be the worst possible heel if I took this as a sign that she's interested in more. Kissing is one thing—it gives a dopamine buzz when we're down, and it makes us feel good. There's nothing wrong with that. But to assume she wants sex would be a big mistake. She might even mean it. But I have no doubt she'd regret it in the morning, and then we're two good friends who have this massive wall between us, and that would make me sad.

But I do want to kiss her. So I take her face in my hands, tilt my head a little to the right to change the angle of our lips, and kiss her properly. I want her to know she's loved and wanted, and I kiss her tenderly, slowly, stroking her cheeks with my thumbs before moving my hands up to her hair. It's in a ponytail, as usual, but I take the elastic in my fingers and slide it down and off her hair, and it falls around her shoulders in a glorious flare of color, like a sunset. I slip my fingers into it, enjoy the sensual feel of the silky strands on my skin.

At the same time, I tease her tongue with mine, and she returns it a little shyly. The kiss deepens, heat rising between us, and she gives an erotic shudder and a moan that makes the hair rise on the back of my neck.

Steady, Kingi.

I lift my head, and she inhales, her eyelids fluttering before she opens them to look up at me. She blinks, then blushes.

"I'm sorry," she whispers.

"Absolutely nothing to be sorry about." I keep her close to me, and continue to run my fingers through her hair. "You know I'm crazy about you."

The thing is… it's true. I'm extremely fond of this girl. I always have been. Circumstances and life intervened early on to ensure we never got together, but it feels as if we've always had a connection, and recently all we've done is rekindle it. I like how down to earth she is. How practical and capable. And our text conversation proved how much deeper that attraction goes for both of us. I want her. And somehow, whereas usually my attraction to women is superficial, this feels different because of our friendship.

Her blush deepens. "Oh," she says.

"We need to talk about that," I tell her. "But not tonight. It's been a huge day for both of us, especially for you, and I think we need to let that settle down a bit before we discuss where we go from here. We need to think with our heads, not with our… you know…"

"Groins?"

"I was thinking a little higher than that, but yeah, those too."

She giggles. Then she says, "I understand."

I move back and take her hand. "You want a coffee? Or a glass of wine?"

"A coffee would be nice."

"Come on, then."

We go into the kitchen and make a coffee, and take them back into the living room with a box of chocolate-dipped shortbread I found in the cupboard that my housekeeper bought for me. I sit in the corner of the sofa, and this time Chessie sits in the middle. When I lift my arm, she curls up and snuggles against me, and I lower my arm around her. We choose another movie, a romcom this time, sip our coffees, and eat the shortbread while we watch.

Halfway through, Chessie goes and checks on Thea and comes back with a smile, saying that Bearcub has curled up in front of her, and Thea's hand is resting on him.

"She's sound asleep," she says, curling up beside me again. "Worn out, no doubt, from all the emotion. I just hope she doesn't have nightmares."

"Yeah. Poor girl."

She rests her head on my shoulder as I unpause the movie. "I hope the hospital can help Mark. The whole situation is just so sad."

"I'm sure they will. It was a cry for help, and now you know how bad he feels, it can only get better."

"I hope so." She sighs.

I slide a finger beneath her chin and lift it so she's looking up at me. "Try not to worry. Worry is the darkroom where negatives develop."

She gives a short laugh. "That's true." She smiles. "You are a surprisingly wise man. Sometimes." She wrinkles her nose.

"Cheeky." My gaze slides to her mouth. Without lipstick, her lips are the same color as her cheeks when she blushes. They look plump and soft. I know how they feel when I kiss her. I want to kiss her again. But I shouldn't.

They part, and I lift my gaze back to hers. There's a hint of excitement in them. She wants to kiss me too.

I look back at the TV and don't say anything, and after a few seconds she rests her cheek on my shoulder.

We sit there like that for a bit. But this time, it's difficult for me to concentrate on the movie. I become hyper-conscious of Chessie beside me. The softness of her body where she's pressed up against me. The smell of her perfume, something gentle and flowery, maybe with jasmine, because it reminds me of summer evenings sitting out on the deck. Her hair is draped over my arm, and it feels like a silk scarf on my skin.

My gaze drifts down. She has so many freckles, small and pale, as if someone has flicked a paintbrush full of light-brown paint over her milky white skin. I've wondered many times if she has them all over her body. She has them on her face, with a couple venturing onto her upper lip; they're on her shoulders, arms, legs, and feet. They're probably on her breasts and thighs. And no doubt they're between her legs, among the red triangle of hair, and down on the soft white skin beneath…

She lifts her gaze to mine. "You're making me tingle."

"Sorry."

"Are you?"

"No."

Her lips curve up a little. "If you don't want me to kiss you, you have to stop looking at me like that."

"Like what?"

"Like you want to eat me alive."

I think about getting on my knees and burying my mouth between her legs, and I'm instantly hard. "Fuck."

Her eyes glow.

I study her lips, and imagine pressing mine to them, sliding my tongue against hers. I want to do it more than anything… but I shouldn't.

We sit there in the semi-darkness, with the movie playing softly in the background. Its light falls gently upon us, highlighting her cheekbones, the golden tones in her red hair, the gleam of her soft skin.

"We shouldn't," I say helplessly.

"Why not? We're engaged." Her eyes dance.

I cup her face, stroking my thumb across her cheek. "You've had a terrible shock today. You're looking for comfort, and that's understandable and not a problem. But I don't want you to wake up tomorrow and regret it."

"I won't."

"You don't know that."

"I do." She rests a hand on my chest. "This hasn't just happened today. My feelings for you have been like a long train journey with lots of stops. This is just the last station on the line."

She's right. The journey began many years ago, when we were kids, and innocent of the complications that adulthood relationships would bring. Back then, we loved each other as friends, a wholehearted, gentle, deep love that I don't think has ever gone away. Instead of disappearing with the years, it remained like a plant in the ground that has suddenly seen sunlight and broken through the surface. Or maybe it's more like a volcano that's lain dormant all these years, and now it's leapt into life, bursting with heat.

Was it always going to end here one day?

I think about when we texted one another, our sexual tension spilling out of us like lava. Then, the thought of being able to do things to her for real was what tipped me over the edge. I wanted her then, and I want her now.

"I don't want to lose your friendship," I say desperately, looking at her soft, plump lips.

"Then don't," she says simply, and smiles.

She's implying that we're in control of our feelings and actions. I think she's partly right. Choices appear in front of us, like junctions in the train journey she mentioned, and we are in control of which line we choose. Except that sometimes our feelings make everything except one track feel impossible.

She looks calm, but her eyes are gleaming in the light from the TV. Excitement makes them sparkle. She wants me.

How am I supposed to say no when her hand is creeping down to the hem of my tee and sliding beneath it? When her lips part as she slips her fingers onto my skin? When her teeth tug her bottom lip as she moves her hand up to brush across my nipples?

I shift on the sofa, turning a little toward her, and then lift her legs so they're across my lap. She inhales, her eyes widening, and makes herself comfortable in my arms.

Then she lifts her face, and I lower my lips to hers.

We kiss for ages. Soft kisses. Lazy kisses. Exploring every millimeter of each other's lips and faces.

I press my lips to her cheeks, her temples. Across her brows and forehead. Down her nose. Back to her mouth.

Slowly, I kiss from one corner up over her Cupid's bow to the other corner, then return to the center of her lips.

Tipping my head to the side, I give her long, chaste kisses, just holding my lips to hers for four or five seconds each time. Then, gradually, I let my tongue join in the fun.

Teasing. Probing. Exploring her lips, tracing the tip of my tongue across them before gently delving into her mouth. Sliding it against hers in a movement that reminds me of ice skaters circling each other, elegant and sensual, always touching.

I make sure to keep my hands to myself for a while, although she seems to be enjoying exploring my body while we kiss. I'm not complaining. Her fingers on my skin give me goose bumps all over. She slides her hands around my ribs to my back, runs her fingers up my spine, and skates them across my shoulder blades. She finds each muscle and follows them with her fingers, squeezes my shoulders, then returns to my chest, where she circles the pads of her fingers over my nipples. I twitch, and her lips widen in a smile beneath mine.

I brush my lips over hers. "Doesn't seem entirely fair," I murmur, moving my hands underneath her tee for the first time. I brush my fingers from her stomach around her ribs, and she inhales and moistens her lips with the tip of her tongue.

So I start investigating the soft curves of her body while we continue to kiss. I stroke her waist and ribs, trail my fingers up her spine, and then follow the strap of her bra around to the front. I bring a finger up between her breasts, trace the neckline of her tee from one shoulder to the other, and enjoy the smooth skin of her neck.

Eventually, though, her breasts prove too much of an attraction, and I stroke from one side over the swell of each breast to the other, enjoying the way she murmurs against my lips, squirming beneath my tongue.

I return my hand beneath her tee and around her back, find the catch of her bra, and flick it open.

"Oh!" She laughs. "That was smooth." She slides the straps of the bra down her arms and removes it without taking off her tee.

I smile, deepening my kiss a little as my body stirs at the thought of her breasts being set free, and stroke around to her front, bringing up my hand to cup one. They're high and pert and full and soft, and sit in my hand like heavy fruit, ripe and ready for picking, making my mouth water. Her nipple is swollen and soft, but as I tease it with my thumb, then pluck it gently, she arches her back, and the nipple tightens to a tight bud.

"Fuck." Suddenly remembering there's an eight-year-old in the house, I look over my shoulder toward her bedroom. "Maybe we should stop there…"

"She sleeps very soundly," Chessie says. "I told her to call out if she wakes, but she won't."

She rises then and moves over me, straddling my hips and settling on my thighs. Then she cups my face in her hands and bends to kiss me again. Her hair falls around me like a copper curtain, and the silky slide of it across my skin makes my goosebumps get goosebumps.

I slip my hands up her tee onto her breasts and tease her nipples for a while. Then, unable to fight the urge anymore, I push up her tee and tear my lips from hers. The skin of her breasts and stomach, less touched by the sun, is creamy white with a lighter scattering of freckles. Her nipples are such a light pinky-brown that they're almost the same color as her breasts. Groaning, I lower my head to a nipple, close my mouth over it, and suck. Her hands tighten in my hair, and she arches her back and gives such a sexy moan that it fires both of us up.

By now, I'm so hard that my cock is threatening to break through the stitching on my shorts. Placing my hands on her butt, I pull her toward me, pressing my erection against her soft mound. She exhales, her breath whispering across my lips, and rocks her hips, arousing herself on me. Fuck, that's hot, and it only serves to make me harder.

Suddenly, it's not enough. I want to taste her.

Part of me is conscious that despite Chessie's protests to the contrary, Thea could wake and come in to find us. In my bedroom, we'll be slightly closer so we'll be able to hear her if she calls out, but I can close the door, so we'll have more warning if she does come looking for us. I know parents have sex while kids are in the house all the time, but she's not our child, and we have to show some responsibility.

So I tighten my arms around Chessie and get to my feet, and she squeals and wraps her legs around my waist. I turn off the TV, pick up her bra, then carry her out of the living room, along the hallway, and down to my bedroom. I close the door behind us, take her over to the bed, and lower her onto her back on it.

Next, I unbutton her cut-down jeans, unzip them, and pull them down her legs. Ahhh, fuck, the sight of all that pale, freckly skin makes my heart pound, as does the black G-string she's wearing. Without removing it, I part her legs, drop to my knees, and tug her toward me. I run my hands from her knees up her thighs, then slip a finger beneath the elastic of the triangle of her thong and slide my finger down to the thin line that disappears beneath her.

I look up at her; she's on her elbows, watching me, her eyes wide, her lips parted, and as I move the G-string to the side and drop my gaze to feast my eyes on her, she says, "Ohhh…"

I lean forward and press my lips to the beautiful tiny triangle of curly red hair on her mound, then kiss down the soft skin on either side. Pressing a hand on either side of her, I gently part her and groan at the sight of the swollen skin glistening with her moisture. Lowering my head, I slide my tongue into her, then lick all the way up to her clit.

She gives a soft cry, then a long sigh that turns into a moan as I swirl my tongue over her clit, teasing and sucking.

Mmm… the taste of a woman, sweet and salty and creamy and perfect. Fuck, she's amazing, and I lose myself in the moment, bringing up my hand to join in the fun. Two fingers inside her, stroking up, my tongue flicking, lips sucking, relentless and insistent, especially when she slides her hand into my hair to pull my head closer. I move my other hand up to her breast and play with her nipple through the T-shirt, flicking and tugging it, knowing by her answering moan that she's enjoying the sensation.

I take my time to arouse her. I have all night, I'm in no rush, and I love giving oral. It's not about a race to the finish line. Sex should be a marathon, not a sprint, with plenty of time to look at the view on the way. So I explore her body, discovering all her freckles and kissing them, enjoying the smoothness of her skin, finding out at what pressure and speed she likes to be touched, which turns out to be slow and steady at first, although she also likes flicks of my tongue.

She's close, I can tell by her ragged breathing, the way she's tipped her head back, how she's rocking her hips to meet each thrust of my tongue. My hand is covered in her moisture, and so is my face; I'm probably giving her bristle burn on her thighs, but she doesn't seem bothered by it. I want to make her come. I want to wipe her ex from her brain. I want to know I'm the one who made her feel good… and that she's thinking of me and only me.

I slow my tongue and fingers a little… lift my head and blow lightly on her sensitive skin… coax the pleasure from her. She grabs a pillow, drags it over her face, and groans into it, holding it there with one arm, while the other hand clenches in my hair. She says something, I don't know what because it's muffled by the pillow, but I ignore it and continue to tease, licking until she tenses, pausing for a few seconds until it releases the tension and she flops back, then doing it again, and again, until she's groaning and gasping and her fingers are tight in my hair and her whole body feels as if it's like a tightly coiled spring…

And then I relent, slide my fingers inside her, and cover her clit with my mouth and suck. She gasps, and I feel her tighten around my fingers slowly as the pleasure rolls over her, while she tries to stifle her moans with the pillow. Ahhh it's amazing… powerful pulses rack her body, and she cries into the pillow and shudders with each clench.

I've been rock hard for ages, and I can't wait to slide inside her, but the anticipation is delicious. It makes me feel fantastic to think I've done this for her. As if I've uncovered a wealth of treasure that gleams gold in the lamplight.

And now I'm turning into a poet. This girl has gotten right under my skin. I don't stand a hope in hell.

Chapter Twenty-Two

Chessie

I flop back, limp as a noodle, the pillow still over my face. Fuck, that was a strong orgasm. He's teased me for what seems like hours, although I think it was probably only twenty minutes or so, but that's a long time for me; normally it only takes me five minutes to come, ten at most. The pulses took my breath away, and now my butt and thighs ache with all the clenching. Wow.

The mattress dips, and then he begins pressing kisses up over my hips. He kisses my stomach, my navel, my ribs, then settles down beside me, cups a breast, and teases the nipple with his lips. Mmm… he's slow and gentle, and I feel as if I'm floating in a warm sea, with his warm hands on me, keeping me safe.

I knew he'd be good in bed. He's obviously had a few partners, because he's never going to be short of female company, being good looking, rich, and charismatic with it. But I don't mind that, if it means he can apply the skills he learned to me.

It does make me wonder if I'm experienced enough for him. Wouldn't a guy like this prefer a girl who knows her way around the bedroom and has a few tricks and treats up her sleeve? I've had a few partners over the years, and I like sex, but most of the guys I've been with have been relatively vanilla, glad just to get some sex, and not really bothered about making it fancy. I've never had one of those relationships you see on TV, where you spend whole weekends in bed exploring each other; where you play games that encourage you to try different positions and roleplay. Despite me having given hints, I've never tried any of the more taboo sides of sex. And I'm sure someone like Kingi would prefer to have a girl who had, long term.

But I'm not going to let that spoil tonight. Who knows what tomorrow will bring? Tonight, it's just the two of us, in this quiet bedroom, exploring each other's bodies for the first time. I'm going to enjoy this, and then when the sun comes up, we'll talk and decide where we go from here.

Suddenly, we're wearing too much clothing for my liking. I remove the pillow from my face and push him away, sit up, slide my G-string down my legs, and toss it away. As I move onto my knees, he sits up too and starts undressing, and soon his tee joins mine on the floor, and then he's pushing his shorts and boxer-briefs down his legs.

As he tosses them away, it strikes me that we use clothes to illustrate our status, wealth, culture, and identity, and there's something symbolic about taking them off. It strips away any indications of class, professions, reputation, and money. It makes us vulnerable, exposed, and open. It's not just your body that's stripped bare. Your soul is as well. In here, naked, we're not billionaire and gardener. Rich guy and poor girl. It's just Kingi and Chessie, man and woman, and there's something thrilling about that to me.

Now we're on our knees, and we move close together until our bodies are flush. My breasts press against his bare chest, the nipples brushing against his hairs, and I can feel his erection hard against my stomach. I lift my arms around his neck, and he wraps his around me and lowers his head, crushing his lips to mine.

When he went down on me, he took his time to arouse me, and it's as if all the desire he was feeling had built up inside him as if behind a dam, because now it breaks and all his passion comes pouring out. His kisses turn volcanic—hot, wet, and dirty, his tongue plunging into my mouth, soft groans escaping us, while our hands and fingers tangle in hair and clutch at skin, nails scraping, fingers plucking and clenching, tightening on tense muscles. He cups my breasts and squeezes them and tugs at my nipples; I score my nails down his back and clutch at his ass and then take his cock in my hand and stroke it.

He growls deep in his throat, ohhh… fuck that's sexy, and I continue to do it, enjoying the way his erection swells in my hand and grows even longer and harder.

"I want that inside me," I whisper against his lips.

"Fuck." He throws the word out like a grenade.

"That too," I tease, still stroking him. I want to drive him as mad as he's making me; I want him to feel dizzy with lust and fizzy with desire; I want him to stop being calm and in control, throw me onto the bed, and make me see stars. "You're so fucking hard," I tell him, groaning as my fingers slide up and down his shaft. "Jesus, I want you so bad."

"Be careful," he warns.

I stop stroking for a moment. "Why?"

"Because I feel like I have a feral creature inside me who'll ruin you given half the chance, and you're driving me crazy."

I start stroking him again as I place light kisses over his bottom lip. "You think that scares me, Kingi?"

"It should do."

"Do you think I'm frightened at the thought of you fucking me into next week?"

"Stop it."

"Did you assume I was going to just lie there like a good girl, open my legs for you, and let you do all the work?"

"Chessie…"

"Why would I do that when I have the finest male specimen in the country at my fingertips?" I kiss his jaw and up to his ear, and murmur, "I'm going to make the absolute most of you while I have you… I'm going to ride you until you come so hard it'll make you dizzy."

"Fuck…"

I feel lightheaded with lust. "I want to taste you, too," I whisper. "Can I do that? Can I close my mouth around you and lick up all that precum I can feel here?" I rub my thumb over the top of his erection, feeling the slippery wetness.

"Yeah," he says, unsurprisingly. "If you want." He sinks back onto his heels, and I kiss down his chest, then take his erection in my hand and lower my mouth over the end.

Ohhh… he tastes amazing, and I give a long moan as I tease him with my tongue, then slide my lips down the shaft. He slides a hand into my hair and swears as he tips his head back, and I murmur my approval and continue to suck, loving that he's enjoying this.

He lets me do it for a minute or two, but then he grabs me by the upper arms and lifts me up. "Enough of that," he says in a gruff voice, pulling me close to him again.

"Not nice?" I ask innocently.

He just laughs and crushes his lips to mine again, and I sigh and kiss him back, looping my arms around his neck.

Mmm… I've thought about this for years, dreamed about it at night when I'm in bed alone, touching myself, but the reality is so much better than the fantasy. When you're using your imagination, you plan what the other person is going to do and say, and although you think about touching them, you tend to forget about your other senses. But when they're in front of you, you get to smell them, taste them, and hear their grunts and sighs of pleasure, all of which are also a huge turn on. And they also get to surprise you.

When he grabs me by the waist and twists, pushing me onto my back, I'm not expecting it, and it makes me laugh out loud.

"Sssh," he scolds, then laughs as well as he reaches over to the bedside table for his wallet. "You'll wake Thea." After taking out a condom, he tosses the wallet away and comes back to kiss me.

"We could have an earthquake and she wouldn't wake up," I scoff.

"Even so… you'll have to wait until we're alone next time before you show me how vocal you really are."

I let him kiss me, but inside my mind and heart are racing. Next time? He's not expecting this to be a one-off? Part of me had assumed he'd got carried away and that tomorrow he'd end up regretting it, but that's not what he's implying.

The knowledge that this might not be it, that he's enjoying it and wants to experience it again, is like super-sweet icing on the cake, such a lovely thought that it actually makes my eyes prick with tears. I do my best to contain them, though, not wanting to spoil the moment, and return his kiss fiercely, hungrily. I want to devour him. I want to become one with him, to take him inside me. I want him so badly.

It's not long before he moves between my legs, removes the condom from the wrapping, and rolls it on. He directs the tip to my entrance and pushes in, then lowers down on top of me and kisses me again as he enters me slowly.

I try to relax, but it's hard, because the sensation of him gradually filling and stretching me is so amazing and erotic that my back arches and I shudder with pleasure.

"Fuck, you're tight." He moves back a little, then pushes forward again. "Ahhh…" This time, his hips meet the back of my thighs, and now he's fully buried inside me, right up to the hilt. He looks into my eyes, and I think it's the first time both of us register exactly what we're doing here. We're doing the most intimate thing that two people can do together; he's inside me, and he's going to come inside me, and it's all so delicious and exciting and hot.

He kisses my lips tenderly a couple of times. Then, as he starts moving, he delves his tongue into my mouth and kisses me deeply.

Ahhh… I'm so turned on… I know I'm swollen and slippery, and that's why he's able to move so easily. I wrap my legs around his hips, tilting up my pelvis, and he groans and thrusts forward, burying himself in me. We move together, while he cups my breasts and plays with my nipples, and I run my fingers over his pecs and shoulders and up his back, exploring all his glorious muscles. Ahhh… this feels so good…

Then, out of the blue, he slides an arm beneath me and rolls us so he's underneath and I'm on top. I gasp, but murmur with pleasure and sit up astride him. He stretches out beneath me, pushing up so he's nicely buried in me, and I groan and start moving, rocking my hips to slide him in and out.

He plays with my breasts while I move, and I get to go at my pace. I can angle down a bit so I'm grinding on him, arousing myself, and it's not long before I can feel pleasure building again.

"You like being on top?" he asks as I bend forward to kiss him.

"Mmm."

"I like it too." He rests his hands on my hips, pushing up. "You're so hot," he says. "I've always thought you were sexy, but I didn't know you'd be like this."

He thinks I'm hot? "It's your fault," I tell him, still moving. "You fire me up."

"Do I?"

"You do. I want to fuck your brains out."

"Is that a fact?"

"Have done for some time."

"The feeling's mutual."

"Really?" A thrill runs through me.

"I've thought of little else for ages."

"Ohhh…" I love the thought that he wants me too. I take his hands in mine and pin them above his head, and lift up so I'm just teasing the top of his cock. "I want to drive you mad with lust," I whisper.

"You are." He glances at my hair where it's fallen around his face. "I feel as if I'm on fire."

"I'm going to fuck you till you explode."

"Go for it."

"I want to watch you come."

"That's definitely going to happen."

I sink down onto him, conscious of a sexual flush growing on my face, neck, and chest. "Are you sure? Are you going to lose control?" I bend and kiss him. "Are you going to fuck me hard, Kingi?"

"You betcha."

"Fuck my brains out?"

"Fuck you into next week."

"You promise?"

"Yeah." His fingers tighten on mine, his hips moving to meet mine as I rock on top of him. "I swear."

"You feel so good." My eyelids flutter shut as my attention begins to focus deeper inside me.

"You going to come again for me, baby?"

"Oh yeah."

"God, you're so fucking good."

I open my eyes a little and see that he's watching me, his amber eyes bright and hot. "You want me to come, darling?"

"Fuck yes."

"Right now?"

"Yeah, I want to feel you squeezing my cock."

"I might cut off your circulation."

"Ahhh..." He groans and swells inside me.

I move faster, conscious of my orgasm waiting to take me. I frown, feeling the tightness building inside me, and grind my clit against him, while he cups my breasts and squeezes the nipples...

"Ohhh..." I'm so, so close...

"Fuck," he says, obviously sensing it, "yeah, come for me baby, I want you to so bad, ahhh... you feel so good... go on, take your pleasure from me, make me yours, ride me, baby girl, fuck me as hard as you like..."

His words tease me to the edge, and pleasure rolls over me in heavy, hard waves. I squeal, clenching around him, riding him all the way, and when the contractions finally ease up, I fall onto his chest, gasping.

"Oh my God." I pant, totally spent.

"Good girl." He doesn't give me time to recover, though. He grabs me around the waist and twists until I'm underneath him.

I stretch my arms above my head, reveling in the feel of him, hot and hard inside me, heavy on top of me, then gasp as he holds me there by my wrists and starts thrusting purposefully.

Oh… He bends and kisses me, delving his tongue into my mouth, and I can't do anything but lie there and take it, pinned there and helpless to resist. Not that I'd want to escape… he's so big, so handsome; I can't believe this rich, powerful, gorgeous man wants me. But isn't that the point of being naked? While we're naked, I'm not his inferior, socially or educationally—we're equals.

The thought is like the sun coming up, and it fills me with a surge of excitement and pleasure. He's just a man, and he wants me. I love him—I have no doubt about that now. And although it's too soon to say it, I can show him with my body, and my mouth. I remember him saying that Sabrina didn't say much in bed and wasn't enthusiastic at all. All men like enthusiasm, more than anything else.

"Yeah…" I whisper as he kisses down my neck, still thrusting hard, "oh that feels so good."

"You like that?" He takes big, hungry bites out of my neck. "You like my cock inside you?"

"Ah yes… fuck me, Kingi."

"Yes, Ma'am."

"Hard as you like."

He groans and lifts up onto his hands, still holding me by the wrists. "You drive me crazy."

"Likewise." I look up at him, fixing my gaze on his. "I can feel you all the way up. God, your cock is amazing; it's so fucking hard."

He closes his eyes and groans again. Releasing one wrist, he drops his hand to the back of my thigh and pushes it up, changing the angle so he can plunge down into me. "You're so wet," he says huskily, "that drives me insane."

"That's what you do to me, baby." I move with him, enjoying the heat between our bodies, and the way he's so desperate for me. "I've been dreaming about this for so long."

"Have you?" He kisses me. "You've thought about having sex with me?"

"So many times. Imagining what you'd feel like inside me."

He slows his hips a little. "And how does reality compare?"

"It's so much better than the fantasy."

"Really?"

I nod, wrapping my legs around his waist. "It's much bigger."

He laughs. "Thank you." He finally releases my other wrist, and I slide my arms around him and run my nails lightly down his back. He shivers and kisses me.

I move my hands down to his ass, clutching hold of the firm muscles and pulling him toward me. "I won't break," I whisper. "Fuck me harder."

"Aaahhh…" He grunts and steps up his thrusts.

"Oh God, yes… that's it… please… I want you to let go… I want you to fucking ruin me…"

He crushes his lips to mine, driving into me so deeply I think he's going to spear me to the bed. Oh God… our hot moans mingle… our damp bodies slide against one another… and then he shudders and stills, twitching inside me as he comes. There's no pillow to stifle his groans, so I have to do it with my mouth, and I kiss him, enjoying the way his deep growls reverberate all the way through me.

"Yeah…" I whisper, kissing him, loving the fact that I've given him such pleasure. I suck his bottom lip and delve my tongue into his mouth. "Good boy…"

He gives a short laugh, then lowers on top of me, still inside me. "Minx," he murmurs, kissing me again. "Wow. That felt so good."

"Mmm." I sigh, enjoying his weight pressing me into the mattress. "It was amazing."

He gives long, slow thrusts as he presses his lips to my face—over my cheeks and brows and back to my mouth. "You're so fucking beautiful."

My face is already warm, but I'm sure the flush deepens. "Thank you."

"I mean it, Chess. You really are beautiful both inside and out." He lifts his head to look at me.

My body feels like a bell that's still resonating after being struck, the ripples of pleasure echoing into the distance. "That's a nice thing to say." I like the way he's still inside me. Tamati used to pull out immediately and roll over. It's nice that Kingi wants to prolong the intimacy.

He kisses my nose. "Do you remember at the ball, when I fixed the strap of your sandal?"

I smile. "Yeah. It was a sweet thing to do."

He picks up a strand of hair that has stuck to my hot cheek and brushes it back. "It reminded me of when Cinderella tried on the glass slipper." His amber eyes study me. "It wouldn't fit anyone else. It showed him that she was the one woman meant for him."

My breath stills. I can't think what to say, so I just say, "Oh..."

He stares into my eyes, then drops his gaze to my mouth. He kisses me, then lifts his head again and looks at me.

"What... what are you saying?" I whisper.

He kisses me again. "I don't know. This is very new to me." More kisses. "I've not felt this way before."

"I... um... what way?"

He kisses my jaw, up to my ear, and sucks the lobe, making me shiver. "I don't know." He kisses slowly back to my mouth, and I realize he's thinking about it, trying to make sense of his feelings.

"You don't have to say anything," I tell him, not wanting him to panic at the thought of what I'm expecting him to say.

"I want to." He nibbles my bottom lip. "I want you to know how you make me feel." He touches his nose to mine, then lifts his head again. "I suppose what I'm saying is... maybe... what we're doing... pretending to be together... doesn't have to be pretend."

We study each other in the semi-darkness. He kisses me again.

"You... want to... date me?"

He shrugs. "Yeah. Amongst other things." His lips twitch.

"So you're saying... we get rid of the contract?"

"Yeah. Tear it up."

I love the thought, but something else strikes me. "What about the engagement?" I lift my hand and look at the ring, feeling suddenly sad at the thought of taking it off. "Do you want it back?"

He looks at it, then brings my hand to his mouth and kisses the ring. "No."

"I'm sorry to be so dense, but..."

"Let's get engaged. For real." He kisses me. "Marry me, Chessie."

I stare at him. My heart bangs on my ribs. Suddenly, I can't breathe. I push his chest. "Can you..."

"Oh, sure." He withdraws carefully and disposes of the condom, while I sit up and move back against the pillows, pulling the duvet around me. "Just a sec," he says, and he pulls on his boxer-briefs and leaves the room.

I sit there, stunned, for twenty seconds until he comes back into the room. He's carrying a water bottle, and he closes the door, gets on the bed, and passes the bottle to me. "Drink up," he says. "Need to rehydrate."

I do as he says without thinking, my head full of too many other thoughts to object. When I'm done, he takes the bottle from me, has a few mouthfuls, and places it on the bedside table. Then he lifts an arm.

I move closer to him, and he snuggles me up against him.

"What do you think?" he asks. "Sorry, I know it wasn't the most romantic proposal, but it was from the heart."

"I think it was very sweet," I say slowly. "But it's a bit too soon for declarations like that. We've just had sex, so there are all kinds of hormones shooting around our systems. I think you should wait a while until you're thinking clearly."

"Oh, I'm thinking clearly." He tucks my hair behind my ear. "I'm in love with you, Chess."

That makes me inhale and my eyes widen. "What?"

"I've loved you for a long time as a friend. But tonight I realized I'm *in* love with you. My heart races when I see you. I think about you all the time when we're not together. I love being with you. You make me feel good. You make me laugh. And this…" He gestures at the bed. "It was the last piece of the puzzle."

"We've slept together once. You can't decide you want to marry me after one fuck."

But he doesn't smile. In fact, he frowns at me. "Don't make light of my feelings."

"Oh… I'm sorry. I didn't mean to."

"I know what you're saying, and if you want to wait and date for a while, I'll understand. But I haven't felt this way before. In the past, thinking about staying with one person made me feel uncomfortable and trapped. But I don't feel like that with you. The thought of staying with you makes me feel excited and… whole. In fact… I'd like you to move in with me." He smiles.

My lips part, but no words come out. Eventually, I manage to squeak, "Really?"

"Mmm." He bends his head and kisses me. "Look. I'm not saying we have to get married tomorrow. We can wait until we're both ready. But I am saying I like the idea of staying engaged. Of showing the world that I'm committed to you."

"You haven't dated anyone long term," I point out carefully. "So I can see why the idea of commitment is new to you, and I'm flattered that you feel that the idea of staying with me doesn't scare you. But it's a big step from long-term dating to marriage. I think you're attracted by the romantic notion of the big gesture. I just think maybe you should take it nice and slow."

His lips curve up. "You don't think very highly of me, do you?"

"Of course I do. But it was only just over a week ago that you said at dinner with Orson and Scarlett that you didn't think marriage was for you."

"I know. I'd spoken to my father, and he'd mentioned getting divorced, and I was still reeling from that. I know it seems sudden. But it just feels… right."

I lift his hand and kiss his fingers. "It's a very sweet thing to say. But let's just take some time to think about it, okay?"

He doesn't look angry, or upset. Instead, he just kisses me again, then says, "All right. But I'm not going to change my mind."

Chapter Twenty-Three

Kingi

"I'm going to take Bearcub out and lock up for the night," I tell Chessie. "The bathroom's all yours."

"Okay, thanks."

We get up, and she goes into the bathroom, while I pull on a pair of trackpants, open the door, and go out into the hallway.

I walk quietly down to Thea's room and go inside. She's out for the count, curled on her side with her hand under her face the way you see angels sleep. Bearcub lifts his head as I approach, and I say, "Shh," as I pick him up. He doesn't make a peep, and I kiss his head as I carry him out to the living room.

"You're all warm and snuggly," I murmur in his ear, and he licks my face as I open the sliding doors and take him out. "Thank you for the kiss." I put him on the grass, and he wanders off for a sniff.

Sliding my hands into the pockets of my trackpants, I look up at the sky. The security lights have come on, so it's difficult to see much, but the rain clouds from earlier have cleared, and I can see the moon, almost full, hanging to the west like a tossed silver ball.

I think you're attracted by the romantic notion of the big gesture.

I consider Chessie's words while I watch Bearcub sniffing around. Is she right? Everything else she said is true. It was only just over two weeks ago that I proposed the idea of a fake engagement to Chessie, and now I want to make it real? I can understand why she's skeptical. It's a speedy turnaround for a guy who was convinced that marriage wasn't for him.

I'd always thought proposals and weddings were something that girls wanted because of their romantic nature. For guys, it always seemed as if they were something they had to get through that usually cost a lot of money for little return. To me, a proposal was like

Valentine's Day—a show you put on for everyone else. The wedding was the same; girls like the big dress and being the center of attention for the day. For guys it's just an opportunity for them to hang out with their mates and get drunk. But then I'd always pictured getting married to someone like Sabrina—a woman I was attracted to, but who irritated the hell out of me after five minutes. I understand marrying because as you grow older it seems sad if you stay single, and I can see the benefits of having a companion at your side beyond the obvious bonus of hopefully regular sex, but committing yourself to one woman like that for the rest of your life? Why, why, oh why would you do that?

But standing there in the cool night air, watching the puppy sniff a flowerpot and then sneeze, I allow myself the thought that I've never considered marrying a friend.

It's as if a whole new world has opened up to me. For the first time I think about what getting married actually means: spending the rest of your life with your best friend. The proposal is the moment you see her face when you tell her that you want to marry her. You get to put a ring on her finger so that every time she looks at her hand, she thinks about you. And every other guy she meets will also see that she's yours. I can see the attraction of that, caveman that I am.

And the wedding itself is the moment when, after all that waiting, you finally get the opportunity to stand in front of your friends and family and promise to love your girl and be faithful to her for the rest of your lives. Before, the thought terrified me. But now, with Chessie waiting for me in my room, her body warm and soft beneath the covers, I feel uplifted at the thought of having her by my side. In bed and out of it.

Sure, we've only been fake engaged for two weeks, but our relationship began long before that. We've been friends for twenty years, and the fact that we kissed when we were teens is a sign that we've had deeper feelings for each other for a long time. If it hadn't been for my father…

I frown. Oh, the irony of it. Telling me that I could do better… and then I find out that he cheated on my mother. Anger boils in my stomach at the thought of the years I've wasted because of the implication that Chessie was socially beneath me. She's worth ten of me—no, a hundred… a thousand! I can't believe I let him convince me not to date her. I'm ashamed of that. I didn't think I was a snob, but I am, or I was, anyway. She's helped me see more clearly, and for that, if nothing else, I'm grateful.

Bearcub has had his pee and is trying to get up the steps, so I pick him up again and take him inside. I lock the sliding doors and turn off the lights, then take him down to Thea's room and put him back on the bed with her. He goes over to her and curls up in the crook of her legs again. She doesn't even stir.

Smiling, I walk out, leaving her door open a little, and go into my room. Chessie is back in bed, looking at her phone, and I wink at her before going into the bathroom.

When I come out, she's put her phone down and is on her side, head propped on a hand. She watches me take off my track pants, come over to the bed, and climb in beside her. Then she moves up close into my arms, and we snuggle down together.

"I shouldn't stay the night here," she says. "Just in case Thea does wake and come looking for me early in the morning."

"Okay."

"I'll give it just a little longer." She nuzzles my neck.

I sigh and kiss the top of her head. "You smell nice."

"I smell of you. And sex."

I chuckle. "It's not the worst combination."

"Mmm." She slides her arm around my waist. "Whatever happens going forward, I really enjoyed tonight."

"Me too."

"I hope you don't regret it."

My heart aches at the hope in her statement, and I squeeze her shoulders. "Of course not. Quite the opposite. I was out there thinking I wish we'd done this a lot earlier. If only my father hadn't intervened."

She rests her chin on my shoulder. "To be fair to him, I'm not your equal in that sense."

"If you mean you don't have as much money as I do, that's true. But he married my mother because she was from a good family and was considered his equal. And they've had a relatively unhappy marriage, and are now getting divorced. Their relationship skewed my view of marriage for most of my adult life. I thought that was what happened. But I don't want to live like that. More than anything else, I want to be happy. And you make me happy."

Her face lights up. "Really?"

"Really. I think maybe it's occurred to my dad now that money can't actually buy happiness."

"Kingi Davis," she mocks, "did you really just say that?"

"I know. What the hell's wrong with me?"

We both laugh.

She snuggles a little closer, and I tighten my arms.

"I need to talk to him," I admit. "About Mum. I'll go and see him tomorrow."

"What if he mentions our engagement and advises that you could do better?"

"I'm my own man now. I make my own decisions."

"You make your own mistakes."

"You'll never be a mistake," I tell her fiercely, cupping her face. "Seeing you in the gardens that day was the best thing that has ever happened to me. I'm not religious anymore. Or I didn't think I was. But looking back, I feel as if that meeting was destined. It's like…" I hesitate, struggling to put my feelings into words. "I don't know… as if I was on a train, and I missed the station years ago and went sailing past you. But whoever is watching over us changed the tracks so I could come around again and have a second chance. And this time I took it and leapt off."

"I'm so glad," she whispers.

"Me too." I bend my head and give her a long, lingering kiss.

"I should go," she says when I eventually lift my head.

"Okay."

"Maybe just a few more minutes."

"Mmm." She's warm and soft in my arms, and I kiss her again, in no hurry to say goodnight.

*

In the end, she stays with me until the early hours. We make love again, slowly and sleepily, and then she dozes off for a while afterward. But eventually, when the moon is high above us, she gets up and makes her way to her own room, just in case Thea rises early and comes to find her.

Usually, when I'm with a girl, I'm kinda glad when she goes so I can have my own space. I enjoy my own company, and I rarely get lonely or bored by myself. But tonight I curl up with the pillow, feeling an ache inside at the loss. I want her here. I want to hug her again. I want to sleep with her in my arms and wake to see her bed hair and the creases on her cheek from the pillowcase. I want to smell her warm, sleepy body and wake her with my mouth.

But soon I fall into a heavy sleep, and when I wake it's light, and I can hear the girls talking in the kitchen, and then a high-pitched bark. I get up and pull on my track pants and a tee, and go out to find Bearcub sitting watching the girls cooking breakfast.

"We're making you a bacon and egg sandwich," Thea announces. She's kneeling on a stool, breaking eggs into a dish and picking out the shell before Chessie pours them into the frying pan.

"Fantastic." I start making a coffee. "You can be my full-time chef if you like."

She giggles, and Chessie winks at me before concentrating on frying the eggs.

When the sandwiches are done, we take them out to the table on the deck, and eat them and drink our coffees while Bearcub plays on the grass. Eventually Thea joins him, and the two of them investigate the flowerpots, Thea talking to him constantly.

"Penny for them," Chessie says, smiling at me.

"I was wondering what it would be like to have my own daughter."

Her eyebrows rise, and her mouth forms an O. "Really?"

I nod slowly. "Or son, I guess." I think about having a child—a boy or girl, it wouldn't matter. Maybe one of each. Tossing them a rugby ball on the grass. Taking them with me hiking. Showing the boy how to shave. Hmm. "I used to think children weren't in my stars. I liked teens, but I knew I'd have to start with a baby, and I wouldn't have a clue what to do with one of those. But I can see it now. Watching them grow up. It would be cool to have a kid like Thea."

She looks at her. "I know what you mean. She's so lovely. I wish she hadn't had to go through what happened yesterday."

"No, of course. We'd much rather protect our children. But she will have built a lot of resilience by dealing with that. It will help her in the long run, as she grows up, compared to other kids who sail through their childhood then get hit with all the horrors of being an adult that life throws at you."

Chessie looks back at me with a kind of puzzled smile. "I suppose that's true. You can be incredibly insightful when you choose to be. I guess that's one reason why they wanted you for the CEO job."

"That and my cash, I'm sure."

She scratches at a mark on her cut-downs. "I was thinking about that. I know you talked about tearing up the contract. But I wanted to say that I think we should get Tane to draw up a new one. I want to make it clear that if we part ways, I don't want any of your money."

I sit back, lace my fingers together on my chest, and give her an amused look. "Like a prenup?"

"I guess. And I want you to tell your father about it."

My smile fades, and I frown. "Our relationship is none of his business."

"I know. But I'd like him to know that it's not your money I'm after."

"You want me to tell him you're after my magnificent cock?"

"I'm sure that will put his mind at ease." She giggles, and I grin. "Will you tell him?" she asks softly. "About the money, I mean."

"If you want." If it puts her mind at ease, I'm happy to do it. It won't make any difference. If I want her to have money, I'll find a way to give it to her. No contract is going to stop me from spoiling the girl I love.

*

It's Monday morning, but I call the office and say I'm going to be late, and I spend the morning with the girls. It's only when Chessie gets a call from Nina to say the hospital is releasing both Mark and Joe that it's time to make a move. I give Thea a hug, then Chessie, and tell her I'll contact her later and find out how they're all doing. I wave goodbye to them as Chessie drives off, and then, after putting on a suit, I take my Range Rover and drive to the Midnight Club, Bearcub in his crate in the back.

Orson's waiting in the car park, and he puts Bearcub in the back of his car. "Was he good?" he asks.

"Yeah, and it was the perfect distraction for Thea, so thanks for loaning him."

"How's Chessie?"

My gaze drifts off into the distance as I think about what happened last night. With effort, I drag my eyes back to Orson. "She's... good."

His lips slowly curve up. "Bwah... bwa, bwa, bwa..."

"Yeah, yeah." I give him the finger. "You were right. And I don't care."

He grins. "So what does that mean?"

"Not sure yet. But I'm hoping to make the engagement real. I'm working on it."

His face lights up with genuine pleasure. "Dude, I'm so pleased for you."

I laugh as he gives me a bearhug. "Thank you. We might yet be able to have a joint engagement party."

"Scarlett was hoping. She said Chessie is crazy about you, and girls seem to know these things."

"True." I smile, warmed through at the thought. "Okay, I'll catch you later."

"Yeah, see ya." He gets in his car and heads off home with Bearcub.

I know that Dad had a meeting here this morning, and I'm hoping he's still around. I go to his office, and sure enough, he's in there, at his desk, on his phone. His door is half closed, and I stand in the doorway. He's facing away from me, his feet propped on the windowsill, looking out at the gardens, so for a moment he doesn't realize I'm there.

"…yeah I'll be with you by six," he's saying. "But I need to go home tonight. She's organized a meeting of one of her groups tomorrow and she wants me to be there to meet and greet."

I lean on the doorpost, arms folded. Anger flares inside me. He's talking to his girlfriend in the city.

"I know," he murmurs. "I don't want to do it either, but it's about keeping up a front. We've been through this. You know I'm not doing it to hurt you."

He must have switched his gaze from the view of the garden to the reflection in the glass, because he obviously sees me, and he sits up hurriedly and drops his feet to the floor. "Gotta go," he says into the phone. "I'll call you later." He ends the call, puts the phone on his desk, and gets to his feet.

I slide my hands into my trouser pockets. "Next time, maybe you should think about closing the door."

"I thought I had."

We study each other from across the room for a moment.

"It's not what you think," he says eventually.

"It's exactly what I think. Mum told me."

He stares at me. Then all the fight goes out of him. He exhales, his shoulders slump, and he lowers into his chair.

"You need to sort it out." I go into the room and take the chair on the other side of his desk. "It's not just going to go away."

He looks past me, out to the gardens. "I know."

"You're not treating either of them well, Dad. I don't know who this woman is, but she deserves better, and so does Mum."

He sighs.

"She wants to stay in the house," I say. "She's comfortable there."

"So am I," he snaps. "My family built that house. I don't see why I should give it up."

"You should give it up because she's spent a lifetime with you. She's given you two children. And you're the one who's cheating."

"You don't know the full story. Nobody knows what goes on in a marriage."

"Dad, I spent eighteen years in that house with you both. I know exactly what went on. I know it takes two to tango. She's not an easy person to live with. And she's made mistakes. But she's your wife. And she deserves honesty. It sounds as if your marriage is over. So what's the point in hanging on to it by your fingernails?"

"I've spent years building my reputation. My business relies on me being trustworthy and respectable."

That word again. "Fuck respectability," I say savagely. "It's meaningless if you're unhappy. I don't like the thought of my parents divorcing. But if you're both unhappy, why stay? Who is this woman, anyway?"

He squares his phone on his desk. "Her name's Ataahua. She lives in Wellington, but she travels a lot."

"Where does she work?"

"At… the Beehive." It's our government building.

I blink. "Not Ataahua Ratana?"

He nods.

Shit. She's a top National Party politician. It might be the twenty-first century, but it still wouldn't reflect well on either of them if it came out that they were having an affair.

"Do you love her?" I ask.

He nods. That hurts, but I hide it for now.

"Then you should do what's right," I say earnestly. "Start divorce proceedings. Move out of the house and sign it over to Mum. And show Ataahua that you're serious about her."

He leans forward, his elbows on the table, and rests his face in his hands, then dips his head, running his fingers through his hair. "I didn't want you to find out."

I wonder why. Because he didn't want to lose my respect? Because he feels ashamed? "This sort of thing doesn't stay hidden forever. Look, I know you're worried about the business, but I think being honest and doing the right thing looks much better than being discovered having an affair."

He lowers his hands and gives me a half-hearted smile. "When did you get so wise?"

"Oh, I've made my mistakes, you know that. But I'm trying to learn from them."

"You mean Chessie?"

"She's not a mistake," I snap.

He holds up a hand. "I mean, is she helping you learn from them?"

"Oh. Yes. Definitely."

"You really like this girl, don't you?" he asks softly.

I study my hands for a moment. Then I say, "She's asked for a prenup that states she doesn't want any of my money if we break up."

He stares at me. Then he leans back in his chair. "Really?"

"Yeah. She wants you to know that she's not after my money."

He lowers his gaze. Then he sighs. "I suppose I asked for that."

"She understood why you think that's likely to be the case. That's why she wants the clause. Dad… I think we've both learned that the person who is right for us isn't necessarily the one that seems the most suitable. Love takes no notice of money or social standing. Chessie isn't from my world… but she appeals to me greatly because of that. She's not pretentious at all. She doesn't care about labels or flash cars. What's important to her is her friends and family, and living a good and happy life. She's good for me, Dad. She grounds me, and lifts me up at the same time. She makes me feel like a better man."

He looks surprised. "I never thought I'd hear you say anything like that." His lips take on a cynical twist.

"You taught me how to be respected in business," I tell him. "You made me what I am today. A financial powerhouse. I'm strong, confident, and authoritative. You showed me how to be hard, even brutal, when I need to be. I'll always be grateful to you for that. But I'm not sure you taught me how to be a good man."

His smile fades.

"Chessie said I've always been like a bull in a china shop," I continue, "and she was right. I've barged my way through life, trampling over others to get where I needed to be. But she told me the fable about the North Wind and the Sun—that persuasion is better than force—and she's right. It was like a revelation to me."

"You've always been charismatic," Dad says, "you've always known how to use charm to get what you want."

"Yes, but it's been a tool, the same as brute force when I need it. Chessie's taught me how to genuinely care. And I want to use that going forward, with the Foundation. I don't want to teach the kids how to succeed in business. I want to teach them how to be better people."

The corner of his mouth quirks up. "Maybe she has been good for you after all."

"I don't think Mum made you feel like a better man." It's not easy to say, but I force the words out. "Does Ataahua?"

He looks away, out at the garden.

"Don't see what's happened with Mum as a failure," I tell him. "It's a successful marriage that has come to an end. Let her go, Dad, and move on. She deserves better."

He leans an elbow on the arm of the chair and lifts a hand to rest on his lips. His eyes have turned glassy. Whoa. I can count the number of times I've seen him get emotional on the fingers of one hand.

I rise to my feet. "Think about it," I tell him. "But if you don't let her have the house, I'll tell you now that I'll take her side, and I'll help her fight you for it. I don't blame you for the breakdown of your marriage. But I do blame you for having an affair. She never deserved that."

He doesn't look at me. I wait a moment, then I turn and leave the office.

Chapter Twenty-Four

Chessie

I pull up outside Mark and Nina's house and turn off the engine. After undoing my seat belt, I turn and look at Thea. "Are you ready?"

Her brows draw together. "I don't know." She looks out at the house. "What if he does it again?" she whispers.

It's a valid concern, and I think for a moment before I answer. "I don't think that's going to happen. Kingi said that when someone tries to take their own life, it's often a cry for help. They're hurting badly, and they need everyone around them to understand how bad they feel."

"He could have just said."

"That's true. But I don't think it was a conscious act. It's not as if he thought, 'I'm going to try to kill myself, that'll show them.' When you're in pain, you just want it to stop."

She nods. "I told Kingi that I hated Dad."

I feel a swell of pity. "Oh, Thea… it's okay…"

"He said he understood. But that hate is a negative emotion, and I need to focus on finding the light."

"That's very profound," I say softly. "Deep," I add at her puzzled look.

"I don't want to hate Dad." She swallows hard. "I want to help him."

Tears fill my eyes, and I have to fight hard not to let them fall. "That's a very mature attitude, Thea. He's so lucky to have you."

She rubs her nose. "Shall we go in?"

"Yeah, come on."

We get out, walk up the path, and I open the door with the spare key Nina gave me. Thea holds my hand, and we walk into the living room together.

Nina's in the kitchen, making coffee, while Mum puts some biscuits on a plate. Mark and Dad are sitting in the living room, but they both stand as Thea and I walk in.

Mark is pale, but he looks okay. He glances at me, then at his daughter as she walks toward him. "Baby." He holds out his arms and when she runs into them, he gives her a big hug.

"Daddy." She buries her face in his chest.

I turn away and smile at my father as he comes toward me. "How are you doing?" I ask. He has a little more color than he had the day before, and his eyes are brighter.

"I'm okay." He gives me a hug too. "I'm so sorry for all the worry."

"Aw, it's not your fault."

"I know. I'm still sorry I wasn't there for you yesterday."

"It's okay, Dad. We went to Kingi's house. We had a nice time, didn't we?" I look at Thea, who nods as she moves back from Mark.

"His friend's dog was there. His name was Bearcub. He slept on my bed."

"Oh, that was kind of Kingi." Mark strokes her hair. "I was thinking… maybe we could get a dog?"

Thea's face lights up. "Really?"

"Yeah. While you're at school and Mum's at the supermarket, he could come to work with me. Then I could bring him when I pick you up at school." She hugs him, and he kisses the top of her head. He looks at me. "I'm sorry."

I blink away the tears that sting my eyes. "It's okay."

"It's not. None of you deserved that."

"Honey, you didn't do it to hurt us, I know that." I go over to him and hug him while he's still got his arms around Thea.

We stand there like that for a moment, until Mum and Nina come in with the coffee and biscuits, and then we break apart with a laugh and sit with them.

"We've been talking, the four of us," Mum says.

"Oh?"

Nina looks at Thea. "Why don't you go and play in your room, love?"

"No," Mark says. "I want her to stay. She deserves to know what's happening."

Nina frowns, but she doesn't argue with him.

"I saw a therapist this morning," Mark says. "And I'm going back to see him once a week. I'm also going to a place called Gamblers Anonymous. I'll be talking to other people who have the same problem as me. And we'll try to help each other to get better. I do want to." He looks earnest. "I'm going to try."

"That's great," I say with feeling. "I'm so proud of you."

He swallows hard. "Chess… I didn't say thank you for the money. I want to see Kingi and say thank you to him, too."

"He knows. But yeah, you'll have to come over to his house one day. It's super, looking over the sea."

He studies his feet. "You shouldn't have faked an engagement for me."

"It's not fake," Thea says. "They kissed."

They all look at me in shock. It's clear from their reaction that they suspected the engagement wasn't real. And now they're stunned that it might not be.

I shrug. "It was just a quick kiss." I give them a mischievous smile.

"Really?" Mark's smile spreads. "I always knew he liked you."

He said 'He liked you.' Not 'you liked him.'

"You knew he liked me?" I say, surprised. "How?"

He grins. "He never stopped talking about you. I know he kissed you when you were young. I was surprised you didn't get together after that."

"His father told him he could do better," I say softly.

"Bloody cheek." My father's eyes flare. "You're worth a hundred of Rangi Davis."

I shrug. "Their world is very different from ours. Parties and balls and celebrities and big deals done every day. Our world must seem very small from such a dizzy height. But I think his chickens are coming home to roost." I stop there, not wanting to tell them about Rangi and Huia's divorce in case it doesn't come to pass. I change tack. "Kingi comes from that background, but he wants to expand his world. He's going to be the CEO of a group called the Ngā Whetū Rangatahi Foundation, and he wants to help under-privileged youths get more opportunities and have a better start to life. He has a big heart."

"And he loves you?" Mum asks, eyes wide.

"I think so. He said he's in love with me." I smile, barely able to believe it myself. "Look, we had a bargain—I said I'd help him look more respectable so he could get the job, and in return he said he'd give me some money to help us get back on our feet. The money was nothing to him, but everything to me. And it seemed like a small price to pay. He's a good man, with a heart of gold, and I wanted to help him."

"But now you're engaged for real?" Dad asks.

"We fell in love," I say simply. "I'm nervous that it's just a crush for him, and I want us to take our time. We won't be getting married anytime soon! But we were about to announce the engagement, and he said he still wants to do it, and… he wants me to move in with him."

Nina presses her hand over her heart. "Oh, that's so romantic."

"I'm so pleased for you," Mum says. "I know you've always liked him. Oh, it's so nice to hear some good news."

Dad and Mark exchange glances. Dad lifts his eyebrows, and Mark shrugs.

"What?" I ask.

Dad looks at me. "Well, we had something to tell you, but I'm not sure if this will change it."

"Go on…" My stomach flips with nerves, but they don't look worried.

"It's about the business," Dad says. "The doctors told me that stress was a contributory factor to the heart attack. I'm better, but it's going to take me some time to get back to where I was… if I even can."

"You will," I insist, but he holds up a hand.

"They've given me a healthy eating plan, and I'm going to start walking regularly. But I need help with the business. It's not easy for a man to say to his daughter, Chess. I should be the one looking after you, and you've had far too much on your plate these past few months."

"You've done so much for us," Mark says stiffly. "I'm so sorry you've been under such pressure. But you're so capable. You're much better at running the business than I would ever be."

"So we'd like you to take over," Dad says. "We'll both try to help more than we have the last couple of months. But we'd like you to head the business."

I stare at him. "It's your company, Dad. You built it from nothing. You can still run it, even if we do a bit more of the leg work."

"I'm not going anywhere. I'll still be around. But it's as if you've breathed new life into it. You have new ideas, and boundless energy to implement them. You're good with people, and the staff all adore you. You've handled the books magnificently, and we're actually making a good profit again."

"That was Kingi's doing," I hasten to add.

"Maybe, but don't you see? Making that bargain with him was a genius move. It saved our lives."

"Literally," Mark says, his lips twisting.

I sit there on the edge of my chair, my spine stiff, breathing fast. "I didn't want you to know," I whisper. "I thought you might see it as me…" I glance at Thea, but she's gone into the kitchen to get a drink, so she can't hear me. "…prostituting myself."

"You did what you had to do to save us," Dad says. "You went to a friend and made a mutual bargain. You weren't too proud to do whatever you needed to save us, and I'm so proud of you for that."

My eyes fill with tears. "Don't…"

"I don't mean to make you cry," he says earnestly, "but I want you to know how grateful we all are. And I don't want to pile all the stress on you. If you really don't want to do it, we'll get someone else in. But the fact is that you have proven yourself great at running the company. We'll help you. But I'd like you to pick up the reins."

"Mark should do it," I say, wiping my cheeks, "he's the eldest."

"I'm in no shape, Chess." Mark gives me an open, honest look. "I'm going to have enough to think about with the therapy and meetings. And I'm no good at all the managerial stuff, anyway. I'll still be working for the company. But I don't want to run it."

"Will you do it?" Dad asks me. "For me?"

"Of course." I get up and go over to sit on the arm of his chair and put my arms around him. "I'd do anything for you."

"Don't do it just because I ask you to. Only if you want to, and you enjoy the work."

I move back a little. "I do. It was hard initially, but I'm starting to find my feet."

"I thought so. I'm so glad." He hugs me back. "It makes me feel a whole lot better to know you'll do it."

"Then I'm thrilled to say yes."

It doesn't escape my attention that everyone looks relieved. Mum is happy that Dad will have less stress, so he can concentrate on his recovery. Nina is just exhausted and glad that she won't have to worry about money. And I can see how relieved Dad is to pass on the baton at last, and have someone else run the race.

Mark is trying to hold it all together for the rest of us, but the cracks in his soul are wide, and, like the Japanese art of Kintsugi that Kingi mentioned, he needs time to understand that they're a part of him, and he can't get rid of them—they will also be there, but he has to learn to accept them. But at least he seems to be on the road to recovery.

I think about the fact that they've asked me to run the business long term. It'll be a challenge. I'm still not sure I'm the right person for the job. But I find myself excited at the thought. This time, it won't be about covering until Dad gets back and trying to keep us afloat. I can use the rest of the money that Kingi gave me and really do something with the company. Buy new equipment, and hire more employees.

Something occurs to me then… a flash of an idea. I put it to the back of my mind, though. I'll need to talk to him about that later.

"I've got a bottle of bubbly in the fridge," Mum says, getting to her feet. "I'm going to open it. I think we need to make a toast to a fresh start for all of us."

I watch her go, and then look over at Mark. His eyes meet mine, and he gives a small smile. I know he feels guilty about what he did. I watch Thea go over and sit on his lap, and she gives him a hug, the same way I'm doing with my dad. Fathers and daughters. When we're young, they know they need to protect us, and they try so hard to be strong for us. But they're only human. And sometimes a kiss and a hug from their baby girl is the medicine they need.

*

A few hours later, I get back in Dennis and start driving home. I'm halfway there when my phone starts ringing, and when I see it's Kingi, I pull over and answer it.

"Where are you?" he asks.

"On my way home."

"Come and stay with me tonight."

My lips curve up. "I need some clothes! I'm still wearing what I wore yesterday."

"Then go and pick some things up, but come and stay with me. I need you."

"Aw. What happened today?"

"Nothing bad. I'll tell you about it when you get here. How are you?"

"I'm okay." I think about sliding in bed with him, kissing him, making love with him, then curling up beside him for the night. "Yeah, all right, I'll be over shortly."

"Good girl. See you soon. Love you."

"Love you," I say shyly, and we end the call.

I drive back to the house I share with the girls in a bit of a daze. I'm worried about this moving so fast… but then I think of the fact that my dad asked my mum to marry her just days after meeting her. It obviously happens, and they've been happily married for nearly thirty years.

After parking Dennis out the front of the house, I get out, and it's only then that I see Tamati's car parked just down the road. My heart bangs, but I realize then that I still haven't spoken to Ria. He's probably here to see her. Wow, that's awkward.

I walk slowly up the path and let myself into the house. I can hear voices, and when I go into the living room, I see Tamati sitting on the couch, where he used to sit with me, and his arm is around Ria.

"Hello," I say evenly.

Lisa is sitting in one of the armchairs, and she gets up and gives me a nervous smile. "Hey, Chess. Everything okay?"

I nod and look at the other two. "So… are you dating now?"

Ria lifts her chin. "Yeah. You didn't want him, so I didn't think you'd mind."

I look at Tamati, who just smirks.

Something settles over me then like a soft mist. You're not always aware of the passing of time. Days, weeks, months, even years can go by without much changing. And then suddenly you catch sight of yourself in a mirror, or you see someone you haven't seen for a long time, and it's a shock to comprehend how things have moved on, and how much has changed.

This is one of those moments. Without realizing it, my whole life has subtly shifted. It's as if I thought the stars above my head were static, but I've filmed the night sky on a long exposure camera, and now I can finally see the way the heavens rotate above me. I've moved on. I've outgrown my old life. Running the business and being with Kingi have given me more confidence and an understanding of myself that wasn't there before. I no longer feel that everyone else is better than I am. I've run the company for months and I've done a damned good job at turning things around. I might not have Sabrina's beauty, wealth, or contacts, but I know that's not going to play a part in my relationship with Kingi because I have other things to offer. I have a long way to go, but I've outgrown my old life.

"I'm very pleased for you both," I say with as much graciousness as I can muster. "But I'll be moving out." I walk out of the room and down to my bedroom, go into the bathroom, and pick up the things I need. Afterward, I come out and take a bag out of the cupboard, and start stuffing in some of my clothes.

Lisa appears in the doorway, looking pained. "Please, don't do this. We can work this out. I don't want him in the house either. We'll tell Ria that if she's going to meet him, she'll have to do it somewhere else."

But I shake my head. I like Lisa, and I'll miss her, but I know she would never have the courage to say that to Ria, and anyway, it's time for me to move on. "It's okay, you'll find another tenant."

"But where will you go?"

"I'm moving in with Kingi." I thought I might feel sad as to leave, but my heart soars as I zip up the bag. I give her a hug. "Thank you for everything," I tell her. "I'll be back over the next day or two to pick up all my stuff."

"I'm sorry," she whispers.

"It's not your fault. It's okay. Take care of yourself."

I don't go back into the living room. I walk down the hallway and out the front door, and close it behind me.

*

When I arrive at Kingi's house, he's obviously seen Dennis pull up because he's standing there, waiting. He holds out a hand. Dangling from his forefinger is a key with a white ribbon tied to it. He smiles. "I'm hoping to tempt you."

I take it from him. Then I burst into tears.

"Shit," he says. "That wasn't what was supposed to happen."

"Sorry," I squeak. "It's been a bit of a tough few hours."

"Aw. Come and tell me all about it."

He takes my hand and leads me through the house, and we cuddle up on the sofa. I tell him everything, about Dad and Mark and the business, and about Tamati and Ria. He tells me about his Dad and the fact that he's probably going to move out of the house and start divorce proceedings.

"Everything's changing," I murmur, resting my cheek on his shoulder. It's growing dark outside, the sun about to disappear below the horizon. The sky is the color of an eggplant, with a touch of orange where the last piece of sunlight remains.

"Yeah." He kisses the top of my head. "But it's not all bad."

I lift my face to his, and we exchange a long kiss.

"Oh, I had an idea," I say when he eventually lifts his head. "I was thinking about the gardening business, and about the Foundation. And I thought that if you wanted, you could always ask any of the youngsters if they were interested in gardening and plants, and if they were, we could run some kind of apprenticeship. We could train them in the basics and offer them a certificate at the end, and maybe give some of them a job, if we start growing enough."

"That's a fantastic idea. I was thinking about working with local businesses like garage workshops or electricians to offer the kids different pathways to jobs. Schools tend to drive kids toward university because they need to make their quotas, but university isn't for everyone, and too many kids are leaving uni with degrees and heaps of debt, and they still can't find jobs. So yes. Some kind of gardening apprenticeship would be a great idea."

He kisses me again, then lifts his head and strokes my cheek. "Are you okay about seeing Tamati today?"

"Oh, I'm fine. I was kind of upset with Ria, that she thought that bringing him into the house was okay."

"It was a tad insensitive. What are you going to do?"

I pick up the key where it's resting on the sofa beside me and study it. Then I look up at him. "I thought… that I might move in with you. I don't want you to think this is the only reason… I've been thinking about it a lot, and—"

"I don't care." He shrugs, his whole face alight with pleasure. "I don't mind what the motivation was. I just want you here."

"Maybe we should trial it for a week or something," I say hesitantly, "and if you think it isn't working, we can reassess and talk about it…"

He just laughs. "Whatever." Then he takes my face in his hands. "I adore you, Chessie Ross. Right here, right now, I absolutely adore you. You're the best thing that has ever happened to me. You make me feel complete. I want you… I need you… and the thought of being able to wake up next to you every morning and go to bed with you at night fills me with joy."

He presses his lips to mine, and kisses me, and kisses me, and kisses me, until I'm breathless and laughing. And then he wraps his arms around me and holds me tightly, while the last touch of color fades from the sky, the stars begin to twinkle, and the moon rises over us, casting us in her silvery glow.

Epilogue

December 8th

Kingi

It's a beautiful early summer's day, and as we approach the roundabout to take the turning toward Waitangi, the Bay of Islands lies spread out before us, breathtakingly beautiful.

Orson is driving, I'm in the passenger seat, and Chessie and Scarlett are sitting in the back, chatting. It's Chessie's birthday today, and the four of us have taken some time off work to go on a weekend break together to celebrate. We're staying in a gorgeous exclusive resort outside the small town of Kerikeri, just twenty minutes away, and today we've told the girls that we're taking them to the Waitangi Treaty House.

We're not, though. And Orson and I are both kinda nervous about it.

I glance at him, and he meets my gaze before blowing out a breath and returning his eyes to the road. I chuckle, although nerves bubble in my stomach, too. This is a bit of a risk, but we're hoping it'll pan out well.

"Whoa," Scarlett says, "you just missed the turning!" She gestures as Orson drives past the turnoff for the Treaty House.

"Actually," he replies, "we're going somewhere different today. We have a surprise planned for you."

I look over my shoulder. The girls exchange a glance, clearly puzzled as they both realize the other knows nothing about this. "What's this about?" Chessie asks, looking back at me.

I smile, then gesture at the sign that's approaching on our right. It says, 'Noah's Ark No-Kill Animal Sanctuary.'

She inhales, her eyes widening, and then she gives me a beautiful smile. "Oh my God, seriously! Oh, Kingi!"

About a month ago, she read an article on Noah's Ark in a magazine, and she was captivated by the story of the billionaire businessman, Noah King, who built the animal sanctuary with other members of his family after his wife died giving birth to their baby, who also died. Noah developed acute agoraphobia as a result, but over the past few years he's remarried, and the article explained how intense therapy and his wife's support have meant he's now living a relatively normal life. The Ark was his brainchild, and it's now the largest and most successful animal rescue center in the country.

Chessie loves animals, and she's mentioned visiting here several times, so it's great to see her face as her wish comes true.

Scarlett also loves animals, and she's been using their puppy, Bearcub, for some of the therapy sessions she carries out at her women's shelter. Bearcub is staying with Spencer and Marama while they're away. Chessie has told Scarlett about the article, and so Scarlett also looks thrilled as Orson takes the turnoff and steers the car slowly down the long, winding drive to the Ark.

It sits high on a hill overlooking the Pacific and the Bay of Islands. To the south is Waitangi and the small coastal town of Paihia, across the bay is Russell, once called Kororareka or Little Penguin, and to the north is the tiny village and accompanying cove called Sunrise Bay. It's a fantastic setting, chocolate-box picturesque, and stunning in summer. I've been to the Bay of Islands a few times, but haven't been to the Ark before, and I'm really looking forward to it… and to our secret mission.

Orson drives past the sign for the Children's Petting Zoo and heads for the central block of buildings set around a large square. A big sign out the front declares that this is Noah's Ark, accompanied by a painting of a boat with lots of domestic animals in it—dogs, cats, sheep, horses, and goats, which are presumably the main animals we're going to see here rather than the usual animals you see on pictures of Noah's Ark like lions, tigers, and elephants.

After slotting the car into a parking space in the accompanying car park, Orson turns off the engine, and the four of us get out. We've told the girls we're taking them out to lunch, so they've both taken time over their appearance, and Orson and I are wearing chinos and shirts rather than the shorts and tees we'd probably have worn otherwise.

We make our way across the square to the building marked reception, and we're just about to go in when someone says, "Kingi, I presume?"

I stop and turn to see a guy walking toward me with a smile. He's about six foot tall, and in his forties, with short gray hair and an easygoing smile. "Noah King," he says, and he holds his hand out to me.

"Ahhh, good to meet you at last." I shake his hand. "This is Orson, and this is his fiancée, Scarlett, and my fiancée, Chessie."

Noah shakes hands with them all. When he gets to Chessie, he holds her hand a little longer and rests his other hand on top of hers. "I understand we have you to thank for your interest in the Ark."

She flushes. "Yes, I read the article about you and said I'd love to visit. We weren't expecting to come today though! It's such a lovely surprise."

"Kingi called and explained your interest. I'm so glad to have you here. I thought maybe I could take you on a tour?"

Her face lights up. "Oh, that would be amazing." She glances at me as if to say 'How did you wangle this?' I just smile. Later on, I'll explain how I made a very generous donation to the Ark, and as a result Noah called me, and we chatted for half an hour about this and that before I put my idea to him. He was most amenable, and it's why he wanted to greet us personally.

"Come on," he says. "Let's start with the veterinary clinic."

He takes us into the left-hand building. It's their lunch break, he explains, which is why there aren't many clients around. The vets are catching up on paperwork and a couple are doing operations. We get to meet the head of the clinic, Stefan, and Noah's cousin, Hal, and several of the other vets. Then Noah takes us through to what he calls The Hotel, which is where the animals recover after their operations.

After that, he shows us the offices containing the business side of the Ark—finance, HR, and IT. He explains how he and his cousins initially invested their own money, but it's now self-sustaining, and in fact flourishing following many generous investments. He smiles at me, and I see Chessie give me a suspicious look. She knows me well enough to guess I was one of the investors—I know she'll quiz me about that later.

We then visit the grooming station, where rescue animals are washed and tidied when they're first brought in, and after that Noah takes us into the rehoming facility. Here he introduces us to a guy called Cullen Reeve. Tallish, in his thirties, and well-weathered, he seems gruff, but when he smiles the corners of his eyes show a plethora of laughter lines.

"Cullen used to be a police dog handler," Noah says as he shakes our hands. "He helps us train rescue dogs when they come in, because many of them don't even know basic commands."

"That must be so rewarding," Chessie says. She bends and looks at a German Shepherd lying under the table. His big brown eyes watch her warily. "Hello, sunshine."

"His name is Ghost," Cullen says. "He's a bit wary of strangers."

"I won't bother him, then." She straightens. "Is he your dog?"

He nods. "He was a police dog. We're both retired now." He doesn't venture any more information, but it's clear there's a story there.

Noah smiles. "Is everything ready?" When Cullen nods, Noah looks at us and says, "How about you guys?"

Orson looks at me, and we both nod, while inside my stomach flips.

"What's going on?" Scarlett asks.

Cullen just smiles. "Would you like to follow me?"

He leads the way through the room full of cages with all the animals who are looking for a new home. The girls stop to talk to some of the dogs, and are relieved when he says that the app that the Ark runs means that most of the animals who are rescued take less than two weeks to rehome.

"We're going to get a dog in the New Year," Chessie says. "Maybe we should get a rescue one?" She lifts her hopeful gaze to me.

"That's a great idea." I do like the notion of helping an animal who's had a hard time.

"Sign up for the app," Noah suggests, "and you'll be able to see what animals are available when it's time."

"I will." She beams at him, then at me. "This has been such a lovely surprise."

"Best day ever." Scarlett bends to blow kisses to a fluffy mixed-breed dog who's standing there wagging his tail at her.

Orson winks at me, then takes her hand. I take Chessie's, and we follow Cullen and Noah through the back door and into the sunshine.

The path leads through the animals' yard, then out another gate, and we walk around the building toward the paddock. A fence runs around it, and a large oak tree stands by the gate, its huge arms causing dappled light to fall over the ground. In the distance, the Pacific is a startling blue, only matched by the cornflower-blue sky with its little puffy sheep-like clouds.

Under the tree is a table. Above it, white ribbons have been tied to various branches that flutter in the sea breeze. A man stands by the table. He's wearing a smart navy suit, and he smiles at us as we approach.

"You must be Ian," I say, and I shake his hand. "I'm Kingi, and this is Orson." I then introduce the girls, who look puzzled, but politely shake his hand.

"What's going on?" Chessie murmurs.

Finally, it's time to explain. I take her hand in mine.

Since Chessie and I first moved in together back in May, she's grown in confidence by several hundred percent. Although her father and brother help out at Ross Gardening, she runs the company pretty much single-handed, and she's doing a fine job with it. She also helps me a lot with the work I do at the Foundation, and we're developing various schemes for the youngsters to help them get jobs in the community.

But despite my best attempts at trying to convince her that I love her, her low self-esteem continues to make her doubt my sincerity. It's not that she doesn't believe me… she just thinks I'm eventually going to wake up and realize she's not the girl for me.

Orson has the same problem with Scarlett. We've spoken to both of them—alone and together—about our hopes and dreams for the future, but both of them continue to brush us off in the nicest possible way. Neither will commit to planning a wedding, and I suspect they've secretly discussed the fact that they're both terrified at the thought of a high-society event where everyone will pour scorn on their choice of a dress and their big day, no matter how much money we spend on it.

And so Orson and I decided to take steps. If we can't bring the girls to marriage, we'll have to… well, do the other thing.

*

Chessie

Scarlett looks as baffled as I feel. We both thought we were going to Waitangi today. The visit to Noah's Ark was a wonderful surprise… but it looks as if the guys have planned more than a mere introduction to animal rescue.

"We've talked about getting married," Kingi says. "But I know you've both been reluctant to set a date because you're worried about all the pomp and circumstance surrounding a big wedding."

Scarlett and I exchange a glance and nod slowly. We've spoken many times about the terrifying thought of a big event in front of hundreds of people. Both of us are quiet introverts who much prefer the company of close friends and family, and we've bonded because of that. We've tentatively mentioned the notion of a quiet wedding to the guys, but they both seemed confused, as they're convinced that all women are desperate for the big dress and the grand event.

"We know neither of you want the fuss," Orson continues. "So…" He smiles at Scarlett. "We thought we could get married here today, and then just have a blessing and a small party with our friends and family back home."

Scarlett and I stare at them.

They glance at each other, their smiles fading.

Kingi looks back at me. "It was just an idea," he says worriedly. "I was talking to Noah about coming to visit, and he happened to mention in passing that they sometimes hold weddings here, and I thought what a great idea it would be, and Orson said he thought Scarlett might like it too, and it might convince both of you how serious we are… but if you're not keen it's not a problem…" His voice fades away, and his brows draw together.

I look across at Noah King and Cullen, who are standing a short distance away, talking quietly. Noah glances at me and winks. I'm thrilled to have met him after reading his article. I found it so inspiring, and such a touching love story.

Get married here, to Kingi, today? In this beautiful, peaceful place, where animals come to heal and find happiness again?

I meet Scarlett's eyes, and as one, a smile spreads across our faces before we both turn and throw our arms around our guys.

"Oh my God," I whisper in Kingi's ear, "you really want to marry me?"

"Silly, silly girl." He hugs me tightly. "Of course I want to marry you. I don't care where we do it, or who's watching. I just want you to be mine."

"I am yours, Kingi."

"Then wear my ring and show the world that you're my girl."

I move back a little, tears brimming in my eyes, and nod.

He blows out a long breath, looks at Noah, and says, "Phew!"

Noah grins, and Cullen chuckles and gives a thumbs up to Ian, who I'm guessing is the celebrant.

"I'm so glad." Orson gives Scarlett a long kiss, then grins at us. "Come on, then. It's a gorgeous day. Let's do it."

*

The ceremony is short and simple. Noah and Cullen are the witnesses. Both the guys have brought rings, and after we've exchanged our vows, they slide them onto our fingers, and Ian declares to each of us in turn, "It is my great pleasure to pronounce you legally married."

Kingi takes my face in his hands. His amber eyes glow in the dappled sunlight, and his expression is full of love.

"Now will you believe me?" he murmurs.

I nod, and the tears finally tip over my lashes.

He just smiles and kisses me, and I slip my arms around him, while above our heads a tui bird sings in the oak tree, its song more beautiful than that played by any wedding band.

*

Afterward, we return to the square in front of the Ark. To my surprise, it's all set out for a very small and cozy reception. They did that super quick! Someone has pulled a large canopy over the square to provide some shade, and staff members are waiting to throw natural confetti made from tiny leaves over us. There's a table with a small selection of gourmet appetizers on plates that make my mouth water. Noah opens a couple bottles of champagne and starts pouring it into glasses, along with orange juice for anyone who doesn't want alcohol, and everyone picks up a glass as he calls for quiet.

MIDNIGHT BARGAIN

"I first came up with the idea for the Ark after a difficult time in my life," he says. "I wanted to establish a center that focuses on love and healing for both people and animals, and I'm proud to say I think we've created that here. I think the atmosphere and location make it an amazing place for a wedding, and I hope it serves as a foundation for a long and happy marriage for all of you." He lifts his glass. "A long and happy marriage."

Around us, everyone repeats it and sips their drink, and then a big cheer goes up, and they all laugh and clap.

After that, we nibble on the appetizers and sip our drinks as we mingle with the staff. I soon realize that Kingi must have made a significant donation to the Ark when I hear him talking with Hal, the head of the Animal Rescue Service, about using the funding for a few more animal ambulances. Kingi did that for me. I'm so touched it makes me want to cry.

"Must be an emotional day." It's Cullen, the corner of his mouth quirking up as I laugh and wipe beneath my eyes.

"Just a bit." I smile at him and gesture at the Ark. "This must be a very different job from your previous one."

He nods. "Ghost and I were part of the Pacific Detector Dog Program. We worked at the New Zealand Aviation Security Service and then moved to Fiji. He's trained to detect narcotics and firearms. He's a smart boy, and he was very good at it."

His gray eyes have the distant, haunted look of someone who has suffered a great deal, and the fact that Ghost is now wary of strangers suggest they've been through some kind of trauma. I wonder what happened? I don't want to pry, and I'm sure he doesn't want to talk to a stranger about it.

"That must have been a tough job," I say evenly. "It's much quieter here, I'd imagine."

"It's a great place to work. Very restful."

"And dogs are amazing. I'll definitely sign up for the app. I like the idea of having a rescue dog."

"Yeah, it breaks your heart when you see the animals that come through here. You have to focus on the fact that they all find happy homes and get to live their best lives after coming to the Ark."

I push up to my feet as Kingi comes over, and Cullen excuses himself. I watch him go back inside the building, no doubt to see his dog. "He said that working here you have to focus on the positive things," I say to Kingi, "that the rescue animals go on to find happy homes. It must be very bittersweet."

"Life is bittersweet, don't you think?" He pulls me into his arms and gives me a big hug. "If you think it's all going to be roses, you'll end up very disappointed."

I think he's referring to the fact that his parents finally separated a few months ago. His father has moved to the city and divides his time between there and Wellington, with the woman who works at the Beehive. Huia has stayed at the house, but Rangi is refusing to sign it over to her, and it looks as if lawyers are going to have to get involved. What should have been an amicable parting has turned sour, and Kingi is furious at his father.

It makes what we've done here even more surprising. He's raised the idea of getting married a few times, but when I expressed my doubt, he quickly backed down and didn't mention it again. I assumed he agreed with my reservations, but clearly he decided that he wanted to marry me, and this was the best way to go about it.

I turn my head and rest my cheek on his chest as it finally sinks in that he really does love me. When it comes to it, I think, everyone has scars of varying degrees, and we're all rescue animals looking for our forever home. Finally, I've found mine. Kingi loves me, and we're married, and we've promised to spend the rest of our lives together. He really wants me! The thought is so shocking, so amazing, that I feel as if my heart is going to explode.

Behind us, someone has started playing some music. It's Louis Armstrong's *What a Wonderful World*. Oh… how appropriate.

Kingi chuckles and I move back a little and loop my arms around his neck. Across from us, Orson and Scarlett start moving to the music too, and we exchange smiles, all aware of the magical location and how special this day is.

"Love you, wife," Kingi murmurs.

"Love you, husband." Filled with joy, I lift my face to his for a long kiss as the summer breeze brushes over us, bringing the smell of the ocean.

Newsletter

If you'd like to be informed when my next book is available, you can sign up for my mailing list on my website, http://www.serenitywoodsromance.com

About the Author

USA Today bestselling author Serenity Woods writes feel-good romances full of friends, family, and falling in love. Most of her stories are set in Godzone, aka Aotearoa New Zealand, where she lives.

Website: http://www.serenitywoodsromance.com
Facebook: http://www.facebook.com/serenitywoodsromance

Printed in Dunstable, United Kingdom